Twenty-six ESKIMO WORDS

Also by Caroline McCullagh

Quest for the Ivory Caribou

Sing for Your Supper: Opera Memories & Recipes

With Richard Lederer

American Trivia

American Trivia Quiz Book

COMING SOON

Let Me Count the Ways...

Visit CarolineMcCullaghAuthor.com

Twenty-six ESKIMO WORDS

CAROLINE McCULLAGH

Twenty-Six Eskimo Words is a work of fiction. Names, characters, places, and incidents either are the product of the author's imagination or are used fictitiously. Any resemblance to actual persons, living or dead, events, or locales is entirely coincidental.

Published in the United States by Madura Press
P.O. Box 178812
San Diego, CA 92177

ISBN: 978-0-9993071-4-4 (trade paperback)
ISBN: 978-0-9993071-5-1 (ePub)
ISBN: 978-0-9993071-6-8 (mobi)

Printed in the United States

First Edition
Cover and Interior Design by GKS Creative
Author Photo by Nikki Alexander

To my long-time friend and writing partner, Richard Lederer
—an amazing mind, an amazing man.

Silent stones stacked just so

Speak of love, ephemeral

As the stones themselves

An inuksuk is a stone landmark built by Inuit, Iñupiat, Kalaallit, Yupik, and other peoples of the Arctic region of North America. These structures are found in northern Canada, Greenland, and Alaska.

ARCTIC OCEAN
BEAUFORT SEA
Prudhoe Bay
Kaktovik
Gordon
Deadhorse
ALASKA NATIONAL WILDLIFE REFUGE (ANWR)
CANADA
BROOKS RANGE
ARCTIC CIRCLE
Nome
Fairbanks
ALASKA
YUKON RIVER
Anchorage

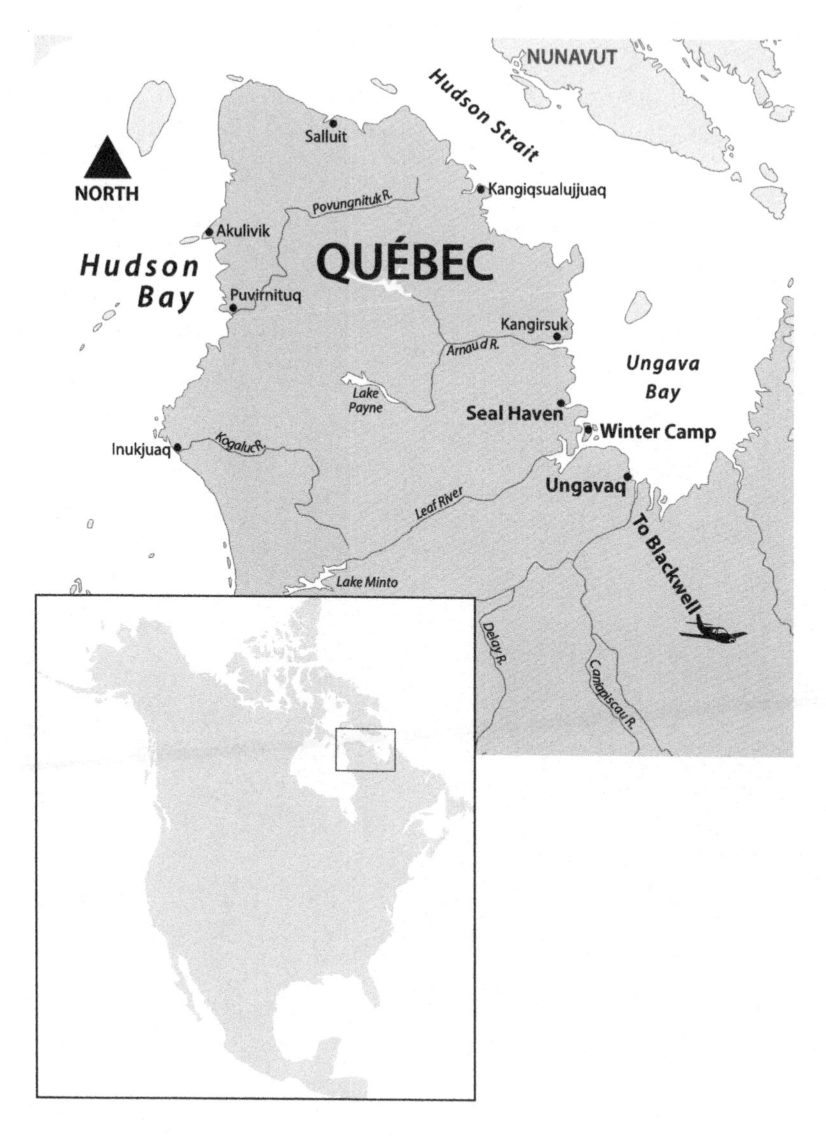

Apologies to my readers who are familiar with Canadian geography. For various reasons, I left the town of Kuujjuaq off the map and out of the story

Chapter One

MARCH 7, 2005

I opened my eyes to the same sense of surprise and wonder I've felt every morning for the past two months. I rolled over, and there was Jack. Sound asleep, he lay on his back, his black hair mussed by the pillow, the covers kicked off because of the warmth of the bedroom—the whole beautiful length of him—the strong muscles of his chest and arms apparent even as he lay totally relaxed, his hands resting loosely on his belly.

His hands are short and broad and powerful. I used to imagine what he could do with those hands. My imagination wasn't nearly good enough.

I love the golden tan color and smoothness of his skin. I've even learned to love those two terrible scars that run from his left shoulder to his right hip, left by the claws of a bear so long ago.

I inched toward him, but before I knew what had happened, he'd turned over, grabbed me, and kissed me soundly. He lay back, laughing. "Anne, you have to be a lot sneakier than that if you want to catch me."

I turned onto my stomach and pulled myself up on my elbows. "In case you haven't noticed, Jack, I've already caught you, and I didn't have to sneak. I just had to wait." I leaned over and kissed him. "Good morning. I love you."

"And I love you." He reached out, touched my face, and gently stroked my hair.

"Do you want to sleep a little longer?" I asked. "You could doze while I fix the tea."

"I have something better to do. Come here."

"You won't get tea."

"Maybe I will . . . later."

I settled into his arms and welcomed him.

We'd arrived in San Diego late the previous night from Pittsburgh, Pennsylvania, where we visited the graves of Jack's grandfather Brendan and great-grandparents John and Ida O'Malley. Visiting graves may seem like a strange thing to do on a honeymoon, but the search for information about Brendan had brought us together. We wanted to acknowledge that.

I picked up the pot, poured two cups of tea, added the milk and sugar, and handed one to Jack. "Come on. We'll walk around the rest of the house and yard."

I showed him the walk-in pantry off the kitchen, the living room, the dining room, and another room—an informal sitting area—the two guest bedrooms, the den, and the laundry room.

A classic Southern California Spanish Colonial Revival style house, it has white stucco walls, arched doorways, and a red clay-tile roof. Built in the 1930s, it sits on the west side of a high peninsula called Point Loma. A huge, sloping back yard more than made up for the small front yard. A mature goldenrain tree, messy but beautiful, shaded the large tile patio. A detached workroom sat farther down the slope at the back of the yard.

Now, we relaxed on the redwood Adirondack chairs my first husband, Robby, had made in that workroom and enjoyed the sunny morning and panoramic view of the Pacific Ocean.

"It's strange to think we've been married two months," I said, "and there are so many practical things we haven't talked about. I know your taste in music and books and about the rather strange foods I need to learn how to fix for you, but we've never talked about money or where we want to live or things like that."

"Anne, I'm committed to six months a year in Ottawa until I retire, but I could retire now. We could live here."

Such a simple statement. Such a major gift of love. I knew how important Jack's job was to him. No way would I take advantage of that offer.

"It almost feels as if our honeymoon will be over if we talk about things like that," I said.

"Not a chance." He took my hand in his.

We sat quietly for a few minutes as an Anna's hummingbird breakfasted on nectar from the scarlet flowers of the salvia bush next to the patio. As he flitted from blossom to blossom, his ruby head and emerald throat flashed in the sun.

"My life's in Canada now, Jack. I know you don't want to retire, although I do appreciate your offer. We should sell this house. If we want to keep a home in San Diego, it should be a condo, so we can lock the door and leave when we want to. We'll have to talk about whether we want even that much."

"We don't have to decide now," he said. "Let's talk about what we want to do today."

"I have a few phone calls to make, and I have to do something about all the mail, but that's it. How about a little sightseeing?"

"OK. I'll call Bob Sumner too. I haven't seen him since the last Archaeology Association convention. I'd like the three of us to get together for lunch."

"Give him a call," I said, "and then we'll decide on what to do with the rest of the day."

We rose and walked into the kitchen.

I'd called Carola to let her know we were on our way to San Diego, and she'd stocked the refrigerator for us. I mixed some water and egg and put bread to soak for French toast while Jack made his call.

When he hung up, he said, "Bob has a class at eleven. He asked if we could meet him for lunch at 12:30. I said yes, but I can call back and change that if you'd like to do something else."

"No, that's fine."

"You'll like him, but watch out. He's really smooth with women. I don't want him luring you away."

I laughed. "Not in a million years."

"He said something interesting. He's had an offer of a job to do an archaeological survey in the Arctic National Wildlife Refuge in Alaska. He doesn't want to do it, and he said he'd recommend me if I did. It sounds like it might be fun."

"How much time would it take?"

"Pretty much the whole summer."

"Oh."

"He's going to give us the details at lunch."

I couldn't stand the idea of Jack going off for the whole summer so soon after our wedding. I knew how lonely I'd be, but I'd known he did field work when I married him. It was part of the package.

I changed the subject. "Shall we go to the cemetery after lunch?"

"OK. Want to take a shower with me after breakfast, since we have time to kill?"

We finished our breakfast and our shower, which took longer than I thought it would. Jack said he had to prove the honeymoon wasn't over.

As we dressed, he said, "Why don't you call a cab? We'll go someplace and rent a car."

"I have a car in the garage."

"What kind?"

"It's an '02 Cadillac Eldorado."

"Great," he said, "but it's been sitting for months. It might not start."

"Ernesto drives it at least once a week to keep everything working. It should be OK. If there were a problem, he'd have taken care of it." The words were out of my mouth before I realized I'd also let the cat out of the bag.

"Who's Ernesto?"

I hadn't meant to tell him this way. I knew it would come out, but I didn't know how he'd take it. I tried to sound casual. "My gardener."

He sat on the bed to put on his socks. "Oh, you have a gardener?"

"Everyone here does."

"But does everyone let their gardener drive their car?"

I shrugged. "He's not totally a gardener—I do a lot of it when I'm here—but he does maintenance and runs errands. There are always little things that need to be done."

"I don't understand. Does he work for you full time?"

"Not now."

"But he used to?"

"He and Carola used to come in five days a week, but they're semi-retired now."

"Carola? I thought she was a friend."

"She is. It's complicated. Ernesto's her husband."

"You had a full-time gardener and a maid?" he said.

"Oh, don't dare call her a maid to her face. She'll skin you alive. She's my housekeeper."

"How long have they worked for you?"

"Since I married Robby."

"Thirty-five years?" He sounded bemused.

I nodded. "A little more. Their oldest child was in my class. That's how I found out they were looking for work. Robby traveled enough that he wanted me to be free to do things with him when he came home. He didn't want me tied down with housework, and he didn't want me alone all the time when he traveled."

"I take it, then, Robby had a bit of money?"

"Mmm . . . yes. He did . . ." I decided I might as well tell him all of it. "And when he retired and asked me to quit my job early, for a hobby, I started buying and selling stocks. It turned out I'm pretty good at it."

"And 'pretty good at it' means . . ."

"Oh, I'll show you the business stuff, but basically it means if you work for the money, you can retire today. But I don't think you work for the money, do you? You'd teach if you had to pay them to be allowed to."

Jack sat quietly.

I knew what he was doing. He was getting control of emotion, as his culture demanded that he do. I just didn't know what emotion. I waited.

"Why didn't you tell me this before?"

"Because it's not important. It's only there to make us comfortable. I was afraid it might get in the way of you seeing who I am—that it would scare you off. Besides, I owed you one, *Doctor* O'Malley."

Jack broke out laughing. "I guess we're even."

I knew he was remembering the look on my face when I found out he was an archaeologist and college professor, not a hunting guide, as I'd assumed.

Well, he took it better than I thought he might. At least, I think he did.

Chapter Two

The car started on the first try. I drove.

"How long will it take to get to the university?" he asked.

"About a half-hour, depending on traffic, but parking's always a problem. If we're lucky and find a space quickly, we can walk around the campus for a while. The architecture's interesting, especially the library. People think it looks like a spaceship."

We did find a parking space and had about a half-hour to walk the campus. The early March day continued clear and fine with a temperature in the sixties, quite a change from Ungavaq, Ottawa, and Pittsburgh, where we'd been the last three months.

I noticed many of the students stared at us. We'd received that same scrutiny in Ottawa and Pittsburgh. I guess we make an unusual couple. I think of myself as a typical older woman. Carola and I like to say we're in late middle age. Jack looks exotic in contrast. Although he has tan skin and black hair, his face is clearly different from the Hispanic and Indian faces common in Southern California, and facial tattoos—two parallel lines—span ear to ear across the bridge of his nose. Some people incorrectly call him an Eskimo, but Eskimos live in Alaska. Jack is a Canadian Inuit.

We met Bob in the lobby of the University of California San Diego Faculty Club.

He hugged Jack. "Well, how's my little Inuit buddy?"

"I'm fine," Jack said, "and how's the weather up there?" and I knew they'd been saying the same things to each other for forty years.

Jack is five eight and muscular, but he did look small next to Bob, who stood at least eight inches taller and weighed at least fifty pounds more. Bob looked solidly built. I guessed that he, like Jack, lived an outdoor life for much of the year. His work kept his body toned.

A good-looking man in a rumpled-scholar sort of way, he had a pleasant face and a warm smile. He was slightly balding, but he didn't seem to care. He didn't do one of those awful comb-overs. His hair was salt-and-pepper like mine, but it appeared to have originally been a much lighter brown than mine had been. He wore it long, but neatly trimmed, as was his dark brown beard.

"And this must be Anne," Bob said, turning to me. "I can't believe I missed this beautiful woman, and she lived here in San Diego the whole time. Jack, you're luckier than you deserve."

He seemed genuinely delighted that Jack had married me and pleased at the prospect that Jack might spend time in San Diego.

Over lunch, they talked shop for a while. I followed most of what they said because I'd read Jack's textbook. And Bob knew many archaeology jokes. I'm sure Jack had heard most of them, but they were new to me. We laughed all through the meal.

Classmates in graduate school at Columbia University, they had done their first fieldwork together at Altun Ha in Belize. They'd kept in close touch ever since.

"We divided up the North American continent between us," Bob said. "Jack took the north and I took the south. I have the better part of the deal. No frostbite." His specialty was Indians of the Southwest.

"Just sunstroke and scorpions," Jack said. "I'll take snow any day."

While we lingered over our ice cream, Jack said, "Tell me about the survey in Alaska."

Bob nodded. "There's talk in Washington again about opening portions of the Arctic National Wildlife Refuge for oil exploration. The companies planning to bid on the development have to do environmental impact studies.

"Allied American Oil approached me to write the part of their EIS having to do with archaeological sites and native antiquities. I tentatively said I'd do it, but Eskimos and Alaskan Indians certainly aren't my area of expertise, and I've had an offer of three months at a dig in New Mexico, so I'm not really interested. You want it?"

"Why do you suppose they wanted to hire you? What do you know about Eskimos?"

"They probably wanted me because I know you."

Jack laughed. "Sure."

"They didn't actually say. I asked, but the conversation moved on, and I never did get an answer."

"I need to know more of the details, and Anne and I have to talk it over."

A little bubble of sadness welled up in me. I knew I'd tell him to take it.

"There's a mystery hanging over the project," Bob said. "The contract was let previously, but there was some kind of accident, and the archaeologist disappeared."

"Disappeared as in 'never found'?" I asked.

"Yes."

"Last summer?" Jack asked.

"Yes. There was a mention of it in the papers at the time, but there wasn't much information."

"His name was John MacNeil," Jack said. "I knew him. I read his obituary in *The Journal of Arctic Archaeology* last fall. And you're right; they never did find his body. It was really too bad. I met him at the annual meeting of the Archaeological Institute of America. He presented an interesting paper on Siberian lithic culture, and we had a good talk about it. I think that was two years ago."

"It's such an isolated area," Bob said. "If you get in trouble, there's no place to go for help. You're on your own. I suppose he could've been taken by a bear."

"Oh, no," I said. "That's horrible."

Jack took my hand under the table. He knew how much talk of bears upsets me. A bear attacked me in Canada. Jack and his brother, Quipac, killed it. I'm working on getting past my fear, but I'm not there yet.

"It's possible," Jack said, "Bears are usually hungry and they're always curious, but they'd have found some sign. Bears make a mess tearing things apart. The obituary didn't mention anything about that."

"But how can someone disappear with no sign of what happened?" I asked.

"They can if they're out in the wilderness," Bob said.

Jack nodded. "But it's a little more difficult on the tundra. Maybe he drowned—swept out to sea or something. It's still odd."

We walked with Bob to his office, and he ran off copies of the information.

As he studied the paperwork, Jack said, "It's unusual Allied American hasn't farmed this out to a company specializing in environmental impact studies."

"They're so big they do almost everything in-house," Bob said. "They're a huge corporation, and they're worldwide, so they have access to people with every skill you can imagine. Let me know in the next few days if you're interested. I'll send your name to Allied American with a recommendation."

"Thanks and thanks for lunch. I'll give you a call."

Jack leafed through the papers Bob had given him as we walked back to the car. "I want you to look at these when we get home, and we can talk about whether it's something we'd like to do."

"We?"

"As I remember, our deal is that we're partners in this marriage. Did you think I'd go to Alaska without you?"

"I assumed you would."

"Well, I wouldn't," he said.

"I guess we have a lot to talk about tonight."

We stopped at the house for a few minutes to pick up the flowers we'd cut and then drove south on Catalina Boulevard to Fort Rosecrans National Cemetery. I parked the car on one of the narrow side roads, and we walked across the neatly trimmed grass to the stark white headstone on Robby's grave.

The rows and columns of uniform headstones seemed to march on forever down the hillside that opened out to a panoramic view of San Diego Bay, Coronado, and the communities to the south. The cemetery included people who'd served as far back as the 1850s and as recently as the present conflict. Robby was in good company. His stone read:

Robert John O'Malley, Pennsylvania
Sgt. - World War II
September 24, 1922 – January 15, 2003
Beloved Husband

We'd stopped and picked up a green cone-shaped metal vase from a storage area when we entered the cemetery. I pressed it into the grass near the headstone and placed the bouquet of flowers in it. Spring always seemed to arrive in San Diego in early March, so we'd managed to find enough gold and white daffodils and blue anemones to make a nice arrangement.

Robby had helped me plant those bulbs.

I started to tell Jack, but . . .

As my tears started, he put his arm around me.

I'd had a difficult time coming to terms with Robby's death. Now, two years later, although I've passed that dark time and moved forward in this new marriage, I still grieve for him. I suppose I'll never get over missing him, his voice, his touch, his love.

We stood awhile, then walked back to the car. This time, Jack drove. As he parked in our driveway, he said, "I'll make the tea."

"Oh, I'll do it."

"We're going to stay here awhile. I'd better get used to the kitchen."

"You'd better not get too used to it because on the two days a week Carola's here, the kitchen belongs strictly to her. She can be quite the tyrant if you get in her way. Don't say you weren't warned."

He laughed.

After dinner, we spent the evening sitting at the oak table in the kitchen and going over the financial aspects of my life. I'd sorted the business mail out of the stack. Jack reminded me that balancing a checkbook was about the extent of his mathematical knowledge, but he didn't seem to have any problem following the intricacies of the most recent stock reports. When we finished, he put down the paperwork and looked at me.

"What?" I asked.

"This is even more than you led me to believe this morning. I'm truly amazed. You're right. We've never talked about how to handle money in this marriage. I never thought about you having money. I assumed I'd take care of you. This will take a little getting used to."

"Of course, if we sell this house, there'll be even more."

"How much more?"

"Prices have gone up and up in San Diego. Homes in this neighborhood are selling for over a million dollars now, and every month they go up more."

"Are you joking?"

I shook my head. "No. Is this money going to be a problem between us? I've tried for the longest time to think how to tell you about it."

". . . No, I don't think so."

His little hesitation made me uneasy.

"I've been worried you might think I'd been deceptive and be upset about it," I said.

"I'm not upset. I'm surprised. We need to figure out things like this. Meanwhile, I think we should leave things as they are. You go on doing what you've obviously been doing so well, and we'll make decisions as they come up."

My tension began to unwind.

He continued, "What do you say? Let's go to bed early tonight. We're pretty tired. We can look at Bob's stuff tomorrow."

"I like that idea."

He turned off the lights, and we went hand in hand to the bedroom.

Chapter Three

The next morning, Jack woke me with a kiss. "My turn to make tea."

"Carola will be here. She'll do it. Don't get in her way. I'll be out in a few minutes."

Jack pulled on gray sweatpants and a blue knit shirt and headed down the hall.

I lay in bed for a few minutes until I was more awake.

When I left the bedroom, I heard voices in the kitchen. I had my fingers crossed that Jack hadn't irritated Carola. She's more family than employee and sometimes can be just a little touchy.

I didn't need to worry. When I entered the kitchen, Jack, Ernesto, and Carola sat at the oak table chatting in Spanish. I hadn't known Jack could speak Spanish, but he later told me that he became fluent when he did his fieldwork in Belize.

Ernesto and Carola rose to hug me and wish me happiness in my marriage.

Physically, they're incongruous together. Carola is short and plump; Ernesto, her opposite, is a tall beanpole.

Carola jokes that she's the same dimension in any direction. Robby used to tell her that she was just a nice armful of woman. Still, she's sensitive about her weight—even though Ernesto thinks she's fine—and she usually wears black slacks to minimize her hips. Today, she had on a green top with gold orchids appliqued on the shoulder.

Ernesto wore khaki work pants, a blue checked long-sleeved shirt, and high-top work boots. His work jacket hung on the back of his chair.

Carola is beautiful, with the round face and classic profile of her Maya ancestors and long, thick black hair she often wears braided, sometimes loose, and today, coiled around her head.

Ernesto's black hair and dark eyes match hers and he has a thick black mustache. Even though they're older than I am, neither has more than a few gray hairs.

Carola is generally good-natured, but sometimes serious, and occasionally snappish. Ernesto is always sunny. He's a joker and a tease. And even after more than forty years of marriage, they're openly affectionate. It's clear they're still very much in love.

When we sat, we switched the conversation to English.

As we talked, I noticed that Ernesto and Carola started out calling Jack "Dr. O'Malley." After a while, they shifted to "Dr. Jack," and finally to "Jack." I recognized their stamp of approval.

After a few minutes, Carola said, "Anne, I haven't seen your ring yet."

I held up my hand to show her my plain gold band, but that's not what caught her eye. I saw the shock on her face and heard the disapproval in her voice. "What's that? Do you have a tattoo?"

"Yes. My mother-in-law made it. Isn't it beautiful?"

I could always trust Carola. I knew I'd have a lot to explain later, but right now, she wasn't going to embarrass Jack or me. Her voice softened. "It is beautiful. Let me see."

I held out my hand.

Jack hadn't missed what happened. He smiled.

"I asked Maata to make it for me after we were married in the village. The older women have tattoos. This is a small one. Maata has tattoos on her hands and arms up past her elbows and on her face too. The younger women don't. It's too traditional for them, I guess. It's gone out of fashion."

Maata had made two parallel lines about an inch apart across my left hand just above the knuckles. Pairs of short parallel lines alternated with y shapes and connected the longer lines.

"What does it mean? Is it symbolic of something?"

"No, it's just a design I liked."

"How did she do it?"

"With a sewing needle and a thread with soot on it. She stitched under the skin."

"Oh, Anne! Eeuw," Carola said. "Did it hurt?"

"Yes, but I managed."

I remembered that time in Maata's kitchen. Maata, Jack's three sisters—Miqo, Saarak, and Allaq—and several neighbor women crowded around the table. They put snow on my hand to numb it and teased me and told me scary stories about getting their tattoos. When Maata finished, they praised me. Their tattoos were more extensive than mine is, but maybe I'm not done yet.

"You're braver than I could ever be," Carola said.

"I don't know," I said. "I don't think I was brave."

Jack beamed.

After breakfast, Jack and I went to the den to read the papers Bob had given us. They were interesting, but I thought what they didn't say was surprising. Jack said this was standard verbiage. The people who did this type of work know the requirements. The proposal was general, but everything would be detailed in the contract.

Allied American Oil wanted to bid on oil exploration rights in the Arctic National Wildlife Refuge. That required hiring experts to identify potential problems, estimate how likely they were to occur, and suggest preventive measures or define counterbalancing benefits. Many people might be hired for an environmental impact study. This one required experts in air quality, water quality, wildlife management, geology, traffic patterns (of all things), and archaeology.

"Why do you think they wanted Bob to do this?" I asked. "It seems unusual. His area of expertise is the Southwest."

"I wondered about that too. I know of several American archaeologists more qualified for a job in the north. Maybe they're all committed to other projects, but still, it's strange. The company's not required to hire Americans, either, but I haven't heard that they approached any Canadians. Word of this kind of thing does get around."

"Why are they required to do this study?"

"These proposals are politically controversial. The law requires it, but even if it didn't, the company needs to do this to answer their critics lobbying in Washington to stop them."

"What's the controversy in this particular project? Who wants to stop them?"

"It's been argued for years. It's between the oil companies, who say they won't do long-term damage to the environment, and the ecologists, who say they will and that the caribou that live in the proposed drilling area during the summer will abandon it." He shook his head. "It's an uneven fight. The oil companies have money and influence."

"I don't understand why something called a refuge isn't really a refuge for the animals there."

"Because of the way ANWR was set up, it can be exploited commercially. But the area they propose to drill in is the birthing ground for a herd of caribou, the Porcupine Herd—more than 150,000 animals.

"The caribou migrate north onto the coastal plain in the late spring to give birth and fatten on the plants growing in the constant daylight. They've done this for millennia. They stay about six weeks. They move south again when the mosquitoes become intolerable. Ecologists say there's no other place the herd can use for a birthing ground. They're the economic base for the Gwich'in Indians, who've hunted them for food and hides for more than a thousand years."

"What would it mean if the herd disappeared?"

"If the herd dies out, as it probably will if the caribou are scared away from the birthing ground, the whole ecosystem over thousands of square miles will change. The Gwich'ins will no longer have a way to make a living, although the oil companies may hire some of them. But the other predators and the scavengers—wolves, bears, foxes, ravens, and wolverines—make their livings from the herd. They'll lose their resources too. They'd disappear after the caribou. Grazing maintains a certain balance of plants, so plant species would disappear after that. Everything would change. It's like the domino thing where they line them all up. One topples, and there's no way to predict where it will end. It would destroy the complex web of life in that whole area of Alaska and Canada."

"I'm surprised you'd consider working for Allied American. I'd have thought you'd be in favor of conserving the herd."

"I am. But as a Canadian, I have no say in American politics. Now, even though archaeology is peripheral to the whole process, maybe I do. I may be able to make a difference. It's unlikely there's anything of archaeological importance up there, but if there is, I think I have a better chance of finding it than almost anyone else. If we can find an important site—some place where people have lived or hunted or butchered their kill—it'll give ammunition to the people fighting against the drilling. One site implies the possibility of others and makes it a little less reasonable to allow people in there with bulldozers.

"I've thought about the ethics of this. I don't see an ethical problem as long as we do what we contract to do to normal professional standards. It doesn't matter if we hope to help the people working to stop them. That's why I'm interested. What do you think? Would you like to spend the summer in Alaska with me?"

"Can we get it done in one summer?"

"Have to. Once it starts snowing, you can't see anything and it's a one-year contract—no second summer."

"It does sound worth doing. If you want me to go with you, I will, but I don't want to be the field cook or something like that. Would there be real work for me to do?"

"Yes. You'd do half."

"Half of what?"

"If we take this on, we'll look at every map, report, and satellite photo we can get our hands on. We'll mark places that have potential. Up there, we'll go by plane, or more likely helicopter, and do a systematic flyover of each section we marked. We'll choose the most promising areas, and then it would turn into a camping trip as we complete the survey."

"Would you need a crew to help?"

"No. Allied American isn't interested in developing archaeological sites. This survey is something the two of us can do. It's not glamorous work, though, and you might get sick of spending so much time with just me."

"Well, camping with you can get pretty exciting. I've done it only once, and a bear almost ate me. I don't know how much of that I can handle . . . But I'm joking and you're not, are you?"

"No. I've been in the field almost every summer for more than thirty-five years, so I see it differently than you would. Since I've known you, life has been interesting. We've traveled, met new people, and had some unusual experiences. This would be the opposite of that. It would be just you and me in a little tent with about a million mosquitoes."

"What's the up side? Why do you want to do it?"

"It's what I love. That's why I've done it for so long. The thought of doing what I love and having you along is more than I could've ever hoped for. But that's me, not you."

"I don't know how to find out if I'd like it without trying it, so of course I'll go with you."

"There's one other thing," he said.

"What?"

"We'll be out in the wilderness again. There'll be bears— maybe polar bears, if we're near the shore, but mostly grizzlies. Since we'll be there in the summer, they'll be awake."

"Do you think it's possible a bear killed Dr. MacNeil?"

"It's possible but, as I said to Bob, it's unlikely. MacNeil didn't strike me as careless when I met him."

"That possibility wouldn't keep you from going?" I asked.

"I was born in bear country. I've lived there all my life."

"Am I allowed to be a little scared?"

"Yes, but I'll take care of you."

"OK."

"OK?"

"Yes. What about Quipac? Won't he want to go too?"

"He doesn't like this stuff. He likes the digging part—the artifacts, not the maps. If you didn't want to go, I could probably talk him into it. I might have more fun with you though."

"I thought we were talking about work."

He smiled. "We might be able to fit in a little work."

Jack called Bob and started the wheels turning. Shortly after we signed the contracts, we received several large boxes of reports, maps, and photos. Jack started teaching me how to analyze the information.

We took a break in the preparations when Bob invited Jack to read his unpublished paper on his latest dig at a colloquium of the professors and graduate students in the anthropology department. I hadn't seen Jack with his peers at a university. People told me he was highly regarded, but for the first time, I saw that they thought his work was special. He answered many questions and participated in a lively discussion.

Several people disagreed with his theories and conclusions. On our way home, I asked him whether that bothered him.

"That's exactly why you present a paper and why you publish, although publishing is a slower process. It's gratifying when someone says your work is good, but it doesn't push you to improve it. Criticism does."

"I guess I'm bothered by that word 'criticism,'" I said.

"Don't be. It just means an analysis of something. It can be positive or negative. Science is really just a long conversation. I'm sure the early Homo sapiens sat around on their rocks and debated just as we did today. This dialogue's been going on as long as humans have been around.

"I was lucky to be able to join the conversation when I went to graduate school. I differed with people on theory and conclusions. Sometimes I was right, and sometimes wrong. Some of the people today are right and some are wrong, but when we challenge each other, as they did, that's when new ideas are created, and we get closer to the truth.

"At some point, I'll drop out, and others will take my place. They'll build on my work, as I've built on the work of those who came before me. It's just the way scholarship works."

Chapter Four

In late May, we headed to Ottawa to pick up the gear we'd need for a season in northern Alaska. The temperatures in the refuge would probably go from the twenties or thirties when we first arrived to the seventies and eighties in August. We could have severe weather including snow at any time though. We needed clothes and equipment for all contingencies.

Ernesto and Carola drove us to the airport.

We left the house in their capable hands. Although we'd talked about it, we still hadn't decided about selling.

As Carola hugged me good-bye, tears came to her eyes.

"Carola, don't cry. Everything will be fine."

She hugged me harder.

We'd had a long talk several weeks previously. She'd finally realized she couldn't talk us out of going when I explained that we'd signed the contracts. Even then, she tried to convince me to let Jack go on his own.

"Why, Carola?"

"I have a bad feeling."

"You're not superstitious."

"I don't care. A bear almost killed you, and now maybe a bear has killed that Dr. MacNeil. I don't think you should go. It's dangerous."

"I'm not going to let Jack go by himself. It would be too lonely for both of us. The idea of someone disappearing without a trace is scary, but the refuge is a big empty area. Any number of things might have happened. It wasn't necessarily a bear."

She rolled her eyes. "That certainly makes me feel better!"

We laughed.

I wish I'd believed what I told her, but the whole thing rattled me too. Dr. MacNeil had been on foot. He couldn't have gone too far from his camp, and if he'd been away from camp, he'd have had a backpack and tools, things not easily destroyed by the elements or bears. Why hadn't they found any trace of them?

But as I said to Carola, we were committed now, so I'd just have to put my doubts aside.

We landed at the Ottawa airport a year and a week after my arrival there when I'd started the odyssey that led to my marriage to Jack. A year ago, I hadn't known Jack existed. Now I could hardly remember the sad, lonely person I'd been then.

Our main job here was to inventory Jack's gear and to decide whether we needed anything extra before we left for Anchorage. We'd brought our sleeping bags and other gear with us from Ungavaq to Ottawa in January. Those items and the equipment Jack had in storage at the university satisfied him. The company would provide our food, but we still had a lot to pack.

We decided that while we were in Alaska, Jack would teach me to shoot. That might help me be less afraid of the bears. One day he went out to buy a rifle for me. When he returned, he said, "You'll never guess who I saw today."

"Who?"

"René. I stopped in at the archives."

Our good friend Dr. René Benoit is chief research librarian at National Archives Canada. I'd met him when I researched there, and we'd enjoyed a brief romance—one more little thing I hadn't managed to mention to Jack yet.

"How is he? I planned to call him."

"Now you don't have to. We're having dinner with him. I called Marcia from his office, and she's joining us." Marcia was Jack's mentor and second mother. Although we'd actually married in Ungavaq, we'd also had a ceremony in Ottawa. Marcia had been my matron of honor, and René had been Jack's best man.

"Where are we going?"

"Where we went on our first date."

"Fujiyama?"

"Yes. You'd better get dressed. Would you wear the blue dress you wore that night?"

"I will. I never told you. Carola and I spent hours on the phone trying to figure out whether that was a date or not."

"I sure thought it was."

"Well, I didn't know if it was a date or whether you were just being friendly."

"I'd have been a lot friendlier if I'd thought I could get away with it."

"Maybe you can. Want to try?"

"It might take a while. I'd have to call and cancel dinner."

"I could be friendly after dinner."

"That's definitely a date."

Marcia and René looked even odder together than Jack and I do.

Marcia is barely five feet tall. Even I tower over her. She's older than the three of us, but she's so vital and energetic you wouldn't think so, except for her hair. It's long and silver. Tonight, she had it done in an elaborate twist with ornate silver combs holding it in place. She wore a long emerald-green skirt and a white lace blouse.

At six four, René is almost a foot and a half taller than she is. Slender and blond, he wore a beautifully tailored navy blue suit. He enjoys wearing good clothes, and in spite of his height and lankiness, they look good on him. He carried a plastic shopping bag.

"What's in the bag?" I asked.

"Ask Jack," he said in his French-accented English. He handed it to Jack. In turn, Jack handed it to me. All three were smiling.

"It's for you," Jack said. "Happy birthday, my darling Anne."

We'd been so busy, I'd forgotten my birthday.

"I never thought I'd be married to an older woman," he said, "but it's turning out to be not too bad."

"Oh, you're not getting away with that remark. I'm only six months older than you are. Anyway, I'm not sure sixty-one is something to celebrate."

"I certainly think you're worth celebrating," he said. "And you have to know the older you get the more interesting you'll be for me. After all, I am an archaeologist."

I laughed. "That's good news. What is it?" I held up the bag.

"Open it."

I took out a package wrapped in silver paper and tied with a blue ribbon. I untied the bow, took off the wrapping and the box top, and saw what nestled in the tissue—a beautifully made ulu, a type of semicircular knife that every Inuit woman has. Her main tool, she uses it for almost every cutting task. I knew it was an important symbol of our marriage—as important as the wedding ring Jack had given me.

I'd been learning to speak the Inuit language, Inuktitut. In that language, I said, "A wife is pleased," and I kissed him.

I turned to show the ulu to Marcia and René.

"Oh, we've seen it," Marcia said. "This has been planned for weeks. Jack called me from San Diego and asked me if I'd buy it for him. He told me where to go and what to look for. Happy birthday, Anne." She and René hugged me.

"There's one important thing I need to do." I reached into my purse, took out three Canadian pennies, and gave one to each of them.

"What's this for?" Jack asked.

"Any time someone gives you a knife, you have to give them money. It keeps the knife from cutting the friendship. And there's a variation on that: If you ever give someone a purse or a wallet, you always have to put at least a penny in it, so they'll never be broke. I learned those things from my mother. There, now I've taught you a little of my culture."

"Interesting," Jack said. "I never heard those before. I'll keep this penny for luck. That I have heard of."

We had a wonderful dinner. Sushi is Jack's and my favorite food. The chef even made a sushi order shaped like a birthday cake with a candle on it. After dinner, we went to Marcia's and had an evening of storytelling. This was our chance to tell Marcia and René more about the month I'd spent in Jack's Arctic survival class the previous December.

"Jack and Quipac didn't expect you to eat Inuit food, did they?" Marcia asked.

"They sure did."

"What food?" René asked.

"There was so much of it," I said. "Raw seal brains mixed with blubber, raw seal liver, caribou fixed six ways. Oh, and fox!"

"I hate fox," Marcia said.

"What's the matter with fox?" Jack said. "I'll grant you, it's not very good in the summer, but it's not bad in the winter."

I made a face.

"Says you," said Marcia. "They didn't make you eat maktaaq, did they?"

"No, I think Jack's saving that for a special occasion, maybe our anniversary."

"What's maktaaq?" René asked.

"Fermented whale skin and blubber," Jack said, "and it's delicious."

"I suppose I'll find out," I said with resignation.

"I'm glad I'm a librarian instead of an anthropologist," René said. "Sushi's about as adventurous as I want to be."

Chapter Five

We arrived at the Anchorage International Airport on May 23.

"There's an old friend of yours here," Jack said.

"Who?"

"Come on. I'll show you." He led me across the concourse.

There, a huge polar bear stood erect on its hind legs. I knew it wasn't alive, but it still gave me shivers. I'll never again think of polar bears as cute, as I had before one charged me. It would have killed me if Jack and Quipac hadn't run between the bear and me and shot it. All this brought my mind back to Dr. MacNeil, but I decided not to allow myself to think about that.

"That can't be the same bear."

"No, this one's been here for years. Besides, remember the women cut your bear's skin up for parka decorations. This one's actually larger than your bear, but not a lot."

Before I had a chance to get too morbid thinking about how close I'd come to dying, we heard Jack's name paged over the public address system. We walked to the Alaska Airlines desk, where Jack identified himself. A young man in a dark green chauffeur's uniform stepped forward. He held a piece of cardboard with "O'Malley" written on it.

"Dr. O'Malley, I'm Jim, your driver from the hotel. I'm sorry I didn't greet you earlier. I was stuck in traffic. I'll be available for your convenience as long as you're here."

"Nice to meet you, Jim," Jack said. "Maybe you can answer my question. We have to claim the stuff we shipped ahead. It'll already have cleared customs. Do you know where we'd pick it up?"

"Gimme your documents. I'll take care of it," Jim said.

"There are a lot of boxes."

"I'll get a cart. I'll store them for you at the hotel if you don't need any of them while you're here."

"Thanks. We won't need them. It's camping gear."

"There's a black limo out front with 'Hotel Captain Cook' on the door. Go ahead. Get in. Leave your duffels and backpacks here with me."

We walked out to the limousine at the curb. Jack opened the door for me, and we slid into the comfortable seats.

"We're certainly getting first-class treatment," I said.

"I've done a few of these environmental impact studies. The companies treat you like royalty before the reports are written because they want you to have happy thoughts about them as you're writing."

"Are we seeing someone from the company tomorrow?"

"Not until Thursday. I thought it would be nice if we had time to fool around. And we have an errand to do."

"What?"

"I thought we might buy a couple of dogs."

"Dogs?"

"Yes, dogs can be kind of handy. One of the world's top breeders of sled dogs lives here in Anchorage. She's won the Iditarod four times."

"I suppose you'd think I was pathetically uninformed if I said I didn't know what the Iditarod was."

"Actually, I happen to be in the education business, so if you did happen to make a statement like that, I'd assume you're pathetically in need of education."

"I believe I will make such a statement."

"OK. The annual Iditarod is an extraordinary and grueling dog sled race of over 1,100 miles from Anchorage to Nome. It starts on the first Saturday in March. It takes anywhere from eight days to a month to complete, depending on the weather."

"Have you ever thought about entering?"

"Oh, no. This is a serious sporting event. You have to spend years building up your team. It takes months of intense training for the musher and the dogs. It's really difficult. More people have climbed Mt. Everest than have completed a race like this."

"What a relief. I thought you were ready to spring one of those little surprises on me."

"We can think about it if you want to give it a try," he said.

"No. That's OK."

"Let's talk about something more immediate. These are one-way windows. We can see out, but nobody can see in. We're like rock stars. We have complete privacy in here." As he said that, he moved over and put his arm around me. "You know what else? I've never kissed anyone in a limousine. My understanding is necking in the back seat of a car is one of the American experiences that shouldn't be missed." He kissed me.

"That and in the front seat too," I said. "Having been an American teenager during the '50s and '60s, I'm somewhat of an expert on the subject. Didn't you neck in a car when you were in New York City or Ithaca?" I kissed him.

"Nobody has a car in New York City, and when I was in Ithaca, I was a professor—much too dignified."

I moved a little away from him. "I'm sorry to hear that, because, as I understand it, you're still a professor. Although I've seen you being dignified on only a few occasions, it sounds like this is going to be one of them."

He pulled me back. "Sometimes, when you travel, you have to compromise your dignity a little to get the full experience." With that, he put his other arm around me, and we stopped talking.

I don't know how long it took Jim to get our baggage, but it wasn't long enough. We heard the trunk open, so we had time to rearrange our clothes before he opened the driver's door.

He asked, "Would you like a little tour of the city, or would you like to go straight to the hotel?"

Looking at me, Jack said, "We'll go straight to the hotel."

Chapter Six

The next morning, Jack called the dog breeder and made an appointment for eleven o'clock.

Jim was waiting for us in front of the hotel when we came out. The day was beautiful and sunny.

The breeder, Karen Adams, had her home and business in the rural area north of Anchorage.

Jack knocked on her front door.

A tense-looking woman opened it. "Can I help you?"

"I hope so. We have an appointment for eleven. I'm Jack O'Malley and this is my wife, Anne."

A look of relief crossed Ms. Adams's face. She invited us in and ushered us to her tiny, pin-neat kitchen. "I was about to have a cup of coffee. Can I fix you coffee or tea?"

I realized this was the opening step in a negotiation that wouldn't be hurried, so I accepted a cup of tea, as did Jack.

Ms. Adams looked exactly as I imagined a serious sportswoman would. She was about my height and weight, and, I guessed, thirty-five or forty years old. She was clearly an outdoors person with a round pleasant face, tanned and lined. She wore jeans, a flannel shirt, and substantial boots—the uniform of the north. Her hands looked strong. Her nails were cut short. She wore no jewelry. Her straight blonde hair was pulled back in a casual ponytail held in a rubber band.

By the time we'd finished our tea, we were on a first-name basis with each other and feeling comfortable.

"You looked a little tense when you opened your door," Jack said, "but when I told you my name you seemed to relax. I wondered why."

Karen smiled and apologized. "The truth is I get a lot of phone calls like yours. People are here on vacation, and they've either heard about me or there's a story in the Anchorage Daily News about the Iditarod, and they think it would be romantic, or adventuresome, or some damn thing to own a sled dog. So they call me. Half the time they've never owned a dog in their lives, let alone a highly bred working dog. I get to spend an hour, or sometimes two, convincing them they should wait until they get home and get a cocker spaniel or maybe a cat.

"When you called this morning, I said to myself, 'Oh, no. Here we go again, and a doctor, no less. They're usually the ones who think they know everything.' No offense."

"None taken," Jack said.

"I set appointments for eleven. I figure I can say I have a lunch appointment at noon and get rid of you if I want to. When I opened the door, I knew I didn't need to worry. An Eskimo's probably going to know a thing or two about dogs and not be too big on romantic notions either. I never would have guessed from your name that you're Eskimo. Are you Yupic?"

"Actually not," Jack said. "We're not local. We're from Québec. I'm Ungavamiut."

"Ah, so you're Inuit."

"Yes."

"I suppose they have dogs in Québec too—just not quite as good as mine."

Jack laughed. "My brother and I have twenty-two dogs—all qimmiq."

"Ah," she said. "I am impressed."

"You probably know of my brother. His name is Quipac."

"Ah, yes. I've heard of him. Now I know why 'O'Malley' seemed familiar."

"He takes care of our dogs most of the time. I'm there for about six months of the year. And you're right about ours not being quite as good as yours. That's why I want to buy a couple, to improve the quality of ours."

"You realize I'm not running a charity here. Dogs the quality of mine aren't cheap."

"I don't think that'll be a problem if you have the right dogs."

"Let's go see if I do." She rose and led the way to the kennels. As we walked, she said, "You know, all my dogs have six legs."

Jack didn't react, but I said "What?"

"Yeah, forelegs in the front and two in the back." She laughed, and I did too when I finally figured it out.

Jack said, "Oh, Anne, I thought you knew that. I suppose that means you don't know why sled dogs are such bad dancers."

"Why?"

"They've got two left feet."

I just shook my head.

Karen laughed. "It's always fun to revisit the world's oldest jokes."

The kennels were spotless. As we toured, the dogs barked in greeting to her and in warning to us. She had them in all sizes and ages. She was proud of them and especially of her Iditarod team.

She put out two folding chairs and went to get the first dog we'd selected to see.

While she was gone, I asked, "Why is she impressed with your dogs, and how did she know about you and Quipac?"

"Only a few hundred of these dogs exist in the world. We call them qimmiq. The official name is *Canis familiaris borealis*, Canadian Inuit dogs. They're an endangered breed. That's why Quipac and I raise them. I could probably name most of the other breeders around the world, and I'm sure Karen can too. She has a particularly good reputation."

I'd kept my mouth shut when Karen made the remark about people who'd never owned a dog, because I never had. I received a thorough education that day. It took Jack over two hours to decide which two he wanted. We finally bought a dog and a bitch—Moose and Kiska.

Moose was black with white patches, Kiska a reddish-brown. Their dense coats consisted of soft fur undercoats and longer guard hairs. They had long hair on their tails that they carried curled over their backs.

Moose was several inches taller than Kiska and weighed about eighty pounds to Kiska's sixty. They looked powerful. In the class last December, Jack had told us that each sled dog could easily pull 100 pounds all day.

They were just short of a year old—they were sort of teenagers—and they'd had some training, but needed more. Karen put them through their paces pulling a small, wheeled training sled so we could see what work needed to be done with them. Of course, we had to meet the parents too.

She sold us a training sled, two travel crates, and food.

The harnesses were set up as part of a gangline so the dogs would pull on either side of a single line attached to the sled, the common rigging in Alaska. The Inuit tie dogs in a fan hitch, each on a line attached directly to the sled. Karen asked if that would be a problem but, after he examined the harnesses, Jack said he could easily rig them the way he wanted.

We planned to pick up Kiska and Moose the day we headed to Prudhoe Bay. Karen agreed the people at the hotel wouldn't be thrilled if we showed up with two big qimmiq in tow.

Chapter Seven

Jack said, "There's a message from somebody named Harold Josephs at Allied American. They want us to come for cocktails tomorrow. It'll be in a private room here at the hotel."

"I don't have anything to wear for cocktails. I didn't expect a party."

"You can wear what you traveled in. It looked nice. I'll tell them we don't have anything but field clothes."

He hung up after making the call. "He said they don't care what we wear. They're looking forward to meeting us."

We ate a late lunch and decided to spend the rest of the day on a tour of Anchorage. Jim knew a lot about the city and its history. He gave us a running commentary as we passed historical buildings, museums, the botanical gardens, the zoo, and Earthquake Park, which commemorated the highly destructive 9.2 earthquake on Good Friday in 1964.

We'd done a lot of sitting and wanted to stretch our legs, so we took a long walk, found a nice looking mom-and-pop restaurant—the kind with red-checkered tablecloths and hanging Chianti bottles—and had reindeer pizza for dinner. I'd never eaten reindeer, but Jack said it was the same as the caribou I'd eaten in Ungavaq. In addition to the very greasy reindeer sausage, they topped the pizza with feta cheese and red peppers. Jack made a bad joke about

Rudolph, the red-nosed reindeer. As much as we like pizza, it was a little odd. I don't think I'd order it again.

The next day, we played tourist and went to the Alaska Experience Center and to the Anchorage Museum of History and Art until it was time to go back to the hotel and get cleaned up for the party.

I'd been surprised to find exhibits on loan from Jack at the Museum of Civilization in Hull, Québec. The Museum here also had exhibits of Jack's finds. He reminded me he'd done a major dig in Alaska. I found some of his books for sale in the gift shop too. One of the clerks recognized him from the picture on the back of the dust jacket, and he ended up signing all their copies for them.

"You're a celebrity, aren't you?" I said.

"Just in the little world of archaeology."

Back at the hotel, we went down to the lobby. As we stepped out of the elevator, Jack patted his hip. "How funny. I've forgotten my wallet. It's sitting on the dresser. You go ahead. I'll meet you there."

"OK."

He turned and reentered the elevator.

I walked down the hall until I saw a sign that read "Allied American Oil, private party." I was self-conscious in my jeans and a yellow floral-patterned turtleneck shirt, but I put on my party smile and walked in.

A bar setup occupied one corner of the room. About thirty people stood chatting in groups, ignoring the chairs set around small tables. The men wore business suits, the women, dresses or pantsuits.

A man broke away from one group and came over, smiling. Forty-five, maybe older, about six feet tall, loose-limbed, slender, and tanned, he had the look of a well-toned athlete. He wore an expensive-looking, well-tailored charcoal gray business suit. His hair was dark with a suggestion of gray at the temples, done in a military buzz cut. He was probably one of the most handsome men I have ever seen—"movie star" handsome—strong jaw, high cheekbones, well-shaped dark eyebrows, and the most beautiful long dark eyelashes. I know women who would kill for eyelashes like that.

His eyes, though, were dark and cold, even when he smiled.

"May I help you?" His voice—a smooth warm baritone—seemed to contradict the coldness.

"I'm Anne O'Malley."

"Ah," he said and smiled again. "I'm very pleased to meet you. I'm Harold Josephs, but call me Hal. I'll be your liaison with Allied Oil during your association with us. Will Dr. O'Malley join you here?"

I nodded. "Yes. He left his wallet in our room. He went back to get it. He'll be along in a few minutes."

"Why don't I introduce you to a few people while we're waiting?"

He ushered me over to the people he'd been talking to. There were six of them—local managers for Allied American and their wives.

His cold eyes were off-putting for me, but what had repelled me seemed to attract the other three women. They fawned over Hal. He treated them with pleasantries and good humor, but didn't respond to their flirting. Their husbands seemed determined to ignore what was happening in front of them.

We'd started to talk about what Jack and I'd seen in Anchorage, when the wife of the senior man present, who seemed to be a couple of drinks ahead of the rest of us, interrupted and said in an irritated voice, "Who's that?"

We all turned to look.

Hal said, "Oh, he's—"

"Probably an employee," the woman's husband said.

"If he's an employee, he should know this room's reserved, but I wouldn't think they'd hire Eskimos here," she said, the pique in her voice rising. "Tell him to leave. What's he doing anyway?"

"I imagine he's looking for me," I said calmly. "That's my husband."

The woman blushed deeply. "I'm so sorry. I didn't think . . . I mean with a name like O'Malley . . ."

I ignored her and waved to Jack.

As he walked over, the woman excused herself and left.

"Well, there you are." I took his hand, drew him into the circle, and introduced him to Hal. Hal introduced him to the rest of the people.

We had a pleasant time with the "meet and greet." Hal introduced us to the other people, and we talked a little with each one. I'd had experience with this kind of event, and Jack obviously had too.

It was interesting to watch the women—some wives, some junior executives—in each of the groups we joined. They competed, in subtle ways a man might not recognize, to stand near Hal and attract his attention. No matter what they did, though, he was courteous, but no more than that. He ignored their subtle and, sometimes, obvious flirting. In fact, he seemed to pay more attention to me than to any of them, although all of them were younger than I was and most, better looking.

After everyone had consumed a couple of drinks, we made a plan for dinner. Hal, the three managers, the two wives, and we agreed to meet at a nearby restaurant in forty-five minutes. Hal offered us a ride, but Jack said we were trying to walk as much as we could. We'd meet them there.

We walked down the street. After a few minutes, Jack said, "Are you going to tell me or not?"

I looked at him blandly. "Tell you what, dear?"

"What was going on when I walked into the party?"

"Nothing." I let go of his hand and turned to look in the window of a dress shop.

"I'm beginning to see I'm not the only one in this family who's skilled at hiding things. Come on. Tell me what it was. You said something, and that woman went red in the face and left."

I turned back to him. "Oh, that. She might have choked a little when she put her foot in her mouth."

"She said something she regretted?"

"Some offhand comment about the hiring practices at the hotel. She didn't think they'd hire Eskimos."

"Aah." Jack nodded.

"We didn't have a chance to get into a more extensive discussion on hotel hiring practices because you arrived, and the conversation was interrupted."

"Aah." He nodded again. He took my hand again, and we continued walking.

When we arrived at the restaurant, the group was waiting for us. The woman had rejoined her husband. Hal introduced Jack to her, and then I watched as Jack maneuvered to get himself seated next to her at the dinner table. Before he turned his attention to her, he winked at me.

The restaurant was elegant, and dinner was on the company. I was petty enough to order salmon caviar for my appetizer. I knew the woman wouldn't know I was getting a little revenge, but still, it made me feel good, and it tasted good too.

I enjoyed the dinner except that every time I looked in Hal's direction, he was gazing at me. He looked away each time. I finally realized he was watching me. I think the other women would have been delighted to be the object of his attention, but it gave me the creeps. I didn't look in his direction again.

Jack and I walked back to the hotel.

"I had a nice evening," Jack said. "How about you?"

"Yes, after that little contretemps at the party."

"I tried to raise the subject, but the lady in question seemed to have lost her interest in service industry employment." Then, a little more serious, he said, "I love what you did, but you don't have to protect me from that sort of thing. I've had a lifetime of it. Most of the time, it doesn't get under my skin—certainly not when it's from someone as ignorant as that woman."

"It shocked me."

"It doesn't pay to be shocked at ignorance. You just do what you can to educate them, even though you can't save the world."

"That's why you teach?"

"Yes."

At eight o'clock the next morning, we had a short and more formal meeting at the Allied American building with Hal Josephs and Robert Hardy, Allied American's top man in Alaska.

"Hal will accompany you to Prudhoe Bay," Hardy said, "and he'll stay there the whole time you're in the field. You'll report to him daily by radio when you're in the camp. He'll fly supplies out to you every two weeks. Each time he visits your camp, I want you to give him a written summary of what you've found."

"That's what I expected," Jack said.

"You have any questions?"

"Not really, except that some of the maps and reports seemed to be missing from the boxes we received." He described the missing paperwork.

Hal said, "Those are for the area where the main buildings for oil processing are to be sited. Maybe the architects have them. I'll find out."

"Give Hal a memo on what's missing," Hardy said. "He'll get them for you."

"OK." Jack said. "What's the story on John MacNeil?"

There was a moment's silence. Hardy shifted in his seat. It almost seemed he wouldn't answer. Finally, he cleared his throat. "Quite a mystery."

Hal took over. "We have no idea what happened. We think he was more than halfway through with his work when we lost contact. We had a big search party up there but never found him."

"You don't think a bear killed him?" I asked.

"The campsite was undisturbed. Nothing tampered with his food supplies. We'd have found something if it had been a bear."

"Yes, it would have been obvious," Jack said. "Do you have copies of his notes for me to look at?"

"We never found his laptop. That's why we've changed our system. MacNeil reported in on his own schedule, which turned out to be not often."

"Odd," Jack said. "I knew him. He was a good researcher."

Hardy started to say something but, again, Hal stepped in. "We wondered whether he really hadn't done the work and chose to disappear because he couldn't fulfill the contract. I guess we'll never know unless he shows up someday."

"That's not the easiest place to run away from," Jack said. "People notice a stranger."

"We thought there was a possibility he'd walked to Fairbanks and caught a plane or a train."

"That's unlikely," Jack said, "but even if he did, I can't imagine he'd carry a laptop with him. He'd have so much other stuff he'd have to take."

Hardy interjected, "Maybe he wasn't thinking clearly by then. In any case, he put us a year behind. I hope you'll be able to give us a full and positive report by September. We need to move forward with this." He stood, so we did too.

"We'll do our best," Jack said.

Hardy shook hands with us, and Hal escorted us to the elevator. At one point, he put his hand on my back to guide me. I pulled away from his touch.

"What do you think?" I asked after the elevator doors closed, and Jack and I were alone.

"They obviously didn't want to talk about MacNeil. And I thought what Hal said about the missing paperwork was nonsense. There's certainly more than one set of all those maps and reports. The architects would have their own copies. Other than that, it's pretty straightforward, although the fact that we met with Hardy is a mark of how anxious they are to have that 'positive report.' I expected we'd be talking with someone at a lower level of authority. I hope this doesn't mean Hal's going to be breathing down our necks trying to hurry us up the whole time we're out there."

"Hal's a little strange," I said, tentatively.

"I can't figure him out. There's something off there, but I couldn't tell you what it is. He certainly wasn't as deferential to Hardy as I'd have expected. In fact, Hardy seemed to defer to him. It almost seemed as if Hardy was afraid of him."

"Yes, it did seem like that. What do you think about what they said about Dr. MacNeil?"

"A man would have to be crazy to choose to disappear. There's no chance he walked to Fairbanks, with or without his laptop. He'd have had to cross some high mountains. I wonder how much they looked for him." He shrugged. "A lot, I suppose, if they were so anxious for that report. Maybe we'll find him, or what's left of him."

Chapter Eight

We returned to the hotel. We'd been staying in a company-leased room, so we didn't have to check out. We called for a bellhop to carry our duffels to the limo. Jim loaded them on top of our field gear, already sitting in the capacious trunk.

Jack called Karen, and we swung by to pick up the dogs. Jack thought it would probably be better if they rode with us, so we left the travel crates unassembled. We'd use them when we took the dogs from Anchorage to Québec after completing the survey.

The dogs were rambunctious at first. Karen reminded us they'd never been away from home. They'd never even seen a car before. After the first few minutes of riding, however, they settled quietly at our feet.

Still, I felt uneasy. I'd never been responsible for a dog. I told Jack he'd probably have to train me more than the dogs.

At the airport, we pulled into the hangar where the company plane sat. Hal waited for us there. He'd been wearing a suit at Hardy's office. Now he wore jeans and a blue polo shirt.

He walked over and opened my door. I stepped out, carrying my backpack in one hand. Kiska, on her leash, followed.

A second man stepped over to help me with the backpack. As he neared me, Kiska moved so she stood between us, flattened her ears, raised her hackles, and snarled.

"Anne, snap the leash," Jack said, as he hurried around the car, all the while holding onto Moose's leash.

I snapped the leash as Karen had taught me. "Kiska, down." I was gratified when she immediately flattened on the ground, but she continued to snarl until I said, "Kiska, no." She stopped snarling, but she kept her eye on the man as I handed him my backpack.

"Well," Hal said. "A dog. That's a surprise. It doesn't seem to like you, Serbin."

The man didn't respond.

"Anne, Jack, this is my assistant, Alexander Serbin. He goes by Serbin. He'll pilot our helicopter out of Prudhoe Bay."

Serbin was clearly not an executive assistant. He was dressed in overalls and had grease under his fingernails. He nodded in our direction.

We said hello.

He was tall and slender—older than Hal, maybe in his fifties. At first, I'd have said he was skinny, but later I realized he was all tense wiry muscle. He had red hair, piercing green eyes, and freckles. At first it seemed almost a boyish face, but there was something that made me think, "No, not boyish," something more adult, even disquieting in a way.

Hal continued. "And this is Kent Richards. He'll be our pilot today."

Kent, a small black man in an Allied American Oil uniform, was more forthcoming than Serbin. He stepped forward and shook our hands. He didn't seem concerned about Kiska.

"Well," I said, "she didn't growl at you."

"Oh, no," he said. "Dogs like me. I don't worry about 'em." He reached down and gave her a rub on the head.

"What'll the flying be like today?" Jack said.

"Ah, it's a gorgeous day. It'll be great. If you want me to, I'll point out some of the sights as we go."

Jack nodded. "We'll look forward to it."

I wondered what it was about Serbin that upset Kiska and what he thought of her behavior with the pilot.

But Serbin hadn't noticed. He stood off to the side with Hal, now deep in conversation. I saw something—I don't know what—maybe it was their postures as they leaned in toward each other. Suddenly, I realized there was something much more equal in their relationship than I'd assumed. I'd thought Serbin was Hal's toady, but that was clearly not the truth of what was between them.

We thanked Jim for his service, and Jack tipped him.

We were still being treated like visiting royalty, so we didn't have to do anything but climb into the plane, settle the dogs, and strap ourselves in. We were in a nicely appointed executive jet—more like someone's living room than like a plane—that seated eight passengers in comfortable upholstered armchairs.

Hal sat with us. He told us it was a little over six hundred twenty miles—two and a half hours—to Deadhorse, the town near Prudhoe Bay.

Jack held Moose's leash, and I held Kiska's. They lay at our feet, alert to what was going on around them.

"Why did Kiska snarl at Serbin?" I asked.

"Sometimes dogs just don't like someone," Jack said. "They sense something. I don't know. We'd better watch her when he's around. I don't think she'd bite, but you never know."

When Serbin boarded, Kiska snarled deep in her chest, but then she quieted down on my command. He ignored her and walked forward to sit with Kent.

We were soon airborne.

"Either of you want a drink?" Hal asked when we'd leveled out. "The plane has a full bar. Better have it now if you want it. You won't get anything in Prudhoe Bay. Alcohol's prohibited there."

We turned it down.

He put ice cubes in a glass and filled it with whiskey—surprising, because at the cocktail party, like us, he drank mineral water. It was mid-morning. I marked him down in my mind as an alcoholic, or at least on his way to becoming one.

The whiskey relaxed Hal more than it should have, and ignoring my presence, he started to tell an off-color joke.

When Jack realized I didn't like it, he amazed me. He took control in a way I'd never seen him do before. When Hal wasn't looking, he winked at me, as he had at dinner the previous night.

He turned the conversation around and asked Hal questions—about the company, Prudhoe Bay, oil drilling, his work. Whenever Hal warmed to a question, Jack would drop the subject and move on to something else. Strangely, Hal had the most trouble describing his own job as a PR rep. Finally, I think just to get away from the interrogation, he excused himself and went to the restroom.

After he walked away, I said, "I bow to the master."

"Oh, no. It's easy. It's what we do in oral exams when we think a PhD candidate is trying to snow us."

"Remind me never to have you as my professor if I decide to work for an advanced degree."

"We'll think about that when the time comes," he said.

"Jack, did you notice that Serbin was wearing a pistol in a shoulder holster under his jacket."

"No. I didn't see it."

"When he backed off from Kiska, his jacket swung to one side for a second. Why would he have it?" I asked.

"I don't know. It certainly wouldn't be useful against anything where we're going except humans."

"I suppose he could use it against Kiska."

"Well, maybe," Jack said, "but that's not what he brought it for. He didn't know about her. We'd better keep an eye on him."

"Do you suppose Hal knows he has it?"

"I think he'd have to know."

"Hmm."

When Hal rejoined us, he said he had reports to read, so he hoped we'd excuse him from more conversation.

Jack said that was perfectly OK.

Hal sat in the seat farthest from us.

Jack turned his attention to me and gave me my first lesson in dog psychology. "Dogs are pack animals. Kiska has shown she already knows you're part of her pack. Every pack has a hierarchy. She'll probably dominate Moose. The females usually dominate."

"That's as it should be," I said.

He laughed. "Well, maybe. You need to make sure both of them know you're above them in rank."

"How do I do that?"

"You've made a good start. Every time you give a command, they must obey. At first, they'll try to see what they can get away with. They might even growl at you, but I don't think so. It's more likely they'll try to ignore you. If they do and get away with it, it'll be difficult for you to reestablish yourself as boss."

"How do I make sure they obey?"

"We'll work together. You'll figure it out and so will they. We can start now, if you want to."

"OK."

Karen taught her dogs in English, but Jack planned to switch them over to Inuktitut.

"Won't that be difficult?" I asked.

"They're intelligent. They'll pick up on what we want. Later, we'll work into teaching the other commands Quipac and I use."

"OK."

Karen had given us a list of the commands the dogs knew. Jack wrote the Inuktitut words next to the English. I practiced saying them, and Jack corrected my pronunciation.

He'd been teaching me Inuktitut right along. Everyone in our village spoke English too, but I wanted to be able to speak to my husband in his own language. Besides, sometimes when we were making love, Jack said things in Inuktitut. I found the sounds and cadence of that language incredibly erotic. He teased me by refusing to tell me what he'd said, but they were verbal caresses, and I wanted to know.

Chapter Nine

The flight was smooth and uneventful, the view out the window spectacular. As when I'd flown across Canada, I saw glaciers, forests, and lakes. We passed over the snow-covered peaks of the Brooks Range and beyond the northern extent of the trees, and then we were over tundra. Although we flew higher than the times I'd flown into Ungavaq, the ground again made me think of a fabulous oriental carpet of wonderful colors, predominantly gray and green, but with touches of red, orange, and yellow. It was fascinating and beautiful.

We finally landed and rolled to a stop on the tarmac at the Deadhorse airport.

"Strange name for the town," Hal said, "especially since, as far as anyone knows, there's never been a horse in northern Alaska, dead or alive. But there are plenty of caribou. Sometimes they wander out onto the runway. We always have to be careful when we land."

Strange thing to have in your obituary, I thought, *killed in a collision with a caribou.*

The plane taxied into a hanger where a van waited for us. Jack and I secured the dogs in a corner of the hangar out of the way and then joined Hal in the van. He sat in the front with the driver. Jack and I sat in the back.

When we drove out, we were in bright sunshine. Hal donned mirrored sunglasses. Then, he turned in the seat to talk to us. It disconcerted me not to be able to tell if he was looking at me or at Jack. He was definitely creepy.

He told us that Deadhorse had a full-time population of about 50, who catered to tourists and the 2,000 to 3,000 pipeline workers who were at Prudhoe Bay at any given time. The town had two hotels, two restaurants, a couple of gas stations, and a general store that had just about anything you could possibly want.

I was astonished when we approached Prudhoe Bay after a short drive. Pipes, chimneys, and huge storage tanks stood everywhere, but I didn't see any houses or stores. "I thought this was a village or a small town."

"The locals call this the Prudhoe Bay National Forest," Hal said. "It's more of an industrial site."

We went to eat in the dining room in one of the large dormitory buildings that housed the pipeline workers. Then we'd return to the airport to head out for our first field site.

Lunch was informal—no suits here, just jeans and flannel shirts. Hal had recovered from the effects of the whiskey and handled introductions to the local managers who shared the table with us. The people were nice enough. We had a pleasant time. Jack said it was unlikely we'd see them again.

Afterward, Hal had the driver take us on a short sightseeing drive to the pipeline, then back to the airport.

Our gear had been loaded into an Allied American helicopter.

The dogs, asleep where we'd tied them, woke, overjoyed, when they heard us. They weren't happy about the helicopter, though, and Kiska, especially, seemed tense being close to Serbin, but again, she obeyed and settled down after a few minutes.

Serbin flew us to the area where we'd start our work and spent more than an hour on a systematic aerial survey before Jack selected a place for our first campsite. Serbin set the helicopter down on a gravel bank near a fast-flowing stream.

A cold north wind blew out of a cloudless sky and chilled my face and hands as I stepped down onto the ground. I quickly pulled my hood up, tied it, and put on my gloves. We guessed the temperature to be in the mid-thirties.

The first thing we did was pound metal pins into the ground for the dog chains and settle Kiska and Moose. Then we off-loaded our gear. While we did that, Serbin set up and tested the radio. Before they left, Hal reminded us that we should radio in tomorrow, and he'd see us in two weeks.

We waved good-bye . . . and we were alone.

As the sound of the helicopter faded, the strangeness of it all overwhelmed me. A few hours ago, I'd eaten breakfast at the Captain Cook. Now, here we were. I'd never been in a place like this before. Except for Hal and Serbin in the departing helicopter, the nearest people were more than a hundred miles away.

The silence was palpable. I heard little noises—maybe insects somewhere—and nothing else. Then I heard some small splashes—something in the stream that flowed nearby—and that stopped. Gradually, bird noises started. They'd been silenced by the helicopter's roar.

I'd read that pioneer women had sometimes been driven insane by the silence of the American prairies. I hadn't understood what that silence was like, but now I did.

Jack looked at me and knew. "The quiet is amazing, isn't it? Sometimes it's wonderful and sometimes it's terrible. I talk to myself when I'm in places like this. It'll be a while before you're used to it, and if it begins to give you the willies, tell me."

"Does it give some people the willies?"

"Yes. Some of my students have had problems dealing with it. The cues you use to structure your day are gone—variations in sound levels, the position of the sun in the sky, things like that. We don't live by the sun in the summer. We eat when we're hungry and sleep when we're tired. Sometimes it's difficult to make the transition if you haven't done it before. We're in the land of the midnight sun. It won't dip below the horizon until the end of July. We may get a little twilight, but not much."

"Do you have trouble sleeping in the light?"

"No. I've done it all my life, but you may. Your body uses darkness as a signal to initiate sleepiness. You won't have that here. Let me know if you have trouble, but I think we'll work hard enough that it won't be a problem."

"OK."

"Let's get busy. We have to make our home."

"We brought all that bug repellent," I said, "but I don't see any mosquitoes or biting flies."

"It's still too cold, but wait a few weeks. You'll be either amazed or horrified when you see how bad they can be. We and the dogs will be OK because of the repellent, but the mosquitoes drive the caribou and other animals here almost insane. Mosquitos normally drink plant juices, but the females have to have a blood meal in order to produce eggs. Each has only one blood meal in her life, but with so many millions of them around, they can debilitate even a large animal like a caribou."

"That's sounds awful. I guess I'll try to enjoy these few bug-free weeks."

We set to work arranging the camp. We put up the tent and a windbreak for our stove, necessary because the wind blows out of the north almost all the time here as it does at home in Ungavaq.

When we stopped for a cup of tea, I asked, "Is this what most of your fieldwork is like?"

"I've usually have at least a few students along. I worked just with Quipac when I did other environmental impact studies, but those projects didn't take as long as this will. The longest one we did was only three weeks—not much more than a hunting trip. This will be most like when I was a kid. In the winter, the families gathered where Ungavaq is now and worked together to hunt seals, but in the summer, we spread out to fish and hunt caribou. Once in a while we camped with another family, but usually it was my parents, my grandmother, and me, and my sisters when they were born, and then, of course, Quipac when he joined our family."

"Do you remember when your sisters were born?"

"Oh, yes. Saarak and Allaq were born in the summer. My father would take me out to fish or something, and we'd go home, and there'd be a sister."

"Was your mother alone when they were born?"

"My grandmother was there. There wasn't anyone else around. Miqo was born in the winter when we were in Ungavaq. I woke up one morning, and she was there."

"Where were your children born?"

"In Ungavaq."

"Did Kaiyuina have help?"

"She didn't think she needed any."

"But, you were educated. Didn't you think she should have a doctor or a nurse?"

"I don't recall anyone being interested in my opinion at the time. That's women's work."

"I hope you won't be too disappointed when you find out I'm a wimp. I like to have doctors and nurses help me when I have a problem."

He sighed a big phony sigh. "I realize I might have to make allowances. As much as I love you, I know nobody's perfect. But I hope you understand all you have out here is me."

"I guess I'll just have to make do. Actually, I've taken a lot for granted. I didn't ask you about the preparations for this trip. And I do need training on what we do if we have an emergency."

"When we get things set up so we can make dinner when we're hungry, we'll go through the medical kit. You're right. Since we have a fifty-fifty chance I'll be the one who needs help, I want my nurse properly trained."

The medical kit was the well-equipped one Jack and Quipac carried whenever they took students to the field. They had to be prepared for almost anything when the nearest medical or dental help could be hundreds of miles away. Jack showed me each item in the kit and explained the uses of the unfamiliar ones. He even had the instruments to take out an appendix if he had to, but so far, it hadn't been required.

The kit held several medicines, including antibiotics and pain-killers. It also included needles and thread for stitches. Since they were usually doing physical labor at the digs, cuts and abrasions were common. Jack had shown me one long scar on his hand left from an injury that Quipac had stitched up. He showed me how to do surgeon's knots, and I practiced on some fabric until they were easy for me.

We prepared dinner, cleaned up, and fed Moose and Kiska. Then we relaxed on canvas chairs in the tent and sipped tea.

"I have a present for you," he said.

"A present?"

"Yes."

He rose and stepped behind me. I could hear him open one of the duffels. He handed me a gift-wrapped box.

"What is it?"

"A little something to tell you I love you. Open it."

I unwrapped it carefully, so I could save the pretty paper and ribbon. I opened the box and laughed. Inside were fifteen bottles of nail polish and a bottle of polish remover.

I've never been able to keep a manicure nice because I do so much gardening, so I make up for it by doing pedicures. After we married, I found out Jack really likes feet.

I took the bottles out one by one—a kaleidoscope of pinks and reds and scarlets and corals and even one blue. Most were colors I'd never have thought of buying.

"Oh, Jack. They're wonderful. Did Marcia buy them?"

"No, I did. It took me a long time to get the right colors. I had to imagine them on your toes." And he actually blushed.

I formed a mental picture of Jack at the Hudson's Bay Store cosmetics counter choosing nail polish colors. I didn't imagine that many Inuit men shopped for nail polish there. I'll bet that gave the saleswomen something to talk about.

He smiled. "There's something else." He handed me a smaller box.

It held a beautiful, intricately designed gold bracelet.

"Oh, Jack. It's beautiful." I wrapped it around my wrist. "But we'll have to shorten it."

"No," he said. "It's for your ankle."

"Oh, but you won't be able to see it under these heavy socks."

"I'll know it's there."

"Will you put it on me?"

He smiled again.

Chapter Ten

The new polish on my toenails—Plum Passionate—was dry. I pulled my socks on. "Tell me what your family did when the work was done."

"The work was never really done for the adults. My mother and grandmother always had skins to prepare and clothes to make or repair. I don't think their hands were ever still. My father carved toys or tools or fixed broken things. As they worked, they talked to each other or to us. They told us stories or we sang. We played games.

"Sometimes we had puppies to play with, and that was fun. You've seen our dogs. Some of them can be pretty rough, but they know from early on they have to be careful with children. I don't recall any of us ever being snapped at, let alone bitten, and we played rough with them."

"I have to admit," I said, "I'm afraid of those dogs in Ungavaq. They snarl and howl."

"I know, but when you learn about Moose and Kiska and build your confidence, you'll get over that. You have to give it time."

"You think they'd bite?"

"When we get them back to Ungavaq, they'll have to find their places in that pack, and that may involve fighting, but they don't ever get to even snarl at you or me. We won't allow that."

"I'll try not to be afraid."

"Good."

"Tell me more about your summers when you were young."

"In the summer there, it's light almost around the clock. We weren't as far north as we are here, so we did have a few hours of true dark, but we didn't have anything like a set bedtime. We didn't have set meal times either, although once a day we'd eat together. Most of the time, we ate when we were hungry. We'd ask my mother when we wanted something. Mother often called us for tea, though, and we'd be together."

"Tea must have been one of the things you traded for at the trading post."

"Yes, we could get it only once a year. Mother used to dry the tea leaves on rocks, and we'd reuse them until all the flavor was gone."

"All those little pieces of tea?"

"No. Our tea came in whole leaves, not in tea bags."

"How old were you when Quipac came to live with you?"

"I was about eight. It was a terrible year. I still remember the hunger. The seals didn't come. Mother gave birth to my brother that year, but she had no milk; he didn't live."

"I didn't know you had a brother."

"I don't remember him very well. I don't think he lived more than a month. Infanticide happened sometimes among the Inuit, but I don't think that's what happened to him. I remember how sad my mother was. That might be the reason Quipac came to live with us. Orphans didn't have an easy time among the Inuit and often had to fend for themselves, but my parents made a home for Quipac even when we didn't have much food. He wasn't related to us. He was one of the boys I played with."

"What happened to his family?"

"His father was a good hunter. I don't know how he died, but they found him dead near a seal breathing-hole. His mother probably died of hunger. She had no one to hunt for her. In a good year, someone would have married her quite soon, but not in a hunger year. People shared food with her but only after they'd fed their own families. So many died that winter—mostly children and old people. She kept Quipac alive."

"How?"

"She smothered his sisters so there'd be more food for him."

"Oh, no!"

"Anne, life was hard sometimes. Quipac lived. She saved one of her children."

"How could she make such a choice?"

"She wasn't given the option of not making the choice, and if she died, Quipac was old enough to have a chance to survive. The girls weren't."

"How many sisters did he have?"

"Two—a baby and a four-year-old."

"Oh."

"That life had a lot of good things, but it had a lot of bad things too. Sometimes the animals cooperated by presenting themselves to be hunted, and sometimes they didn't and people died." He shrugged. "People today tend to romanticize the past, but I don't think many would like to live that way again."

Jack took the last sip of his now-cold tea. "Let's not talk about that anymore. We're fairly well organized. Let's go for a walk around our territory and see what there is to see."

We fastened the leashes on the dogs. They were still too new to trust off-leash. We had a relaxed walk along the stream—snow-melt that flowed north out of the distant Brooks Mountains and across the sloping plain. Large patches of snow scattered here and there also fed the many streams and small ponds we saw in every direction.

Brilliantly clear air allowed us to see for miles. The gravel-strewn ground made the walking easy. Jack said that later, when our work required us to walk across marshes, the walking wouldn't be so effortless.

Birds flitted and called everywhere. I recognized some: sparrows and redwing blackbirds. Of course, there were ravens. Ducks sat on the gravel bank a hundred feet upstream of us. They were too far away for me to see what kind they were. Jack told me that more than two hundred species of birds ate, mated, and raised their young here during the height of summer. Most were migrants that came for the abundance of food—the millions of mosquitoes and flies. They left for the south when the weather turned harsh. Some flew as far as the tip of South America.

I received a thorough lesson on Arctic flora that day too. Plants were greening up. They hinted of the lush growth to come, but the permafrost started as little as a few inches down, leaving scant room for anything to root. The shallowness of the usable soil dwarfed those that were normally taller. Nothing grew more than about eighteen inches high.

Jack said the plants' ground-hugging size protected them from the drying effects of the almost-constant wind from the north, and it allowed them to make maximum use of the insulation of the snow cover in the winter.

He named some of them for me: grayleaf willow, dwarf Arctic birch, sedge, the ubiquitous Arctic cotton grass, and many other dwarf shrubs, flowering plants, lichens, and moss.

I could see how attractive this area would be to grazing animals. The succession of plants allowed the caribou to eat their way through one kind as a different one sprouted. The North Slope provided a bountiful feast, necessary if the caribou were to store enough fat to survive the subsequent winter. Each of the tens of thousands of caribou soon to be here could eat as much as ten pounds of plants a day. In spite of the abundance, however, the caribou would start to leave in mid-July when the flies and mosquitoes became intolerable.

When we returned to camp, Jack went into the tent while I lit our stove to make tea. Suddenly something jumped off the worktable and ran across my feet.

I screamed.

Jack came running. "What's the matter?"

"Something ran across my feet!"

"Was it a bear? That certainly was a bear-sized scream."

"No, it wasn't a bear!"

"Can you describe it?"

"It was small and brown, and it had a short tail, and it ran very fast."

"After your scream, it's probably still running."

"I have a feeling I'm not getting much sympathy here."

"Oh, no. On the contrary. It was either a lemming or a vole." His voice became serious. "I hope it was a vole, because lemmings are actually quite dangerous, especially for white women wearing short boots and long trousers. You know, that's why the Eskimo women around here wore short pants and boots that came up over their knees. Otherwise, the lemmings would crawl right up."

I laughed. "You just wait. The day will come when you'll want a little sympathy."

In spite of Jack's story about lemmings, I didn't have any problem getting to sleep when we went to bed, but I woke up thinking about Quipac's sisters. The bright daylight confused me, and I didn't know whether I should go back to sleep or get up. I finally decided I'd wait for Jack to roust me out of bed, and I closed my eyes again.

The next thing I knew, I heard Jack's voice say, "Sleeping all day?"

I yawned and stretched. "I might get up."

"I'll just leave your tea over here."

I groaned. "No tea in bed?"

"Not here. Get up, Lazy Bones. It's after six. We're on the clock. Time to get to work."

I managed to drag myself out of the sleeping bag before the tea cooled. We had a quick breakfast and then took out the maps and planned our day.

Jack knew the background of the Arctic National Wildlife Refuge, and he'd taught a mini-class for me, including several reading assignments, before we left Ottawa. I learned ANWR was established in 1960 in the extreme northeast corner of Alaska and covers more than nineteen million acres. In addition to the caribou herd, it accommodates thirty-six species of land mammals. So far, I'd only seen a vole or a lemming or whatever it was, but I could anticipate seeing many more kinds.

We wouldn't survey the entire refuge. Oil exploration was prohibited in the area covered by the Brooks Mountains. The oil companies could explore only the coastal plain, from the lowest slopes of the mountains to the shore. Even within that limited area, we could only sample likely spots, not really do a complete survey.

Jack explained that if a university or research institution funded this project, an excavation crew might come behind us. But they wouldn't do a full dig on each site we identified—no matter how rich in potential it might seem—because of the cost. A dig in permafrost requires thawing the ground by pouring heated water on it, a slow, expensive, and messy enterprise. They'd do sample trenches to see what they could turn up. If they found something important, a full dig might be done in the future.

"If they find something, who does it belong to?" I asked.

"If it's found on federal land, like ANWR, it belongs to the funding institution, assuming they have the proper federal permits."

"You mean the oil company?"

"In this case, they are the funding institution."

"What would they do with a find?"

He shrugged. "Beats me. My guess is they'd destroy it. They don't want to encourage archaeological interest up here. That's why, when I negotiated the contract, I reserved the right of ownership of any artifacts we find. I also got the right to write scholarly papers without having to wait until the environmental impact study becomes public record and without them having the right of censorship."

"They agreed to all that?"

"They didn't want to, but it was getting late. They needed us, so they were willing to make concessions."

We'd divided the coastal plain into sections on the map. We planned to hike to the most likely places in a section to look for signs of ancient habitation.

I understood what to look for on the satellite photos and maps, but I hadn't learned how to translate that two-dimensional information into three-dimensional geographic features. Jack taught me patiently, though, and I soon began to understand what I saw.

We walked a lot those first two weeks but found no clear sign of human occupation. A couple of times we carried our sleeping bags and stayed overnight.

Jack called in every night on schedule to report to Hal, except for those nights when we were away from camp.

We did see bears, but each time, we waved and shouted and jumped up and down. The bears wanted no part of us. They turned tail and left.

As planned, Hal and Serbin showed up in the helicopter two weeks later. We had our trash and laundry bagged up and everything else packed and ready when they arrived.

The minute Serbin stepped out onto the ground, Kiska started a low rumbling in her chest.

I double-checked her leash. "Serbin, you're going to be in camp every two weeks. Would you like to make friends with Kiska? I could help you."

He looked at me coldly. "No." He turned and walked away.

The transfer to our new site worked out as we'd hoped. It took less than an hour to load the helicopter. We repeated the aerial flyover of the next section until we saw a likely campsite; they set us down with our bag of mail and our new supply of food and clean clothes.

When we'd off-loaded everything, Jack said, "Hal, did you bring copies of the missing maps and photos?"

"No. Those idiots couldn't find them. My guess is they haven't looked very hard. I'll get on their tails about it. Somebody needs to give them a kick in the butt."

I liked everything we did, except I came to dread the transfers because they involved time with Hal. I tried to like him, but he always gave me the creeps.

He continued to tell dirty jokes, and when Jack made his lack of interest clear, Hal told them to Serbin when he stood near me and Jack couldn't hear. He watched me as he talked to see how I'd react. I felt like I was in high school again, and that helped me realize he did it for attention. After that, I tried to be so absorbed in something else that I appeared not to listen. He gave it up after a while.

He also sometimes touched me "accidentally." More high school stuff. He'd hand something past me to Serbin, or walk past me, or hand me something and brush his hand or arm across my breast or some other part of my body. He never did this when Jack watched. He seemed to have an uncanny ability to hide his actions.

The first time he touched me, I didn't think anything of it. Accidents happen. Neither of us commented or even said, "Excuse me." The second time, I thought, *Gosh, I really seem to be in the way here.* The third time, I realized they weren't accidents.

After Hal and Serbin took off that day, I told Jack what had happened.

He didn't react in anger. Jack, as did the Inuit in general, made a practice of suppressing anger.

"There are men like that everywhere. Getting away with little things stimulates them, especially if they can do it when another man's present. Is Serbin a problem too?"

"No. He avoids me."

"I think it would be better if we don't confront Hal directly. We have to work with him until September. We have no way to go over his head and get him reassigned. We'll just make sure I'm between you and him when he's in camp."

"Why would he do this, Jack?"

"You don't know?"

"No."

"He's attracted to you."

"I don't think that can be true. He's so much younger than I am."

"Believe me, Anne, you're very attractive. I fell in love with you the first time I saw you. Robby did too. Something similar happened with René. I asked him how he met you. He said he didn't normally pick up women wearing wedding rings, but he saw you in the lobby of the Archives, and something about you drew him to you. You have a quality that appeals to men."

"I never knew."

"Well, I sure know it, and apparently Hal does too. It's OK. We'll take care of it."

During our next transition, Jack stayed between Hal and me. It worked. We had only one more unpleasant incident. As they were getting ready to leave, Hal stood with his side toward me, exposed himself, and urinated.

Jack saw.

"Hal, that's inappropriate. Anne's right here. You go to the other side of the helicopter in the future."

"Hell, Jack, we're all friends here. I don't think Anne minds."

"I mind. You won't disrespect my wife again. Are we clear?"

"All right. All right. Sorry, Anne." He turned to Serbin, "Let's go."

He didn't try anything else after that.

Chapter Eleven

Other than the problem with Hal, we enjoyed our days.

We'd marked sites on the maps that looked interesting, and Jack prioritized them as to the likelihood we'd find something there. I didn't help with that. Jack said there wasn't any way to teach me how to do it from the maps and photos. I had to get field experience before I'd have a sense of what to look for.

As we worked, we found artifacts in some places and not in others we thought had potential. "It never pays," he said, "to be too invested in a site until you actually find something."

I was thrilled when I made my first find. We were on our hands and knees probing the spongy ground with our trowels. I hit something. When I unearthed an edge of stone obviously worked by human hands, I called him. Together we finished excavating a carved soapstone lamp, called a *qulliq*.

"That's wonderful," he said. "Now you're a real archaeologist."

"Do you think it's old? I mean, it could be sort of modern, couldn't it?"

"Sure, it could. My family used these when I was a kid, but this one's not recent. From the shape, I'd say it's early Eskimo—about four thousand years old. We can't know for sure until we get that residue on the edge carbon dated. If we had time, we could do more of a dig here to see what other artifacts it's associated with, but I think I'm not too far off."

"Oh, Jack, this is so exciting."

"Now you know why I like to do it. You never get over that excitement. You've found something special. You can be proud of yourself.

"Archaeologists build a picture of an ancient society one clue at a time. Something like that lamp implies a lot about a culture. I don't think any deposits of soapstone exist nearby. That lamp tells us these people traveled or else traded with others who traveled to acquire it. If we had some money and time, we could figure out where the raw material came from. Each deposit of mineral or rock has a unique chemical signature. Trade patterns can be defined by knowing where this soapstone came from. Now, Madam Archaeologist, it's your turn to make an entry in the log."

So I wrote the entry—the date, the place, an identification number, and a description of what I'd found, plus my initials. We wrapped the lamp carefully, and I put it in my backpack.

I couldn't wait to get back to work.

When we weren't prospecting for sites, we took time to have fun. We worked on training the dogs to respond to Inuktitut commands, and Jack taught me how to handle my rifle, a 38-55 Winchester 94 Legacy. We shot at targets every day, and I improved to where I could hit the empty food cans more times than I missed. Sometimes I watched him stand in an icy stream and fish with his spear. We ate that fish—usually Arctic char—raw as soon as he brought it out of the water, the ultimate sashimi. We talked more and more in Inuktitut. I had to switch back to English when I couldn't express myself, but I improved with practice.

In spite of what Jack had told me, I wasn't prepared when the mosquitoes and biting flies finally started to hatch. Early on, they were sort of slow and sleepy, maybe from the chill, so we weren't too bothered by them. Later, they swarmed around us in a cloud when we were outside, and when we were in the tent, they sounded like rain hitting the nylon sides. We had to renew our bug repellent and that of the dogs several times a day. Bathing—what little we did—was a challenge.

The mosquitoes annoyed me, but I came to hate the flies, not for what they did to us, but for what they did to the caribou. They laid their eggs in the caribou's nostrils. When the larvae hatched out, they burrowed in and ate the living flesh. Jack told me that in the late summer, the larvae would eat their way out from under the skin of the caribou and drop to the ground to pupate. In the old days, skins of caribou killed during that part of the year hadn't been usable for clothing because of the holes.

I did have trouble sleeping sometimes. Jack had told me to wake him if I had a problem. When I did, he held me, and we'd talk quietly with our eyes closed. Sometimes we made love, but most of the time, I'd drift off to sleep as he told me stories in Inuktitut. They were about the great shaman hero Kiviuq, who traveled many miles, lived many lifetimes, and may still be alive. He had dangerous adventures, but used his magical powers to escape each time.

One time, Kiviuq was traveling in his kayak when he saw a stone hut. He pulled ashore and went to investigate. In the hut, he saw an old woman. She invited him in. She put his *kamiik*—his shoes—and his stockings to dry on the rack above the qulliq, while he settled in to take a nap. When he woke, he tried several times to get his kamiik, but the rack moved out of reach each time. He realized that the woman was a witch and a cannibal. She intended to eat him. He called upon his familiar, a polar bear, who approached the woman and roared at her. This frightened her so much that she gave Kiviuq his clothing, and he escaped back to his kayak and the safety of the sea. That was just one of his many adventures.

Jack told me later the stories were the ones you told small children when they were relaxing and getting sleepy in the igloo or tent. They certainly worked for me.

I knew I was like a child in Jack's world, and he was helping me grow into my Inuit identity. I understood I couldn't become Inuit. Still, as his wife, I had to find my place in his society, and this whole process was part of that.

One day, when we were walking, I asked, "What's that strange clicking noise?"

Jack called the dogs and attached their leashes.

"Look." He pointed. "You're going to see your first caribou. The pregnant females have arrived. That sound happens when they walk. Tendons in their ankles snap across a bone each time they take a step."

Ahead, on a slight rise not too far away, there she was. She wasn't in a hurry, but she seemed to be walking with purpose. Then there were two . . . then ten . . . then hundreds . . . and, finally, thousands. It's almost impossible to describe that flood of brown cresting the hill and flowing onto the plain.

I'd never seen anything like it. There's no way to express the thrill I felt.

A few had new-looking calves, and most of the others were obviously pregnant. I knew the bulls, juveniles, and nonpregnant cows would arrive later.

"They'll all drop their calves in the next ten days or so," Jack said.

"They're synchronized?"

"Yes. Nature doesn't give much leeway here."

They were smaller than I expected. They look so big in photographs, and if I'd stood next to one, its antlers would have towered over me, but its head would be only at my chest level.

Some glanced at us, but didn't seem to be the least bit curious or concerned, even about the dogs.

Kiska and Moose were terribly excited though. Jack ordered them to lie down. They obeyed, but lay trembling and panting with the desire to give chase.

"They don't react to us or the dogs," I said.

"We're far enough away that they don't consider us a threat. The dogs are lying down, so they know they're not hunting. If they'd moved toward the caribou you'd have seen different behavior."

We waited and watched until the caribou had passed.

"This is just the beginning," Jack said. "We'll see many more. They're heading closer to the coast. They'll give birth and spend the next six weeks or so fattening for the winter."

We started to walk again. We hadn't gone more than fifty feet when I saw a newborn calf that stood shivering and bleating for its mother. The umbilical cord still hung down.

"Would you like fresh meat for dinner?" Jack said.

"Would you kill that calf?" I was shocked.

Jack answered my question with a question. "Have you ever eaten veal? You need to think about this. That calf will die if the mother doesn't find it, and it's unlikely she will. It may starve, but more likely wolves or an eagle or a bear will get it. That's what life is like here. We're just one more predator. The dogs and I are going to eat caribou this summer. You don't have to, and you won't go hungry. But you remember about the seal we killed during the class and the foxes, and even the bear. We're Inuit. We hunt. That's what we do."

"Can you give me more time? Could you not kill that one?"

"Of course."

And so we walked on.

I understood what Jack had said. The difference between us was that I'd always had a middleman between my food and me, so I didn't have to think about where it came from. I knew Jack was more honest than I was, but still, I needed more time to think about it.

Chapter Twelve

Finally, the helicopter set us down in the mystery section, as we'd come to think of it—the one for which we'd never received the maps and photos. We were to camp here for three weeks and maybe even longer, depending on what we found.

In the middle of the second week, we hiked out to a place near a stream. We planned to stay overnight.

"I'll walk up the stream bank to see if I find a better camp site," Jack said. "Do you want to rest or go with me?"

"I'll sit here a little. My dogs are barking."

"What does that mean? The dogs aren't barking."

"It means my feet are telling me they've had enough walking for a while."

Jack smiled. "I've never heard that one before. Sometimes, I think you make these things up. We'll be back in a little while." He whistled to the dogs. They'd been running, playing, investigating, but came immediately. Jack and the dogs turned south and walked upstream.

I sat a while and then began to be bored, so I started to entertain myself by throwing things into the stream. My mother would have said, "Simple things for the simple mind." Well anyway, I was having fun. I put leaves in to see them float downstream. And I tried a few sticks, and that was fun. Then I decided to throw pebbles to see how far I could make them go.

I'd thrown three pebbles, getting a little more distance with each one. A sort of grayish-white pebble caught my eye. I tried to pick it up, but it wouldn't come. I said to myself, that's strange, so I tried a little harder, but it still wouldn't come. I leaned down to look at it and felt a chill go down my spine and the hair on my arms stand up. It was a tooth . . . and it looked human!

I had a trowel and a little brush in my backpack. My hands shook so much I could barely hold them. I gently loosened the soil and pebbles around the tooth the way Jack had taught me and brushed the loose material out of the way. When I saw that the tooth was embedded in a piece of bone, I knew I shouldn't do anything more.

I stood and, leaving my backpack to mark the place, walked quickly upstream until I saw Jack coming toward me.

He walked casually until he was closer. I must have looked as upset as I felt, though, because then he began to run. When he reached me, he put his arms around me. "What's the matter?"

"Oh, Jack. I may have found Dr. MacNeil."

"What do you mean?"

"I found a bone, a jaw with a tooth in it."

"Show me."

We walked quickly back to where I'd been sitting. I pointed to the tooth.

Jack knelt next to where I'd dug. "OK, you can relax. It's not Dr. MacNeil."

"How do you know?"

"Because you just found your first fossil. It is human though. You have sharp eyes."

We spent the next hour carefully excavating the jawbone.

Jack never touched it with his hand. He used a small clean towel we'd brought. When I asked why, he said, "There's a small chance that there's some retrievable DNA left in these bones. They probably have our DNA on them already, but we don't want to contaminate them any more than necessary. Try never to put your hands directly on them."

"I touched the tooth."

"That can't be helped. We'll just be careful from now on."

It was an entire left mandible, a lower jaw, and it had two more teeth in it. What I'd seen was a molar. The jaw also had a premolar and a canine tooth. The bone was broken in three pieces, but it was all there. We dug around and found one more molar. That made four teeth. The two incisors—the teeth in the front—were missing.

Jack said the person was probably a girl and a teenager when she died. He showed me that the wisdom teeth had started to erupt.

"I can understand how the teeth would relate to age, but why do you think it was a girl?"

"It's just a guess based on all the skulls and jawbones I've seen. I'd say that this one is more gracile than robust, so it indicates a girl. We'd need the pelvis or some DNA to know for sure."

His hands shook as he held the piece of jaw, but I realized it was from excitement—not fear, as my shaking had been. I'd never seen him like that before.

"Is this important?" I asked.

"It's too early to know exactly how old it is, but it's old. It'll require testing to establish a date. We don't often find something old in such good shape. The glaciers were pretty good at grinding things up, but this has only a little wear on it. I'm torn. This is exciting, but we don't have the tools to do a proper excavation. We shouldn't dig anymore."

"Let's take a break and make tea. It'll give you time to think it over."

"Good idea," he said.

I dipped water out of the stream with the teakettle and set it to heat on our little portable white-gas stove. When it was ready, we sipped tea and looked at the pieces of the jawbone on the ground between us.

"Do you always get this excited when you find a fossil?" I asked. "You weren't like this about the other things we found."

"You're right. I need to calm down and think like a scientist. The right thing to do is to get a GPS reading on this spot and then leave it alone, so it can be properly excavated later. There's erosion with each snowmelt. That's what exposed the tooth, but any other bones under there will be safe for the time being."

"What are we going to do?"

"We'll stay here tonight. We need to see what else we can find. We're so lucky you spotted that tooth, but I want you to know it wasn't just luck. Most people looking at that little white pebble would never have stopped to ask what it was. You have the right instincts, and we can develop them if you're interested. If you were a student, I'd be so pleased if you asked me to be your graduate advisor."

"What's a girl going to do with praise like that except say of course I'd like to learn. It's like finding buried treasure. Every time we find something, I want more. I feel greedy."

We wrapped the three pieces of bone and the tooth and put them into Jack's backpack. He also took soil samples from where we'd dug out the jaw. Then we refilled the holes we'd dug and stacked stones into a cairn to mark the place.

We examined the surrounding area downstream that evening and the next day, but didn't find more bones or any artifacts.

We did discover something else, though—signs someone had camped nearby. Jack said it looked as though that person had been digging, but if so, it wasn't this year. There weren't many people on the refuge, and there weren't many reasons to dig. Had Dr. MacNeil been here? It seemed likely.

Chapter Thirteen

It's strange how two people who love each other can hurt each other, and the hurt is so much more because of the love.

We stayed in bed late—at least late for us. We had a day off because, although it was the end of a two-week period, we weren't moving camp, though Hal and Serbin were bringing supplies. We almost felt guilty, but we talked ourselves into snuggling a while.

The dogs were up and ready to go, but Jack told them to quiet down, and they more or less did.

We cuddled and kissed and dozed.

When we decided it was time to get up, I was relaxed and happy. I guess that's why I was unprepared when, as he handed me my cup of tea, Jack said, "I want you to go back with the helicopter today, first to Prudhoe Bay and then to San Diego."

"What?"

"You didn't hear me?"

"No, I heard you. I didn't understand."

He switched to English. "It would be better if you go back to San Diego."

"But I don't want to go back."

And then it happened.

I used to say to myself that sometimes a switch would click, and Jack would change. I'd seen him change from villager to urbanite and from villager to college professor, but I hadn't seen one of those changes in months, I think because we were away from the places that required them. Now, I saw a change that was different. Jack looked at me and said formally and quietly, "It is unusual for a wife to disagree with her husband. Perhaps she knows better than he does."

For a moment, I didn't understand, and then I realized I'd somehow touched the Inuit part of Jack, and that switch had clicked. I knew Inuit women were expected to be subordinate to men, but this was the first time since I'd met Jack that it had become an issue. I thought carefully about what to say.

"A wife is confused. A wife understood the word 'partner' to have a certain meaning."

He said brightly and with a big false smile, "Partner . . . yes. But when a woman doesn't need her husband to hunt for her and doesn't need him to protect her, maybe her husband can sew for her. Ah, yes. Maybe she needs a wife instead of a husband. Do we have needles in the camp? Perhaps I can learn." And he laughed.

If Jack had hit me, it wouldn't have hurt as much as those words did. His "jolly" statement betrayed deep anger. The Inuit value suppressing anger. They reveal it through ridicule. I hadn't realized before this moment how wounding ridicule could be.

I was at a loss. I couldn't say anything. In all the time we'd been together, we hadn't argued. I know all married people argue sometimes, but I didn't know the rules of this kind of fighting or what I could say that wouldn't make things worse. So I said, quietly, the only thing I could. "A wife will do as her husband wishes."

I set my cup down on our small folding table and walked away to sit in the camp chair near the tent with my back to him. I felt hollow and empty. Against my will, tears started to trickle down my cheeks. I tried to stop them so he wouldn't know, but I couldn't.

After a minute, without saying anything more, Jack walked over and sat next to me. He had my cup in his hand. He put his arm around me gently, tentatively. "A husband wishes he had not said what he said." He drew me close and, as he had one other time, turned and kissed my tears away.

"A husband who is loved can hurt a wife more with words than with blows," I said.

He pulled me a little closer, and we sat quietly and gradually relaxed.

After a while I said, "Please tell me why you want me to go back."

He shifted and looked at me. He took my hand. "I've been a bachelor too long. I should have told you what I've been thinking." He handed me my cup. "There's something wrong with this whole deal." He shook his head. "I can't put my finger on it, but I don't feel good about the way the company's been behaving—wanting to hire Bob when he wasn't qualified, the missing maps and reports, and Hal's lame excuses, that strange story about MacNeil, and especially Hal's attitude toward us. That's why I want you to go back."

"Then you should go back with me."

He rose, walked over to get his tea, returned, and sat again. "I have to stay to complete the contract. There's something else. You may have found something important. I didn't say anything the other day, because I didn't want to jump the gun, but I've been thinking about it, and we may have found an Early Man site."

"What do you mean? An early Eskimo site?"

"I mean something a lot older than that."

"How much older?"

"Many anthropologists think humans came to the Americas about thirteen thousand years ago or so, during the last ice age, although there are some sites that may prove to be earlier. We're not sure. Thirteen thousand years ago, much of the world's water was frozen into glaciers, and the sea level dropped all over the world. Most of Alaska was covered with glaciers, but this area along the Arctic Ocean and a corridor down the west side were relatively ice-free."

"You're saying they got here somehow?"

"You know that now there're only about fifty miles between Siberia and Alaska in one location. When the sea level dropped, a land bridge formed between eastern Asia and Alaska."

"Bridge? Like the bridge between San Diego and Coronado?" I asked.

"That's a narrow bridge. This land bridge was twelve hundred or more miles wide. And people wouldn't have crossed it as if they were commuting to work. They'd have drifted across it over a period of years and decades as they followed the herds and hunted. The herds were just moving and grazing in new areas where there was no competition."

He sipped his tea. "For years, anthropologists argued over this. Some insisted thirteen thousand years wasn't enough time for people to get from Alaska to the tip of South America and that humans must have come over at some time before that in a previous migration. Others disagreed.

"In 1996, someone found a fossil skull along the Columbia River in Washington State that they called Kennewick man. Well, the you-know-what hit the fan. Arguments raged about the dating, and then the Native Americans jumped in. The Umatilla in that area claimed the skull as an ancestor, and under US law, something called the Native American Graves Protection and Repatriation Act, if that were true, they had the right to rebury it according to their religious rites. This would have prevented scientists from having access to it. The skull was locked away, and the whole thing was fought through the courts. Ultimately, in 2004, the Umatilla lost."

"That law sounds like political correctness gone berserk," I said.

"But it had a real basis. Congress enacted the law because it had been usual for scientists to dig up Indian burial grounds, even recent graves, and take grave goods and bones and mummified bodies to display in museums. Museums all over the United States had thousands of skulls and skeletons and artifacts from burials in their collections. Many of those bones and bodies belonged to family members of living people. Think how you would feel if someone decided to dig up Robby and display his body in the Museum of Man in San Diego."

"Oh, I see what you mean."

"The Indians lost in court. The judge ruled there had to be proof of a connection between that skull and the current tribe, beyond the fact that the skull was found on tribal land, and there couldn't be evidence either way until the scientists did their analysis.

"The Kennewick skull created a lot of excitement. People thought it might push the dates back beyond thirteen thousand years. When it was properly dated, it turned out to be about nine thousand, three hundred years old, not as old as some people hoped, but still one of the oldest human fossils found so far in the Americas.

"The same year Kennewick was found, someone found more fossil bones in southern Alaska. Those were ultimately dated at ten thousand, three hundred years old.

"You may possibly have discovered a site at least that old, or maybe even older. If I'm wrong, then it's an early Eskimo site, but it's still old and important. The fact that we've found anything is a problem for opening this area for oil exploration. Remember, this is the area where the processing facilities are to be located. If this should turn out to be an Early Man site, it would be explosive news all over the world. It probably wouldn't stop talk of opening this area, but it would slow it up considerably."

I set my empty cup down on the ground. "What does that mean?"

"We're talking about the oil companies potentially losing billions of dollars because of the delay."

"Then this fossil is a real threat."

"I didn't tell you, but I'm sure you realized we were sent here to find nothing. My report was supposed to say I'm a big expert, and I looked at everything, and there's nothing here of interest or value. And, in spite of my hopes, that's the kind of report I expected to write. I thought the odds were in favor of us finding a few relatively recent sites. Anything like that could probably have been fenced off and protected."

"Can't they fence off the jawbone site?"

"Finding the jawbone makes the whole coastal plain important. We wouldn't know where we might find something else of value until the whole plain was surveyed and all potential sites tested. It would have to be off limits to the oil company. It might be years before they knew for sure where oil equipment could be sited.

"I thought of this survey as an extension of our honeymoon. You could learn more about camping, working with the dogs, how to shoot, and we could have fun. But that's not the way it's turned out. Now, I can't write that report they want so badly."

"Couldn't they fire you and bring someone else in to write their report?"

He shook his head. "It's too late. I know what I know. I wouldn't be quiet about it even if I did get fired."

"What do you think they might do about it?"

He shrugged. "I don't know. I'm bothered by the fact that they never found the maps and photos for the area where you discovered the jawbone. I don't know if that means they know about the site. I may have read too many political novels, but I can't put John MacNeil out of my mind. I think there's a possibility they might try to silence us. I'm worried about your safety. I think it would be better if you went back to San Diego, even though it means riding with Hal."

"What about you?"

"I'll finish the survey. It's only four more weeks. I don't intend to tell them what we've found until I'm back. I didn't mention the jawbone in the daily report when I radioed in, and I didn't include it in the log I'll give to Hal. I'll wait until I turn in the final report.

I've written a short summary. I want you to carry it and the jawbone back with you. If necessary, give it to Bob Sumner. He'll know what to do with it."

"What do you mean 'if necessary'?"

"Well, in case I . . . have a problem getting back."

I looked into his eyes. "You mean in case you don't come back, don't you?"

". . . Yes."

"Come back with me. We'll tell them I'm sick. We'll say we found a lump in my breast, and you have to take me home. Then we'll keep quiet about it."

"Anne, I can't do that. I'm a scientist. It's not always easy, and the greatest dangers aren't necessarily things like frostbite and bears. Archaeology can become political sometimes. But it's what I do. Besides, I might be completely wrong about this."

"You've made up your mind, haven't you?" My tears started again.

Silent, he drew me close and held me.

"If this is what you do," I said, "then of course I have to support you in it. I'll do what you ask. I'll go back. We'll tell them I didn't know how dirty and buggy it would be and that I'm going home to get my nails done, but Jack, I'm afraid for you."

He kissed me. "It'll be OK."

Chapter Fourteen

I packed my gear. We wrapped the precious bone, teeth, and soil samples in clothing and cradled them in the center of my duffle. I added Jack's hand-written report to the other items.

"When you get to Anchorage, go to one of those packaging stores, and mail the jaw home. We can't chance you being pulled out of line during the airport security check because of the way the jawbone looks on a scanner. We don't want you to have to explain why you have a human body part in your luggage, even if it is a fossil, and we certainly don't want it confiscated."

As I started to stack my gear in one place, Jack said, "You won't need your rifle. I'll keep it. Let me have your field knife too."

I didn't say anything. I just handed them to him. But what I was thinking chilled me.

We spent the rest of the hours after breakfast talking, talking, talking, but not about the oil company or the survey. We talked about us—about how much we loved each other and what we wanted for our future—trying to reassure ourselves that there would be a future for us.

Jack told me stories about growing up he hadn't told me before. He'd planned to tell them to his son and daughter someday. He worried about his children. He felt they were losing their connection to the community that was so important to him. He was depending on me to tell them the stories if he couldn't.

I wavered back and forth between being scared and thinking I was being silly and overly dramatic.

That all stopped when we saw the dot of the helicopter in the distant sky.

I panicked, but I quickly regained control. We had to pull this off. Even without proof, I knew Jack was right. We were in a fight for our lives. If we couldn't convince Hal that the story we'd concocted was the truth, it might be the end for us, as it had been for Dr. MacNeil.

"Anne, come in the tent."

In the shelter of the tent, Jack took me in his arms. "I want to remember your scent, your hair, your eyes, your mouth. I love you, my darling Anne."

"I love you, Jack . . . Four weeks isn't long," I said, lying to myself. It was an eternity.

"No, not long. Keep the bracelet on your ankle, so I can think about it."

"I'll never take it off."

He kissed me, and we held each other until we heard the helicopter touch down.

Maybe my teary eyes would convince Hal that our story was true.

As we off-loaded the boxes of food, clean laundry, and mail, Jack said, "Anne's going back with you today."

"Back?" Hal asked. "Back where?"

"To Prudhoe. Then she's going home."

"That's a surprise. You never said anything on the radio."

"We made up our minds this morning. She's going to take a little break from field work."

Hal looked at me but made no further comment.

Serbin stowed the dirty laundry, trash, and my duffle. As usual, he didn't speak to me. He climbed aboard and the helicopter rotors started to turn again.

I said goodbye to the dogs. Silly, I know, but you never know what another creature understands.

Nothing seemed real. We'd been acting a little stiff with each other. We wanted Hal and Serbin to think we'd had a fight and that was the reason I was leaving.

"I'm going now," I said.

"Yes, you're going." Jack gave me a formal kiss on the cheek as our last contact before I climbed into the back behind Serbin.

Hal shook hands with Jack, climbed into the seat next to Serbin, and shut the door.

The helicopter lifted off the ground.

We'd agreed that I wouldn't look back or wave. I concentrated on not crying. It was almost more than I could manage.

I hadn't liked Hal much when I met him in Anchorage. My impression of him hadn't improved as I'd become better acquainted with him. By the time this flight was over, I loathed him.

He turned sideways in his seat so he could look at me, put on his headphones, and pointed to the headphones on the hook next to me. He wanted to talk.

He looked at me long enough that I began to feel uncomfortable. Finally, he spoke. "Well, Anne, you and Jack have a little problem? You didn't seem very friendly to each other when you were saying good-bye."

"I don't understand why that's something you and I should talk about, Hal."

"I thought we were friends by now, Anne. You know—just a little conversation between friends. It's a long ride back to Prudhoe. We have to talk about something. You and he had a little fight? It happens to everybody."

Oh, boy. How do I handle this?

"Jack's not always the easiest man to get along with," I said.

"I've noticed that. I suppose you'll miss him though. Or maybe I'm wrong. Maybe you've been together too much, and you'll enjoy a little time away from him."

"Yes, that's what we need. A little time apart, or maybe a lot of time. I don't know. I don't think I even care. I'm going to take time for myself and do things I like. I've never had to work like that. I mostly stayed home before I married Jack."

"You don't seem like a camping type of woman to me. You're more the kind of woman who would look right in a boudoir with silks and lace and candles. You're a beautiful woman, Anne. You don't need to be living in a tent."

He actually sighed.

Oh, disgusting. He's been fantasizing about me in a "boudoir."

"That's a compliment, I guess. I suppose I should thank you."

"You don't need to thank me for telling the truth. You're a very attractive woman. Any man could see that. You'd look lovely in blue silk. Maybe I should buy you a little farewell gift. I suppose we won't see each other again."

"I don't think a gift would be appropriate. I'm married, after all, even if we're spending a little time apart."

"Ah, Anne. Again, you forget we're friends. Friends can give each other gifts. Maybe there'll be something you'll want to give me."

His double-entendre was not subtle. I could see where this conversation was going. It surprised me, in spite of what Jack had said. I was much older than Hal. How could he be interested in me? I guess there weren't many available women in

Prudhoe Bay. So it was any old port in a storm, with the emphasis on "old."

"The first time I saw you at that party in Anchorage," Hal said, "I wondered what kind of man Jack must be to take you out into the wilderness. Many of our brown-skinned brothers don't understand how to treat a woman of quality, and you are definitely a woman of quality."

There! I'd reached my limit. As a white person in a predominantly white society, I'd been much more insulated from racism than I'd understood. Now that I was with Jack, the things people said without a second thought astonished me. My feeling was that most of those people were ignorant, but well meaning. They had no idea what they were saying. Some were vicious though.

"Hal, we'd better put an end to this conversation. You don't know how Jack treats me, or what he understands or doesn't understand. I find this conversation offensive."

If I'd thought that would stop him I had another think coming, as my mother often said.

"We don't have to talk about Jack if you don't want to. We'll talk about you, instead. You're a little up tight." He nodded. "I don't think you've had any fun in a long time. Prudhoe Bay isn't Paris, but I'd be glad to offer you a drink when we get there."

"I thought alcohol was prohibited in Deadhorse and Prudhoe Bay."

"It is for most of the people there, but we can make a little exception for you. It might help you relax a little. We could have fun. Even in Deadhorse, I could show you how a man should treat a woman like you. Come on. Say yes. We'll have a good time."

"Look, Hal, I'm tired and I'm dirty. I want to get to Anchorage, go to the Captain Cook, get a massage, a manicure, have my hair done. Then I'm taking the next plane home."

He smiled. "That's even better. I'll ride back to Anchorage with you. You get cleaned up. I'll do a little shopping. They have good stores in Anchorage. I'll bet I could find something really nice for you. Then I'll take you out for a five-star dinner, and we'll spend a little time together—a little time to say good-bye."

He spent the rest of the flight trying to convince me I "deserved a little fun" that he'd be willing to provide. I knew what kind of fun he was talking about.

Mostly, I spent the time looking out the windows, marveling at how what had seemed so beautiful before, now seemed so empty.

At one point, I saw him wink at Serbin.

I thought he was a disgusting toad.

Chapter Fifteen

Hal seemed sincerely disappointed with my refusal to see him. I don't know if his technique worked with other women. It sure didn't with me. I couldn't get away from him fast enough.

Ernesto picked me up at the San Diego airport on Sunday. I couldn't tell him the real reason I'd come back, but at least I didn't have to lie about being at odds with Jack.

The house felt so empty. Jack had filled it with life and love. Now that feeling was gone. I missed him so much. I couldn't settle down, and I couldn't follow through on anything.

Tuesday, the first day Carola was there after I returned, she put up with me until early afternoon, when she'd finally had enough. "Anne, you go sit in the living room right now. You're driving me crazy."

I meekly obeyed.

Carola and I have an unusual relationship. She and Ernesto have been the constants in my life from the day I married Robby. She and I know she's an employee, but she's sometimes my mother and sometimes my sister and always my best friend, and like a mother or a sister or a best friend, sometimes she bullies me, usually for my own good.

She brought in two cups of tea and handed one to me.

We sat quietly for a while. I just stared into my cup.

Finally, she said, "OK, out with it. What's going on?"

"I miss him so much, and I'm worried about his being up there by himself."

"You could get on a plane and go back."

I shook my head. "I promised him I'd be here. This is where he wants me."

She took a sip of tea and set her cup down firmly. "In that case, I'm going to have to find some work for you to do. It's that or let you drive me insane. Maybe it's time for us to do a spring-cleaning of this entire house. You and Jack are talking about selling. If you're going to do that, there's a lot of preparation to be done. We'll get started this week. I'll have to be here with you cleaning until he gets back."

The idea of anything being dirty with Carola around was a joke, but I knew what she meant. She meant sorting and discarding. I could be a little bit of a pack rat. "Maybe you're right. I need a job to keep me busy."

"No time like the present." She stood. "We'll get started right now. We'll clean out the closets and storage areas. I've had my eye on a few items I think you could send off to charity."

So we started sorting "stuff." It sometimes seems possessions multiply themselves in the dark and quiet of closet life, but when I looked at the first closet, I couldn't see anything to discard.

"You're not concentrating," she said. "We'll reverse the system."

We emptied everything out of the closet.

"Now put something back."

I picked up a winter coat I hadn't worn for about fifteen years.

"Why are you keeping that?"

"Well, I might need it someday."

"Could you wear it in Ungavaq?"

"Aah . . . no, it's not warm enough."

"How about Ottawa?"

"It's not really in style. But it might come back in style. You know, everything cycles through."

"Not acceptable. Out it goes."

"Carola, it's a perfectly good coat."

"Then there's somebody out there who really needs it. Out."

She was strict with me and didn't give me any slack until, with one item, I said, "Just because!" She let me keep that one.

We had battles, with a little bit of sulking on both sides, but we made progress. She was right. It took my mind off my worries. Periodically she'd remind me we were making room for Jack to put his things. That felt good.

I don't believe in premonitions, but sometimes, strange things happen. Two weeks after I came home, the house phone rang as we were stacking up our first boxes of discards for the day. If it had rung a minute earlier, I'd have told Carola to let the machine pick it up. She'd just set down her box, so she stepped over to the small table next to the sofa to answer it.

I suddenly had a terrible feeling. I shivered.

She listened a moment. "Yes, just a minute please." She turned to me. "It's Harold Josephs for you, Anne."

My face tightened. I walked across the room and took the receiver from her. Trying to keep my voice from being too frosty, I said, "Hello, Mr. Josephs. This is Anne O'Malley."

"Anne, you don't remember me? It's Hal."

"Oh yes, Hal, I remember you, but I didn't think I'd hear from you. I did expect to hear from Jack by now. What's going on?"

"Well, there's no way to sugar-coat this, I'm afraid. I have bad news for you."

I thought my heart had stopped. For a moment, things started to go gray. I frantically gestured to Carola to come back. It was all I could do to say, "What's the matter?"

"We've lost contact with Jack. He's stopped calling in, and he doesn't respond to our calls. When we couldn't reach him, we flew to the camp. It's undisturbed, but there's no sign of him there."

"What about the dogs?"

"They're gone too."

"I suppose he's out looking at sites or hunting. He'll probably be back tonight or tomorrow."

"Actually, Anne, that's what we thought, so we waited a few days before calling you."

"A few days? How long is a few?"

"Actually six."

"Are you telling me you haven't heard from him in over a week, and you waited this long to call me?"

"Well . . . yes. We didn't want to upset you. I'm sure there's a reasonable explanation for this. We'll wait a while longer. I'm sure we'll hear from him—maybe today or tomorrow."

"Have you looked for him?"

"Yeah, but so far, no luck."

"Luck! I'll be in Anchorage on the next plane."

"Oh, Anne," he said soothingly, "that's not necessary. I'm sure Jack would be much happier knowing his little wife was safe in San Diego. I don't think you should trouble yourself. I'm sure everything will be OK."

"Hal, you're sure of a lot of things. Do you have anything more to say?" My voice was definitely frosty now, but he didn't seem to notice.

"Not really, Anne. You relax and stay by the phone. I'll call you as soon as I have news, and maybe we'll get together one of these days."

I hung up.

"Sit down, Anne!" Carola said.

I sat with a thump. My legs wouldn't hold me up.

"What's happened?"

"Jack's been missing for more than a week. Josephs says I shouldn't worry. He's certain Jack will be happier if his 'little wife' just stays by the phone!"

"Oh, dear," said Carola, "I guess he doesn't know much about Jack's 'little wife' if he thinks you're buying into that nonsense. What are you going to do?"

I thought for a moment. "I have to go there. Pack a bag. I'm going to Ottawa. I don't want anything dressy—strictly outdoor clothes and my boots. Pack that stuff I brought back from Alaska. Oh, and my sleeping bag too."

"OK. Would you like Ernesto and me to stay here at the house in case Jack calls?"

"I'll have my cell phone."

"If you're going back to Alaska, you might be someplace that doesn't get reception. He might call the house."

"You're right. Yes, please."

"You get ready. I'll pack the bag. Ernesto can drive you to the airport."

I called my travel agent. The next flight connecting to Ottawa was leaving in four hours.

When I went to tell Carola, she asked, "Would you like Ernesto to go with you?"

"No, I'm going to call and see if I can get Quipac."

"Quipac? Is that Jack's brother-in-law? I still get the names mixed up."

"Yes and his adopted brother. He and Jack did a dig in Alaska."

"That's good. He'll know more what to do than Ernesto would. Will he meet you at the airport tonight?"

"I don't think he could be there before tomorrow at the earliest. Laura Chandler would have to fly to Ungavaq and pick him up."

I dialed the phone.

Laura picked up on the sixth ring. "Northern Air."

"Laura, it's Anne. Thank God, you're there."

"Anne, what's the matter? Where are you?"

"I'm in San Diego. They just called me. Jack's missing in Alaska."

"What can I do to help?"

"Would you fly as soon as possible to Ungavaq?"

"And then?"

"Pick up Quipac, take him back to Blackwell, and get him on a plane to Ottawa. I'll meet him there. If he's away on a hunting trip or something, talk to Maata. See if there's someone else in the village she could send."

"I'll radio the village as soon as we hang up. Anything else?"

"Tell Quipac to bring his rifle and his field gear. We're going to Alaska."

"OK. Will do."

After I hung up, I sat, took a deep breath, and said a little prayer. I knew how competent Jack was in the outdoors. He'd spent most of his life in the north, but accidents can happen even to the most prepared people. If what he'd told me was true, other things can happen too.

I decided to call René. Maybe he could get information for me.

"I'll pick you up," he said. "What time?"

"I don't want to inconvenience you."

"What time?"

"Eleven, but what about Yvonne?" His mentally disabled sister couldn't be left alone.

"I'll ask my neighbor to stay with her. She'll be asleep by then. She won't even know I'm gone, eh?"

"I'll be so glad to see a friendly face, but I really called to ask another favor of you."

"Of course, Cherie. Anything. You know that."

"Will you look up Allied American Oil and see what you can find out about them? I have the business cards of the people we were introduced to in Anchorage and Prudhoe Bay."

"OK. I have a pencil. Read them to me."

When I hung up the phone, Carola said, "I'm going to fix you something to eat."

"Don't bother. They'll serve something on the plane."

"You need to eat before then."

"I'm too jumpy to eat."

"Why don't you sit in the garden for a few minutes?"

"All right. Maybe it'll help me calm down."

"You go relax. I'll make some sandwiches."

I walked through the house, out the French doors, and across the patio to the glider. The crimson bougainvillea, in riotous bloom, had dropped blossoms onto the seat. I brushed them aside and sat.

The day was clear and hot. I could see the ocean. On the horizon, a ship sailed south. For a few moments, I imagined that Jack was leaning on the rail of that ship looking in my direction, and it would round the point and dock safely at the pier downtown.

Suddenly my face was wet with tears. Hysteria rose in me like a flame.

I'd come out here so many times when Robby was ill. The garden gave me the strength to go on then, but now here I was again, this time weeping for Jack. I couldn't stand the thought that he might be gone. I didn't think I could go through another loss. Maybe I'd used up my strength with Robby. Maybe if Jack needed me, I wouldn't be able to do what was necessary.

. . . But I would do what was necessary.

And I realized that if I went to help Jack, I might not come back either. That meant there was something else I needed to do. I went into the house and found Bob Sumner's phone number. I had my fingers crossed he'd be home. I didn't want to leave Carola with this responsibility.

I was lucky; he answered on the third ring. He started to say, "How are you?"

I interrupted. "Bob, I need to talk to you. We've had an emergency. Could you come over right away?"

"What's the matter?"

"Jack's missing in Alaska."

"I'll be there as soon as possible."

Less than a half-hour later, he knocked on the front door.

He hugged me. He'd never done that before, but I must have looked like I needed it.

We sat on the sofa in the living room.

"So what's going on?"

"I'm hoping this turns out to be nothing, but Jack has been missing from our campsite for over a week. They finally called to let me know."

"Damn! And you mean you didn't know until today? I saw a backpack and a sleeping bag by the front door. Are you going up there? Do you want me to go with you?"

I set a box in front of him on the coffee table. "You have a more important job to do. Jack gave me this to give to you if I needed to. Look in there."

I handed him a pair of disposable plastic gloves.

"Bones?" he asked.

I nodded.

He pulled the gloves on and lifted out one of the pieces of the jaw and then a second one, wrapped in dishtowels. He unrolled them one at a time. His eyes widened in surprise. He set them on the coffee table, took out the third piece and the tooth, nested in cotton in a clear plastic box. He looked at me, his face flushed with excitement.

"Oh, my god, Anne. Jack told you what this is?"

"He thinks there's a possibility we've found an Early Man site."

"Jack's the best. If he says it's an Early Man site, there's no 'possibly' about it. What does he want me to do with these?"

I handed him a manila envelope. "Here's his handwritten report. We've signed it. It authorizes you to handle this for him if necessary. I typed a copy for you. The disk is in there along with two hard copies. He wants you to take care of these bones, hide them. Bob, you might be in danger if anyone finds out you have these."

He looked at me, disbelieving.

"It's essential you keep this secret. He said you'd know what to do later about getting the report published and the site excavated if he doesn't come back."

"What do you mean 'if he doesn't come back'?"

"He thought there was something fishy going on up there. That's why he sent me home. The oil people tell me not to worry. They want me to be a good little wife and sit by the phone. I'm going to Ottawa. I'm hoping Quipac will meet me, and we'll go on to Anchorage. I don't know what we'll do when we get there, but we'll figure it out."

"Quipac's smart. He'll know how to handle this. And the oil people will help too."

"I don't want them to know I'm in Anchorage. They're the ones Jack doesn't trust. I hope he'll be able to explain this to you later. Don't let anyone know you have the bones. That's crucial."

"Anne, these bones are important, but Jack's more important. Are you sure you don't want me to go with you and Quipac?"

"Jack thought it was much more important for you to have custody of these fossils. That's what he wants, and I hope you'll help us."

"But if he sent you home because of the danger, he won't want you to come back."

"Bob, he's my husband. Of course I have to go back. Will you take care of the bones for him?"

He nodded. "If that's what you want, yes, I will. And when you and Jack get back, the three of us can have lunch together, and you two can explain this whole thing. I'd say bring Quipac too, but I know you'll never get him this far south. Everything will be fine, Anne"

Chapter Sixteen

I cleared customs and saw René waiting. He kissed me, and his kiss had an echo of the passion we'd shared the previous summer.

"Ah, Anne, I didn't think we'd meet again under circumstances like these."

"René, I'm frantic."

"For now, relax a little. Jack will be all right. You just keep thinking about that."

"I'll try."

He picked up my backpack and sleeping bag. "I want you to tell me the whole thing again."

We started walking, and I told him what had happened. Then I asked whether he'd found anything useful in his research.

"I've been on line almost the whole time since I talked to you. I have a folder of printouts for you to look at. I found a lot about your Dr. MacNeil."

"That whole thing is so odd. The oil people said they think he'd decided to disappear and just walked off the job."

"He was young, only thirty," René said. "He must have been a relatively recent Ph.D. Maybe he couldn't handle the loneliness, but walking off the job sounds like a career-ender—not something a person in his position would do."

"What about the other people?"

"I did a little hacking and managed to get into the Allied American personnel files."

"René! I didn't know you knew how to do that."

"It's not a skill I include on my résumé, eh? Their security is shockingly bad."

"Will they be able to trace it back to you? Will you get in trouble?"

He laughed and shook his head. "No."

"What did you find?"

"Most of the names you gave me were run-of-the-mill business types who've worked for the company for years, but I found two men who don't fit that profile."

"Who?"

"Your liaison man, Josephs, and his assistant, Serbin. Allied American hired them together about eighteen months ago to work on a project in Colombia—I couldn't get details—but they were transferred fairly quickly to the Alaska Division. They were working out of Prudhoe Bay when MacNeil disappeared. In fact, Josephs was in charge of the search."

"Could you find any other details of his work assignments?"

"No. But whatever he does, it's important. He reports directly to the man in charge in Alaska."

"What else did you find?"

"I found stories from, of all places, your newspaper in San Diego. Josephs started out in the US Navy as a SEAL. He must have had talent because he was promoted rapidly, but in 1986, he was bounced out with a dishonorable discharge. There was a drug-smuggling bust in a city called Coronado. The whole thing blew up because one of the smugglers was murdered. Josephs was accused of being involved, but the civil authorities didn't prosecute him."

"A murderer? Oh, no!"

"We don't know, Anne. Let's not borrow trouble. Anyway, he's been in more scrapes with the law over the years, but he's managed to get by without jail time. He can't seem to hold a job for long, though, and he has long gaps in his employment history. He doesn't look like the kind of person I'd want to hire. His longest tenure ever has been this job with Allied American. Most of his jobs have been in security. He started in security with the oil company. If he's been shifted to public relations, it doesn't show on their company roster yet."

"What about Serbin?"

"Serbin has evidently been his assistant on all his jobs and came with him to Allied American. His employment history is a duplicate of Josephs', including the same gaps.

"Also, according to the things I've been looking at, this company is highly connected in Washington. The consensus is they're a shoo-in to get the contract for the oil exploration. The work Jack's doing is one of the hoops they have to jump through before the lease is awarded, but essentially, it's a fait accompli. Of course, this hinges on your Congress allowing oil exploration there at all."

At the car, René opened the door for me and then put my gear in the trunk.

As I waited, I felt overwhelmed by fatigue and fear. I closed my eyes and tilted my head back against the headrest. I could feel tears again.

René slid into his seat. "Anne, you're so pale."

I opened my eyes and wiped the tears away. "Too much worry. Too much traveling."

He took my hand in his. "Did they give you dinner on the plane?"

"They served something, but I couldn't eat."

"When's the last time you had anything to eat or drink?"

"Breakfast."

"How many hours ago was that? You'll be no use to Jack if you keel over."

He opened the glove compartment and took out a package of Smarties, the Canadian version of M & Ms. I could have predicted he'd have something. He snacks all the time.

"I'll fix myself a little something when I get to the condo. There's canned food and stuff in the freezer."

"Don't be foolish, Cherie. You eat some candy, and we're stopping for something to eat before I take you home, eh?"

We went to the twenty-four-hour coffee shop where we'd eaten so many times the previous summer. Then he took me to the condo.

"I'll call you in the morning. Do you think you can sleep?"

"I'll be OK. Thank you, René."

"Cherie. I'll always be there for you. You know that. Call me any time, day or night. Don't worry about Yvonne. My neighbor can take care of her on short notice."

He hugged me with the love and tenderness I knew he felt for me. He kissed me on the cheek—"One from Jack," he said—and he left.

I called Carola.

She hadn't heard from Jack or Hal.

I hadn't been in the condo long enough after we were married to put much of a stamp on the rooms. Some of my clothes were in the closets, some of my toiletries in the master bathroom, but mostly it was Jack. It almost distilled his essence—bright, warm, strongly masculine, full of books and music, organized, and neat.

I walked through the living room, dining room, kitchen, den, guest bedroom, and, finally, our bedroom. I stood and looked at the double bed—our bed. It was covered with a Hudson's Bay point blanket—creamy white with one broad stripe each of green, red, yellow, and indigo. I remembered one lazy morning on our honeymoon. He stayed in bed and I made tea. When I entered the room with the two mugs, he was sitting up with the pillows tucked behind him. That beautiful blanket covered him to the waist, but I knew what he looked like, and suddenly I wasn't interested in tea anymore. My heart welled up with love and desire. My marriage to Robby had been good, but I hadn't known it was possible to feel like that.

As I walked around now, I felt sadness and fear rising again. But René was right. If Jack were alive, I couldn't help him if I didn't pull myself together, so I visited each room again. This time I stayed until I had a happy memory of something we'd done or said there. That wasn't difficult. We'd been married for two weeks when we returned from Ungavaq. We made love on every horizontal surface and on some of the vertical ones too. We couldn't get enough of each other.

Jack was too alive in these memories to allow thoughts of anything else. I slept well.

Chapter Seventeen

The next morning, the phone awakened me. I grabbed it. "Jack?"

"No. Quipac."

"Oh," I said, disappointed.

"I'm on my way. I'm ready to board here in Blackwell. Air Canada flight 1433. Can you meet me at the airport at noon?"

"Yes. I'm sorry I sounded the way I did. I am glad you're coming. I don't know what to do."

"It's OK. You can tell me about it when I get there. I'll see you at baggage claim at noon. Do you want to talk to Laura?"

"Please."

"Hi," Laura said. "How are you doing?"

"Besides being scared out of my mind, I'm OK."

"Quipac looks pretty determined. I think you can relax a little. You called for the right person."

"Thank you for what you did. I hope you didn't lose a charter."

"Don't you worry about that. Call me when Jack gets back."

"OK."

I called René and told him about Quipac arriving.

"Do you want me to pick him up?"

"I'll do it," I said. "It's something I can do so I won't sit here and worry. I shouldn't say that. I'm sure everything is going to be OK now. Quipac will know how to handle things."

"Yes, he will."

"I don't know how soon we'll be heading out. I'll call you before we go, but I've been thinking about this. If you don't hear from one of the three of us within two weeks, I want you to go to the authorities with everything you know. I'm going to put it in writing and mail it to you."

"Anne, I don't think that's necessary."

"Look. Everyone tells me everything's going to be OK. But Jack's missing, and that's real. He sent me home because he didn't know what might happen, but he was worried."

"OK. But when it turns out to be a tempest in a teapot, I'm going to say 'Told you so.'"

"Duly noted. Thank you, René."

I spent time writing out the details, then repacked my backpack and set it with my sleeping bag and parka by the door to be ready when Quipac said it was time to head out. Then I sat down to read the papers René had given me.

I'd considered renting a car to pick up Quipac, but I didn't think we'd be in Ottawa long enough to need one. When the time came, I took a cab.

As I walked up to Quipac, tears of relief came to my eyes. We shook hands gently. Jack had taught me the Inuit don't hug in public.

When he saw my tears, he said, "Remember, we Inuit are supposed to be unemotional. Let's not disappoint all these people around here."

I couldn't help but smile. He always said the right thing. And I noticed he'd said "we." By coming into Jack's life, I'd changed his relationship to Quipac, especially the amount of time they spent together. During a usual year, Jack would be spending the summer in Ungavaq or on an archaeological dig with Quipac, but, instead, this year he'd been with me. By saying what he did, Quipac gave me a welcome message that I'm family—not an interloper.

If there was anyone in the world who cares as much about Jack as I do, Quipac surely is that person. Jack has many friends and family who love him, but Quipac is the special friend of his childhood. They've been close all their lives. They're brothers by adoption, but closer than most brothers.

Quipac looks similar to Jack. The most noticeable difference is his mustache and wispy goatee. He wears his black hair in a sort of bowl cut, and even though he's the same age as Jack and me, he has no gray hair. His eyes are black, where Jack's are hazel, and he's a little shorter than Jack's five foot eight, but still taller than I am. Both have beautiful golden-tan skin.

He wore Levi's and a maroon plaid flannel shirt with the sleeves rolled up—a little warm for Ottawa, but it had undoubtedly been much cooler when he left Ungavaq.

He picked up his backpack and his rifle case. "Come on. Tell me what's going on. How is it you're here and not in Alaska? You must have left after Jack wrote his last letter to me."

"Quipac, this is more than Jack just being missing."

"I'm listening."

"I think . . . I think there's a possibility he's dead."

He took my hand and led me into an empty waiting area. "Tell me."

I wasn't crying now, but I was shaking. He took my other hand in his too and held both gently.

"We found a human jawbone and teeth. Jack thought they were important, and he thought the people from Allied American might try to stop us from getting the news out. Two weeks ago, he sent me back to San Diego with the bone and teeth. He said he had to stay and finish the contract. He was going to keep what we found a secret until he was safely back, but I don't think that worked. When the man called yesterday to say Jack was missing, he said Jack would want me to stay in San Diego where I'd be safe. That was a strange thing for him to say. It felt like a threat, and the archaeologist who had the contract before us also disappeared."

"Jack wrote about him. And it does sound like the man from Allied American . . . what's his name? Josephs?"

I nodded.

"It does sound like he threatened you. Why did Jack think what you found was important?"

"He thought maybe we'd found an Early Man site."

"Aah! That would start a debate about the damage building an oil processing facility would do to a site of worldwide importance. I can see why Jack would be worried. Now, I don't want you to think about Jack being dead. You think about how I'm going to find him."

"I have my things packed. I'm ready to go."

"Go?"

"With you . . . to Alaska."

"I don't think so. From what you say, there might be danger involved. I don't think Jack would appreciate it if I brought you."

"I'm going."

"Don't you remember I told you Inuit women are expected to be subordinate to men in public."

Ah, he was clever! He'd made me feel included. Now he reminded me that inclusion requires conformity with community standards. Almost any other time it would have worked—but not now.

"I'm going."

He thought a moment. "I'm not going to argue with you, so I guess you're going."

He smiled and I sighed in relief. I felt like I'd been holding my breath since I received the call from Hal, but now everything was OK. Quipac would find Jack and I'd help.

"First," he said, "I want to go back to Jack's—I mean your place . . . you know what I mean—and look at his maps."

"OK."

"Did you bring that beautiful teal blue parka?"

"Yes. I did."

"Then we have a little shopping to do. You need something not quite so noticeable, maybe a nice dark green." He nodded to himself. "Now, when you were in our class, I had the impression you didn't really know which end of the rifle the bullet came out."

I laughed. "I don't think I was quite that bad but, more or less, you're right. Jack bought me a rifle, though, and taught me how to shoot."

"Where's that rifle now?"

"He kept it. He kept my field knife too. He said he wanted them in case he mislaid his. I thought that was a strange thing to say."

"We'll add a rifle and a knife to our shopping list. What kind of rifle did he buy?"

"The same as he has: a 38-55 Winchester."

"Are you sure? That's a big gun for a beginner."

"I know," I said, rubbing my shoulder. "I still have the bruises to prove it. He said he thought about it a lot, but he didn't want to give me a gun that would just irritate a bear. After I shot it the first time, I was afraid to shoot again, but he helped me get over my fear."

"Anything else we might need?"

"A first aid kit. Oh, and we'll need bug repellent."

"No, it'll be cool enough up there now that the mosquitoes will be gone, but we'd better take food for you. I don't know whether you'll want to eat the things I would."

"I'll eat what you do."

He shrugged. "OK, let's get lunch and go shopping."

We took a cab to a restaurant. After we ate, we walked to the camping supply store.

Quipac asked for the manager.

A man of sixty-five or seventy came to greet us. He was white-haired, tall, and a little paunchy, but he had the hands of someone who did work more demanding than stocking store shelves—maybe an outdoorsman who was beginning to slow down a little. "Quipac, my old friend, don't tell me you've run out of camping equipment."

"No," he said. "We have enough of your equipment in Ungavaq to outfit the village. Anne, this is Al Sanford. Al, this is Jack's new wife, Anne."

"Well, Mrs. O'Malley, what a pleasure," Mr. Sanford said. "Where's Jack?"

"That's why we're here," Quipac said. "Jack's out wandering around someplace in Alaska, and he's stopped reporting in. We thought we'd better go find him. We need a few things."

Mr. Sanford quickly provided the items we needed. In spite of what I'd said, Quipac had him include freeze-dried food for me.

"Don't worry about a thing," Mr. Sanford said. "I'll put them on your bill."

"Oh, no," Quipac said, "you put them on Jack's bill. He'll be in to pay you soon."

Mr. Sanford smiled at me. "I'll look forward to seeing him."

We hailed a cab and went home.

Quipac had reminded me it was my home too—not just Jack's, and I had a job I knew how to do. I was his hostess. The normality of that made things easier.

While Quipac put his things in the guest room, I cut the tags off my new parka. When he returned, I asked whether he'd like a cup of tea or would rather start work immediately.

"Tea, I think, and then we can talk awhile."

I understood what he was doing. These rituals of greeting and shopping and tea made things better. They anchored us in the familiar and gave us strength to strike out into the unfamiliar. It let us feel more as if we were in control, and that felt good.

We sat in the comfortable chairs in the living room and sipped our tea from Carleton University mugs. At first, even the gentle clink of his spoon stirring sugar into his tea made me jump, but with the warmth of the mug in my hands and the sweet smoothness of the liquid, I began to relax. I could hear a voice in my head say, "Be more Inuit, Anne."

"You live in two worlds," I said, "the way Jack does. When you're in Ungavaq, you're that 'simple hunter,' as I described you that time. When you're here, you're like a city person."

"Did Jack tell you what it's called, what we do?"

"No."

"It's called 'code switching.' You do it every day, but you're not aware of it. You talk to your best friend differently than you do to a police officer or to your minister. I've thought about this. Jack and I do an extreme form. It's more than just language for us. It's linked into the way we see the world. We each see the world in two ways—the Inuit way and the white way. He's had even more exposure to the white way than I have. Those ways of seeing the world are sometimes hard to integrate, and some things don't translate at all."

"May I ask you something?"

"Maybe." He smiled. "I know this is going to be about Jack."

"When we were in Alaska, I said something that, I guess, hit a nerve. In terms of code switching, Jack switched from 'us' to 'Inuit.' He was speaking English, not Inuktitut, but he had switched, and I knew he was angry because he used ridicule in a way that left no doubt. What I want to ask, I guess . . . I don't know how to fight in the Inuit way."

"That's one of those things that doesn't translate. I don't think married people can fight in an Inuit way, at least not the way I think white people fight in their marriages. I've seen Jack switch the way you describe. There's one thing you can do. You can get him to switch to 'professor' and debate him. He's good at that." He laughed. "You worked it out, I assume."

"I guess I used the ultimate white woman's weapon. I didn't do it on purpose, but I cried."

"And that took care of it?"

"Yes, but I can't do that every time. I have to learn how to switch to Inuit with him."

"You're asking me for advice about something I've never done. I've never had a fight with a white woman. The only thing I can say is trust him. I don't think it's possible for a man to love a woman more than he loves you. You know, in the survival class, most of the time when he was speaking Inuktitut, he was talking about you and how wonderful you are. Men aren't supposed to be that aware of women, at least not overtly. We're certainly not supposed to talk about them endlessly. I told him I was going to rub his face in the snow if he didn't stop." He chuckled.

"I didn't know."

"He's crazy about you, in both the Inuit and the white world, and I don't think that's going to change. Trust him." He sat forward in his chair. "Now the fact that you asked me about Jack shows you're feeling a little more positive, so it's time for us to get busy finding him. Tell me what you've done so far."

I told him what René had found with his computer search.

"What does it mean Josephs was a seal?" he asked. "That's a strange title for someone from the United States."

"He was a member of the US Navy's elite special forces—a commando. He would have had extensive training in infiltration and killing. They're called SEALs because they specialize in underwater warfare, but it's an acronym for Sea-Air-Land. I've met some SEALs over the years. They're based near San Diego. They're perfectly nice when you meet them in the regular world. Still, they're kind of scary people when you think about what they've been trained to do."

"This Josephs doesn't sound like he's perfectly nice. He sounds like a person to be careful of and not underestimate." He rose. "Well, it's time to do a little work. I'm going to look at the maps." He started toward the den.

"You know where they are?"

He nodded.

"I'll go to the store and get us something for dinner."

He stopped and turned. "I remember there's a drug store somewhere close."

"Yes."

"While you're out, would you go there and buy several large bottles of face makeup? Get a color as close to the color of Jack's or my skin as you can."

"What are we going to do with that?"

"If we're out on the tundra, it would be fairly easy to spot you as a white woman. Your hands are so pale they'd stand out even from the air. We're going to make you look a little more Inuit. Your hair color's OK, but can you straighten it?" You won't want to have your hood up all the time.

"I can dampen it, pull it straight, and spray it with hair spray."

"You better get a can of that too."

"I'm surprised you know about such things."

"Many of the hunters and fishermen we get in Ungavaq bring their wives and girlfriends. You'd be amazed at the things I know."

"I'll bet I would," I said, laughing. He was right. I did feel a lot less scared and a lot more positive.

When I returned, Quipac was in the kitchen. He'd spread the maps on the table. "How good are you with these?"

"I'm pretty good. Jack had me do the mapping of the sites we visited each day."

"OK, show me where your last camp was, and then mark the Early Man site and any other sites you remember."

"How will that be useful?"

"We have to start somewhere. It's guesswork, but it's possible everything is as it's supposed to be, and Jack's just out doing his survey. He can live off the land, no problem. He wouldn't have needed to take a lot of stuff from the camp. Or maybe he's injured, and he's sitting out there waiting for us. That's why I changed my mind about you going. If he's hurt, he might need someone to care for him while I go for help."

I sat with the maps and a red pen. He put the groceries away while I worked. First, I marked out the sections Jack had defined, and then I marked sites. I might have missed one or two, but not many.

He looked at what I'd done. "You may not have realized it as you were marking, but you've confirmed what I suspected. Jack's using the grid survey pattern he usually uses. It's easy to predict where he'd go after you left. All we have to do is follow his pattern."

"What if things aren't as they're supposed to be?"

"Then either Jack is hiding from the oil people, or they've put him someplace. Jack told you he didn't want the oil people to know about the Early Man site. If he's hiding, he'd head away from there."

"Then you think he'd be OK?"

"Yes."

"But what if things aren't OK?"

"The only reason I can think of that the oil people would put Jack someplace is if they found out about the Early Man site and thought he might know about it too. They might want to silence him."

"Kill him, you mean." I felt sick to my stomach saying the words that had been whirling in my brain.

"Yes, but Jack's important in our specialized world. They'd have to know there'd be an intensive search. They'd know they couldn't afford to do anything that would cause an investigation after his body's found. That means they can't shoot him or anything like that."

"Couldn't they make him just disappear?"

"Since they've already had one archaeologist disappear, I don't think they can afford to have a second one do that and especially not one who's well known. That would really get attention. That's the last thing they want. They'd have TV reporters from the tabloid shows racing all over the place doing broadcasts about mysterious disappearances and who knows what—maybe even aliens and space ships. They can't afford that."

"How do you know about tabloid shows?"

"All airports have TVs."

"If they weren't going to make him disappear, what would they do?"

"They'd leave him out there. They'd think he'd starve to death, and then they'd say they hadn't found him in time. Or they'd think the wolves or the bears would get him." He snorted. "What do you think the chances are of any of that happening to Jack?

"They'd have to keep him in the area where it would be logical for him to be found. They'd remember they have you to contend with. If Jack's body were found a long way from where he was expected to be, you'd be able to tell the authorities something wasn't right. They'd also want to get him as far away from the Early Man site as possible. They wouldn't want searchers stumbling across the site, and they probably don't know how easy it would be to recognize. We know where the site is in relation to your last camp. It's most likely he's in the opposite direction."

"So, you don't think he's dead?"

"He's not dead. He's OK. Maybe a little hungry. We'll just have to walk out and find him."

That's what I wanted to believe. I turned my head so Quipac wouldn't see the tears of relief in my eyes.

"It's all right, Anne," he said gently.

Chapter Eighteen

"Now we have to talk about something that's not my business. I don't know what arrangement you and Jack have made about money, but this is going to cost a bit, and I don't have much. Do you have access to his checking and savings?"

"That's something we don't have to worry about. I don't care what this costs. I can pay it. What are you proposing?"

"OK. We can't trust the oil people, so Anchorage and Prudhoe Bay are out. We'll go to Fairbanks. We'll have to go through Anchorage, but it's not likely anyone at the airport will recognize you. In Fairbanks, we'll charter a helicopter. It's just short of three hundred miles to your campsite, but one of the big choppers can do it."

"What if we charter a plane from here? We wouldn't have to go to Anchorage."

"You can afford that?"

"Yes," I said. "I'll get on the internet and see what's available. Maybe we could go tonight."

"I don't think we'd gain anything by doing that. We have to sleep sometime. We'll be more comfortable here than in a motel in Fairbanks. We'll get to the camp about the same time, no matter what. We'd do better to go in the morning."

Chartering a plane turned out to be simple. It's amazing what you can do with a credit card. There'd be a bit of red tape about crossing the border from Canada into the US, but we had our passports, and we were told it would be handled after we landed in Fairbanks.

The plane was red and white like Laura's plane, but the resemblance ended there. It was a small executive jet, mostly used to carry upper-echelon businessmen. We even had a flight steward who said he would serve us grilled steak for lunch and snacks when we wanted them.

After take-off, Quipac stretched out on the comfortable seat. "This is great. The three of us should travel like this from now on. But it'll be up to you to talk Jack into it."

He never even hinted that he thought Jack might not come back or that we were going to do anything other than walk out and find him.

"Tell the story of your summer from the beginning," he said.

I told him how our camp was set up, how Josephs and Serbin had treated us, and details of the survey. He knew Jack so well that I told him things I might not have shared with anyone else.

"Jack must be so proud of what you've learned," he said. "You're the kind of student a professor dreams about. Jack has a good student and an even better wife."

In the terminal at Fairbanks, we were shunted to the Customs and Immigration counter. I just had to show my passport, but Quipac had to fill out a form since he was Canadian. When he handed it in, the agent said, "Thank you, Mr. O'Malley. That's all we need."

We turned to walk down the concourse.

"That's a mark of my ignorance," I said. "It never occurred to me you had a last name."

"I don't use it much. I didn't need it at all until the government said we had to have them. First we had to have numbers and then names."

"Numbers?"

He nodded. "The government decided they had to keep track of us, so in the 1940s, everyone got a number. It was called *ujamiit*—the Eskimo Disc System. We had to wear the numbers on tags around our necks or sewn into our clothes until 1978."

"How awful."

"Yes. We thought so. Later they came and told us we had to have last names."

"And you chose O'Malley?"

"I didn't choose it. That's my name. Jack's father, Piuvkaq, had the last name O'Malley because his father told his mother everyone where he came from had two names, their personal name and their family name. So when Ivala gave birth to Piuvkaq, she gave him two names, and when Jack was born, Piuvkaq and Maata gave him two names. That's how I knew I was adopted, because they told me O'Malley was my name too."

"But you don't normally use it?"

"Of course I have it on my passport, and I use it at the bank, and it's on my paychecks from the university—things like that."

"There's another thing I didn't know. I never thought about whether you were paid for the classes, but I suppose you'd have to be."

"Even though I don't have any degrees, I'm officially Jack's co-teacher. I'm listed in the university catalog as adjunct faculty. I'm an official professor."

"Wow! I never thought about that . . . But getting back to your adoption. Wasn't that a problem when you wanted to marry Miqo? She's your sister by adoption."

"My adoption happened because Piuvkaq and Maata said it happened. There wasn't any paperwork or official approval. And our marriage was the same way. We're married because we said we are, and the community agreed. I knew her from when she was born. I never thought about marrying anyone else. I always liked her, then I loved her, and she felt the same way about me. I made a good choice."

"That's the way Jack and I are married too. Even though we had a ceremony later in Ottawa, we were married in Ungavaq at that party. Jack stood up and announced to everybody I was his wife, and so I was. It was funny. We sort of did it backwards, because later he asked me if I'd like to be his wife."

"Well, that's Jack, isn't it. You'll notice he does a lot of things that way."

"I have noticed."

We'd been directed to another counter to check into chartering a helicopter, and that too, turned out to be easy. It had never occurred to me you could call for a helicopter the way you call for a cab.

Quipac showed the pilot, Ernie Latham, the place on the map where we wanted to go, and Ernie said, with a smile, "No problemo."

"How soon can you take us?"

"We have a lot of daylight left. The bird's gassed up and ready to go now if you want."

I called René and Carola, and we boarded the helicopter and headed for camp. "The bird" was an Augusta A109 Power helicopter. It had room for seven passengers. It was bigger than we needed, but it had a big gas tank and a range of almost 600 miles when carrying just us.

Ernie was a short, pleasant-faced blond with what seemed like an endless enthusiasm for conversation. He and Quipac talked man-talk—engine power, rifle types, that kind of thing. Ernie had flown in the Gulf War, and Quipac was interested in his experiences.

After a while, I tuned them out. I didn't doze. I turned inward and tried to think about the good times with Jack. Mostly that worked, but every once in a while, like an electric shock, a voice in my mind would say, "He's dead," and I'd have to grit my teeth and shake it off.

Ernie was true to his word. The sun was low in the southwestern sky when he spotted the tent.

I looked where he was pointing. "Oh, Quipac, there's someone standing there! Can you see? Is it Jack?"

He looked. "It's not Jack. It's not a person."

"Not a person? What, then?"

"Stones."

"Not a grave!"

"No. You'll see in a minute. It's OK."

Ernie set the helicopter down.

The three of us climbed out and moved away from the downdraft of the slowing rotors—Quipac and me to stay, Ernie to stretch his legs before heading back.

"Come on, Anne," Quipac said. "I'll show you what it is."

We walked over to a pile of stones near the tent. I could see now why I'd thought it might be Jack. Big flat stones were stacked about five feet high, roughly in the shape of a person with two legs, a body, rudimentary arms and one large stone for the head.

"This wasn't here before."

"He must have built it after you left."

"What is it?"

"*Inuksuk.*"

"Why did he build it?"

"They're often used to mark things—a good place to beach a kayak, a meat storage site—but I think he built this one to be a companion."

"A companion?"

"He was lonely."

"Oh, Quipac . . ." I turned away.

I finally blotted my eyes with my sleeve and turned back, all business. "We'd better get our stuff out of the helicopter."

"Before we do that, do you notice anything else different?"

I looked around the camp in the twilight. "It looks the same."

"No sign bears have been here," he said.

We'd asked Ernie if he'd stay to fly us around in a search pattern after we'd had some sleep, but he had another charter commitment.

"You can catch a ride out of Prudhoe if you want," Ernie offered. "I'll take you over there. I'm going over to refuel. I don't want to land in Fairbanks on fumes."

"No, thanks," Quipac said. "When you're there, it would be better for us if you don't mention you dropped us at this camp."

"Don't worry. My business affairs are confidential. I won't tell anyone."

We arranged for him to come back in one week and again in two weeks, in case we wanted a ride back.

He waved as he left.

"We'd better not light a fire," Quipac said. "We don't want to announce that we're here."

"I'll open canned food. We can eat it cold."

We settled in to sleep soon afterwards.

I was exhausted. I slept in Jack's sleeping bag. I could smell him in the fabric. It made him seem both closer and farther away—a bittersweet experience.

Chapter Nineteen

Quipac was up first and woke me. "I saw the chains. I suppose the dogs are with him."

"Oh, Lord, I forgot about them."

"If they're with him, he's in even better shape than we thought."

"Why?"

"If he gets hungry, he can eat them."

I looked at him, amazed. "I guess you're right."

He laughed. "I'm teasing. He hasn't been out there long enough to eat the dogs. Let's look at those maps."

I fixed breakfast while he pored over the maps. They confirmed everything I'd said.

We finished eating. "We're going to start in this direction," Quipac pointed to the southwest, "and walk a big zigzag pattern to see if we can find some sign of him. I have more stamina than you do. It won't help if we push today and can't do anything tomorrow. I'm going to set a pace that may seem slow to you. Every two hours we're going to stop, and you're going to rest while I do a little extra scouting."

I started to say something, but Quipac held up his hand. "And this is where you get to demonstrate you know how to be subordinate."

"A woman understands her place," I said in Inuktitut.

He laughed loudly. "You are full of surprises," he said with delight. "OK. Let's make you Inuit."

I worked on straightening my wavy hair. Then he rubbed a thick layer of makeup on my face and hands.

"Good enough," he said. "Let's go!"

We put on our backpacks, picked up our rifles, and started out.

When we'd walked about a half-hour, he said, "It's time to teach you to sing."

"Sing?"

"Yes."

"Boy, I sure . . ."

He gave me one of those looks.

"If my brother says sing, I'll sing," I said quickly.

He smiled and nodded. "You're doing better than I thought you would with the subordinate business. This walk may even turn out to be fun."

"I think you're pushing your luck!"

He laughed again. "I do want us to sing though. Jack might not respond to a shout if he isn't sure who it is. He'll know we're Inuit if we're singing Inuit songs."

I saw the sense in that.

So as we walked, he told me about a song and what the Inuktitut words meant. Then he sang it for me, and I sang it for him with a little prompting. Then we sang it together. The first one we worked on was a hunting song created by the famous shaman Igjugarjuk:

Yai—yai—yai
Ya—ayai—ya
I ran with all speed
And met them on the plain,
The great Musk Ox with brilliant black hair—
Hayai—ya—haya.

It was the first time I had seen them,
Grazing on the flowers of the plain, Far from the hill where I stood,

And ignorantly I thought
They were but small and slight . . .

But they grew up out of the earth
As I came within shot
Great black giant beasts
Far from our dwellings
In the regions of happy summer hunting.

I was surprised how fast singing made the time go, and it was fun. It took my mind off the worrying. At the same time, we watched the ground carefully for a sign Jack or the dogs had been there.

I saw a number of marks, and from time to time we'd see scat, but Quipac showed me that the signs were of caribou or bear or wolf or some other animal. Nonetheless, he complimented me on my sharp eyes and encouraged me to keep pointing out marks.

We'd eaten a cold lunch, and we had a cold dinner. During the short dark night, the glow of a fire would be like a beacon visible for miles. During the day, campfire smoke would be even more visible.

He told me not to worry. We weren't far from camp yet, and there was plenty of territory left to cover.

We slept close to each other as we had those weeks in the survival class in December. As we relaxed before we fell asleep, I told him more about our summer. He questioned me about the details of our archaeological finds. He was delighted for me when I told him how excited I'd been when I found the soapstone lamp. Some of his questions were quite technical, so I began to see how broad his knowledge of archaeology was and how much he loved it, a side of him I hadn't seen before.

The second and the third days of the search were similar. We sang and we scanned the ground. I wasn't discouraged yet, because he wasn't discouraged. I didn't think he was just acting to keep my spirits up. He was sure we were going to find Jack.

The first three days of our search had been chilly and overcast with a continuous drizzly mist that soaked through everything, but the fourth day arrived with clear skies and bright sunshine. It was warm enough that I didn't even have to zip my parka. I thought this had to be an omen.

After our break for lunch, we'd started to walk again.

I saw something. "What's that? A wolf track?"

He looked. "That's what we've been looking for."

My heart rate shot up.

"Is it one of the dogs?"

"I think so. And look over there. There's something else."

"What do you think it is?"

"It's the marks made by something large moving through here. I'd say it was a person crawling. Come on. We'll track a little way and see what we find."

What we found was an odd collection of stones. Quipac bent and picked up one to examine.

"What is it?"

"Jack had something cached here. Given the shape the stones form, I'd guess it was a rifle, maybe yours."

"How do you know it was Jack and not someone else—maybe even an Early Man?"

"You know it's not old. Look at the rocks. Some of them have been turned upside-down, and the lichens on the sides facing down aren't dead yet. It's possible other people are walking around out here caching things, but I'll bet this was Jack. You sit right there where you are. I don't want you accidentally destroying any marks. I'm going to look around."

About ten minutes later, he called. "Come on. This way."

"How do you know?"

"Jack is expecting us. He left a mark for me. I guess he thought the rather obvious track he left by crawling wasn't enough." He laughed.

"You're sure it's him?"

"Yes. We used to play a kind of hide-and-seek when we were kids. One person would hide, but he'd leave a trail of marks. It was up to the other to find him. We played that all the time. Now watch for a plant that looks like something's been gnawing on it. That's what we're looking for now."

We cast around, and sure enough, we found some willow branches that had been marked.

I didn't think my heart could beat faster than it had been, but it did.

"OK, now we're going to walk in this direction."

"We could run."

He laughed, angled off from our previous path, and started walking faster. "It's time to start singing again. This is what all that practice was for."

So we started singing and it wasn't long—not more than a half-hour—before a third voice joined in.

Chapter Twenty

I had such a rush of relief that I was the closest I have ever come in my life to fainting. My legs went wobbly, and I started seeing stars. I stopped singing. Quipac looked at me, and he was back and holding me up before I had a chance to fall. He pulled off my backpack and made me bend over and put my head between my knees, and all the time he kept singing.

When he saw I was OK, he took my backpack and rifle, and we started walking again.

. . . And there was Jack.

He sat on the ground with the two dogs. They sat on their haunches and sort of smiled at us the way dogs do, tongues lolling, tails going side to side. When they recognized me, they rose and yipped with excitement, but when Jack said in Inuktitut, "Quiet. Down," they obeyed.

I thought my heart would burst with joy, but I remembered that I was an Inuit wife, and I should not show emotion in front of Quipac.

Still, I ran to him.

As I knelt, and he put his arms around me, he said, "I like your song."

"She's a good singer," Quipac said. "You know, I'm almost sorry we found you. I was beginning to think about taking her on as a junior wife. She has some good qualities, although she does have a tendency to be a little emotional, and she doesn't quite have a handle on 'subordinate' yet."

"How, exactly, were you going to break that to Miqo?"

Quipac shrugged. "I hadn't worked that part out yet. You OK?"

"The bastard broke my ankle." Jack's voice was calm, but I was astonished. I'd never heard him use profanity.

"That would explain why you've been crawling instead of walking. Your trousers need a little repair around the knees, and you're looking a little skinny too."

"I did manage to crawl back to the rifle and the knife, but no game was kind enough to stop in my sights. These dogs have scared off everything within twenty miles. They need a little discipline."

"Why didn't you eat one of them?" Quipac asked.

"It's obvious you don't know how much we paid for them, but I was thinking about it."

"What have you been eating?" I asked.

"The only things that have dropped by for a visit have been voles. There're lots of them here, although not as many as there used to be."

"Jack, I hate eating voles," Quipac said. "They're just little bones and fur and those nasty little tails. If that's all you have to offer, I'm going hunting. I'll be back in a couple of hours. Don't you wander off! I don't want to have to find you again." With that, he set my rifle down with the backpacks, turned, and walked away.

The whole time they'd been talking, I'd sat with Jack's arms around me as tears streamed down my face.

"Are you going to cry like this all through our marriage?" he asked.

"I don't know. Maybe . . . Are you going to keep doing things like this?"

"No, I don't think I'll do anything like this again. What's that stuff on your face and hands? It's gone all stripe-y from your tears. It's really strange."

"Quipac wants me to look like an Inuk."

"I don't know about that. I've never seen any striped Inuit."

"It wasn't striped when I started."

"You know, I appreciate Quipac's efforts to make you more attractive, but I like you better the other way."

"Let me look at your ankle. And your knees are abraded. We brought a first aid kit."

"My ankle can wait. It happened ten days ago. I cut strips off my shirt and bound it up. It's already started to set. You stay here where I can hold you. It's been too long since I've been able to tell you how much I love you."

If anything, I was crying harder now. I blubbered, "I didn't know . . . if we'd find you . . . I didn't really think . . . Quipac could be right . . . when he figured out where to look . . . I thought you could be any place out here."

"Well, they didn't really have as many options as you'd think. Whatever they did with me had to look reasonable. I knew you and Quipac would come, but I didn't know when. I didn't know if I'd get a chance to see you again. I waited for you all my life, and I'm not willing to lose you now that I've found you. I'm not going to do anything foolish like this again." And with that, he turned me around, gently tilted me across his lap, leaned down, and kissed me as only he could. I melted into his arms, and I was home again.

I don't know how long he held me, but then he sat me up. In Inuktitut, he said, "But, woman," and his voice changed to a stern tone, "a husband is shamed to hear his friend say someone's wife 'doesn't quite have a handle on subordinate yet.'"

I lowered my eyes and said demurely, "A wife is doubly shamed."

"A husband thinks it's time to practice. Move over here," and he gestured to the space between his outstretched legs.

"What are you going to do?"

"I'm going to take your clothes off."

"I might get cold."

He smiled. "I won't let that happen."

"Don't you think Quipac might come back?"

"Yes, in two hours. That's what he gave us. Let's not waste it. Turn around and kneel here."

I knelt between his legs and let my unzipped parka drop on the ground behind me.

For a few moments, he looked at me. Then he reached out and touched my hair. He smiled when he felt the stiffness of the hair spray. He reached for the top button on my shirt and undid it. And the next. And the next.

I reached for his shirt too.

"No. I'll tell you when you can do that."

He slid my shirt off my shoulders and off each arm and then took off my long-sleeved silk undershirt. He kissed my right hand . . . first the back . . . then the palm. He ran his tongue slowly from my palm up the inner side of my wrist and kissed that and then to the bend of my elbow and kissed that. He did the same thing with my left hand.

If I'd thought I might be cold, I was wrong.

He reached around and ran his hands slowly and gently down my shoulders and back. Leaning forward, he reached past me, picked up my parka, and draped it on me.

Then he put his hands under me, lifted me, and set me astride his lap.

My nipples were hard in anticipation.

He cupped my breasts, stroking and feeling. He kissed my right nipple . . . and then the left.

I was so excited I could hardly breathe.

"Now," he said. "Now you can take my shirt off."

I was fumble-fingered as I undid the buttons of his shirt. I pulled his shirt and his undershirt off his arms and let them drop.

I couldn't keep my hands off him. Everything about him excited me.

"Unroll your ground sheet and your sleeping bag here next to me and lie down," he said.

I rose and unrolled the ground sheet on the pad of brush he'd made to insulate himself from the cold of the permafrost. Then I opened out the sleeping bag and lay down.

Careful of his ankle, he took off his boots. Then he undid the button at his waist and opened the zipper, slid his Levi's and his briefs down, and pulled them off.

He turned carefully, knelt at my feet, and took off my boots.

"Take off the socks," I said.

He did, and then he breathed out in a long sigh.

When I'd gone to the drugstore in Ottawa to buy the makeup, I also bought nail polish—"Dragon Fire." Before Quipac and I left, I painted my toenails—a little act of faith that we'd find him.

He undid my jeans and pulled them and my long silk underpants down around my ankles and off. He kissed each of my toes and my insteps and ran his fingers along the ankle bracelet. "I thought about this," he said.

"Please, please."

I thought I'd go crazy if I had to wait a second more.

And he said, "No. Not yet."

He moved until he was between my legs as I had been between his. He bent and kissed slowly from my knee up my inner thigh, first on the left, then on the right . . . and then in the middle.

I was dizzy with desire.

"Now," he said. "Now."

And he lay on me, but before he had entered me completely, I had an overwhelming wave of sensation. He felt what had happened. Suddenly his breath was ragged, and he thrust into me and started moving strongly—oh, I had dreamed about this. He moved faster and faster, and I knew, and I went with him.

We'd made love in so many ways and in so many places. I hadn't thought it could be new and different, but we both knew it was a miracle we'd found each other a second time.

We lay exhausted under the sleeping bag and dozed for a while.

"See, it's not so bad being subordinate," he said as he ran his hand gently down my cheek.

"Some scientist you are!"

"What do you mean?" he asked.

"You're coming to a conclusion with insufficient data. That's what I mean."

"What other data do you think I need, then?"

"I'll show you." I started kissing him as he'd kissed me, touching him as he'd touched me, and I wouldn't allow him to touch back. I made love to him as he had to me.

When we finished, he said, "You might have a point there."

Chapter Twenty-one

Quipac was as good as his word. Two hours after he left, he returned, making a great deal of noise. He'd shot two hares.

Jack was eating jerky we'd brought.

I sat, relaxed, petting the dogs.

"I found your stream," he said to Jack.

"That's why I came here from the rifle cache. If I'd been smart, I'd have left the rifle and the knife nearer the stream, but I didn't actually plan on having a broken ankle."

"This isn't where they left you?" I asked.

"No, they left me about six miles from here."

"You crawled six miles?"

"More or less. I had to. I couldn't survive long without water."

"Anne, can you eat raw hare?" Quipac asked. "I'm not sure it's a good idea to light a fire here."

"I don't think they'll be back yet," Jack said, "and we're going to get out of here as soon as we eat. A small fire might be good."

"OK," Quipac said. "So, tell me what happened."

As we talked, he started a fire, skinned and gutted the hares, and set one to cook. The dogs ate the offal.

"Hal and Serbin came five days after Anne left," Jack said. "That was ahead of schedule, but I thought it was a delivery of supplies. I wasn't as suspicious as I should have been."

"But you did expect something to happen?" I said. "That's why you cached the rifle?"

"Yes."

"And they broke your ankle?" Quipac asked.

"Not at the camp. Hal held a gun on me and made me load the dogs into the helicopter and climb in myself. They flew me out here. I thought they were going to kill me, but they just wanted to get me far enough away from the camp that I couldn't crawl back. Then Serbin held a gun on me, and Hal stomped on my ankle twice."

"Why?" I asked.

"I thought I was being so smart not letting them know about the Early Man site, but they already knew about it."

"How?"

"MacNeil told them."

"They admitted causing his disappearance?" Quipac asked.

"They dumped him out of the helicopter into the ocean."

"Oh!"

I was sickened at the thought.

After a moment, I said. "How did they know you knew about the Early Man site?"

"They didn't know for sure, but they guessed I must have found it, based on the stuff I did report. They know its significance, and they're desperate to keep it quiet. They took a big gamble hiring us to come out here, but they had to have that report for the environmental impact study. They had their fingers crossed that we wouldn't find the site. That's why they never gave us those maps and photos. They were afraid we'd see something crucial in them."

"Now they're back to square one," I said. "They'll have to hire a third person."

"Hal said they have enough of my interim reports now that they can put together a final draft. They're going to forge my signature."

"Why didn't you tell them you'd already sent a report out on the Early Man site?"

"Because the only way I could've sent it out was with you, and I didn't want them coming after you. I don't think for a minute Hal is some sort of rogue acting on his own. That company has long arms, and they could've easily reached out and harmed you in San Diego. I kept hoping they wouldn't wonder if you knew about the site."

"Hal asked me in the helicopter if we'd found anything interesting. I told him it was just a bunch of old trash."

"He must have believed you. You created a bigger problem for him than I did. It would be impossible to explain if you died or disappeared too."

"I think he wanted to believe me. He tried to get me to go out with him when I got back to Anchorage."

"So that's why they didn't respond when I tried to call in the next day after you left. They took you to Anchorage. I didn't know what to think."

"Yes. I finally convinced him I wasn't going to go out with him. Then when he called to say you were missing, he even said maybe we could get together some time. I couldn't believe it."

Jack didn't say anything, but he spread his fingers out momentarily the way he does when he suppresses emotion.

"It still seems strange to bring you out here and break your ankle."

"They need to be able to find a body. They plan on me dying from lack of water and food. They're coming back soon to see if I'm dead yet. They think by the time I'm dead, the bruises from the stomping will be healed, and Hal said he hoped my body would be chewed on by the dogs and other animals. It didn't occur to them that I could get to the stream or that I could eat the animals that were supposed to eat me.

"Anyway, I'd been studying the maps. I knew I wasn't far from where I'd cached the rifle and the knife. That was pure dumb luck! I haven't used the rifle, but I needed the knife to cut strips off my shirt to tie up my ankle and make the kneepads and to cut this brush we're sitting on. I rested a day to let my ankle be less painful. Then I came over here to the water.

"I debated about moving on, but I figured even in a week I couldn't get farther than they could get in a couple of hours in the helicopter, so I decided to wait for you to show up. I've been sitting here snacking on voles ever since."

"Did you truly eat voles?" I asked.

"Sure. You want to see me do it? Quipac can get one."

"Ugh, no! And let me think a minute about whether I want to kiss you again." I'd meant to joke, but I couldn't repress a shiver of revulsion.

"Anne," Quipac said quietly, "remember my parents died during a hunger year. That's how hungry you have to be before you try to live on voles, but voles are fat and protein, like caribou. Wolves and foxes can live on them, and we can too. They're not bad. It's just that it takes so many of them to fill you up, and you spend a fair amount of energy catching them. You don't usually eat them until after you've eaten the dogs, and you can guess how desperate we had to be before we did that. Once the dogs were gone, we couldn't travel to hunt, even if the game returned."

His gentle chiding left me ashamed. "I understand."

"Anyway, Jack," he said, "now we've found you, we need to figure out what to do with you."

"I've been thinking about that."

"I figured you might."

"We could try shooting their helicopter out of the sky. That's what I planned to do if you didn't get here in time. It's risky though. We're more vulnerable than they are, and we have Anne to think about. Brown or not, she makes a good target."

"Our pilot's coming back."

"Anne told me. Unfortunately, he may be coming back the same day Hal is. If we make ourselves visible to a helicopter, we have a fifty-fifty chance it's the right one. That seems like pretty low odds. If we're wrong, it takes us back to the problem of shooting them out of the air."

"So it's better we run?"

"Yes, but in different directions. It'll be too easy to catch us if we stay together. We need to split up. Brother, let me see your map."

Quipac spread the map on the ground.

"You go west to Deadhorse. They have law enforcement there." Jack pointed at the map. "Anne and I'll take the dogs in the opposite direction. We'll head toward the Early Man site. Look for us around here," and he pointed again. "We can pass through camp and pick up supplies. I'll be slow, but I can make better time than they think I can, and they'll probably spend time making sweeps here looking for my body before they'll think of looking elsewhere."

"They may spot me before I can make Deadhorse."

"Be sure your hood is down, so they can see you're not me. If they land to question you, tell them you're Iñupiat. They won't know the difference. Smile and be cooperative, but act a little slow. They'll probably ask you if you've seen me, but they'll have no reason to bother you. They're not in the business of murder for the fun of it."

"OK, that about covers it," Quipac said.

"What about the radio in camp?" I asked.

Jack shook his head. "They took the battery, just in case."

Quipac took the hare off the fire, and we ate. Jack ate slowly, but he ate more than Quipac and I did together. As Quipac had pointed out, the voles hadn't been very filling.

Kiska and Moose sat, looking anxious. They knew better than to beg. Their good behavior paid off. They ate the leftovers.

After we finished, Quipac wrapped the second hare in its skin and tied it to his backpack. He stood, hefted his backpack and rifle, and said the Inuit version of good-bye, “I’m going now.”

We responded, “Yes, you’re going.”

He turned and walked away.

I called out, “Quipac! Thank you.”

Without turning, he waved and kept going.

Chapter Twenty-two

I unwrapped Jack's ankle. The bruise, now yellow, was much worse than I expected. It spanned from his instep to his calf. I could even recognize the pattern of Hal's boot soles in the bruising. The brutality it indicated sickened me. I couldn't understand how Hal could do that.

Jack soaked the ankle for a while in the icy water of the stream, as he'd been doing right along to reduce the swelling. Then I wrapped it with an Ace bandage.

He scattered the remains of the fire and the bedding to disguise the fact that we'd been here.

"We'll experiment," he said. "I'll carry your pack, and we'll see if it slows me down."

His boot gave the ankle some support, and he used me as a crutch, but walking was difficult.

After a while, I said, "Let me take a turn with the pack."

He slid the straps off his shoulders and handed it to me.

As we continued to walk, he didn't say anything, but I could see that his face had relaxed. The pain had eased.

This whole thing was strange. We were in danger and fleeing for our lives. I was afraid, yet I was as happy as I have ever been in my life. I was with Jack. Whatever we had to face, we'd face together.

Quipac and I had walked in a big zigzag pattern to find Jack, but Jack and I went in a straight line back toward the camp.

When his face began to look strained, we stopped to eat a cold supper from food in my pack. I told him I was too tired to go on, so we piled up small branches as padding to protect us from the chill of the permafrost, put the ground sheet down, and used my sleeping bag as a blanket. We slept in each other's arms.

Jack woke me. I have no idea when, but it was during the twilight time. I think he had a nightmare, and he called my name. I stroked him and kissed him until he finally relaxed. I don't think he ever properly woke up. The next day he didn't remember it.

We started again almost as soon as we woke and arrived at camp in the late afternoon.

Jack changed clothes. Although he'd washed in the stream, he'd been wearing the same things for almost two weeks and was glad to see the last of them. He also was happy to be able to shave and brush his teeth.

I opened the medical kit and rewrapped his ankle, and he took half a dose of Vicodin for the pain. He'd never taken Vicodin before. He didn't want to be groggy and was concerned that if he knocked the pain back too much he might reinjure his ankle with overuse.

He told me there was no further value in disguising me, so I took a few minutes to clean off most of the makeup and get my hair part way back to normal.

We loaded the training sled with our backpacks, rifles, ammunition, food for us and the dogs, ground sheets, and sleeping bags. We added a map, compass, and some things from the camp medical kit.

"If they check, they may notice that the training sled and my sleeping bag are gone," he said. "We'll have to keep our fingers crossed."

I thought after almost two weeks with no practice, Moose and Kiska might be unruly, but they pulled that sled as if they'd been doing it all their lives. This is what they'd been bred to do, and they seemed to know it. Even without snow on the ground, the pulling was easy because the sled was lightly laden, and the dogs were strong.

Jack used his fishing spear as a walking stick to ease his progress.

We continued east. The helicopter would come from the north-west and stop first at the place where they left Jack. Then they'd start looking. They might be able to spot us with binoculars. Our goal was to get farther away from where they might logically search as fast as we could, but it was difficult sometimes for Jack to see where to put his foot down. Stepping on ground a little higher or a little lower than he expected jolted him with pain. It didn't take us long to figure out that going that fast wasn't worth it.

When I thought he'd had about as much as he could manage, we stopped, fed the dogs, ate, and rested.

In spite of the pain, this day had been easier for Jack. His ankle had another day of healing. The walking stick helped too. But the strain still showed in his face.

We continued walking after dinner. At about midnight, during the twilight time, we settled down to sleep. We were tired, but couldn't let go of being awake. Before, I'd thought everything was a nightmare. Now everything felt like a dream. I didn't want to wake up to find Jack still missing.

I think he felt the same way. He kept kissing me and touching me.

"This whole experience made me think about my life and what's important in it," he said. "It's you. I've had a lot of time to think about what happened between us before you left."

"Me too."

"I was wrong. I've had a whole lifetime to learn how to live in your world. You've had less than a year to learn to live in mine."

"I don't care who was right or wrong," I said. "I care about you. What I feel for you is overwhelming. I don't know how to handle it.

I'll do my best to be what you want me to be and do what you want me to do. I'll be subordinate if that's what you need of me, but you have to help me understand what that means, and you need to allow me to make mistakes. I never thought I could say something like this to a man, but I'll make any compromise for you."

"I didn't fall in love with you because you were subordinate," he said. "I just fell in love with you. I don't want to change you."

We were silent for a while.

"You said something we need to talk about," I said.

"Go on."

"You said I didn't need you to hunt for me. That was about the money, wasn't it?"

"I was surprised when that came out of my mouth. Yes, it was about the money."

"What do we do about it?" I asked.

"I don't know."

"I had a little talk with Quipac."

"Oh?" he said.

"He explained about code switching. I'd never heard of that before. He said you and he have to do that because you both live in two separate worlds. He said some things in the Inuit and white worlds are comparable, but some don't translate at all.

"I told him I didn't know how to be in the Inuit world with you. He said to trust you. I know he's right. I want to hurry things along and, I guess, for us to be like old married people now, instead of in five years or ten years or whatever. But it doesn't work that way. I have to trust you, but you have to trust me too. I didn't marry you because I was lonely. I didn't marry you because I need you to take care of me. I married you because I can't imagine life without you. It's mysterious, but it's not complicated."

Jack nodded. "We know there's a possibility Hal's going to make these problems moot for us. But if he doesn't, you're right. It's mysterious, but not complicated. We'll learn how to handle these things."

"Quipac said something else that made me think," I said. "I asked him how to fight 'in Inuit,' and he said he didn't think it was possible to fight in Inuit the way white husbands and wives fight. He said he'd never had a fight with a white woman. I wondered, have you?"

"Not with any woman. That's not the way we do things."

"Never with one of those women you dated? Never at a faculty meeting with one of the other professors? Never with a student?"

"Sometimes the male students can be belligerent when they come in during an office hour. The women cry or flirt. And both men and women try to butter me up. Don't get me wrong. Most of them come in with genuine questions, and they want to learn, but a few are interested only in the grade, not in the learning."

"What do you do about the belligerent ones?"

"The males of every species bluff, and that's what most of them are doing, so I ignore it. For those few who aren't bluffing, I don't worry about being able to handle them."

"How did you date and never get in a fight?"

He shrugged. "I don't know."

"I've never asked you, and your life before me isn't my business, but . . ."

He nodded. "Go ahead."

"You once said Maata never thought the women you brought to Ungavaq were potential daughters-in-law, but you must have been serious about someone to introduce her to your mother."

"Not really. In your society, meeting the parents is the last step before an engagement, and I might have thought of it that way except for my experiences dating. All the dating I did was with white women and black women. I didn't find a whole lot of Inuit women in New York—or in Ottawa, for that matter. Anyway, I learned—rather painfully—most of them just looked on me as an exotic adventure. I was looking for someone to share my life. I didn't want to be someone's trophy.

"That's why I married Kaiyuina. Of course, I'd known her from childhood. Miqo told me she was marriageable. It hadn't occurred to me that she'd still be available. We didn't love each other when we married. We assumed love would come in time."

"And it did?"

"For me, yes, but . . ." He shook his head. "It was such a relief to be with someone who didn't think I was a savage. What I didn't recognize was that half of my life was as alien to Kaiyuina as my Inuit life was to the other women. Kaiyuina didn't think I was a savage, but she didn't think I was very Inuit either."

"So no one accepted you for who you were?"

"Until I met you. Before I married Kaiyuina, I learned taking a woman to Ungavaq was a quick way to find out what her feelings were. After Kaiyuina died, I didn't bother to do that. I gave up on the idea of ever meeting someone I could marry."

"You still dated, didn't you?"

"Oh, yes."

"Did you ever date Laura? She's single, isn't she?"

"She has a partner named Helen. They've been together for about fifteen years."

"Oh, I didn't know. Who did you date?"

"Now I was older, there were women out there who didn't especially want to get married, and they weren't looking for a trophy either. They just wanted an evening's or a night's companionship. I was lonely too. I was willing to provide what they wanted."

"When I met you, I didn't sense that."

"That's because it was different with you. I've never been as happy in my life as I have been since the day I met you. Even when I thought you couldn't love me, it was better being with you than with anyone else I ever knew. You know what was important for me?"

"What?"

"When you told me you weren't dating René."

"Why?"

"I knew how much you liked him. I thought it was more than liking. When you introduced me to him, though, it showed you cared enough about me to do that. You didn't have to invite me along, but you wanted to."

"I wanted René to know you because I already loved you, and I wanted to see what he thought. I finally figured out the two of you were jealous of each other, but still, I could see he liked you. I was in a funny situation. Going to Ungavaq was like a romantic dream. It was so different from anything I'd ever known that I was afraid maybe I was getting carried away."

"René showed you I was real and not a dream?"

"Real and a dream too."

"Now, answer a question for me," he said.

"Sure."

"What's the truth about René?"

Suddenly my heart raced. Evasion was impossible. I was in his arms. He could feel the sudden tension.

". . . We were lovers."

"I thought so from the way he kissed you that day I met him."

"Not then. Later, after I made up my mind you couldn't be interested in me."

"You said you weren't dating, but I didn't believe that. The way he kissed you wasn't just friendship."

"I didn't actually lie. We didn't date, but we did see a lot of each other."

"I guess you did if you were lovers." He laughed.

"That's not what I meant."

He laughed again.

"Is it a problem that we were together?"

He became more serious. “That was then. That’s over. Is he a problem for us now?”

“He’ll never be a problem for us. When I came back to Ottawa last November and the two of you met me at the airport, I told him how I felt about you. He already knew. He’s a dear friend, that’s all, and this time I’m not hiding anything from you.”

“I’m glad that’s the way it is. I like René. Tell me about fighting then.”

His change of subject startled me again. “Tell you what?”

“Did you and Robby ever solve anything by fighting?”

“Sometimes. Nothing that couldn’t have been solved another way if we’d tried. Fights were difficult for me. My father used to get angry, but my mother was never allowed to, and my sisters and I weren’t allowed to, or at least we were never allowed to show it. I read someplace that women cry sometimes because they don’t have another way to let out anger.”

“Is that why you cried after I was so harsh with you?”

“No. I was sad. Things were out of hand, and I couldn’t think of a way to make them better, and I didn’t want to go away from you.”

“We should find another way to do things.”

“If we do that, my thirty-five years of training on how to fight with a husband will go down the drain. It’ll be totally wasted on you. You won’t even recognize my skill.”

Jack laughed. “No, I don’t think I’d recognize quality fighting if I saw it. I’m going to have to take your word for your skill level. And I do believe you.”

He pulled me closer. We cuddled together and finally drifted off to sleep.

I woke with a start. The sun greeted me, as did a soft breeze on my cheek— another glorious summer day. I immediately felt hopeful.

Jack was already up and had breakfast prepared.

"Can you handle the dogs on your own?" he asked.

"I don't know."

"You'll have to. We don't know how long we're going to be out here. We can't depend on the food on the sled. I need to hunt, and the dogs are excitable when they sense other animals. Pack up and go east. I'll find you."

"Can't I go with you?"

"No."

"Why not?"

His jaw tightened, but with visible effort, he relaxed. "Last night you told me about Quipac saying some things don't translate from Inuit to white."

"Yes."

"This is one of those things. It's offensive to the animals for a woman to hunt. When they're offended, they no longer make themselves available. That's the way it is. Now, I'm educated, and in my mind I think the caribou doesn't concern itself with who fired the bullet, but I'm also Inuit, and in my soul, I know the caribou's spirit can be offended. You can't go."

When I'd seen Jack tense up, I realized I'd challenged him again. The challenge wasn't the fact that I'd asked, but the way I'd asked, the abruptness and petulance of my phrasing and the tone. This time, however, he let me make that mistake, as I'd asked him to.

"A wife understands," I said.

He hugged me to him and kissed me. Then he picked up his rifle and started walking away.

This was the first chance I'd had to watch him from a distance, and I wasn't happy seeing how much he struggled. He was in pain already.

And I could do nothing about it.

Chapter Twenty-three

If Jack had asked me to be responsible for the dogs a few weeks ago, I think I'd have panicked, but by now I had experience with them and with a compass. I decided I'd have to manage what he asked.

I finished my breakfast, rolled up the sleeping bags, and packed the sled. That done, I picked up most of the broken branches we'd used for padding and insulation and threw them as far as I could in different directions, so they wouldn't immediately draw the eye by being massed together.

When it came time to put Kiska and Moose into their traces, they decided to be playful, but I managed to let them know who was top dog in the pack and get them settled and hooked up. I was pleased with myself as I cracked the whip and started them off.

Twenty minutes later, I found Jack sitting, resting his ankle. Like Quipac, he'd shot two hares. I'd heard the shots and, for a time, after the first one, I was afraid it might be Hal—but then I realized I'd have heard the helicopter.

We walked on until we were hungry, found a stream, drank, and refilled our canteens.

Then I went to work. It was my responsibility to clean the hares. This was my first real test preparing an Inuit meal. I'd never done anything like this before, but I'd watched Quipac. Without saying anything, I took the hares off the sled. As I gutted and skinned the first one, I thought about the choices I'd made. When I married Jack, I'd chosen to live in a patriarchal society. Our time in Alaska was an extension of village life with its sharp division of labor between men and women.

Jack watched but didn't take the carcass out of my hands when I was slow and clumsy with my ulu, nor did he offer advice. With his OK, I gave the parts we didn't want to the dogs, then handed him the dressed carcasses. I felt like a child learning a new skill, and I was happy when he praised my work.

We didn't dare light a fire, so I had to eat the hare raw. I'd tried different things in the class—raw seal, caribou, fox, and of course, fish and a number of strange combinations, but they were just tastes, one or two mouthfuls. This was a whole meal. Jack reminded me I had to take in enough calories to keep my strength up. So I did.

He helped by cutting little pieces of the parts he said were most tender.

Well, I don't think hares live the kind of life that leads to tender meat.

"Things could be worse," I said. "This could be fox."

"Keep your fingers crossed that we keep finding hares. I don't like the taste of fox in the summer."

"I don't think it tasted all that good in winter."

"We may see a caribou, but it's late in the season, so most of them have started moving south. Anyway, I don't want to leave a carcass obviously butchered by a human. We couldn't be sure the foxes and ravens would do a good enough job on it before Hal spotted it."

"You know, I was thinking about something."

"What?"

"All that money is absolutely no use to me now. I do need you to hunt for me."

Jack nodded. "I understand. A husband needs a wife, and a wife needs a husband."

I wrapped some of the meat in one of the skins, so we'd have something for dinner. Jack gave everything else to the dogs. He told me you usually feed them every other day when you're traveling, but they hadn't had much to eat during the last ten days. They were skinny. He said they wouldn't pull as well with food in their bellies, but the sled was so light, he didn't think it mattered.

Normally we would have walked beside the sled, but now we were in front of the dogs. Jack moved so slowly that we couldn't have kept up with the dogs if they'd set the pace. Even though he used the fishing spear as a walking stick, the walking was difficult, and later in the day, the strain reappeared on his face. I asked for a rest at about four o'clock, earlier than the previous two days.

We put down one of the ground sheets and a sleeping bag so we'd have something comfortable to sit on.

Jack anchored the sled, so the dogs wouldn't take off with it. In spite of the light load they'd been pulling, they seemed glad for a chance to nap. Their harnesses gave them enough slack to lie down comfortably.

I sat. Jack lay with his head in my lap.

"I know what you're doing," he said.

"What?"

"Do you think I've forgotten how far you can walk? I know you're saying you're tired so I can rest. I want you to know I appreciate it. For a little while, I'll stop pretending I'm so tough and tell you this ankle hurts all the way up my leg."

I had known Jack for a little more than a year. He had never before indicated he needed my help. He always noticed the things I did. He was quick to praise when I accomplished something new like preparing the hares, and he was quick to thank me when I did something for him, like bringing a cup of tea, but he was one of those men who needed to be in charge and never show weakness. It was difficult for him to take rather than give. I was thinking all that, but said only, "I suppose at this point I could say something about lemmings and women's boots."

He laughed. "You have a long memory!"

"Instead, I'll say if you were one of my first-graders, I'd probably put a kiss on it."

"Hmm. We know what that would lead to, so maybe you'd better not."

"OK," I said. "We'll rest a while. You know you haven't told me yet what our plan is."

"Are you going to make me pretend to be a tough guy again and say I have everything worked out?"

"Not really. Go on telling me the truth, like you did about your ankle."

"We're just running," he said. "We're trying to keep out of Hal's sight until someone rescues us."

I looked around. The tundra that had always seemed so spectacularly beautiful to me now looked barren and exposed. The tallest of the vegetation was no more than eighteen inches high. There was nowhere to hide.

"Let's look at the map." He sat up, took it out of his pocket, and unfolded it. "We started here." He pointed. "Quipac is heading west to Deadhorse to find the police."

I shook my head. "He has all those rivers to cross."

"It's late in the season. They'll be low. He can do it. We're approximately here." He moved his finger across the map. "We're actually only a few miles from where we camped a few weeks ago. I wouldn't be surprised if you started thinking things looked familiar fairly soon.

"North of us is the Beaufort Sea. If we were a little later into the fall, it would be frozen, and we'd have more options. We could have gone to Kaktovik. It's not very big, and I don't know if there's law enforcement there, but the people could have hidden us. As it is, the sea is a barrier for us."

"We can't go south because of the mountains," I said.

"Right."

"That leaves east or west."

"The truth is we're going east as a delaying tactic and hoping for the best. If we're lucky, Quipac will bring someone before Hal finds us."

"If we keep going this way, and Hal doesn't catch up with us, what then?"

"We'll cross into Canada. Of course, that's no barrier to Hal. North Yukon National Park here on the border may have a ranger station. Nothing shows on the map, but if there is one, chances are it'll be on the coast. It's cheaper to restock a facility like that by ship than by air. Sometimes the tourists come in by ship too."

"What about this village, Gordon, here on the Alaskan side?"

"Up here lines don't mean much. Canadian park rangers might be located there by agreement with the American Government. They'd have police powers. It's all guesswork, but the coastline swings so far south, if we keep going east, we'll get pretty close to Gordon. I guess that's our destination."

"OK," I said. "We'll go to Gordon. Which way is home?"

"Ungavaq?"

"Yes."

He pointed slightly south of the direction we were going.

"OK, then. We're walking home."

"Yes." He smiled.

"But now we should get the other sleeping bag out and sleep for a few hours. It wouldn't hurt us to have a real rest."

We piled up branches, rolled out the other ground sheet, and zipped the two sleeping bags together. I convinced him to take another pain pill. That, combined with the warmth of the sleeping bag, helped him relax.

"I wish you'd tell me something," I said.

"What?"

"Since there's a chance I might not have much more time to learn Inuktitut, I want you to teach me the words I can say to you when we're making love. Teach me how to tell you how much I love you in your language." So we lay close together, and Jack taught me. And then I told him the things he'd taught me. And we slept.

Chapter Twenty-four

I woke. Jack was dozing. When he felt me shift, he opened his eyes. It was getting close to seven. We ate what was left of the hare for dinner and started out. Jack seemed better. I was relieved to see the pill and the nap had helped him.

After four more hours of travel, we slept again.

When we woke in the morning, Jack said he was going hunting. We'd do things as we had the previous morning. He'd walk out while I loaded the sled and hitched up the dogs.

We breakfasted on beef jerky and canned peaches. I longed for a cup of tea, but I knew that even if we'd brought tea, it was too dangerous to have a fire, even for the short time it would take to boil water.

Jack picked up his rifle and walked away. He wasn't limping as badly as he had been. That made me more hopeful.

I set about cleaning our campsite. I had the sled loaded and the dogs hitched up when I heard something.

I turned.

It was what I'd been dreading . . . the familiar sound of a far-off helicopter. I saw a dot in the distant sky.

I knew it was futile, but I looked for a place to hide. Even if I lay flat on the ground, though, they could spot me from the air. And I didn't have time to hide the sled.

I had no options.

The only thing left was to turn the dogs loose. Hal had no reason to hurt them. Maybe they'd be able to survive on their own.

I made sure my rifle was loaded. They weren't going to slaughter me like a sheep. Then I sat on one of the rolled-up sleeping bags on the sled and waited, a terrible fear in the pit of my stomach.

The helicopter flew closer and closer. Finally, it was north of me. For a moment, I thought it was going to pass by, but it made a big swing and came back.

I stood, rifle in hand, and considered trying to shoot it down. I didn't know what to aim at, though, and I'd never fired at a moving target.

Finally, it circled low. The sound almost overwhelmed me. I closed my eyes against the dust from the rotor wash. I hadn't seen Hal or Serbin, but I didn't need to.

I heard Serbin bring it in west of me. He hovered momentarily, and then the helicopter rose into the sky again.

When I opened my eyes, Hal was crouched where he'd jumped to the ground.

I'd never fired at anything living before, but as Hal straightened, I swung my rifle up. I didn't wait to talk. He'd already tried to kill Jack. I didn't think he'd show me any mercy. I aimed and pulled the trigger . . . but my hands shook so much that even though he was close, I missed. I saw a little puff of fabric go up from his right shoulder, but he didn't flinch.

Before I could lever another shell into the chamber, he said coolly, "That wasn't quite good enough, and you don't get another chance. If you don't put the rifle down now, I'll shoot you where you stand."

He was aiming his rifle at me. His hands weren't shaking. He had that cold look in his eyes—the look I hated.

I considered whether I could shoot again before he could kill me. That would leave just Serbin. Maybe Jack would have a chance.

It was as if he could read my mind. "You're not going to get another shot off. Don't even try."

I'd seen Jack shoot caribou. I'd seen the way the bullet jolted them. Sometimes they struggled against their approaching death. Sometimes they just fell and didn't move again. That was what was going to happen to me.

I heard the helicopter touch down again, this time behind me. The dying noise of the rotors covered any sound Serbin might have made getting out, but I was sure he had and that he was armed.

I stooped and laid my rifle on the ground. I hoped Hal wouldn't see how much my hand shook, but he probably had.

I guessed they hadn't seen Jack. Perhaps they hadn't looked in the right direction yet. Jack surely heard the helicopter. Had he heard the gunshot? I didn't know. All I knew was how frightened I was.

Hal didn't recognize me in my new green parka.

I reached up, pushed my hood off, and removed my wraparound dark glasses.

His jaw dropped in astonishment.

I'd heard that clichéd phrase before, but I'd never actually seen someone do it. Now I had.

And he laughed. "Anne. You shot at me." He lowered his rifle.

"Hello, Hal." My throat was so dry I almost couldn't speak.

"What are you doing here?"

"Looking for Jack."

He shook his head. "I'm disappointed you'd think I'd fall for that, especially after you shot at me. You're not out here by yourself looking for Jack. Not unless you brought two more dogs that look just like the ones you had before. And you have two sleeping bags there."

"A girl can always hope, Hal."

"Ah, there's the Anne I like. I didn't expect to see you so soon. This is a surprise."

"I'm supposed to be waiting by the phone while you rescue Jack. Wasn't that it?"

"You do add a complication. I suppose people know you're here."

"A lot of people."

"Well, yeah, a complication, but not insurmountable."

"What are you going to do?"

"I'm going to have to kill you. It's only a question of how. I don't want to shoot you." He stood thinking a moment. "I hadn't anticipated this possibility, but I guess there's a question of what we do before I kill you too." He smiled that cold smile.

It took me a moment, but suddenly I realized the implication of what he'd said. In the helicopter those weeks ago, he'd asked if I wouldn't like to have "a little fun" with him, and now I couldn't even put it into words in my mind. It was too grotesque. Whatever courage I'd mustered to face him was seeping away.

He continued to talk. Time seemed to slow down. It was like being a mouse in front of a swaying cobra. His gentle low voice was calming and soothing. Only his words were terrible. I almost couldn't register what he was saying, until he mentioned Jack.

". . . and when you and I are done, we'll leave you someplace, like we did Jack. I won't have to break your ankle though. You're a city girl. You've been with Jack for a while, but I'll still bet on you not making it if we leave you somewhere out here by yourself. Of course, we have to find Jack too. I wonder how you found him. He has to be close by. He wouldn't leave his new bride on her own on the tundra."

"How do you know these things?"

"Oh, we've been checking up on you, Anne. There's not much we don't know about you. I have friends in San Diego."

"I know."

"So, I'm not the only one who's been doing some checking."

"That's right."

"Well, there's a lot more to you than I thought. The last thing I ever expected was for you to come out here by yourself and find Jack. Maybe I'm going to have to rethink my idea of just leaving you someplace."

He shook his head. "I'd like to think we have all the time in the world to chat, but I'm a working man, and I do have to get that report written. I've invested more time in this than I thought I'd have to. I'd like to get back to Anchorage. Prudhoe Bay is the ass end of nowhere. We need to get on with this. Why don't you come over here?" He leaned down and set his rifle on the ground.

I looked at my rifle.

He shook his head. "You don't want to get in a race to see who can get a shot off first."

His voice had softened even more and become caressing, like a lover's voice. The contrast between his voice and his intentions was almost more than I could bear.

"Anne," he said gently, "I don't want to hurt you, but I can. Or I can just put my hands around your neck and squeeze until you pass out. Then you won't be any trouble to me. I don't want to do that either. I'd rather you were awake." He said it as if he were coaxing me.

I was so afraid I felt nauseated, but I didn't want him to know. I don't know why I thought it made a difference, but it did, to me, at least. I suppose it was just pride. I didn't want to make it easy for him. "You're going to have to do that, Hal. I'm not coming over to you."

I had focused so much on Hal that I hadn't been paying attention to anything else. If I had, I'd have heard Kiska growling, and I'd have had warning of Serbin coming up behind me. Suddenly, he twisted my left arm back and up. I cried out in pain.

At the same moment, Kiska moved toward us, barking. Moose stood staring, hackles raised.

Serbin balanced his rifle, one-handed, on his hip and pointed it at Kiska.

"Serbin, no bullets," Hal snapped.

"You'd better quiet that dog down, woman, or I'll shoot it no matter what the boss says."

"Kiska," I said, "Moose, down . . . stay . . . quiet."

They obeyed, but trembled with tension.

"Boss, we don't have time for this shit."

"Yeah, we do. I'm going to spend a little time with Anne."

"Come on, Boss. Let's kill her and get it over with. I can smother her. That won't leave much in the way of marks, especially after the animals get done with her."

Without waiting, Serbin bent to put his rifle down, straightened, and put his right hand across my shoulder. I had just enough time for a whiff of the motor oil on his hand, and then I couldn't breathe.

I pulled at his hand with my free hand as I tried to lean away from his grasp, but that pressed me tight against his body. I tried to wriggle away from him, but it seemed each time I moved he pressed harder. He was so strong. I panicked, but I couldn't even scream.

"Serbin, that's enough!"

"Aw, come on, Boss."

"Enough!"

Serbin let go.

I gasped for air, panting and shuddering, my heart pounding. I'd never felt so totally helpless.

With icy calm, Hal said, "We do have time. Don't hurt her anymore. I've told her we don't have to do that. Bring her here."

Serbin moved me toward Hal and then gave me a push. I stumbled forward. The stumble wrenched my shoulder. Serbin hadn't let go of my wrist.

I cried out again.

"Serbin!" Hal reached for my free wrist and held it firmly. "Let go of her now," he said, in a voice frightening because of its calmness.

I heard Serbin's anger as he stepped back. "I still think you oughta kill her."

"Serbin. Let it go. This isn't going to take long." Hal's voice had switched from ice to exasperation.

He turned to me.

I was still shaking and my shoulder and elbow throbbed.

"Calm down, Anne. He won't hurt you again. I won't allow it. You don't need to worry about him. He's not part of this. It's just you and me."

"I wouldn't touch her with a pole. Fuck her and get it over with." Serbin sounded like a sulky child.

Hal ignored him. "Everything's going to be OK, Anne. I don't want to hurt you. I'll be gentle."

"I don't understand, Hal," I said, my voice trembling.

"Don't understand what?"

"Why you'd be interested in me. I'm older than you are by at least ten years, if not more. You can't be that desperate for a woman."

"Oh, Anne, you underrate yourself. You're beautiful; you're smart; you're brave. I noticed all that in Anchorage when you put that bitch in her place at the cocktail party. I meant what I said about you being a woman of quality. Jack doesn't deserve you. You're too good for him."

"But not too good for you, I suppose."

He gave it a moment's thought. Nodding, he said, "Oh, yeah, you're too good for me too, but . . ." and he shook his head, "that doesn't seem to matter now, does it?" He pointed. "Serbin, unroll that sleeping bag. Then get back in the helicopter. Anne deserves a little privacy."

Serbin did as ordered, but not without glaring at us and giving us the finger as he picked up his rifle and turned to walk away.

As he passed the dogs, they rose and snarled.

He raised his rifle.

"Moose, Kiska, down," I said.

Again, they obeyed.

Serbin swore as he walked toward the helicopter.

Hal ignored him. He pointed to the sleeping bag.

"Oh, Hal. Don't do this . . . Please."

He moved toward me.

I thought he was going to follow through on what he'd threatened, but he wasn't rough. I tried to move to the side out of his way, but I couldn't. His hand on my wrist was like a steel bar. I had to either move back or let his body press against me. I moved back.

We finally stood next to the sleeping bag.

"Relax, Anne. I'm not going to hurt you. I'm going to undo your coat now." He unzipped my parka with his free hand.

He looked with interest at the field knife on my belt. "Ah. You weren't thinking of using this, were you?" He pulled it out of the sheath, and tossed it aside. He focused on me again. "So frightened, but defiant too." He nodded. "I can see it in your eyes. You were going to, weren't you? It's not that easy to stab a person, Anne. I wouldn't have let you do it. It's better you didn't try."

I tried to turn away, but he took my face in his free hand and forced my head back so I had to look at him.

His thumb and fingers dug into my cheeks. His other hand never loosened its grip on my wrist. "I'd like to see tenderness in those beautiful eyes." He had a faraway look on his face. He shook his head, refocused, and leaned forward to kiss me.

I pulled away as much as I could.

Again, he paused. "A kiss is too personal, isn't it? I won't force that on you. I do wish you wanted my kiss." He sighed deeply, moved his hand, and caressed my cheek gently. "Ah, Anne, how I wish things were different."

Again, he hesitated. Then his expression changed. "Well, things aren't different. They're what they are. Sit now."

I stood looking at him.

"You will do what I say." His hand closed tighter on my wrist until the pressure made tears come to my eyes, but I just looked at him.

Perversely, he admired me for defying him. "See, I said you were brave." He reached up and gently took one of my tears on his fingertip. He looked at it and shook his head. "There's no need for this though. You don't have to fight me every step of the way. I don't enjoy inflicting pain, especially on you. I will if I have to though. Why don't you make this easy on yourself?"

I stood mute. More tears trickled down my cheeks.

He increased the pressure again.

Finally, I cried out, my knees buckled, and I fell onto the sleeping bag.

He'd let go of my wrist, so I made one last effort. I turned and tried to crawl away. My right hand wouldn't hold me though. Then he moved around to block my way, so I sat.

"Anne, this is going to happen. Don't fight me. It won't be that bad."

"I guess that's your version of pillow talk, huh, Hal?"

He unzipped his coat and dropped it on the ground. But when he started to bend toward me, suddenly he was falling away, and there was Jack, with his knife in his hand!

I'd never seen Jack like that. His face was a twisted mask of rage. He slashed at Hal.

Hal tried to get the knife away from him.

They rolled back and forth on the ground as Hal tried to kick Jack's injured ankle.

The dogs circled the two men, snarling and snapping.

I wanted to get one of the rifles, but my right hand was numb. I couldn't move my fingers. I couldn't have held a rifle or pulled the trigger. My left hand wasn't numb though. I hit Hal's face as hard as I could with my left fist as he and Jack rolled on the ground.

Then, things changed again. I felt arms pulling me away from Hal. *Oh, my God, I forgot Serbin again.*

Chapter Twenty-five

An authoritative voice boomed out, "Police! Get up off the ground!"

At first, I couldn't take in what I'd just heard.

But the second man, the one not holding me, repeated, "Police! That's enough!"

Then Quipac's voice said in Inuktitut, "Jack! Jack! It's over. It's all over."

I realized the arms holding me tight were uniformed. I stopped struggling.

I couldn't believe it.

About fifty yards beyond Hal's helicopter sat a second one.

Jack and Hal stood.

Quipac stepped between them. With his back to Hal, he took the knife from Jack's hand and gave it to the officer. Then he took Jack's hand in his. "Let me help you, my brother."

The rage disappeared from Jack's face, and his usual calm demeanor reappeared, although his breathing remained deep and ragged.

The officer released me, and I ran to Jack.

Quipac stepped aside, and Jack put his arm around me. For a moment, I thought he was going to fall, but he pulled himself together and managed to balance on his good leg. He said, "Down," to Kiska and Moose who still had their hackles up and, as before, they settled immediately.

"My" officer had followed me. He frisked Hal and took a pistol from a shoulder holster on his left side. Then he frisked Jack and me.

In spite of being out of breath, Jack said calmly, "Officer, I'm Dr. Jack O'Malley. This man was going to rape my wife, and he has killed someone."

The other man said, "I'm Sergeant Arthur Brooks of the Alaska State Police, and this is Corporal Robert Davies. We've been looking for you, Dr. O'Malley. Why don't you sit? I've been told you have a broken ankle."

"I'm OK. Let me see to my wife." He turned to me and gently traced the places Hal's and Serbin's hands had touched my face. It was as if he were erasing whatever they had left behind. His touch made my world right again.

"Where's Serbin?" Hal asked.

"In the chopper," Jack said.

Hal seemed as concerned about Serbin as Jack had been about me. I had suspected there was more to their relationship than what showed on the surface. The thought struck me that they were lovers. But if that were true, why would Hal want me? Nothing made sense.

He hurried to the helicopter.

The police indicated we should follow.

Quipac, Jack, and I stood back while they tended to Serbin.

Jack held me tightly.

Serbin sat slumped over the controls, his chin on his chest. I thought he was dead, but when Hal put his hand on his shoulder and spoke to him, he stirred, then lifted his head slowly. He seemed only semiconscious.

Hal breathed a big sigh of relief, pulled himself together much as Jack had done, and turned to Brooks.

"Sergeant, I'm Harold Josephs. I work for Allied American Oil Company. Dr. O'Malley is one of our contract workers. He's been missing. Perhaps the stress . . ." He shrugged. "Of course I haven't done any of the things he said."

"You liar!" I said.

"Anne," Jack said softly. I knew he was telling me to calm down, to be more Inuit.

I moved a little closer to him and didn't say anything more.

Quipac nodded, and I felt a moment of pride. I was learning.

"Folks," Sergeant Brooks said, "we'll get this sorted out, but first you all need medical attention. Dr. O'Malley, Mrs. O'Malley, you and Quipac come with me. Corporal Davies will fly Mr. Josephs' helicopter back."

"I don't think the corporal will be safe with those two," Jack said.

"I don't think Mr. Serbin is a threat to anyone right now, and I'm sure, Mr. Josephs, you realize even if you've done what Dr. O'Malley says, there's no place to go except Deadhorse."

"But I didn't do—"

Corporal Davies shook his head and gestured toward the helicopter.

Hal shrugged and went to retrieve his coat.

He and Corporal Davies helped Serbin move out of the pilot's seat and strapped him into the back.

We moved away, and they took off and headed west toward Deadhorse.

Quipac called the dogs and loaded them and the gear into the police helicopter.

Sergeant Brooks picked up the two rifles—Hal's and mine—my knife, and then Jack's rifle, which was on the ground where Hal's helicopter had been.

"It's good you didn't shoot someone, Dr. O'Malley."

"I couldn't get a clear shot without endangering my wife."

Sergeant Brooks started to unload the rifles. He stopped for a moment as he unloaded mine, then continued without comment. He put the cartridges in his coat pocket and handed the rifles and knife to Quipac to put with the rest of the gear. The four of us climbed in, Quipac in front, Jack behind Sergeant Brooks and me to his right.

Jack leaned over to look at my wrist. I winced when he touched it. It was badly swollen. He bent and kissed it and then my cheek.

He strapped me in and then himself and put my headphones on my head and his on himself so we could hear each other above the din of the rotors. He took my left hand in his and sat back as the helicopter rose.

As Sergeant Brooks turned the helicopter in the direction of Deadhorse, he said, "Dr. O'Malley, I know who you are. I've even read one of your books—the one on your dig here in Alaska. I enjoyed your ability to see the beauty of this land. You write so clearly. It's easy for someone not trained in archaeology to understand. I hope we can apply that clarity to this situation later, but for now, you just try to relax."

"Yes, we will and thank you," Jack said.

"Quipac told me you were doing an archaeological survey here on the Refuge. I don't think that falls under the purview of the investigation of what happened today. Did you find anything of interest?"

I said a quiet thank you to Sergeant Brooks under my breath. I couldn't think of anything better to get Jack's mind off the ugliness of what had happened. The three men spent the rest of the flight to Deadhorse talking about archaeology.

I was OK for a while, but then those darn tears started again. Quipac was right. I did have a tendency to be a little emotional.

Jack noticed. He took off his headset, leaned over, and kissed me on the cheek again. He moved my earpiece and said, "I love you."

Chapter Twenty-six

When we arrived in Deadhorse, the Allied American Oil helicopter was on the ground. Hal and Serbin were gone.

A car waited to take Jack and me to the hospital at Prudhoe Bay. The officer who drove us introduced himself as Paul Apatok, the North Slope Borough police officer.

We told our story to Dr. Fitzgerald as he examined my shoulder. It was strained, nothing worse, and my right wrist only badly bruised—no broken bones. The same was true for my left hand, the one I'd hit Hal with.

The doctor photographed all my bruises—and later, Jack's. He explained that the state police had requested he do that. Finally, he gave me an ice bag and pain meds, then turned to Jack.

"So you're the one who hit Mr. Serbin?"

"Yes," Jack said.

"You really belted him."

"I did my best."

"And you gave Mr. Josephs that shiner?"

"No. My wife gets credit for that."

He smiled. "Aren't the two of you little old to be fist fighting?"

"Didn't seem so at the time."

Dr. Fitzgerald chuckled. "Yeah, well . . ."

"I broke a finger in the process, I think."

"Let's have a look."

He examined Jack's hand and ankle, then did x-rays.

"I'd say you're very lucky," he said.

"I think so too. What's the story on the ankle?"

"Look here on your X-ray. The ankle joint is complex. It's made up of three bones plus tendons, ligaments, and muscles. The two lower leg bones, the tibia and the fibula, come down to the talus, the anklebone, right here." He pointed. "The tibia is also called the shinbone."

"Yes, I've seen a skeleton or two in my time," Jack said.

Dr. Fitzgerald nodded. "Then you know the fibula's thinner. This little bump here on the outside of your ankle is the end on the fibula. It's positioned in the outer portion of the leg. That's what broke, down low here near the talus. If it had been the tibia, it would have been physically impossible for you to walk. The tibia carries about ninety percent of your body weight with each step. As it is, I don't understand how you could tolerate the pain, but the fibula's healing nicely."

"What do we do now?"

"I'll put you in a walking cast, but I want you to rest the ankle as much as you can."

"When do I get the cast off?"

"We'll let your doctor at home decide that."

"I may not be near a doctor."

"Well, you keep that cast on for at least six weeks. You have the tools to get it off?"

"I'll manage."

"Tough guy, huh?"

Jack and Dr. Fitzgerald laughed.

He applied the cast, cleaned the abrasions on Jack's face and knees, and splinted the broken ring finger on his right hand. After he had provided Jack with a pair of crutches, he wished us good luck and said good-bye.

Lunch in the hospital cafeteria was a lot better than raw hare.

Officer Apatok drove us to the Public Safety Office in Deadhorse and ushered us into his office. Sergeant Brooks sat at the desk.

Brooks gestured to two chairs in front of the desk.

Officer Apatok sat on a folding chair next to him.

Brooks turned on a tape recorder and spoke. "My name is Sergeant Arthur Brooks of the Alaska State Police. Also present is Borough Police Officer Paul Apatok. The date is August 12, 2005, and the time is 4:15 p.m. This is an official inquiry. I'm recording this interview. Please identify yourselves for the record."

We did.

"Normally we'd have separated the two of you and questioned you individually as we did Mr. Josephs and Mr. Serbin, but I think that's not necessary. My superiors concur. Where were you going?"

"Gordon," Jack said. "We didn't know whether there'd be police or park rangers there, but we were hoping somebody would be."

"It's good we found you," Sergeant Brooks said. "There's nothing in Gordon. It used to be a trading post, but it was abandoned decades ago. There's one tumbledown building left. What happened that made you travel toward Gordon?"

Jack told the whole story from when we first arrived at the refuge.

"What happened today?" Sergeant Brooks asked.

"I was hunting. I heard a helicopter and saw it land near where Anne was. I came back as fast as I could and saw that Hal Josephs was going to rape her."

"How did you know that?"

"He was forcing her down onto a sleeping bag."

"What did you do?"

"I climbed into the helicopter behind Alexander Serbin. When he turned to see what the noise was, I punched him. I was going to shoot Josephs, but I couldn't get a safe shot, so I tackled him."

I filled in the rest of the story, telling Sergeant Brooks what happened before Jack had arrived.

When I finished, Sergeant Brooks clicked off the recorder. "I want you to understand I have a strong opinion about who's telling the truth and who's lying here. I said before I know who you are. We also know a thing or two about Josephs and Serbin. Deadhorse may be out in the boondocks, but the computer here is hooked up to the rest of the world.

"The problem is with evidence. It's no different in my profession, Dr. O'Malley, than in yours. I have a hypothesis, but no data. You say Josephs told you he and Serbin dropped Dr. MacNeil into the ocean. I believe you, but we have no body. I don't think that case will ever be closed. You say Josephs broke your ankle and left you to starve. I believe you, but there's no evidence I could take to court. You say Josephs was going to rape your wife. I believe you, but again, there's no evidence. The bruising on her wrist and her face is not enough. In all these things, it's your word against his. You're more credible than he is, but it's not enough.

"Now here's the real problem. As we were flying in, we saw some things. We saw Mrs. O'Malley on the sleeping bag with Josephs leaning toward her. We saw you attack him, and we saw Mrs. O'Malley hit him. You've told me you attacked Serbin. Those attacks are assaults. They're felonies, and for those we have our observations. Because you had a knife, the attack on Josephs could be construed as attempted murder."

I had a sudden sick feeling in my stomach. I'd thought this was over, but Hal was going to use the police against us.

My feelings must have shown on my face. Sergeant Brooks said, "Mrs. O'Malley, it's OK. I've explained to Josephs how important Dr. O'Malley is. If he were arrested, it would make headlines everywhere. Josephs is still hoping to salvage his environmental impact study. It's not to their advantage to damage Dr. O'Malley's credibility with a criminal trial. Josephs has declined an opportunity to sign complaints against either of you, so you won't be prosecuted. At this point, though, there's nothing I can do to help you press charges against them either."

I sighed, and my body slumped in relief, but Jack sat upright, his face immobile.

"You're free to go if you want," Sergeant Brooks continued, "but I suggest you stay here at the Public Safety Office. There's a little dormitory in the back. It's not great accommodations, but you can have a decent meal and a clean bed.

"I think you may still be in danger. If you stay here, we'll be able to protect you. I hope Josephs wouldn't do something stupid, but there's a lot of money at stake. I sent Corporal Davies and Quipac out to pack up your campsite. We can take you to Fairbanks tomorrow when we go."

I waited for Jack to speak.

He sat silent.

"I know this can't seem right to you. And I know your custom is to not show anger. I also think it's not right, but my hands are tied. I'm honored to have met you, Dr. O'Malley, Mrs. O'Malley, and I hope ultimately this has a much better ending."

Jack rose, so I stood too. He shook hands with Sergeant Brooks and Officer Apatok. "I thank you for your help. We'll stay here tonight and go with you tomorrow. No matter what happens, we're better for having met you, and I hope we'll see you again in happier circumstances."

Chapter Twenty-seven

The dormitory was where the Safety Office staff stayed when duty or weather required it. Officer Apatok ushered us in. He asked us to call him Paul. "We'll have a meal ready for you soon. While you're waiting, is there anything else I can do for you?"

"Where are our dogs?" Jack asked.

"I put them in the yard where we store the snowmobiles. They're OK. Those are sure good looking dogs."

"We just bought them. They were bred by Karen Adams."

"Aah! No wonder they're so good looking. I'll make sure they get fed."

"Thanks."

"Anything else?"

"Paul," I said, "I'd almost sell my soul for a cup of tea,"

"That's easy. How about you, Dr. O'Malley?"

"I guess if we're going to call you Paul, you'd better call us Jack and Anne, and yes, I'd really like some tea."

"You want anything in it?"

"Sugar for both of us, thanks."

"OK. I'll be back in a few minutes."

The small dormitory, crowded with four cots, wasn't luxurious, but was neat and clean. The minimal decoration included a photo calendar of Iditarod winning teams, something of local interest. I leafed through. Sure enough, one of Karen's teams was the picture for April.

Typical of buildings in the north, the windows were small and covered with heavy curtains to keep out the midnight sun of summer.

The room also had a small sofa with a coffee table adjacent. We sat. Jack leaned back and put his arm around me. I rested against him. We were quiet. I don't think I could have talked without breaking down in tears again.

Paul brought two mugs of tea and told us he'd be in the next room if we wanted him. He now wore a holstered pistol on his belt

The tea's warmth and fragrance were what I needed. I began to relax.

Jack shifted so that he could look at me. "We're alone. Tell me what you didn't say to Brooks."

". . . I don't want to talk about it."

"I need to know," he said quietly. "I know it upsets you, but I need to know."

"Are you going to look for Hal?"

"No. I told you I'm not doing anything foolish anymore. But I think it's important we don't have secrets. Please."

I had that sick feeling in the pit of my stomach again. "I shot at him. I tried to kill him."

"Ah, Anne. I heard the gunshot. I thought maybe you were dead. I can tell it upsets you, but I say 'Good for you.' I'm surprised at something though. When Brooks unloaded your rifle, he could smell that you'd fired it recently. And he saw the cartridge casing on the ground and picked it up. When he questioned us, he didn't ask about that. I wonder why not."

"Maybe he felt sorry for me."

"He's a good cop. That wouldn't make any difference. He didn't hold back on any of the other things. I think Hal must not have mentioned it. Strange . . . Is that why Hal hurt you, because you shot at him?"

"No. He didn't duck or flinch or anything, even though I hit the shoulder of his coat. When he realized it was me, he laughed."

"It's too bad you missed. He wouldn't have been laughing if you'd hit him."

"It was horrible."

"He would have killed you."

"He told me that. Then he said he was going to . . ." I couldn't go on. Jack put his arm around me again and drew me close.

"It's over. It's all over. You don't have to be scared anymore."

I nodded.

"Why did he hurt you?"

"I kept saying no to him. I never did anything he told me to do until he forced me."

"And that made him angry?"

"He never seemed angry. The more I defied him, the more he seemed to admire me. It was a contest of wills he knew he would win, but he liked that I tried. When he hurt me, he didn't seem to enjoy it. I don't think he's sadistic. Pain was just a tool he was using to get what he wanted."

Jack shook his head.

"He said I was brave."

"He's right."

"I didn't feel brave."

"Well, you are."

"The thing that was really odd . . ."

"What?"

"He was going to kiss me, but he didn't. He seemed sad. Then he said he wished I wanted his kiss. He wanted me to want him. I don't understand."

"Maybe he's used to women wanting him. It probably boosts his ego. He thought you'd be an easy conquest."

"Let's talk about something else. I don't want to talk about him."

I wiped my eyes. "Did you hear the helicopter?"

"That's why I came back."

"Not theirs. The police helicopter."

"The first thing I heard was Quipac," he said.

"That's so strange. I didn't hear it either."

"That's the adrenaline. I've never been that angry before. Now I understand what rage is. I didn't even realize I'd hurt my hand until we were on the way back here."

I sat up. "I'd better call Carola and René." I wiped my eyes again. My cell phone wouldn't work, so I opened the door and asked Paul if I could make two long-distance calls.

When I returned to Jack, I said, "I made a decision. We have a flight for the three of us out of Fairbanks to Ottawa tomorrow."

"That's good news."

"Carola and René send you their love."

Paul arrived with our meal: steak, salad, fried potatoes, green beans, and apple cake from the local coffee shop. It was delicious.

We sat up and listened to the local radio station playing "golden oldies." Maybe it wasn't so golden for us; it was rock and roll. But at least our food had time to settle. Then we pushed two of the cots together and went to sleep holding hands. We slept ten hours.

When we woke, Quipac was asleep on one of the other cots. The fourth cot had been used, but its occupant was gone.

Jack moved closer and slipped his hand up under my shirt to touch my breast.

"Quipac's here," I whispered.

"He's asleep," he whispered back.

"He might wake up."

"It doesn't matter. We'll pretend we're in an igloo."

"We'll pretend we're in a public safety office and wait," I whispered with emphasis.

Jack burst out laughing, and that woke Quipac.

"See, I told you so," I said.

Jack's only response was more laughter.

When Corporal Davies brought our breakfasts, I asked when we were leaving for Fairbanks.

"As soon as you're ready, but don't hurry. Enjoy your food."

We took his advice and savored the bacon, eggs, potatoes, and toast.

Jack and I told Quipac what had happened to us before he arrived, and he told us about his trek to Deadhorse.

"It wasn't difficult," he said. "I walked about twenty hours. Then, I slept for a few hours and walked the rest of the way."

"I guess we're lucky Paul was in his office," Jack said. "He told me he's out in the district most of the time."

"He called Fairbanks," Quipac said. "Brooks and Davies arrived a couple of hours later. I thought I might have trouble getting them to believe me, but Brooks knew who I was because of your book. MacNeil's disappearance was still fresh in his memory. He was concerned that a second archaeologist was in trouble.

"They confirmed Hal and Serbin had gone out in the company helicopter. We went straight to where I estimated you might be and spotted it on the ground."

"Were we ever glad to see you." Jack said.

"You didn't look like you were having much fun."

"Oh, I'd have beaten him."

"Sure," Quipac said. They laughed the easy laughter of men who know each other well.

Sergeant Brooks arrived to escort us to the airport. He'd no sooner entered the room than Corporal Davies appeared behind him. "Sergeant, you need to come. Josephs is in the lobby."

It was like a blow to the stomach. Suddenly I couldn't breathe.

Sergeant Brooks hesitated a moment. Then he said, "Davies, give them their rifles." He went out the door.

Jack started to follow.

"Please don't go. Please."

"Brother, your wife needs you," Quipac said.

Jack returned and put his arms around me. "You're OK. Everything's going to be OK. I'll stay here with you."

Davies brought our rifles.

We loaded them and waited. Quipac stood against the wall to the right of the door. Jack stood next to me facing the door. My hands shook so much I didn't think I should be even holding a rifle.

It seemed like forever before Sergeant Brooks returned. "He's gone. He asked for you, Mrs. O'Malley. He said he wanted to make sure you were OK."

I moaned.

"It's all right, Anne," Quipac said. "We won't let him bother you. He sure has nerve though."

"I'm astonished he'd come to the police station," Sergeant Brooks said. "That's a measure of the power he feels as a representative of Allied American. This is a company town. The sooner you're out of here, the better. Let's go now."

Chapter Twenty-eight

When the helicopter landed in Fairbanks, the executive jet waited for us on the tarmac. Quipac wasn't surprised, but Jack definitely was. "How'd you manage that?"

"I hope you don't open the credit card bill this month."

"Oh, well."

While I went into the terminal to tell Ernie, our helicopter pilot, he didn't need to make the last trip out to the campsite, the men shifted our baggage and the dogs into the plane. We said our good-byes to Sergeant Brooks and Corporal Davies, and we were back in the air in less than an hour.

Home in Ottawa, we took turns showering.

I looked in the bathroom mirror. There along my lower jaw were five round bruises: one, the mark of Hal's thumb, on the left and four others on the right. I felt sick when I saw them. I cried the whole time I stood in the shower.

There wasn't much food in the cupboards, so we went out to dinner. Afterwards, Quipac walked Moose and Kiska to the grocery store to buy them some meat. When he returned, we had tea, listened to a CD of Chopin etudes, and talked. Then

Quipac excused himself, took the dogs, and went to bed. We soon followed.

After we closed our door, Jack said, "Now we'll pretend we're in our own bedroom, and we won't worry about Quipac."

I took off my earrings and set them on the dresser. "I don't know. The doctor said you should rest. This might not be good for your ankle, not to mention your broken finger."

He chuckled. "I'll risk it."

He opened the drapes and the sliding glass door onto the deck to let in the night. We were getting toward the end of summer, but the air was still balmy. A slight breeze riffled the sheer under-drapes.

"What is that wonderful fragrance?" I asked.

"Ah, our neighbors have a jasmine tree on their deck when the weather's warm enough. They probably hadn't put it out yet when we were here in May."

He walked to the bedside table and turned on the CD player. A Brahms piano concerto softly filled the room. Then he dimmed the lights.

"Wow! I'm getting the full treatment."

"Yes. All this and even a bed. Nothing's too good for you." He propped his crutches against the wall, pulled me into his arms, and kissed me the way he does, and, as always when he does, some little switch turned my brain off and my body on. My heart filled with love and desire.

He gave me gentle little kisses—my ears, my eyes, my cheeks, my neck. By the time he reached my mouth again, I was ready to beg, but I felt his hand come up between us to unbutton my blouse, and that was enough of a distraction to make a thought pop into my mind. I pulled away a little. "Would you really have made love to me this morning with Quipac in the room?"

"Sure. Why not?"

"Why not!"

"Think about what we did in the igloo. Quipac was there."

"But you were quiet and secretive about that, and besides, it was dark."

A look of resignation came over his face. "I guess we're going to have 'a discussion.' Well, at least I'm going to be comfortable."

He undressed.

I did too.

"Before we talk, I'm going to have one more kiss," he said. He pulled me onto the bed, and it was a lot more than one kiss. When he stopped, I tried to kiss him again.

"Oh, no. You wanted to talk. We'll talk. What was it you asked? Oh, yes. I have no doubt Quipac knew what we were doing. I wasn't quiet and secretive because he might hear. I didn't want the students to know. Professors are supposed to behave themselves when they're in a classroom, even if the classroom is an igloo."

"So if it'd been just Quipac, you wouldn't have cared?"

He lay beside me now. He turned and kissed me again and brushed his hand across my breast.

I touched him too, but he took my hand and put it back where it had been. "Uh-uh," he said, shaking his head. "None of that. I can't concentrate on talking when you're doing that. You keep your hand up here. Now, as I was saying, no, not really."

"No, not really what?" I'd completely forgotten what we were talking about.

"No, I wouldn't care if Quipac saw us making love. He and I have no secrets. Remember we grew up in an igloo. I've made love to women with him there."

"Women? More than one?"

"One at a time."

"More than one time?"

"Many times."

"When you were with Kaiyuina?"

"No, we had a separate house by then." He leaned over to kiss me, but I shook my head. "Uh-uh, none of that. I can't concentrate when you're doing that."

He laughed and sat up. He turned on the bed so he was facing me and sat cross-legged, moving his ankle in the cast carefully.

I curled onto my side. "When, then?"

"When we were teenagers. We had a lot of freedom. Sex was considered normal. We built our own igloos where we went to socialize and part of socializing was sex. It's not like that now, not since we've had the missionaries."

"Oh. Well, I don't know . . ."

"What?"

"How I feel about that."

"I can tell you Quipac wouldn't comment to you about it, or to me, for that matter. And I wouldn't share you with him, as men used to do with their friends. I've already told him that."

"You what?" Now I sat up. "You and he were talking about sharing me?"

"No. We were talking about not sharing you."

He looked so innocent, but I saw that a tiny smile played at the corners of his mouth.

"When did you talk about this?"

"At night. In the igloo. During the class."

"Those times you were speaking Inuktitut?"

"Yes."

"Were you already planning to marry me?"

"I didn't think you'd have me. I was dreaming."

"So, even though you wouldn't share me, you would make love to me in front of him."

"Sure. I don't care what he sees. What's private for me is what we talk about, what we share that way."

"But isn't that secret from Quipac?"

"Private and secret aren't the same. Quipac understands. He doesn't tell me what goes on between him and Miqo."

I moved to the head of the bed and rearranged the pillows. He slid back and leaned against them. I snuggled up to him, and he put his arm around me.

"Did you share Kaiyuina with your friends?"

"No. That was part of a way of life that disappeared when we settled in Ungavaq. Before that, sometimes a man exchanged wives with a friend."

"Why?"

"If the friend were going on a long trip and his own wife was pregnant or ill, he needed someone to sew for him and provide sex for him. Or sometimes men exchanged wives for a night or a week or even months as a mark of friendship. It signified a lifelong relationship between the men."

"What if the wife got pregnant?"

"We all knew a wife could only get pregnant by her husband, so it was the husband's child."

"Didn't the wives mind?"

"I don't think so. It was just the way things were done. Now we do them differently. I don't know for sure though. It was said men made those kinds of decisions, but it's hard to believe women had no say in the matter. I was young, and women didn't talk to me about such things. Ask my mother. She'll tell you."

"Oh. I don't think I could ask your mother about her sex life."

"I don't think she'd mind."

"Maybe not, but I might."

"Well, suit yourself."

Something had been on my mind for a long time. I was glad he couldn't see my face, but I knew he could feel my tension. He never seemed to miss physical signals, and his arm was around me. I finally worked up my courage.

"Can I ask you something else?"

"Of course."

"Were you . . . faithful to Kaiyuina?"

"That's a big question for you, isn't it?"

"We didn't talk about these things before we married."

"No, I wasn't faithful. I was at the beginning, but not after she refused to come back to Ottawa. We never discussed it. I don't know if she expected me to be faithful . . . One of the other professors and I had an arrangement."

"Did you love her, the professor?"

He shook his head. "No."

"Did she love you?"

"No." He shook his head again. "It was an arrangement of convenience. We were friends. We knew what it was."

"Is she still in your life?"

"No, she's no longer in Ottawa. She moved on to a different university."

"Then I'm not likely to meet her?"

"You won't have to meet her."

"Were there other women?"

"Not while Kaiyuina was alive."

I hadn't expected to be jealous of his past, but I was. This talk about the past, though, was just a prelude to talk about the future. Now I had to find my courage again. I turned to face him and ask the question this had all really been about.

"Will there be other women?"

He looked at me quizzically for a moment. "You want me to be faithful, don't you?"

"Yes, but I don't know what you want. I'm still learning about you. I don't know what you're going to"—my voice faltered—"require of me."

"Ah. I understand. When we had that ceremony here in Ottawa, we said, 'forsaking all others.' I made a vow to you, and I'll keep that vow. I love you, and I'll never hurt you that way. And even without that vow, I can't imagine a time when I'd prefer another woman to you."

He saw how relieved I was. He kissed me tenderly.

I'd been worried about this since we'd married. I'd known I was marrying into a different culture. I did it with my eyes open, and I'd already made up my mind that I'd have agreed to whatever he asked of me. But I hadn't known how to ask him.

"If we've finished with that," he said, "I want to talk about privacy again."

I shrugged. "OK."

"I can honor your wishes about privacy, but we do have one problem."

"What's that?"

"We have the survival class in December, and I assumed you'd be participating again, this time as a teacher. You made a big difference during the last class. It was more relaxed than it's ever been before. You were a calming influence."

"Ah. I guess I hadn't thought that far ahead. What did you think we'd do for three weeks in an igloo with the students?"

"I thought sometimes we'd be quiet, and other times we'd ask Quipac to find some activity to take the students away from the igloo."

"Hmm." I nodded. "I guess this is one of those things we're going to have to work out. You're right. There's no way we're going to go a month without touching each other. We can't even go a day without touching." And to prove my point, I reached down and caressed him again.

"Would you like to talk about it now?" he asked.

"About what we're going to do for the survival class?"

"Yes."

"Not now."

Instead, I told him in Inuktitut how much I loved him. We made love slowly and gently and beautifully. When we finished, he held me close.

"I wasn't brave, you know. I've been scared to death this whole time, ever since Hal called and said you were missing. I'm not over it yet. I spent my time in the shower crying."

"Being brave is doing what you need to do, especially when you're scared. Even crying is OK. But you don't need to be scared now; I'm here to take care of you."

"We're still in danger, aren't we?"

"We are until we get something published about the find. I'm going to call one of the science reporters I know and give her an exclusive. After that, I think we're OK. Harming us or not is strictly a business decision for them. They don't care about us. They care about the report . . . But I wish I didn't have to."

"Why?"

"It's unethical. Something this important should be published in a peer-reviewed journal first. But we'll do what we have to do. Don't worry anymore."

He drew me close, and I drifted off in his arms.

Chapter Twenty-nine

The next morning, we considered sleeping in, but we heard Quipac go out the door with the dogs. We thought we couldn't very well lie in bed while he was up working. We dressed and went to the kitchen.

As I mixed pancake batter, my phone rang. I asked Jack to get it. He answered, talked briefly, and hung up.

"Who was that?"

"Carola. Bad news. Someone broke into the house yesterday."

I stopped stirring. "Oh, no! Were they hurt?"

"No, they're OK. They'd gone home early. They went back this morning because Ernesto didn't get a chance to mow yesterday. The back door was standing open. Carola wanted to talk to you, but the police arrived. She said she'll call you later."

"Was anything missing?"

"They went through everything in the den and stole your computer."

"Not my jewelry? Not the silver?"

"Just the computer. Not even the peripherals. That has to have been one of Hal's friends. He didn't waste any time. He's determined to find out what we found at the site."

My stomach clenched. "He said he'd been checking up on us. Maybe he knows about this condo too."

Jack shook his head. "He probably doesn't have friends in Ottawa the way he does in San Diego."

"He might find us with a Google search. We're not safe here."

"What will you have lost on your computer?"

"Nothing. I always keep it backed up. I keep the backup in a file box in the bedroom. But the Early Man site report was on there. I typed a copy for Bob."

"So Hal knows what we found. Was there anything that links the report to Bob—a transmittal letter or a note or something? Could he be in danger?"

"No, and I told him not to tell anyone he has the bones. Do you think Hal will give up now?"

Jack shook his head again. "No. He tried to kill us once. I don't think he'd hesitate to try again, to keep us from giving the report to someone. That makes it all the more important we get to that newspaper office today. How did we ever get into this? I'd rather face a bear any day."

"I don't think we should see anybody we know," I said, "and we shouldn't even use our phones. If someone's watching us, we don't want them to think we've given information to anyone. And now they know about Quipac. He's not safe either."

"It'll take them a while to figure out we've come to Ottawa," he said, "but a while may be just a few hours. It's probably better to be too cautious than not cautious enough."

When Quipac returned with the dogs, I gave him a cup of tea, and Jack told him the latest news.

Quipac frowned. "I thought this was all over."

"So did we," Jack said. "We think you might be in danger too, since they know you now. It's not a good idea for you to walk the dogs by yourself. I'm going to talk to a reporter today and see if we can get a story about the find in the paper. Once that news is out, I don't think they'll have any more interest in us, but meanwhile the safest thing for you is to go back to Ungavaq today. Whatever their resources, Ungavaq is so remote, and everyone knows everyone. That's our safest place."

"I'll head out right after breakfast," Quipac said. "I'll take the dogs."

"We'll follow you as soon as we talk to the reporter," Jack said.

I looked up flight times on the internet.

We finished breakfast, and while Quipac packed, I called a cab.

Before he left, I said, "Thank you for everything, and I want you to know if I weren't otherwise committed, I'd be honored to be your junior wife—as long as I didn't have to wear that makeup."

"I'll reconsider the makeup," he said, with a smile, "but this better be our little secret, and none of us needs to mention it to Miqo."

We had a one o'clock appointment with Jack's friend Susan Flannery at the *Ottawa Citizen.*

Sue was different than I expected. I'd thought a reporter for a major urban paper would be sleek, sophisticated, fast-talking—like the women on the news shows on TV. Sue was the opposite. She was middle-aged, motherly, relaxed, and friendly and clearly liked Jack. I warmed to her immediately and felt tension draining out of me. When Jack told her the story, she was excited to have the exclusive. She knew this was big.

"Would you be willing to talk to my editor?" she asked. "Allied American Oil has major business interests in Canada."

"Sure," Jack said.

Sue's editor, Art Greene, was definitely interested. He invited us to his office and asked us to tell our story to one of the business reporters, so we went through it a second time.

I finally felt a sense of relief. I knew it was premature. We weren't really safe until the story was published, but at least we were on our way.

When we finished with the reporter, Mr. Greene said, "You're going to want to do something to prevent Allied American from faking up that final report."

"I'm not sure how to handle that," Jack said.

"I'll tell you what. I'll put in a call to our attorney. He'll call you back in Sue's office and advise you on next steps."

"Thank you. I'd really appreciate that."

"I really appreciate you bringing us this exclusive."

Sue settled us in her office, and we thanked her for her help. She left to start her research on Allied American.

Jack had a conversation with the attorney. He said he'd start the process by sending Allied American a letter. Then we could go from there. After that, I called René to tell him we were heading to Ungavaq and didn't think it was a good idea to see him before we left. Then Jack thanked him for his help.

As usual when Jack talked to René, the conversation branched off in all directions. I'd learned early on that Jack and René always had things to discuss. I'd brought them together as friends, and now, every time they were together, I had to wait patiently until they'd talked themselves out. I had worried, but it didn't sound as though what I'd told Jack about René and me was going to change their friendship.

I phoned Carola, and Jack called Bob Sumner. He told Bob what we'd been doing and emphasized how important it was that he keep secret that he had any knowledge of the bones. He also asked Bob to send them and the report to him in Ungavaq.

As we left the newspaper office, I mentioned buying the rifle and parka from Mr. Sanford, so we went there to pay our bill. Mr. Sanford was delighted to see Jack, although he said he'd never had any doubt about Quipac's and my ability to find him.

We'd packed our bags and cleaned out the refrigerator before going to the newspaper office. After a late lunch, we checked into a hotel.

Chapter Thirty

The next day, we caught the same flight Quipac had taken.

In Blackwell, we walked down the concourse to Northern Air, and Jack called out to Laura, "Hey, Lady, I hear you charter planes."

Laura looked up and smiled. "Well, Jack, it's good to see you, even if you are on crutches. Quipac told me you'd be coming. That's one tough wife you have there, going out and finding you in the middle of nowhere."

She came around from behind the counter and hugged us. I always smiled when I saw Laura and Jack together. She was so petite she made Jack, who's five feet eight, look huge. You wouldn't think a tiny feminine woman with short curly brown hair and lots of jewelry would be adept at "manly pursuits" like engine repair, but she did that and was a first-rate pilot too. She had two planes and was always tinkering with one of them if she didn't have a charter.

"Want to go up to Ungavaq today? I don't have any charters, but I already have one for tomorrow."

"Today's great," Jack said.

"What do you want to do with those dog crates? Quipac left them here. He didn't think you'd need them."

"Do you know anyone who might want them?"

"You could donate them to the Humane Society. Want me to do that for you?"

"Thanks. Yes."

She took us to her floatplane, a red and white Cessna 185 Skywagon, docked at a nearby lake.

I sat in the front with her. Jack sat in the back and after takeoff, when we'd leveled out, he turned a little sideways and stretched his sore leg out on the empty seat.

We told Laura about our adventures.

"Boy," she said. "I'll bet you're ready for the peace and quiet of home."

Well, "peace and quiet" is a relative term. In Ungavaq, the story telling began. You wouldn't think there'd be so much social life in a village that small, but everyone had to hear the story. We were invited for tea somewhere almost every day.

I had a lesson in perspective. We were telling the same story, but the police had asked us one set of questions, the newspaper reporters a different set, and Laura a third. Our family, typical of the Inuit, never asked any questions, but made their areas of interest clear.

They wanted to know about Karen Adams and her dogs. People were especially interested in the Iditarod team. Jack remembered details I hadn't even noticed. He described many of Karen's dogs and the differences between them. He had a clear explanation for why he'd chosen Moose and Kiska, instead of the others available. I saw lots of heads nodding when he talked about that. They'd all already inspected the two dogs and agreed with what Jack was saying. .

Our family and friends were also interested in the quality of the hunting in the refuge and in the condition of the caribou herd. They had a more sophisticated understanding of the ecological problems than I did. I learned a lot by listening to their discussions.

They didn't think there was anything surprising about what Jack had done to survive. It was "business as usual" for them—just the kind of thing you had to do sometimes.

I received lots of praise, but not for the things I'd have thought. Going there and finding Jack was what a wife would do, but the women were very interested in my experiences cleaning and eating the hares, and they wanted to see the ulu Jack had given me. I knew the women liked me, but I also knew they still thought of me as foreign. My status in the village went way up, though, because of those hares—they all agreed most white women wouldn't have been able to manage.

I even told them the story about lemmings and women's boots, and they thought that was hilarious. They especially liked the fact that I'd mentioned it again when Jack wanted sympathy. That particular story went a long way toward bringing me into full membership in the Ungavamiut branch of the "International Sisterhood of Women Who Have to Put Up with Men's Foolishness." For a long time after that, someone had only to mention lemmings to get a good laugh out of any woman present.

Life settled down. When we'd first returned, Ungavaq was ablaze with color. The leaves had turned. The greens and grays were almost gone. In their place, golds, reds, and oranges delighted our eyes. Shortly after we came home, though, the first snow fell, and it was no time at all until the saltwater bay was frozen enough to walk on.

Jack received the jawbone and the report that Bob mailed to him.

He, in turn, wrote a scholarly description of what we'd found and sent it off to a professional journal. He credited Dr. MacNeil as the original discoverer of the site, and I was proud that he put my name in the report too.

He sent a copy to Dr. MacNeil's family with a letter telling of our experiences. We debated about whether they'd want to know the details of how he died and what the Alaska police had said.

We decided we'd want to know if we were part of his family. Jack wrote that information on a separate page, in case they didn't want to read it.

Dr. MacNeil's widow wrote back and thanked us.

Jack also wrote a report for Allied American in which he emphasized the importance of finding the jawbone and teeth. He said it would be insult added to injury if they sued us for breach of contract. Hal had left Jack's computer at our camp, although he'd deleted all references to the find. He'd evidently learned from the search for Dr. MacNeil that it looked suspicious for a scientist's computer to be missing. He'd done the same thing with Jack's written notes and logs. But we had all the information in the report Jack had written for Bob.

Jack and Quipac did a fair amount of hunting, and I gained more experience preparing seal, hare, ptarmigan, and even walrus.

I spent time with Jack's mother, Maata, sewing and learning to cook his favorite foods. I never did have the courage to ask her about wife trading.

I wrote letters to Carola, René, and other friends. I restarted my story hour for the village children.

Jack and I worked together to train Moose and Kiska, and I learned to hitch up and drive a full team with confidence.

Life was good.

Chapter Thirty-one

When Jack's away, I don't fix meals. I snack whenever I'm hungry. I was in the kitchen making a cup of cocoa and thinking about cutting a slice of bread off the loaf for toast when I felt a cold draft. Then I heard the front door close and footsteps cross the living room. I thought it strange that whoever it was hadn't stopped to take off their boots. They'd be leaving wet prints on the carpet.

I called out, "Jack, are you and Quipac back already?" I didn't get an answer. That was strange too.

I turned to see who it was, and my heart almost stopped.

Hal stood in the kitchen doorway. He smiled. "Hello, Anne."

I looked at him for a moment.

"Are you crazy? What are you doing here? Get out of my house!"

I turned to put my cup and saucer on the counter. With the same motion, I grabbed the bread knife, but when I turned back, he had a pistol pointed at me.

I froze.

He kept smiling. Finally, he shook his head and gestured at the knife with the pistol. He said in a conversational tone, "There *is* a difference between being courageous and being foolish."

I stood, debating my chances.

"Anne." He shook his head again.

I set the knife on the counter.

"Well, what kind of greeting is that after all the work I've done to find you? Haven't you missed me even a little?"

"My skin crawls when I think about you."

I heard a bark of laughter from the living room—Serbin.

"That's not a nice thing to say." Hal actually sounded hurt. "I've been thinking about you. You don't make my skin crawl. Quite the opposite."

"How did you find us?"

He hadn't moved, but I'd backed up until I was pressed tight against the counter. My heart beat faster and faster. I didn't care how he'd found us. I wanted to stall for time . . . to wait for the miracle of rescue . . . to figure out a plan of escape . . . something! I was trapped with no way out except past him.

"It's surprising how easy it was, once I thought of it," he said. "I called the University and asked for Jack. That nice secretary in the Anthropology Department was very helpful.

"She told me he wouldn't be back until January, but that he lived in Ungavaq when he wasn't in Ottawa. She said if I wanted to get in touch with him, I should do it before his class started next month.

"Ungavaq's a long way out of the way, isn't it? It took Serbin a while to find it. It's lucky we arrived before everyone turned off their lights and went to bed. And we took a bit of a risk with the landing. But what's life without a little risk?"

He didn't seem to recognize my growing panic.

"Don't you get bored here?"

"No." I could barely speak.

"In any case, maybe I can make life a little more interesting for you. I have time for this little project because I'm currently unemployed. Allied American didn't think I'd done my job well. They said they didn't need my services any longer. They didn't like the fact that

Jack put that story in the paper before I could stop him, and they especially didn't like the investigation that followed." He shrugged. "I guess it's still going on. I don't know."

"I don't understand. If you're not working for them, why have you come to kill Jack? Do you want revenge for losing your job?"

"I haven't come to kill Jack."

"Then why are you here?"

"I've come for you." He seemed surprised I hadn't realized that.

". . . For me?"

"Yes."

"Why?"

"Because I want you . . . " He shrugged. "And because I can."

He unzipped his coat.

"Are you going to kill me?"

"Not now."

I shuddered. I knew what that meant.

Suddenly, horribly, something occurred to me. "How did you find this house?" I had an awful feeling Hal might already have hurt someone in the village in order to find me.

"That's interesting. I learned a thing or two about Eskimos—oh, excuse me, Inuit—from my time in Alaska. They're courteous, and they don't like to ask questions. Would you believe I picked a door at random and knocked? I told the woman who answered I was looking for Jack. She pointed out the house, but said he wouldn't be home until tomorrow because the men were out seal hunting. She said you'd be here though."

"Jack's coming back tonight. He and Quipac should be here very soon." I heard the quaver in my voice.

"Anne, Anne, Anne." He shook his head. "I thought in Alaska we established that you're not good at bluffing, and I'm not stupid." His tone became peremptory. "It's time for you to put on your snow clothes. We're going for a walk."

"Going? With you? No. I'm not going with you."

He shook his head again. "I'd forgotten how contrary you are. I won't take the trouble to force you into your parka, but you are going with me. You know I can make you do that. You can go cold if you want. It probably won't kill you right away. I think you're too smart for that though."

"No. No. Hal, no. I don't want to go with you."

"It's not your decision."

"I'll sit on the floor. I won't go."

"Anne, now you're being silly. I'll carry you if I have to." He sounded like a patient father talking to a petulant child.

"You can't take me away. I'll scream and yell."

He shook his head and smiled. I could see he enjoyed this debate. "Anne, you know me. You can assume I'm rather good with a pistol. You wouldn't want to be responsible if I shot one of those nice polite women between the eyes for putting her head out her front door, would you? You know I'd do it."

Suddenly, my panic disappeared, and I felt cold all over. There'd be no rescue. There'd be no escape. He'd won.

I walked past him and then Serbin.

I heard the snick of the knife on the cutting board as he cut himself a slice of bread. Then he followed.

I stood by the bed. I hated being there with him. It was an invasion of my private space with Jack, and I was afraid of what he was going to do to me.

But he didn't try to touch me. Again, it was as if he could read my mind. "Ah, not here." He shook his head. "Not in Jack's bed. In our bed."

"Our bed! Are you delusional?"

He stood, eating the bread. "Did you make this?"

I didn't respond.

"It's good. I didn't know you could cook." He nodded at the closet. "Get your parka."

With the pistol at his side, he watched me get my parka and snow pants. He knew I wasn't going to fight. Jack had his rifle. Mine was in the gun cabinet in our den. Even if I had one in the closet, I don't think I could have brought it to bear on him before he shot me.

I walked back into the living room—past Serbin, who stood scowling—and sat in my chair. I slipped my feet through the legs of the snow pants, stood, pulled them up, and put the straps across my shoulders. As I did that, I asked, "Serbin, why are you involved in this?"

"I should've killed you, bitch, when I had the chance."

I recoiled in shock.

Hal said, "Serbin, would you just give it a rest!"

Serbin didn't respond. He just glared at me.

"Anne," Hal said, "before we go, you can write a note to Jack if you want."

"Why would you let me write a note?"

"Because I want Jack to know. He took you away from me. Now I'm taking you back."

Suddenly my hands were shaking, but with anger, not fear. I made a fist with my left hand and shook it in his face. "Do you see this ring? Do you see it? I'm not a toy for the two of you to fight over. I'm his wife."

"Ah, you've got your dander up. I did remember how brave you are—maybe more than you should be right now, considering the circumstances. But you're right. I shouldn't trivialize this. It's not a fight between little boys. It's about you, and you're not trivial. I should show you more respect."

"You're controlling me with a pistol. Where's the respect in that?"

I walked into the kitchen, took a notepad and pencil out of a drawer, returned, and sat at our dining table. My hands shook so much I almost couldn't hold the pencil. I wrote, "Jack, Hal and Serbin are here. They're taking me. Anne." In Inuktitut, I wrote, "*Nagligivegit*" I love you.

I turned to Hal with the notepad in my hand.

"I don't care what you wrote. It won't make any difference. They never found MacNeil, and when I'm done with you, they're never going to find you, either."

"You're crazy," I said with contempt, as I set the note on the table.

"No, I'm not. When you get to know me better, you'll understand."

"What is it *you* don't understand? I don't want to know you better. I don't want anything to do with you. Go away. Leave me alone . . . Please." I was determined not to cry, not to give him that satisfaction, but it took all my effort to prevent it.

He gestured again with the pistol.

I replaced my house shoes with boots, put on my coat, zipped it, adjusted the hood, pulled on my gloves, and walked out the front door.

Serbin led the way with a flashlight, and Hal walked beside me. I thought about running, but I didn't think I could outrun him in the snow.

I felt numb. I couldn't comprehend what was happening.

We walked past several houses and turned to go through my sister-in-law Saarak's yard. Some of the village dogs yipped, but most were curled up asleep under the snow. No one looked out to see what was going on.

After a while, I saw something bulky ahead that was darker than the background—an airplane.

I stopped.

Hal said something, and Serbin stopped too and shone the light on me.

I've watched all those TV shows. I know the worst thing you can do in a situation like this is to allow "the perp" to take you somewhere else. I had considered resisting, but I'd had no doubt he'd shoot one of the other women, so I'd walked. And I'd done what I wanted. I'd gotten him away from the village. But I didn't want to die somewhere a long way from my family—a long way from Jack. It would be better to die here, close but far enough away that none of my family would hear the shot and come out to see what had happened.

Hal gestured.

I didn't move.

"You're really frightened, aren't you," he said in a surprisingly gentle voice. "Go on, Anne. Get in the plane."

"Don't take me away. Please don't take me away from my family. I'll give you what you want here at my house, and then you can leave. Please."

"No. Get in the plane."

"Then shoot me. I'm not going."

He stepped forward and reached to push me.

I recoiled from his touch.

"We've already talked about this. You have to get in the plane."

"No, I won't go. Shoot me. Kill me now. I won't go." I grabbed at the pistol, but he just held it above his head.

"Shoot her, Boss!" Serbin said.

"Shut up, Serbin. Calm down, Anne," he said, as I continued to grab for the gun. "I'm not going to shoot you. And I don't want to have to carry you into the damn plane." He sighed. "Maybe if you go, you'll stay alive, and you'll see Jack again."

I stopped trying to pull his arm down. I turned and looked at the ladder on the plane. I thought about Jack . . . and reached for the handhold.

Hal put his hand out to help me.

I slapped it away.

He smiled.

He'd defeated me . . . but at the same time, he'd given me hope.

The plane was a single-engine, four-seater. I sat in the rear on the left. Hal sat next to me. He unzipped his coat and put his pistol into the shoulder holster on his left side. I thought briefly about trying to grab it away from him again, but I knew that wasn't going to happen.

Serbin climbed into the pilot's seat in front of me.

Hal pointed to the seatbelt buckle. "Fasten it, Anne."

I did. I didn't want him trying to help.

Serbin pushed the starter button.

In my mind, I was saying *don't start, don't start, don't start* . . . but it did.

The plane began its acceleration. The vibration changed as the skis lifted off the snow.

Hal, half turned in his seat, looked at me and smiled.

No one spoke for a long time.

I watched out the window as Serbin circled Ungavaq and headed south. The lights faded away behind us. I didn't want to cry, but I couldn't stop myself. Finally, I wiped my eyes with my sleeve.

"What are you going to do with me?"

He put on his earphones and pointed to mine.

I put them on and repeated my question.

"I'm going to finish what I started."

"Why?" I shook my head.

"You're not like any other woman I've ever met. I know you're older than I am. You said ten years—in fact it's fifteen—but you fascinate me."

"Are you doing this to punish Jack?"

"I don't care about Jack. He was an inconvenience, a work assignment I didn't handle well. But I don't care . . . Well, maybe I do care, but not because of Alaska, because of you."

"Why are you taking me with you? Why not handle that 'unfinished business' back at my house?" The thought was so distasteful I could hardly get the words out.

"Because I don't know how long it'll take me to get you out of my mind, maybe a long time—weeks, months. I don't know."

"And then you'll kill me?"

"Yeah."

"So as long as I keep you interested—entertained—I get to stay alive?"

"That's the plan. You'll be a sort of modern-day Scheherazade, I guess. It's strange, isn't it? It even seems strange to me." For the first time, he didn't look quite so sure of himself.

"As long as we're doing literary references, maybe I'll be a modern-day Jael," I said.

"Who's Jael?"

"From the Old Testament—Judges. She drove a tent spike through the brain of an enemy general while he slept."

"Well, I think it's unlikely that I'd let you do that, but you can try, I suppose."

"Things aren't going to get that far," I said.

"What do you mean?"

"I'm probably not going to stay alive long enough to do that."

"Why do you say that?"

"Because I'm not going to give you what you want."

"Maybe you'll surprise yourself. Maybe you'll get to like me."

"Is that what you want?"

He didn't answer. His silence told me more than any answer would. This wasn't just about sex. I hadn't understood that.

"Where are we going?"

"Serbin and I have a house in Mexico."

"Mexico? You came from there?"

"Yeah."

"How are you going to get across the Canadian border into the United States?"

"Serbin knows a thing or two about getting across borders."

He had all the answers. There was no use talking, so I stopped.

He didn't though. Just as the last time I'd been with him in the air, he couldn't keep his mouth shut. "Oh, Anne, you'll love Mexico. It's a great country. I'll bet you've never been away from the tourist areas."

When I didn't respond, he continued.

"We have a beautiful home, and I've fixed a room just for you. It's done all in peach-colored silk—almost the same color as that shirt you're wearing. There's a big four-poster bed with down pillows and a nice down duvet for the cold nights. We're up on the side of a mountain there, so it can get chilly.

"Of course, what you're wearing now will be way too warm, so I have clothes for you. Beautiful clothes. Lingerie from Paris. Lots of lace. I bought you some silk stockings, not nylon, real silk. I guessed at your size, but I think I got it right. I even got you a pink feather boa just for fun.

"I didn't know your shoe size though. We'll trace your feet and send the tracing to the man in New York who makes my shoes. He does wonderful work. I've never seen you in high heels. Black patent leather high heels. Oh, I can hardly wait." He was silent for a moment, maybe thinking about it.

"I'll be good to you, Anne. I won't hurt you. I know I was a jerk in Alaska, but I'll treat you right. I've dreamed about this since the first time I saw you. I'll treat you like a queen. You'll find out what kind of a man I am, and you won't be afraid of me anymore. When you find out you don't have to be afraid, we can be friends, and then we can make each other happy.

"You're so beautiful. I can see you on that bed in a deep blue negligee. I'll kiss you like you've never been kissed before. I'll hold you, and I'll touch your beautiful breasts through the silk. Just perfect." He took a deep breath. "And then you'll take that negligee off for me . . ."

I'd thought at first that he was courting me in some weird way, but if so, he had to think I couldn't remember he was going to rape me and kill me. How strange. How repulsive.

I decided he was really talking for himself, teasing himself, exciting himself, and maybe Serbin too. It was nauseating.

I tried to drown his voice out in my mind, but I couldn't, so at last I said, "You might as well shut up. You can force me, you can kill me, but you'll never make me like you or what you do to me. Never."

I took off the earphones.

He smiled.

Serbin snorted with disgust.

The only sound now was the engine.

Chapter Thirty-two

Life is always so strange.

We'd been flying a little more than an hour.

As the three of us sat silent, I considered jumping up, throwing myself across the front seat, and trying to force Serbin to crash the plane. Then I pictured the plane hurtling to the ground, and I knew I was too cowardly. I'd meant it when I told Hal to shoot me, but I couldn't bear the thought of falling through the sky for as long as that would take.

I thought about all those things my mother had taught me. In those days, a girl was expected to fight to the death for her "virtue." I remembered talking with my friends about that and our swearing that we'd die fighting if we had to, but I knew, now, how foolish that was. I wanted to stay alive. No matter what else happened, if I were alive, I might see Jack again.

Then it was as if someone up there decided to give me what I wanted, but happened to be a few moments behind my train of thought. The engine sputtered.

Serbin started adjusting knobs.

"What's the matter?" Hal asked.

"Nothing, Boss. We emptied one of the fuel tanks. I have to switch over to the other."

The engine sputtered again.

"Is there a problem?"

"I don't know, Boss. I can't get the switchover to work. Give me a minute to figure it out."

The engine sputtered a third time and went silent.

"Serbin!"

Serbin said calmly, "It's OK, Boss. We have plenty of time. I'll get it going again."

But he was wrong.

He fiddled and fussed and nothing happened. Finally, he said, "Check your seat belts. I'm going to land this thing. We're a glider now, but I can do it. I'll figure out what's wrong when we're on the ground."

The only sound was the whoosh of air across the wings and fuselage.

I held my breath.

Finally, the landing lights illuminated the snowy tundra.

Serbin was good. The plane touched down without a bump.

I exhaled.

We glided along on the skis. Since the engine was dead, Serbin had no way of feathering the propeller. He'd lowered the flaps manually to slow the plane. He said he'd let it ski to a stop.

Maybe we'd have been OK, but tundra isn't always as smooth as it looks from the air.

Serbin suddenly shouted, "Hold on, Boss, I can't steer away from—"

The left ski caught on something, probably a rock. The plane tilted to the left, and I heard the shrieking of metal as the wing tore off. The lights went out. Then one more sudden sharp jolt as the propeller hit the ground and we came to a violent and twisting halt.

The plane stopped nose down.

Silence.

We had a moment of respite from the horrible metallic grindings. Then another sound, even worse, started.

Chapter Thirty-three

I don't know how long it took me to realize that what I was hearing was Serbin, first screaming in agony, now moaning.

The smell of blood was strong.

I undid my seat belt and fell against the back of his seat.

He screamed again.

I braced myself with my arms, trying to escape that sound. It was high-pitched, horrible. I'd never heard a man scream before. I couldn't think of anything but getting away. I've seen movies of animals thrashing in nets and traps. That's what I was doing. The more I thrashed, the more he screamed. I wanted to get out, out, out, but in the dark, I couldn't find the door handle, even though I knew it was right next to me.

When my eyes had had time to adjust, I still couldn't see anything, until at last, I managed to orient myself by seeing the line of the horizon and stars dotting the sky through the tilted windshield.

I remembered Serbin had a flashlight. With difficulty, I climbed into the front seat, rummaged around, and found it. I turned it on and looked at him.

I wish I hadn't.

He was silent now. He was twisted in the seat. I could see his face, lacerated and so bloodied that I could hardly recognize him. It didn't look like a face. Blood dripped slowly off his chin, staining his pant leg with a widening circle of gore. Even his hair had changed from its usual orangey-red to blood red.

He tried to say, "Help me." The effort made him groan in pain.

I turned and moved the flashlight to look at Hal. He was slumped sideways in his seat with his eyes open. I thought he was dead. Then I saw he held his pistol. His hand lay in his lap, the pistol pointed at me.

For the first time in my life, I had a moment of blind rage. "I've had enough, Hal," I shrieked. "Damn it. If you're going to shoot me, get it over with."

His hand relaxed. He let the pistol rest on his leg. He said slowly, "What's the matter with Serbin?" He sounded half-asleep.

My dismay about Serbin drove away the rage. "He's bleeding. It's awful."

Serbin moaned again. He was trying to say "Boss," but even that little bit of movement hurt too much.

"He's trying to call for you. Can you sit up?"

"I don't know . . . I hit my head. Can't see very well . . . Dizzy . . . I'll try."

I shone the light so he could see, but he couldn't control his hands enough to find the seat belt. I knelt on the front seat, leaned over the back, and helped him put a hand on the buckle.

"Be careful," I said. "The plane's tilted nose-down. When you release the seat belt, you'll fall forward and to the left. Brace your legs."

To my surprise, he thanked me.

He finally managed to get the belt undone. Then he said, "I can't tell which way is up. I need your help. I need to see Serbin."

Serbin was moaning again—awful, agonized moans.

I put one hand on Hal's elbow to steady him as I pointed the light up to orient him.

He inched toward Serbin.

"Shine the light over there. I can't see him."

When I shone the light on Serbin, Hal fell back almost as if he'd been hit, then leaned forward again.

"Oh, Serbin! Oh, my god, can you hear me?"

Serbin managed a yes. Then he said something else so softly Hal couldn't hear it.

"What?"

"I think his back is broken," I said.

Again, Serbin said yes and then something else.

"He said 'Fix it.' Fix what? His back?"

The color drained from Hal's face. "Oh, Serbin. No. I can't."

Serbin moaned.

"What does he want?" I asked.

"He wants me to fix the pain."

"Can you do that? Do you have drugs?"

"No."

"Nothing?"

Hal's eyes were shiny with tears. "You have to help me," he said, emotion gone from his voice.

"What?"

"You have to guide my hand to the back of his seat."

I realized he meant the hand holding the pistol.

"What are you going to do?"

He took a deep breath. His voice broke. "I'm going to do what he asks."

Now I was horrified. "You can't do that."

"I can't do anything else." The sadness in his voice was heartbreaking.

"Please," Serbin said.

"I need your help," Hal said. "I don't want to have to shoot him twice. Please."

I hesitated.

"Please." Serbin said again.

Hal lifted his hand. It wavered badly.

I hesitated a moment more. Then I reached out with my left hand and grasped his wrist. I moved it until it was resting on the top edge of Serbin's seatback.

"Is it where it needs to be? I can't see," Hal said.

"Yes."

"Please, don't let go."

"Wait!" I wedged the flashlight between Serbin's seat and mine. Then I reached over with my right hand and took Serbin's hand in mine. I'm not a saint, but he was a human being; he needed to know he wasn't alone.

He squeezed my fingertips.

"All right," I said.

"Good-bye, my friend," Hal said softly. He hesitated, then pulled the trigger.

There was almost no noise—just a strange popping sound.

Serbin pitched forward. His hand spasmed in mine, then went limp. He didn't move again. He didn't make any more sounds. Blood dripped onto the floor. The smell of gunpowder filled the plane.

I let go of Serbin's hand and then Hal's.

Tears ran down Hal's cheeks.

I'd never seen a violent death before. Oh, I'd seen thousands of them on TV, but this was nothing like those. I'd seen Robby die. He was peaceful in his own bed at home. It was gentle. But this . . . My mind was numb.

After a while, Hal asked, "Are you OK?"

"I think so. I'm not bleeding, and I can use my arms and legs. What about you?"

"I don't think I'm bleeding, but I'm so dizzy. I have a concussion, I think. When the plane hit, my head slammed hard against the door."

I almost started to feel sympathy. Then I noticed the pistol pointed in my direction again.

I lost it again. Anger rose in me like a flood. It engulfed me. "Damn you, Hal! Shoot me. Shoot me now. Let's get it over with."

But he didn't shoot. With effort, he reversed the pistol and held it in my direction with the butt toward me. "I can't see well enough to shoot you even if I wanted to, and I don't. You might as well have it. I don't think it's of use to either of us now."

"You're going to have to tell me how this thing works so I don't shoot you by accident."

It was a semiautomatic. He explained the safety, how to check to see if the chamber held a cartridge, how to cock it. I went through the sequence several times until I was sure of it, then held it pointing away from him, my finger on the trigger.

"No," he said. "You don't put your finger on the trigger until you're fully committed to firing the weapon. And when you do decide to shoot me, steady your hand like this." He demonstrated cradling one hand in the other. "Don't hold it near your face or you'll get a powder burn."

I took my finger off the trigger. "I don't want to shoot you."

"Well, then, why not unload it?"

". . . No, I don't think I want to do that."

He smiled.

"Do you have other cartridges?"

With effort, he reached into his parka pocket and gave me a handful.

"Any more?"

He nodded, then groaned. "In my suitcase."

"I'll get them later. Does Serbin have a pistol?"

"Shoulder holster, left side."

That was the side away from me. I shuddered. I couldn't look for it.

I heard a sighing sound.

I shone the flashlight in Hal's direction. He was slumped again, but this time his eyes were closed. Again, I thought he had died. I shook uncontrollably as the horror of being alone in the dark with two bodies overwhelmed me.

Then I heard another sound.

Hal's mouth hung open. I could hear him breathing. It was a rattling sound, almost like a snore. I thought, *he's not dead, but if I leave him alone, he'll be dead pretty soon.*

Because of the angle of the plane, it was a long drop to the ground from the door next to me, so I pulled myself upright to climb into the back where I'd been sitting before, to get to the door on the lower side . . .

But I couldn't leave him to die. I'd helped kill Serbin, but another person? I just couldn't.

I leaned over the seat back again, shook his shoulder hard, and called his name.

He opened his eyes, slowly.

"You have to stay with me."

"I'll try. I'm sleepy." His speech was slurred like a drunk's.

I snapped at him, "You're not going to get me into this and then go off and leave me by myself. Don't you dare!" I wanted to slap him.

"No, no, I won't do that."

"What are we going to do?"

He sat silent for a time. Finally, he said, "I don't know."

"You were a SEAL. Didn't you have survival training?"

He nodded. "Oh, shit, I can't do that."

It took me a moment to realize he meant he couldn't nod his head.

"My training was for jungle and desert warfare. We weren't at war with anyone in the Arctic. I don't know about survival in snow. I know I shouldn't go to sleep though."

Well, there it was. I'd led a sheltered life. Robby had expected me to provide him with companionship and love, but not much else. He'd hired Carola and Ernesto to smooth out the day-to-day aspects of our lives. Life with the Inuit was so different, but Jack, too, had taken care of me. Now I was on my own. No Robby. No Carola. No Ernesto. No Jack. No one to step in and make decisions for me or give me direction. It was all on me.

OK, then.

"What time do you think it is?" My watch sat next to the sink in Ungavaq. I'd taken it off to wash dishes. That seemed so long ago.

"I can't read my watch," he said. "I can't focus."

"Give it to me."

He fumbled with the band. "I can't."

"Put your arm up."

He held out his arm. It wavered as I yanked the watch away.

"Hey! Take it easy. That's a Rolex."

I glared at him and he glared at me. At least I think he did, though it's hard to tell with someone who can't focus.

"Well, I guess murderers make a good living," I snapped.

"Well, I guess they do," he snapped back.

"A lot of good it does you now, Mr. Bigshot."

He didn't respond.

I'd had the last word.

I felt childish.

I took a deep breath. I needed to remember I'm an Inuit wife. Anger wouldn't help. Survival is what counts now. I needed to control myself.

I buckled the watch onto my wrist. Even using the smallest hole, it hung loosely. The illuminated dial read 12:15. Not as much time had passed as I thought.

More civilly, I said, "Daylight won't come for another seven hours. I don't think we can afford to wait. We need to build a shelter. We'll freeze in this plane. The metal will suck the heat right out of us."

"What the fuck are we going to use to build a shelter?" he said.

"Last time I looked, we had a lot of snow."

"I suppose you think I know how to build a goddamned igloo."

"What's with the swearing? You don't normally talk like that. I don't like it."

"So?"

"So maybe there's something you haven't quite recognized. Right now, you're incapacitated and I'm not. That puts me in charge, so knock it off."

Surprise replaced the belligerence on his face. He started to nod again, but caught himself in time. "OK."

He looked relieved. I guess he'd thought that as the man he had to rescue us, or at least himself. Well, I couldn't expect him to fix everything. I was going to have to do that.

"I hadn't even considered the possibility you might know how to build a snow house, but I do. I need a knife with a long blade. What kind of knives do you and Serbin carry? Don't tell me 'Swiss Army.'"

"I don't carry a knife. Serbin has one strapped to his right ankle."

I didn't think I could stand to look for it. I didn't want to touch him.

But I had to.

I told myself it was just a leg. When I finally worked up my courage, it felt bony and hairy and warm. It was hard to understand he was really dead. This touching seemed so intimate, and I didn't want any kind of intimacy with Serbin.

I found the knife.

"I don't understand. There's a handle, but no blade."

"Hold the handle away from you and push the button."

I heard a click and, abruptly, the blade appeared. My heart practically pounded out of my chest.

"Switchblade," he said. "Point the blade up and press the button again. The blade will go back into the handle."

"Oh." My heart began to slow down. "I guess it'll do. Now I need something long and skinny I can use to probe the snow."

"I can't think of anything like that—maybe a screwdriver. Oh, wait a minute. There might be a dipstick in the engine. There's probably a radio antenna someplace too. Did you try the radio? Maybe we can call for help."

"We can let people know we're down, but we can't tell them where we are. Were we headed to Blackwell?"

"Yeah, to refuel. We were only in the air about an hour. We can't be more than 150 miles from Ungavaq."

"I don't suppose you filed a flight plan."

"No."

"I'll try the radio." I swung the flashlight around.

The copilot's headset was spattered with blood. I picked it up and then had to wait until my nausea receded.

I put it on. The switch on the instrument panel was in the "off" position. I turned it on and then turned the volume up. Nothing happened. "Shouldn't a light be on or something?"

"The dial should light up, like that radio you had in Alaska."

I turned the switch off and then on again. "Nothing lights up. There's no power to anything. All right, I'll have to see if I can find the dipstick."

Chapter Thirty-four

I climbed over Hal's legs into the back and tried the door next to where I'd been sitting. I was surprised when it opened easily.

Suddenly, the smell of gasoline was almost overwhelming.

"Hal, gasoline! It's strong. Get out of the plane."

I lowered myself to the snow. Because of the strange tilted angle of the plane, it wasn't far. I zipped up my coat, pulled up and tied my hood, put on my gloves, then stepped back and held the light so he could see.

He eased himself out and tried to stand.

He fell.

He tried again and fell again.

He sat, legs splayed out in front of him.

For a moment, I saw fear on his face. Then he said in a firm voice, "I can't tell which way is up. I can't stand, and I can't steady my hands enough to zip my coat. I don't think I can help you."

"Just a minute."

I set the flashlight down, bent and zipped his coat, put his hood in place and tied it, and helped him with his gloves. I don't know how many children I helped the same way. I could feel my attitude toward him softening. What a sucker I was for someone who needed a little mothering. The last thing Hal wanted was for me to be his mother.

"You lean on me. We need to move away from the plane in case it catches fire."

I helped him stand. He put his hand on my shoulder, and we walked slowly away from the plane.

Suddenly he said, "Oh, damn. Anne, move!" and he pushed me away. Then he fell to his knees and vomited. When I thought he'd finished, I started toward him, but he held up his hand, so I waited. He had another bout that continued until he had the dry heaves.

I finally went to him. "What's going on?"

"I think it's that hit to my head. It's better when I keep my eyes closed."

"Keep them closed then. I won't let you fall." I helped him stand and moved him away until I thought we were at a safe distance from the plane.

"Are you still queasy?"

"It's over."

I helped him sit, then took off my glove and picked up a handful of snow.

His eyes were still closed.

"I'm going to wash your face. This is going to be cold."

He winced when I put the snow on his skin. I washed his face, then picked up another handful. "Put this in your mouth. It'll help you feel better."

He took the snow in his gloved hand. "I'm sorry."

"Well, it's not like you did it on purpose. You stay here. I'll see what I can manage."

The full moon began to rise in the clear sky. It was like being in a spotlight. I hadn't been using the flashlight because the bowl of stars we were in gave off so much light, I could even see faint shadows.

The moon added to that light, but it didn't matter. There really wasn't anything to see but snow. Whatever animals had been in the area were long gone or hiding in their burrows, and no people lived between Ungavaq and Blackwell.

I did take some time to look at the stars. I saw Niqirtsituk, the North Star—a familiar friend—almost above my head. Whenever Jack went hunting, he and I took time to look at the sky before we went to sleep and remember that the same stars were shining down on both of us. It took some of the loneliness out of separation, even in these circumstances.

The temperature was well below freezing, and a stiff breeze blew. I was right about the necessity of building a snow house.

I walked to the nose of the plane. The snow was deep, deeper than in Ungavaq, so even that much walking was a challenge.

I unfastened the cowling on the right side where it wasn't buried in the snow, conscious of the fact that if I made a spark, I might start the fire I feared. I had my fingers crossed, and my luck was in because there was the little handle, like the dipstick on a car. I had to stand on tiptoes to reach it. I pulled it out carefully, trying not to get oil on my gloves. Silly, I finally realized—whoever found my body, whether animal or human, wasn't going to care if my gloves were dirty.

The dipstick wasn't as long as I'd have liked, but I thought I could make it do. I called out. "I found the dipstick. You stay there. I'm going to look for the right kind of snow."

"I won't leave without you."

"You can't be hurt too badly if you can joke."

"I'm OK." There was no hint of fear in his voice.

I admired his courage. Here he was, injured, in the middle of nowhere, with nobody to depend on but a woman who despised him, but you wouldn't have known from the way he answered.

I started to walk and probe the snow. I didn't actually know if the dipstick would work, but I did find some compact, fine-grained snow I thought would be OK. I said out loud, "Well, Jack, this is where

I find out if I learned anything in your class." I called out, "I found snow that'll work. Can you get over here?"

"I'll try."

I'd participated in building almost a dozen snow houses in the class last year so I was sure of the technique, but I'd never done it by myself. The igloos we made had to be big enough for eight people. This one was going to be much smaller. Still, I hoped I had the strength to build it alone. Whatever adrenaline rush I'd had from the crash had dissipated, and I was getting tired.

I paced the outline of our igloo in the snow.

I'd lectured Hal about swearing, but now I swore a blue streak—at him, at the plane, at the snow, at the cold, at the knife—furious at this turn in my life. "I thought things had finally settled down. I just want to be a damn housewife. I want to fix some damn seal meat for Jack. I don't want all this damn drama!"

I laughed. I was getting a little crazy talking to myself, and I wasn't doing well as an Inuit wife if I swore. Oh, well.

Hal called out, "Anne, where are you?"

I went to find him, following my trail back to the plane and then his to him. He had crawled off in the wrong direction

I helped him stand and walk back toward the building site.

"I could hear you talking," he said, "but I couldn't make out what you were saying."

"I was swearing."

"That doesn't surprise me. This probably isn't what you planned to do tonight."

"I'm not supposed to swear though. Inuit wives aren't supposed to show anger."

"But the men can?"

"No, not them either."

"That explains something."

"What?"

"When I broke Jack's ankle, I expected him to be angry, but he didn't show it. He didn't act frightened either."

"He probably wasn't frightened. And it's not just that he doesn't show anger, he doesn't usually feel it. You gave him enough provocation to make him mad. Still, it's important to him not to show it."

"Can you learn to be like that—to not show anger?"

"The Inuit do. They don't get angry easily the way we do. They're more . . . accepting of what life gives them. But they learn that from childhood. I'm not having much luck so far."

When we reached the site, I helped him sit. "I guess you're not going to be able to help me with this, but at least you can talk to me. That may make the work easier."

I started to cut the first block with Serbin's knife.

"What do you want to talk about?"

"Tell me about Serbin. It seems strange that we . . . that he died, and we went off to do other things. I think we ought to—" I sighed. "I don't know what."

"What do you want to know?" He sounded guarded.

"Why did he hate me?"

"He didn't hate you."

"He did a pretty good imitation of someone who did."

Now it was his turn to sigh. "He was pretty rough on you, wasn't he?"

"Why? I don't think I ever did anything to him."

"I wanted you. He was jealous."

"Jealous? Were you and he a couple?"

He laughed. "Of all the things you could've asked. A couple!"

"Yes or no?"

"No. What made you ask me that?"

"I thought it might be a possibility."

"We were friends."

"Does he have family?"

"No one who'll care he's dead, if that's what you're asking. I guess we were each other's family." He stopped talking and looked down. After a moment, he cleared his throat. "Tell me what you're doing."

He wanted to change the subject.

"I'm making an igloo."

"I know that, but what in particular are you doing? I've never seen it done before."

"They don't build these much in Alaska, just in Canada, and not often here anymore. You pace out the outline where you find the right kind of snow. It has to be in thick enough layers, and it has to be dense. Some snow won't hold together."

"So, there are different kinds. You hear about how the Eskimos have all those different words for snow."

"They don't really. That's an urban legend. They don't have any more words than we do. They just use them differently. Anyway, you cut blocks and lay them on the outline. Then you trim them to a slope and start laying up a decreasing spiral. Cutting the slope is tricky. It has to be right for the diameter and height of your igloo. If you build it correctly, people can stand on top of it, and it won't collapse because it's a true arch."

"You're kidding, right?"

"No. I've seen it."

I worked steadily.

At one point, I saw a satellite shoot across the sky from northeast to southwest. It seemed a strange contrast to the fact that the only way we were going to survive was to fall back on Stone Age technology.

"I haven't quite figured out how I'm going to do this. I've never done it alone. Usually, someone cuts the blocks, and another person stands outside and lays them in place. It doesn't matter on the first three or so courses, but when you want to close in the roof, I don't know if one person can do it. Is your stomach OK now?"

"I think so."

"If I were to show you how, do you think you could cut blocks sitting down and hand them up to me?"

"I'll try."

I cut blocks from what would become the floor of the igloo. Then Hal took over. He was slow, but with a great deal of effort and concentration he was able to cut blocks from a separate "quarry" area.

I finally closed in the roof and made a small vent hole so we wouldn't have a buildup of carbon dioxide.

I showed Hal how to fill the chinks outside between the blocks with snow. I'd done the ones inside while he cut blocks. He was still having trouble controlling his hands and arms, but he worked on the lower tiers slowly and steadily. I did the higher levels and dug and roofed an entry tunnel below the floor level. It was to keep wind from blowing directly into the interior. Also, the dip in the tunnel trapped cold air and kept it from coming into the igloo, and it prevented whatever warmer air we might have from escaping. I didn't have the usual tool, a type of scoop, so I had to do it with my gloved hands.

I was getting so tired, but there was still more to do.

Inside, I finished digging more snow out of half of the interior to make the floor space, the *natiq*. Hal helped as much as he could. It was an agonizingly slow process. We tamped that excavated snow into the other half of the igloo to make a raised platform, the *ikliq*. I finally patted the last handful of snow down. We'd done it.

We sat on the natiq for a few moments of rest.

I hoped I'd have the strength to get up again.

"Here's how it's going to be," I said. "We sit and sleep on the ikliq. It's up in the warmer air."

"If it's warmer up there, why aren't we sitting there now?"

"We have to put something on it to insulate it so we don't melt it with our body heat. What do you have in your luggage?"

"There's a canvas tarp in the plane."

"A tarp?"

"We were going to use it to cover you when we had to stop for fuel."

"You were going to tie me? And gag me?"

"Yes."

A rush of fear hit the pit of my stomach. For a while, the business of making the igloo had allowed me to forget why we were here.

"I'll look for it. Anyway, if you have to answer nature's call, go outside—a little distance away if you can manage."

"Maybe we don't have to," he said. "We weren't going to let you off the plane when we stopped to refuel. We bought a woman's urinal for you. We could use that."

"You think I'd take my pants down with you here? Not going to happen, Hal."

When I said that, I realized if he hadn't been able to zip the big zipper on his coat, he wasn't going to be able to unzip the smaller one on his fly. Even in the dim moonlight that filtered through the snow blocks, I could see he knew it too and was humiliated by that knowledge.

There were so many little ways I could get revenge on him now for all he had put me through, but I didn't want to.

"Hal, I had to help my first husband, Robby, many times when he was ill. I'll help you. It'll be OK. Let's go outside now."

We went out and took care of what was necessary. He was grateful and didn't try to make anything sexual out of it.

"Now, you go back into the igloo. I'll go get the tarp."

"What about the gasoline?"

"We need the tarp. I'll be careful."

"There's a bag of food and bottles of water too."

"OK. You stay inside. I'm taking the flashlight. I need it to see inside the plane. You'll be OK. We're too far from Ungava Bay to worry about polar bears."

"What about wolves?"

"There won't be any wolves around here, and besides, wolves don't eat humans."

"I guess we were due for some good news," he said.

Chapter Thirty-five

On the way to the plane, I stopped to pee. Everything seemed to function OK. I turned on the flashlight and checked. There was no blood in my urine.

I left the flashlight on. I didn't know if I could make a spark when I pushed the switch, and I didn't want to find out by doing that in the plane.

The smell of gasoline was still strong. I wondered about the safety of getting in, but as I'd said to Hal, it had to be done. I hoped as long as I was careful it would be OK.

The plane was at such an odd angle. I also worried that it might shift position when I climbed in, but it was firmly wedged in the snow. It never even wiggled.

I tried to avoid looking at Serbin. I wasn't afraid of his body or of his ghost. It was the horror of his death—his moans and that gunshot—that had anchored itself in my brain.

I found the tarp, shoved it out the door, and opened it out on the snow. I dropped Hal's and Serbin's suitcases, the bag of food, and the water onto it and dragged it back to the igloo.

There, I pushed everything inside and closed the doorway from inside with the block of snow I'd cut to make the opening.

As I distributed things around the floor, Hal tried to fold the tarp to fit the ikliq. He seemed to be having trouble.

"What's the matter?"

"My hands. I can't feel them."

"Let me see."

He couldn't get his gloves off.

I knelt in front of him and helped him with the gloves. His fingers were a dull white. "Oh, Hal, you're getting frostbite!"

I couldn't let him lose his fingers. I removed my gloves, took his hands in mine, and placed them on my cheeks, as Jack's mother, Maata, had taught me to do. That's what Inuit do to warm the hands of children when they get cold. I kept my hands on top of his.

I couldn't turn my head to avoid his eyes. This seemed even more intimate than when I'd helped him outside. I guess he could see how much it distressed me. After a moment, he looked away.

We waited.

After several minutes, he said, "The feeling's coming back." He moved his hands. His fingers were getting pinker. He wiggled them to get the circulation going even more.

"They're going to hurt."

"They already do."

"That's a good sign."

"Well, they're not dead, anyway."

I helped him put his gloves back on. "Let's finish here." I turned to the suitcases. "Did Serbin have a favorite shirt?"

I opened the bag he indicated.

He rummaged through it and pulled out a black turtleneck. "What do you want it for?"

"I'm going back to the plane tomorrow. I thought I should cover him. It's the respectful thing to do." I folded the shirt and set it aside.

"Thank you for thinking of that."

He handed me clothes, and I put them in layers on the ikliq. Then we folded the tarp to fit properly, and I laid it on top.

Finally, we were sitting on the tarp on the ikliq, our work done.

We agreed not to eat anything, but I handed one of the three plastic bottles of partially frozen water to Hal.

"Drink some. If you get dehydrated, you may throw up again."

He sipped the water slowly.

I drank too.

It was at least twenty below outside. The temperature was probably between twenty and thirty degrees above zero inside the igloo. Our body heat had warmed it as we worked. I'd heaped a pile of snow on the natiq. It was frozen, of course, but warmer than the snow outside. I took handfuls of this "warm" snow and refilled the water bottles.

"Put your bottle under your shirt." I said.

"It's cold. I'm not going to do that."

"You are if you want to live. You know we can't last long without water. We can't drink it frozen. You have to thaw the bottle with your body heat. We don't have anything else."

"Then give me yours too. I can't do much else for you, but I can do that." He took the bottles from my hand.

I hadn't expected that.

"Thanks . . . Now, it's time to go to sleep. You get to make a choice. We can sleep together and help keep each other warm, or we can sleep as far apart as possible. If you touch me in a way I don't like, I'll get up, walk out of this igloo, and keep on walking. Maybe I'll survive and maybe I won't, but I'm sure you won't survive without me. What's your choice?"

I wasn't bluffing and he knew it.

"I won't touch you without your permission."

"I'm exhausted." I lay down.

He lay next to me.

"Come closer," I said. "We need to keep each other warm."

"I'm so cold. May I come really close?"

". . . Yes. Come as close as you can."

He moved closer. We were spooned together. We lay in silence for a while.

"I don't know what to do with my arm," he said.

". . . Put it around me."

He put his arm around my waist, then asked softly, "Why are you helping me? I saw in your eyes how difficult it is for you to touch me. I know I disgust you. Why are you helping me after what I've done to you, what I was going to do to you?"

"Because you cried for Serbin and reminded me you're human too. I won't be responsible for another death."

"Anne . . ."

"Go to sleep," I said, not unkindly.

He was injured. I didn't think he could be thinking about sex, but I couldn't be sure. Two sets of snow clothes separated us. Still, his proximity made me rigid with tension. Yet sleep overtook me as I thought about Jack.

Chapter Thirty-six

Hal woke me just as the sun was rising. He knew we needed to use the daylight.

I woke up confused. I didn't know who was calling my name or why it seemed so cold. I sometimes have vivid nightmares and, for a moment, I thought that's what this was. Then I remembered, and I was overcome by rage. What had he done to me? But again, I reminded myself, *you're an Inuit wife now. Anger won't help.*

When I tried to move, I almost couldn't. I was so stiff and sore. I hadn't noticed it before, but I sure did now.

I struggled to sit up.

"Do you need help?" he asked.

"No."

I didn't want him touching me.

The block of snow covering the doorway had been shifted.

"Have you been outside and taken care of what you needed to?" I asked.

"I tried. I couldn't manage the zipper or the buttons."

"OK, come on then."

He was red-faced with embarrassment.

"Hal, don't worry about it. We'll just do what we have to do."

We went out and when he'd finished, I helped him adjust his trousers and then get back to the igloo. "Let me borrow your dark glasses. You stay here. I'll be right back."

I went out. While I had my pants down, I looked at the parts of my body I could see. I had a huge bruise on my right hip. I suppose that might have been from the armrest on the seat. I also had a bad diagonal bruise across my belly that had to have come from the seatbelt. I wondered about internal injuries, but decided it didn't pay to speculate.

Back in the igloo, I saw he was sitting with his eyes closed.

"Are you feeling sick again?"

"No, I'm OK. I'm resting my eyes. I was thinking about how hot our apartment in Rangoon always was."

"You lived in Rangoon?"

"For a while."

"I thought Myanmar was a closed society."

"For most people. It's certainly wasn't any place you'd want to go on vacation at that time."

"What were you doing there?"

"It's not something I can tell you about."

"Oh . . . I'm going back to the plane. Do you want to go?"

"I'll stay here, unless you need me."

"Do you know anything about radios?"

"How to turn them on and off."

"You don't know anything about the wiring or what could go wrong with it?"

"That was Serbin's area. He was a mechanical genius. He could do anything with a machine or a radio."

"I don't know anything about it either."

"You know, last night you tried it, but if there's gasoline, I don't think you want to do that again. We don't know what might create a spark. I don't want you to get burned."

"I'll be careful." I took Serbin's shirt and crawled out through the tunnel.

As I walked, all I could hear was the wind, my heartbeat, and the noise my boots made on the snow—nothing else. The silence bothered me. As much time as I'd spent in Ungavaq and Alaska, I still wasn't used to it.

When I reached the plane, I smelled the gasoline again, but not so strong. I took Hal's warning to heart though.

First, I wanted to cover Serbin's face. I did think it was the respectful thing to do, but also, he looked awful. I couldn't do anything about the blood and other matter sprayed all around though. I'd have to ignore that.

Serbin was as we'd left him. The foxes and ravens would find a way to get to him eventually, but I didn't plan to mention that to Hal. I laid the shirt over his face.

I wanted to get his pistol. I didn't doubt Hal's ability to take the other pistol back when he wanted it, and I didn't for a minute think I could stand him off. I wasn't worried about that, because I knew he needed me. He'd kill me if it were to his advantage, but right now, it wasn't. I did want the second pistol, though, because we had to hunt. Perhaps the animals wouldn't take offense at my hunting if they knew we were desperate.

I took a deep breath and reached under Serbin's coat. I could touch the grip, but his left arm was partly over it. His body had frozen in the night. There was nothing to use to pry his arm up and I wasn't strong enough to do it without a tool. I berated myself for being such a coward the previous night, but I realized that was foolish. I'd done what I could.

I did remember to take his watch. It had only a little blood on it. It showed the same time as Hal's, so I knew it was still working. It hadn't frozen. It was also a Rolex. Looks like murderers' assistants were well paid too.

His dark glasses lay on the floor by his right foot. They'd fallen out of his shirt pocket. Luckily, they weren't broken, so I took them. Serbin had been a smaller man than Hal. His glasses were a better fit for me.

I found Serbin's toolbox, but nothing else I thought might be useful.

I smiled when I saw how irregular the igloo looked in the daylight, but I still patted myself on the back. We had, after all, built it in the dark. Of course, because of the long nights and short days of the Arctic winter, most igloos had been built in the dark at the end of a long trek next to a dog sled. Still, I thought we'd done OK.

I called to Hal, moved the block of snow, and pushed the toolbox in through the tunnel.

He was holding it when I crawled in. He gently rubbed the name-plate. "He never went anyplace without this."

"I really am sorry for your loss, Hal."

"Thank you."

"Have you eaten anything?"

"I waited for you."

"What's in the bag?"

"Six sandwiches we bought in Blackwell. I didn't know what you liked, but I remembered you weren't a vegetarian, so I bought turkey and chips, candy bars, and cookies."

I took everything out of the bag to do an inventory. First came six packages of potato chips. The label said there were 150 calories per package. For the first time ever, I wished for more grease. The cookies were those giant chocolate chip oatmeal ones you see in big glass jars on deli counters everywhere—loads of calories. There were six assorted chocolate candy bars. The sandwiches were the kind you see in every airport—a squashed croissant with a few layers of salty sliced turkey breast, lettuce, and bright red slices of tasteless tomato. There were also long thin sections of pickle, probably kosher dill. Everything was frozen. The lettuce had that translucent look it gets, and where in the world did tomatoes come from in Canada in November? There was a handful of little plastic packages of mustard and mayonnaise. We'd lick those out. Those packets made me think of something else.

"Do you and Serbin have toothpaste in your suitcases?"

"Yeah. Why?"

"I read someplace about someone surviving by eating toothpaste. I suppose it has sugar in it. It's designed to go in your mouth, so I don't suppose it can hurt us."

"Maybe in the old days," he said, "but that's one thing I did learn in survival training. The fluoride in toothpaste is toxic, and some of the other ingredients will hurt you too, if you eat much of it."

"OK, we'll pass on that. What else do you have that might be edible?"

"Tums. They have sugar in them, and they won't hurt us."

"For now, let's split a sandwich and drink some water."

I used the knife to cut a sandwich. I gave him the paper plate with the bigger piece on it.

"You didn't cut it evenly," he said.

"No. You're bigger than I am. You need more calories to survive."

"I don't think that's fair. You're doing all the work. You need more calories."

"No."

"Yes," he said.

"Well, I'm the boss here, and this is the way it's going to be."

"Well, you may be the boss, but I know about fairness. Be fair, or I'm not eating anything. I'm going on a hunger strike." He closed his mouth and crossed his arms on his chest.

I sighed loudly. I took his plate back, cut a little piece off his half of the sandwich, and put it on the napkin I was using as a plate. "All right. Back to first grade. One cuts; the other chooses. Which one do you want?"

He pointed to the plate, and I put it back on his lap.

"Do you want help?"

"Let me try first. Would you cut it in smaller pieces?"

I did, and he ate slowly, one small frozen fragment after another.

"You're sure we're between Ungavaq and Blackwell?" I asked.

"There weren't any other options, and Serbin wouldn't have drifted off line."

"If they don't find us, we're going to die. I can try to hunt, and I know how to trap foxes, but I don't know if I can catch enough food to keep us going. The weaker we get, the harder it'll be to feed ourselves. It takes a lot of calories to keep warm in this weather."

"Why trap foxes?"

"Because there are some out there. They came sometime in the night and investigated where you threw up. I saw their tracks. We can eat them. They don't taste good—they're gamy and stringy—but if you're hungry enough, you won't care."

"What else is there to hunt? Are there caribou?"

"Nothing so grand. The caribou have gone south. That's why there won't be wolves here. They follow the caribou. It would be hares and ptarmigan . . . and ravens—small game. I know how to shoot a rifle. Jack was teaching me. I'm reasonably good at it, but I've never shot a pistol."

He nodded. "I can teach you, but handguns aren't as accurate as rifles, especially at a distance. I don't know whether you'd be able to get close enough to anything to hit it."

"Hares are nervous. They run at the least thing."

"So someone has to find us or we starve."

"I think so," I said. "The question is, are we better off staying here or walking toward Ungavaq? You said last night you didn't think we were more than 150 miles away."

"How would you find it in all this whiteness? Everything looks the same."

"It's not possible to navigate by the land, but I'm pretty sure I can navigate using the sun and the stars. Jack was teaching me how to do that too. The other thing is the wind almost always comes out of the north, so that would help. I don't have to be all that accurate if we go in the right general direction. Ungava Bay is big. We just need to go a little bit east of north. It would be hard to miss. Once we find the shore, we follow it. We might have a problem with polar bears there, but I can only handle one crisis at a time."

"OK, Boss. What about the compass in the plane?"

"It's damaged. My friend Laura has one in her plane. The needle's supposed to float in oil, but it's leaking away. Since we were flying to Blackwell, the ski tracks from our landing would be coming from the north-northwest. I don't remember the plane turning. And I looked at the stars last night. I have an idea of the orientation of the igloo and the plane. The compass isn't right."

"Should we wait for rescue? Aren't we supposed to stay by the plane so they can spot us more easily?"

"They'll find where we took off at Ungavaq, but they won't have any idea how far we've gone. When the police don't find a place we stopped for fuel, how long will it take them to think of the possibility of a crash and, even if they think of it, where will they look? We could be anywhere in the world. There might be a locator beacon on the plane, but that's no use unless they're looking for us in a certain area."

"I suppose the rental company in Blackwell will notify the police when we don't return the plane."

"Did you tell them you were going to Ungavaq?"

"No."

"The police might link up the idea of a plane missing from Blackwell and a plane missing from Ungavaq, but how long will that take? There's another possibility. My friend Laura flies this route on Fridays. She might notice the wreckage. But she takes off from

Blackwell in the dark this time of year and gets to Ungavaq not long after daylight. She might fly over this area before sunrise. Maybe she'd see our flashlight. But if she doesn't, she goes northwest to a second village. She won't fly over this spot on her way from there to Blackwell."

"What you're saying is we need to start walking. I guess this is payback time."

"Payback?"

"I know you've been saying 'we' in this conversation, but isn't this where you say 'Adios. See you 'round, Buddy'?"

I shook my head. "I'm not going to leave you. I said it before and I meant it. I'm not willing to be responsible for another death. It's still 'we.' I'll make fox traps, and we'll hope your dizziness diminishes before we get too weak to walk."

He looked relieved, as he had last night on the plane when I said I would take care of us. He took a deep breath.

"We ought to set a time limit," he said. "If I don't improve in, say, three days, you show me how to make traps. After that, you walk to Ungavaq. If I get worse instead of better, you leave before then."

"All right. We usually use seal blubber for bait, but I guess we're fresh out. I'll use some of the meat out of one of these sandwiches instead. We'll have to hope the foxes will come to it. If we catch even one, we can use part of it to reset the traps. How's your vision?"

"Better."

"Here's your watch." I handed it to him. "I took Serbin's. It hadn't frozen."

"There's nothing in it that can freeze. It's glass, metal, jewels, and oil."

"Oh. I hadn't thought of that."

Neither of us commented on my implication that Serbin's body had frozen.

"Can you read the dial?" I asked.

"It's an effort, but I can make the double image go single if I work at it. Maybe that's a sign I'm getting better."

"I bet it is. When we finish eating, I'm going to go make those traps. Is there any way to make the pistol louder?"

"Yeah. Why?"

"If I'm not back in, say, three hours, I want you to go outside and shoot the pistol every ten minutes."

"You're giving it back to me?" His voice showed his surprise.

"Yes. I could say something all noble about trust, but the reality is you need me. I don't think you're suicidal, and you're smart enough to know that harming me will also harm you. For now, we're in this together. Maybe that'll change later, but that's how it is now."

Chapter Thirty-seven

I headed out to make the traps. At first, I was afraid to get out of sight of the igloo. Everything looked so much the same. The plane, behind a slight rise in the ground, was invisible. There weren't any useful landmarks.

I finally realized the obvious. Coming back, I could backtrack my own trail. There was a big "if" and that was if the wind didn't blow the snow so that it covered my tracks and those of the plane. But I could still see the ones we'd made last night. I had to gamble, and I had to hope the trail would still be obvious tomorrow when I needed to check the traps. I looked up to see if I could see any weather coming in and started walking toward the plane.

Last year in survival class, when Quipac had taught us about the deadfall traps, we'd walked a long way from our igloo before setting the first one. Maybe it was because the foxes were afraid to come near the dogs. I wasn't sure. But walking meant using energy, and I needed to conserve energy, so I wouldn't go far.

One last fleeting thought. I was walking toward Ungavaq. I could just keep going . . . but I'd already made that decision.

I couldn't remember how Quipac handled the bait. The foxes out here were unlikely to have had contact with humans. Even so, I'd used a piece of the wrapper to take the meat out of the sandwich to keep my scent off it. Maybe whoever had made the sandwich had worn those plastic gloves food handlers often wear. No point worrying about that now though.

I had a mental image of the *A* I'd earned in class morphing into a *B* and then into a *C*. Jack had said if you received a *B*, you were having serious problems—well, I was—and if you received a *C*, you needed to start thinking about a different career path. That was a good idea. I certainly didn't like the path I was on.

Thinking about the class made me think about Jack again. My mind had come back to him over and over. It felt like I'd been away forever, but, in fact, it had been only twelve hours. Jack probably didn't even know yet that I was gone. He and the other men might be on their way back from seal hunting by now or maybe just reaching home if they came back a little early. He and Quipac would unhitch the dogs, get them settled and fed, and pack the gear for storage.

Then Jack would go into the house. He'd expect to find me sewing or cooking or reading. He might think it was a little odd that I hadn't come to greet him, but if I weren't there and he didn't notice the note, maybe he'd think I was with Maata or Saarak or Miqo. He might joke with Quipac about women spending so much time socializing. He'd ask him to send me home if I were at his house. Maybe he'd take off his boots and parka and settle down in his chair with tea to wait for me to come home, or maybe he'd walk to Maata's to see if I was there.

I didn't know if someone would mention that a man had been looking for him. News of a stranger would certainly have been all around the village by now. People would comment on their surprise that I hadn't come yet to tell who he was and why he was there. And people usually came into the village with Laura. How could a stranger have found his way there on a day other than Friday? Would that have worried Jack? Maybe.

Maybe he'd have found the note by now. My heart hurt with the pain I knew he'd feel. I couldn't imagine what he'd do.

Saarak would certainly have noticed that people had walked past her house. Everyone would recognize the tracks my boots had made and the fact that the other two sets belonged to strangers. The trail would be easy to follow, and the plane's landing site easy to interpret. But what then?

I had a little cry as I walked along. My heart ached for both of us.

I finally saw what I was looking for—the long slender depression that marked a frozen streambed. I needed ice to make the traps. I'd refused to think about the possibility that I might not find a stream. I just had to.

I swept the snow off the surface of the ice with my gloved hand and went to work with Serbin's knife. Making a trap isn't complicated—I made one in class last year—but chipping the ice block is tiring.

Once I got a big enough block chipped out, I manhandled it up onto the bank and went back to the streambed to find a round, water-washed stone. Then I dug around under the snow to find a sturdy stick. The bait is tied firmly to the stick. I was using a strip of dental floss for the tie—I hoped the odd smells wouldn't scare the fox away.

I started assembling the trap, balancing the block on one end of the stick, then balancing the stick on the stone. If I made the trap correctly, when the fox pulled on the bait, it would pull the stick out and the ice block would fall.

I made three traps and started to return to the igloo, but a thought stopped me. I went back to the stream and searched for more stones, ones that were just right. I filled my pockets with them and carried some in my hands.

When I reached the igloo, Hal called out, "Is that you, Anne?"

"Yes, I'll be in in a minute."

I stacked the stones carefully against the part of the curved wall that faced Ungavaq—the legs, the body, the rudimentary arms, the head—to make a small inuksuk for Jack. Maybe he would find it and know how much I had longed for him.

When I went in, Hal said, "I knew you were back. You cast a faint shadow through the wall. What were you doing?"

"Nothing much."

He handed the pistol to me.

"It feels different," I said.

"I took the suppressor off. It's lighter, easier to aim."

"Suppressor?"

"The silencer."

"Oh. The gun's so small."

"It's a Smith & Wesson .22 Mag. You don't need a big gun. A little one's better, easier to keep out of sight. You just need to put the bullet in the right place."

"Oh . . ."

Those words brought back with overwhelming vividness what this little pistol had done to Serbin. I started to shake.

"Let's not talk about these things," he said. "It upsets you. You're thinking about what happened and about what might happen. We have a truce. We don't need to think about those things right now."

I couldn't speak.

He waited.

After I'd calmed myself, I said, "I didn't see any hares or signs of them. The crash might have scared them off."

"Do you think they'll come back?"

"Probably. This is home. I want to tell you how to make a trap."

"Don't you want to wait till later?"

"No. When you're feeling better, I'll show you too."

"Why would you tell me?"

"Why wouldn't I?"

"You might want to save that information as a bargaining chip. Didn't you think of that?"

"Hal, I'm not naive. I thought about it. Last night, I thought about leaving you in the plane and letting you die in the cold. But I told you, I'm not going to be responsible for another death. Whatever you decide later, before then, something might happen to me, and if you can't catch food, you'll die. You need to know how to catch the foxes."

"All right."

When he had a clear idea of how to make the traps, I said, "We have daylight left. Do you want anything from the plane? I could help you get over there."

"I don't want to see Serbin again. I . . ."

"Hal, there's a good chance we're not going to get out of this. Just say what you want to say. I can't ever be your friend, but I don't want to hide things, even from you, if these are going to be my last few days alive. I'd think maybe you wouldn't want to either."

"I'm not in the habit of telling the truth," he said, all expression gone from his face.

"The offer's there."

"Don't patronize me," he said coldly. "You're not my mother. I don't need you to— I'm sorry. That was out of line."

I changed the subject. "I've been thinking about sleep. It's important for keeping up our strength. We should eat a little something, maybe share one of the cookies at bedtime so we aren't kept awake by hunger. In the long run, we might lose a day of food, but we'll probably be more productive."

"OK."

"Can you can manage on a small amount of food?"

"I'll tell you something that is the truth. I was thrown out of the Navy because of the marijuana, but I was proud to be a SEAL, and our most important strength was self-discipline. I'll do whatever is necessary."

"What about alcohol?"

"What do you mean?"

"Is it a problem if you don't have something to drink?"

He looked surprised. "Why ask me that?"

"You had that big glass of whiskey on the flight from Anchorage to Deadhorse. I thought there was a possibility you were an alcoholic."

"You do lay your cards on the table, don't you? No, I'm not going to have trouble. I don't normally drink. Alcohol doesn't mix well with my work. That trip was a perfect example. I was tense about being with you in that plane. I felt almost like I was back in high school. I didn't know how to behave around you. I thought maybe a drink would help, but it sure didn't. Jack really did a number on me, didn't he?"

"He knew I didn't like those dirty stories. Why did you keep telling them?"

He looked rueful. "I was trying to get your attention. I knew I was doing it all wrong, but I couldn't stop. I'm not . . . experienced with caring about a woman."

I tried not to show my surprise. He'd said on the plane that maybe I'd get to like him, and now here he was saying he had feelings for me. I knew he meant something other than "fascination," as he'd called it.

"Well, if you care about someone, maybe it would be better not to plan to kill her."

He looked down, embarrassed, and changed the subject. "Speaking of food, I'm sorry I didn't tell you this morning. Serbin is . . . was . . . always eating candy. He'll have a pocket full."

"On the right side or the left?"

"On the right. He was right-handed. It's probably in his coat."

Seeing Serbin was easier now that his face was covered, but it was repulsive putting my hand on him.

Hal was right. His pocket was full of individually wrapped, fruit-flavored hard candies. This would mean an extra day of life for us. He had more candy in his shirt pocket. Blood had soaked through his shirt and dried on the wrappers. I scratched it off. It seemed unnecessarily cruel to leave it there for Hal to see. And Serbin did have a Swiss Army knife. I took that too.

Chapter Thirty-eight

I showed Hal what I'd found, put the candy in the bag with the other food, and settled onto the ikliq with him.

"Robby had a Swiss Army knife, but it was smaller than this one."

"This one has tools for everything." He started to open the various thingamajigs to show me. "It even has the tool for getting stones out of a horse's hoof. He actually used that one. We kept horses. We used to ride a lot. Oh, look. I forgot. It has a magnifying glass. We could light a fire."

"It's a good idea in theory, but not really. We couldn't find enough dry fuel under all this snow. The time it would take us out in the cold and the calories we'd spend to keep warm while we were searching wouldn't be worth it. And if we built a fire, the igloo would start to melt. We can't let it get above 32° in here. If you think we're uncomfortable now, try being here in wet clothes."

"How do you know all this?"

"I took a survival class," I said.

"I might have guessed. It's how you knew about igloos and foxes."

"One of the problems we had was 'cabin fever.' Spending too much time together made us testy, and there were a few little spats. We handled it by keeping busy. But you and I don't have anything to keep us busy. We're just waiting for the foxes to show up. We have to be alert to what boredom can do to us."

"There's a deck of cards and a cribbage board in my suitcase. Serbin and I always played cribbage whenever we had time to kill. We each had a book too."

"Oh. Is your book interesting? I could read to you."

"Very interesting. Colin Powell's autobiography, *My American Journey*."

"What about Serbin's book?"

"I don't think you need to bother with that. He liked to read about killers."

"You're right. I'll pass on that."

"Let's play cribbage for a while."

"I don't know how." I said.

"I'll teach you. We can play as long as we have enough light—penny a point. You can owe me."

"Hah! You're so sure you're going to win? Bring it on, Mister!"

He smiled.

If anyone had asked, I'd have said it would be impossible to relax and have fun with him, especially in our circumstances, but I did. And when I stopped feeling so defensive, I began to recognize a side to his character I hadn't expected. He was self-disciplined. He'd been able to control his fear, and he did things at high personal cost without slacking off or complaining. And his concern for Serbin had been a revelation. I even noticed a little thing: he never failed to thank me when I did something for him.

I understood that didn't mean he'd show me mercy if he thought he needed to hurt me, but still, I found I couldn't ignore his good qualities.

He even teased me. We'd played only a couple of hands of cards when I realized he could see well enough to play. I'd been dealing out the cards and moving the pegs on the board for him because of his hands, but I hadn't thought about his eyes.

"You can see the cards!"

"I wondered when you'd catch on. You weren't trying to take advantage of a poor disabled man, now were you?" He laughed, and his laugh was warm and joyful. "I still have double vision, but it's getting easier to bring things together."

"You haven't laughed before. I think you're getting better. Maybe you'll be able to walk soon."

"I hope so."

"I'll tell you one thing. When you start eating foxes, you'll be motivated to walk anywhere where there's something else to eat."

About two-thirty, when it was too dark to see the cards anymore, we stopped. This was the first time I'd been relaxed in his presence since I met him. I guess I was at the point where I had nothing else to lose. If I irritated him, he couldn't hurt me without hurting himself. That thought was quite liberating.

"I didn't think we'd ever be able to talk like this," he said.

"Me either."

"You said you'd tell the truth about things. Did you mean it?"

"Yes." I nodded, even though he could barely see me in the gathering dark.

He hesitated a moment, then quietly asked, "How do you feel about me?"

"Oh, Hal."

"Would you tell me?"

". . . Yes, I'll tell you. You've been very cruel to me, Hal, in Alaska and in Ungavaq too. You terrorized me. I said you made my skin crawl. That was true. I loathed you. I guess I'm too worried about our survival now to have those kinds of emotions, but I still couldn't ever like you."

"Why not?"

"Because of who you are. Because of the things you've done. They're not tolerable."

"Maybe I could change. They always talk about how a man can change with the love of a good woman."

"If you're going to change, you need to do that for yourself, not for someone else. And, anyway, you seem to think I'm going to make the jump from 'I can't like you' to 'I love you.' It's not going to happen."

"Why not?"

"Of course, there's Jack. We're . . . I don't know how to explain it to you, partly because it's too personal and partly because I don't think it can be put into words. I don't think I could explain the passion I feel for him. We're a fact. But even if Jack weren't in my life and even if I could get past the idea that it didn't bother you to talk about killing me . . ."

"Go on."

"I didn't expect you to ask me this. I haven't thought it out . . . There's a fable. A scorpion comes to a deep and fast river, and he can't get across. He asks a frog to carry him over on his back. The frog says, 'No, because you'll sting me.' The scorpion says, 'I promise not to.' Finally, the frog agrees. He's halfway across the river when the scorpion stings him. 'Why did you do that?' the frog asks. 'Now we're both going to die.' 'Because it's my nature,' the scorpion says, and they drown.

"You're who you are. It's your nature. I don't think your nature will change, and I couldn't ever accept it. I don't think you could learn any other way of dealing with people besides forcing them to give you what you want."

He was silent for a long time. Then he said, "Thank you for being honest."

"Do you want to try?"

"What?"

"Telling the truth about something."

"What do you want to know?"

"Tell me more about Serbin. I know it's difficult for you, but I'm deeply troubled about what happened. I don't know if we did the right thing. I've never seen anyone die like that."

It was full dark now. Outside, the stars shone, but their light couldn't penetrate the snow blocks. The moon would provide a dim light, but it wouldn't be up for hours. Even though we were right next to each other, it was too dark to see him.

I think it must have been like being in one of those sensory-deprivation chambers. There was no ambient noise. Once in a while, I became aware of the muffled cry of the wind, but if we weren't talking, the only sounds I could usually hear were our breathing and my heartbeat.

He didn't answer for a while. Then he took a deep breath. I could hear the tension in his voice when he said, "It's never easy to see that, but I do know we did the right thing. I've been in battle. I've seen many injured men. Serbin wouldn't have survived."

"People survive broken backs."

"Anne, we had no pain meds. We had no way to keep him from going into shock. No way to keep him warm or hydrated. No way to feed him. All he had to look forward to was agony for as long as it took him to die. He knew it. That's why he asked me to help. At first, I said I couldn't. That was selfish. I couldn't stand the thought of him dying . . . of losing him. But I had to do it. How could I not? He was my friend. You don't have to worry. I'll never tell anyone you helped me. This won't come back to you."

"But I did help you. I helped kill a person. I don't know if I can work that out to where I can understand it."

"Understanding it leads to explaining it away. It might be better for you if you don't do that. You don't ever want to be hardened to something like that. You don't want to be like me."

"But you cried."

"Still . . ." He shook his head.

"I don't know. It was so quick. One minute we were flying through the sky, and then he was dead. It almost seemed trivial."

"Death is like that sometimes," he said. "But it's always important. It's always life-changing for those of us who are left."

"For you?"

"Yeah, for me."

"You mean with Serbin."

"I mean every death."

"You cry?"

"No. That was for Serbin. But every death changes me."

"The ones you cause?"

"Yeah," he said.

"I don't understand."

"I can't explain it. That's just the way life is, I think."

"Would you tell me the truth about something else?"

"Maybe. I can try." The tension was there again. It seemed these questions threatened him.

"How did you get to be what you are?"

"Do you mean what were my career goals?" Now he laughed, the tension gone.

"I guess . . . Yes."

"This wasn't what I had in mind for myself."

"Was Dr. MacNeil the first person you killed?"

He hesitated.

"I mean since you got out of the navy."

He was silent.

I waited.

"No."

I was glad we were in the dark. I wouldn't have wanted him to see my reaction. Even though that was the answer I expected, it horrified me.

In spite of that, I felt compelled to ask more. But would he continue to answer? Answering was risky for him. He was revealing things he'd probably never told anyone else, things that could send him to prison or even execution.

"Why did you kill him?"

Silence.

Then, "He radioed in to say he'd found something really important. Serbin and I were pulled off another job to take care of it. He'd found teeth. Maybe they came from that jaw Jack found. He was so excited. He wanted to share his happiness and excitement with us . . . He was so naive." He sighed. "We couldn't let him tell anyone else."

He sounded sad. That didn't make sense. Now I sat silent for a while as I tried to figure things out. I didn't know how much latitude I had, but I figured that if we didn't die of starvation, he'd still kill me. I wanted to understand why.

"Anne? Are we done?"

"No."

"All right. Go on."

He was inviting me to ask a question.

"Are you a contract killer, a hit man?"

"Anne, I . . . I shouldn't . . ." He sighed again. "I don't think you'll understand. I'm not trying to defend myself. I don't think of myself as a hit man. A hit man is someone who works for a mob, like an enforcer. I've never worked for organized crime—I wouldn't—unless you count the drug thing when I was in the Navy, but that was just of bunch of guys who wanted easy money, and it got out of hand."

"Then, what do you call yourself?"

"I guess you'd say my job description is 'troubleshooter.'" He gave a short, sardonic chuckle. "No, I suppose that's not a very good word either. I'm a consultant—a security specialist. I work for big corporations. I've never been hired to kill someone. I get hired to 'handle situations,' and it's up to me to figure out the best way to do that."

"Does that always involve a death?"

"No . . . Not even often."

"Ah. I see. It's OK, then, because you only kill people once in a while."

He didn't respond.

Had my sarcasm made him angry? Maybe he wouldn't answer again.

"Do the people who hire you know what you do?"

He was silent for quite a while.

I waited him out. I had no place to go.

"Of course they do, but part of what they pay me for is never having to know the details. That's why Allied American fired me. They found out the details."

"May I ask another question?"

"We've started. We may as well finish. I can always take the Fifth. I've never been able to talk to anyone about this. You can't take a woman out on a date and tell her this kind of thing. Serbin was the only one who knew, and he knew everything about me. He was my friend. I'll bet you didn't realize that. You never saw him as he really was. He was shy, and he wasn't comfortable around women."

"He didn't like me."

"He didn't. But he was shy around everyone. I guess you noticed he didn't do much talking. That's why I was the front man for our team. He called me 'Boss,' but I wasn't his boss. We were partners. In our line of work, there's a lot of down time, like when we were waiting for you and Jack to call in each day. If we didn't have anything else to do, we'd read or play cards or talk. We talked about everything."

"About me?"

"Yeah. He didn't like this plan. He didn't like the idea of kidnapping you. He didn't like my first plan either. I said we'd go to San Diego after we found Jack's body so I could offer my condolences. Of course, that didn't work out. He thought I was making a big mistake. He tried to talk me out of this whole thing, but when I said I wanted to do it, he backed me up. He always did. I admit he wasn't very nice about it. He was jealous of you. We'd been kind of a closed unit for so long. I really screwed things up."

"Were you going to give me to him when you were done with me?"

"I don't know that I'd ever have been done with you, but I wouldn't have given you to him. Never. I wouldn't treat you that way."

I wasn't being sarcastic this time. I'm sure he could hear my anger when I said, "You wouldn't treat me that way? You'd terrify me and kidnap me and rape me and kill me, but you wouldn't treat me that way?"

He didn't say anything for a while, then softly. "Not very logical, I guess. Serbin was right."

"Were you really going to kill me?"

". . . In Alaska? Yeah."

Now it was my turn to sit in silence. Finally, I had to ask. "Would you still do that?"

He shifted a little. "You want the truth?"

"Yes."

He took a deep breath. "The truth is . . . I don't know."

I thought that over. It seemed so odd to sit with this man in the intimate dark, close enough that I could have touched him by moving my little finger. In my entire life, being with a man in the dark had been good—first my father telling me stories at bedtime, then my boyfriends and lovers, and Robby and Jack . . . and now this man.

"Anne?"

"Maybe I didn't want the truth, after all. Maybe I wanted you to say, 'Of course not.'"

"I can't say that, Anne. I've lied to you before, but I won't lie to you again. I've never met anyone like you. I just don't know. But at least I'm a little more honest than that scorpion."

"When you make up your mind, maybe you'll let me know."

He laughed, but it was a bitter laugh. "I promise."

The silence stretched out as I thought about what he'd said. Maybe I should have let him die in the plane. I could do that now. I could just wait until he fell asleep and take the food and the knife and leave. It would be easy. If I got a few steps away from the igloo, he could never catch up with me. He couldn't stand upright by himself, and he couldn't catch me by crawling.

But I couldn't any more do that today than I could last night. I'd claimed the moral high ground for myself when I lectured him about his behavior being "not tolerable." You don't always know when God or Life or whatever is testing your character, but this time it was obvious. I failed the test last night. I was not going to fail again.

Chapter Thirty-nine

We didn't speak for a long time. We sat, and we shifted, and we repositioned, and finally, I couldn't stand it anymore. Maybe he'd answer another question.

"You didn't tell me yet how you chose this line of work."

"It wasn't what I planned. I was good at math in high school, and I thought I'd go to college and become a banker. I wanted to earn lots of money. My mom worked. It was just the two of us. We got by, but we had to be careful about money, and I always wanted to have enough so that I wouldn't worry." He added ruefully, "I haven't figured out yet how much that is.

"I had a girlfriend named Crystal in high school. We dated for two years, and we talked about getting married after we finished college. I thought I had my life planned out. Yeah, well, that's how you make God laugh."

"How?"

"You make a plan."

"Oh. Go on."

"During our senior year in high school, Crystal was with a guy, and they were killed in a street racing accident. Afterward, I found out she'd been seeing him, and she'd been getting ready to break up with me.

"Then, just after I graduated, my mom had a heart attack and died. One day she was there, and the next day she was gone, like

Crystal. Everything in my life changed. I wasn't eighteen yet, but they didn't put me in foster care because I'd graduated from high school."

"Didn't you have relatives to live with? What about your dad?"

"No relatives. My dad was a drunk. He wouldn't have been fit to take care of me, even if he'd been interested—which he wasn't—so college was out, and the Navy was in. I loved the Navy. I'd have made it a career, but I got involved in that stupid drug thing."

"It wasn't just stupid. Someone was killed."

"But I didn't do it, if you're wondering. I know who did, but I found out after it was done. And that's true. Some things—I guess lots of things—I won't tell you. I wasn't joking when I said I'd take the Fifth. But it's true that I didn't do it. That was one of the few times in my life I've been arrested though. They finally had to release me. I've never spent any time in prison. I've never even been brought to trial for anything."

"What happened?"

"You don't have many career choices when you have a dishonorable discharge from an organization that primarily taught you a whole lot of ways to kill people. Serbin was one of our pilots. He brought the marijuana across the border. He didn't get caught when they shut down our business. That's when we linked up and drifted into this. Our skills complemented each other. We were one hell of a team."

"What do you mean 'drifted'?"

"That's something I really can't tell you about."

"Oh . . . You seem more educated than someone who's only finished high school."

"I had to educate myself."

"How?"

"I read. Much of my work's been outside the United States, so I've needed a pretty good idea of the politics and culture in the various countries where I've worked. I know a lot about psychology. I'm fluent in German and Spanish. I don't take assignments in Mexico though, since we . . . since I live there. We didn't have retirement plans—not that we really thought we'd live that long—so I read a lot on economics and investing. I work exclusively at the executive level—I'm not hired for minor problems—so I've had to be knowledgeable about things at that level. I have to know the right wine to order and one caviar from another. I'm a man of the world." He laughed.

"Why did you say you wouldn't work for organized crime?"

"Because I was a SEAL, and I fought for our country, and organized crime and drugs are destroying us. That's why I'm ashamed I was part of that drug operation. I'd never do anything like that again. I was young and very stupid."

"I'm surprised to hear you say you're ashamed of the drug thing."

"Why?"

"Because I thought people who earn their living the way you do don't have feelings about what they do. I thought they didn't feel guilt or shame."

"Anne, I know what a sociopath is. I'm not a sociopath. I have feelings, or maybe I should say I did. I've had to learn how to disregard them."

"You have feelings about the people you hurt?"

His voice dropped. "I know it's wrong. Sometimes I even like the people—you, for instance. But it's what I do. I'm a little like a soldier that way. Most of them don't like killing, but it's their job."

"So you're saying that doing those things isn't your nature; it's something you learned? But you do those things. How do you justify them?"

"It's big corporations. It's one shark after another shark."

"I'm not a shark. Jack's not a shark. Dr. MacNeil wasn't a shark!" My voice became shrill. *Calm down. Be more Inuit.*

"No . . . I guess not . . . I hadn't thought about that."

"I don't know much about you, but it seems to me you haven't thought much about a lot of things. When we were in Alaska, you told me you didn't enjoy inflicting pain, but you were going to let me starve to death. That's painful."

"Letting you starve to death was what I had to do for my job. What I meant when I said that was that it wasn't a turn-on for me to hurt you. I've known men who like the hurting more than the sex."

Again, I sat for a while without saying anything, thinking about what he had just said.

He didn't move.

Finally, he said, "I know there's something else you want to ask. I can feel it. We're not done yet."

"I wasn't going to ask, but I really need to know. Jack told me you dropped Dr. MacNeil into the ocean. Was he alive when you did that?"

"No . . . I wouldn't do that. That would be torture. I don't do that. I don't take that kind of job."

My anger flared again. "In Alaska, you said you'd hurt me to get what you wanted, and then you did. Where's the line, Hal? What you did to me was OK, but you wouldn't torture someone? Where's the line?"

He was silent for a long time. I didn't know if I'd made him angry, but I didn't care.

Finally, he cleared his throat. His voice was subdued. "You're right. There isn't a line. I guess I was fooling myself when I thought at least I had some ethics . . . This is something I shouldn't talk about . . . He didn't suffer. It was quick. He never knew."

"I don't know whether to be afraid of you or not anymore. You confuse me."

"I won't hurt you again, Anne."

"But you might kill me."

"I don't know if this is reassuring, but I'm very good at what I do. If I had to, you'd never feel any pain and not even fear. You don't need to be afraid anymore."

"So you'd give me a good death?"

He sighed. "Sometimes this telling the truth gets complicated, doesn't it?"

"Maybe it's time to stop," I said. "It's early, but I might sleep a little. I'm so tired. Do you want to sleep?"

"No, but if you don't mind, I'll lie close to you. Maybe you'll be a little warmer."

I thought about refusing him, but I didn't. I needed his warmth, and I needed not to feel alone.

I lay on my left side. He lay behind me and put his arm around me as he had in the night.

When he did that, in spite of the fact that I wanted the human contact he could provide, I tensed up and leaned away from him. We lay like that for a while, not speaking.

When he didn't do anything else, I began to relax.

He knew.

He exerted a very gentle pressure with his hand on my belly.

I resisted.

He didn't increase the pressure, but he didn't decrease it, either.

After a few moments, I relaxed again.

He still didn't increase the pressure.

Finally, I moved closer to him.

"I won't hurt you," he said softly. "I promise."

I didn't really understand what had just happened. Had he forced me or had he encouraged me? I was too tired to make sense of it. I slept, cradled in his arms.

Chapter Forty

The next day, we woke in the dark. It was Friday, the day Laura flies from Blackwell to Ungavaq. I walked around outside the igloo with the flashlight in my hand, ready to signal, but I never saw or heard a plane. I was there almost two hours until the sun rose. By then, she'd be in Ungavaq.

I took the flashlight back inside and told Hal I was going to check the fox traps.

When I got there, I couldn't believe it. I'd caught three foxes! This time I was lucky. All three were dead and frozen. It hadn't occurred to me until now that I might have to kill one if the trap didn't do it.

I reset the traps, and then I had to figure out how to get the foxes back to the igloo—another thing I hadn't thought about. I ended up taking the drawstring out of my hood and tying their tails together. They weighed about seven pounds apiece, so not too heavy for me to manage.

I slung them across my back and went back to the igloo. By the time I got there, I was so excited I was almost giddy.

"I've never seen you happy before," Hal said. "I wish I could make you feel that way."

"We've been through that."

"Yeah, I guess we have."

I untied the foxes, then sat on the ikliq next to him and turned one of the fox carcasses on to its back on my lap.

"Anyway, I'm glad you're back," he said. "It's difficult when you're gone."

"Because of your head?"

I opened Serbin's knife, this time without scaring myself, and started my initial cut down the fox's chest and belly.

"No. It's too quiet. There's no sound at all once you leave. When you're here, even if we're not talking, I can hear you breathing and moving. When you're gone, it's kind of creepy."

"It takes getting used to. It bothered me in Alaska, and Jack was close by most of the time. And we had the dogs. I sang a lot, but then sometimes a song would get stuck in my head. That's almost as bad. Anyway, you might want to try singing."

"I will the next time you go," he said.

"It's strange using a different knife to gut and skin the foxes. I'm used to my ulu."

"You're good at that," he said, with surprise.

"I've had a lot of practice in the last few months."

"With foxes?"

"Foxes, hares, birds, seals. I haven't done a caribou yet. They were gone by the time Jack and I got back to Ungavaq. The men do the walruses and, once in a while, a bear. Those take more strength than I have."

"You don't eat foxes do you?"

"No. In the winter, when the fur turns white and the skins are at their best, they bring money into the village."

"That's why you're being so careful now?"

"It's the way I was taught."

"How are we going to cook them?"

I shook my head. "We can't. There's no fuel. That's why the Inuit used to eat much of their food raw. And really, they wouldn't taste better cooked."

I finished the skinning and butchering and cut one of the shoulders in small pieces.

We had to hold the pieces of meat in our mouths until they thawed enough to chew. Hal gagged on the first bite, but he managed.

We decided to save the meaty back legs to eat while we walked, but we ate everything else edible on the carcasses and I even scraped the fat off the skins. We sucked the bones of the spinal column, and I did something I'd only done once before—on a dare from Jack. I ate the eyes. Inuit children eat eyes as a special treat, so I figured I could do it. Jack didn't think I could, but I showed him. It wasn't something I thought I'd ever do again.

Hal thought it was really disgusting, and I could see I rose in his estimation because of it.

"Well, I bet you wouldn't eat a bug," he said.

"Shoot! I should have bet you about the eyes. I could've won the money back that I lost at cribbage."

"Too late now. What about a bug?"

"Put your money where your mouth is and find a bug."

We laughed.

It came to me suddenly that I wasn't afraid of him. It was like having an enormous burden, a physical weight, lifted off me.

In addition, at least for now, we were holding our own. We weren't hungry, and we were a little less cold because of the food in our bellies. For the first time, I had hope we might survive. I might see Jack again.

I decided to go make three more traps, but before I could do that, I had to put the drawstring back in my parka hood. I was surely learning a lot of lessons about planning ahead. Hal couldn't put it back because his hands still weren't that coordinated, and I didn't want to take my parka off for the time it would take to restring it. A further difficulty—we were without the usual tool used to restring hoods, a big safety pin.

We poked through Serbin's toolbox. Hal came up with the idea of attaching the string to Serbin's skinniest screwdriver with electrical tape and poking it through that way. I got the string most of the way around, and then the screwdriver worked its way out of the tape. After that, it was just patient effort, moving the knot at the end of the string a quarter of an inch at a time until it came out the hole on the other side. I was able to do that without taking the parka off.

That done, I went out and made three more traps.

As the day wore on though, and in spite of the food, I began to feel chilled again. Hal said he did too. From time to time, our teeth chattered. We took turns standing and moving our arms around to keep the blood circulating. When Hal stood, I'd stand too, so he could hold onto me with one hand while he swung the other arm. Other than that, there was nothing to do but ignore the cold. To keep our minds on other things, I read to him for an hour, and then we played cribbage until the early sunset, shortly before three o'clock.

"I feel better when the sun goes down," he said. "It's so tiring to try to focus my eyes, but I can't seem to make myself not try. When it's dark, they relax."

"Does your head hurt?"

"The bruised part only hurts if I touch it. The headache's not so bad now, either. If I move, I still get a wave of dizziness, but not the nausea."

"You're improving. That's good."

"I did a lot of talking yesterday," he said. "Maybe it's your turn."

"OK. I'll try. I won't take the Fifth, but I won't tell you things that are too personal."

"You told me why you couldn't like me. Would you tell me why you love Jack?"

"I would if I could, but I don't know why." I shrugged. "I met him and it was right."

"Is it because he's a professor, you know—important?"

"When I fell in love with him, I thought he was a hunting guide. I didn't find out he was a professor until later. Did you know Jack and I are related besides being husband and wife?"

"Wait! How'd you get related to an Inuit?"

"Jack's three-quarters Inuit. His grandfather was my first husband's father, so Jack is my half-nephew-in-law."

He chuckled. "Well, pretty complicated. So you've known him for a long time?"

I shook my head, then realized he couldn't see me in the dark. "I met him a year and a half ago."

"Oh. You married him fairly quickly then."

"Yes, I met him in June and married him in January. Alaska was part of our honeymoon."

"I guess I ruined that for you."

"Not entirely."

I smiled as I thought about Alaska. Jack had worried I might get tired of being with him every day, but each day we woke up eager to be together.

One of the strange things about being there was that we had been so totally alone—much more alone than we'd been in our condo or in our houses in Ungavaq and San Diego. That solitude gave us complete freedom to explore our sexuality together. We came to a level of intimacy and comfort it took me years to achieve with Robby. I was wearing Jack's ankle bracelet under my sock. And the polish I had on my toenails was one of the colors Jack had given me in Alaska—"Scarlet O'Hara." In the evenings, if we didn't have anything else to do, he'd change the color of the polish on my nails. More often than not, that led to making love. One evening when we were feeling particularly silly, I painted his toenails—a different color on each toe. He really loved that. Those were some of the things I wasn't going to tell Hal.

"I knew you hadn't been married long," he said. "Is the tattoo for him?"

"It's to make me more beautiful for him."

"Anne, you don't need it. If he can't see how beautiful you are, he's blind."

"It's not that; it's that beauty is relative. Do you remember that when you found me in Alaska, I had dark makeup on my hands and face?"

"I forgot about that. I wondered about it at the time."

"Quipac asked me to wear it so if you flew over in the helicopter, you wouldn't see my white skin. You'd think I was an Eskimo. When we found Jack, he made a joke about Quipac trying to make me more attractive. That set me to thinking. He'd complimented my body, but he'd never said I was good-looking. So I asked him about it."

"And he said you were beautiful, didn't he?"

"No."

"No?"

"No. I don't look Inuit. My eyes are wrong. My nose is too big. They value small flat noses. Mine's too pointy. I'm the wrong color—too pale. My hair's not right."

"He said that to you?"

"Not in so many words, but I figured it out. I don't look like his mother or his sisters or the other women in the village, but he loves me anyway."

"I don't know what to say to that. I think you're beautiful."

"Thank you."

"Other than being kind of a dumbshit about that, Jack's one hell of a man, isn't he? His file said he was sixty. I couldn't believe he managed to walk so far on that broken ankle. And he took me on, and I'm fifteen years younger and bigger. He's really tough."

"More than you know. Jack grew up as a traditional Inuit. When he was a teenager, he killed a polar bear with a spear. Life was hard but people endured. When we went home and told our family what happened in Alaska, they said, 'You do what you have to do.' They didn't think it was especially tough. The younger ones have had an easier life, but many of the older ones have been through experiences just as hard as that."

"How did you find Jack in Alaska?"

"Quipac found him. We were at the camp by the evening of the second day after you called. He found Jack by knowing how his mind works. I couldn't have done it."

"Quipac? That's the guy who came with the police?"

"Yes."

"So they're a good team too."

"Yes, and they're brothers."

"They didn't look much like brothers."

"Quipac was adopted. He's Jack's friend the way Serbin was yours. They're that close."

"What happened to your first husband?"

"Robby died three years ago. We'd been married thirty-five years."

"I guessed you were loyal because of the way you stood by Jack."

"It was a good marriage. We were happy. I almost didn't make it after he died. But I decided to try to finish some genealogy work we'd been doing. That's how I found Jack."

"What do you mean you 'almost didn't make it'?"

"... It's hard to explain. I'll tell you something I've never told anyone. When Robby finally died, for a while I was happy. We'd been so sad for so long, and I was so scared. It was a relief when it was over. He didn't want to go to the hospital. He was afraid they might prolong his dying. So I promised him I wouldn't let that happen. But even though he and I had agreed on no treatment, every moment I didn't ask them to do something—anything—I felt like I was killing him ... But I did what I promised. He stayed at home, even after he went into a coma. I had nurses, and the hospice people came in to help.

"For a little while after he died, it was OK, and then it just wasn't. I lost interest in everything. I've never told anyone—not even Jack—but I did think about killing myself. I didn't know how to be alone. It was like I'd had an amputation, and half of me was gone. I don't know if that makes sense to you."

"I remember when my mother died," he said. "It was kind of like that. I've never cared about anybody except Serbin since she died . . . and now you. I feel like that now—like I've lost part of me. All these years, I've been with Serbin almost every day. Our lives were so connected. I can see why you thought we were a couple. He's been gone less than two days, but it feels a lot longer. I'm glad you're here. It makes it a little easier."

"You have no one else?"

"I never tried to make other friends."

"Why not?"

"I didn't imagine anyone would want me in their life . . . in any role."

"Didn't you date or have women friends?"

"Not really. I dated a little when I was in the Navy, but usually we were too busy with training or on a mission. After that, when I linked up with Serbin, it became clear I'd chosen a lonely profession. There's a quote from Groucho Marx. He said he wouldn't want to join the kind of club that would have him as a member. I didn't want to date the kind of girl who'd think what I did was OK.

"Since we're telling the truth, I'll tell you Serbin and I always had money, so we spent time with high-class call girls when we wanted company. You can take them places, but they don't expect your life story or a commitment."

"What will you do now? You can't be alone the rest of your life."

"I don't know. It never occurred to me I might have to start over again. I thought I'd be dead by now. I've had too much good luck, if you can call surviving Serbin good luck. But you found Jack, so who knows?"

As he had several times before, Hal changed the subject. "I've been wondering. The survival class—I guess that's where you learned about igloos and foxes. Did you take that class since you've been with Jack?"

"Jack and Quipac teach it every December. I took it last year. I'm going to help teach this year . . . Well, anyway, I was supposed to. That's the class the department secretary told you about."

"You have a lot of confidence for someone who's just had one class."

"It wasn't just in a classroom. We built igloos and lived in them for more than three weeks. I can tell you they're a lot more comfortable with a little heat and light and sleeping bags. I know I put on a confident front. I don't feel quite so confident inside."

"You're always surprising."

"You do what you have to do in life. What's the other option? Quitting? I tried that after Robby died. It didn't work. So you just move forward and keep moving."

It seemed like time to take a break from this conversation, so we decided to sing until we were sleepy. I sang the Inuit songs Quipac had taught me and told Hal how we had used them to find Jack.

Then we tried to remember the words to some of the old songs we knew. Although I was fifteen years older than Hal, we had a lot in common when it came to popular culture. Of course, we knew many Beatles songs, so they sustained us for a long time. It turned out Hal had a mellow baritone singing voice. It blended well with my alto, or at least we thought so.

One of the songs we sang was "Strawberry Fields Forever," and that brought us to talking about food.

I was uncomfortably hungry all the time. He said he was too. I'd never been really hungry before. Hal had. He said that after a few more days we'd probably start obsessing about food: thinking about it, dreaming about it, talking about it. We weren't there yet, but we did talk about our favorite meals.

"My mother was an OK cook, not spectacular," I said. "Whenever my dad was home, it was meat and potatoes. When he was out, though, we had tomato soup and popcorn and ice cream."

"That's really strange."

"It sure was good though. They were all foods my dad didn't like, so we didn't get them any other time."

"What did Jack say when you told him about that?"

"I've never told him. If I have a chance, maybe I'll fix it for him. I haven't thought about it in a long time. Our favorite now is sushi."

"I like that too. I spent time in Japan when I was in the Navy."

"What's your favorite meal?" I asked.

"Pot roast. I'd rather have that than the best steak any day. My mom was a really good cook. She'd make pot roast and mashed potatoes and gravy, with vegetables cooked in with the meat. We'd have sweet potato pie for dessert."

"That's a Southern recipe."

"We were from Louisiana," he said. "We moved to San Diego when I was in fifth grade."

"I always thought I heard a little 'Southern' in your voice."

"You have a good ear."

"Why San Diego?" I asked.

"I don't know. There was nothing to hold her in Louisiana, no relatives or anything. Maybe it looked like there'd be more opportunity there. It was kind of tough for me. I wished we'd stayed in the South."

"It is tough for a child to move and leave friends behind."

"Well, I survived."

"I used to teach first grade," I said. "I saw what a move like that could do to a child. Some don't seem to mind any change; they just accept whatever comes. But others are really knocked off kilter. They need a lot of special help to adjust."

"You really love children, don't you," he said. "I can hear it in your voice."

"Yes."

"Do you have any?"

"Children? No, no children."

"Ah. Your voice changed again. Why not?"

". . . Robby didn't want children."

"That's the first time you hesitated before answering a question."

"It's my one regret. It's the saddest part of my life besides Robby's death. I suppose you don't have any."

"No, although they say a man never knows for sure."

"Have you ever wished for children?"

"What kind of a father could I be? 'Come on, son. I'll teach you how to kill people.'"

The bitterness in his voice was a revelation.

"You don't like your life, do you?"

"Ah, I'm telling you more than I should, aren't I?"

"Yesterday, we talked about what you do, and you answered my questions. Today, we talk about what you feel, and you don't like to give away that secret."

His voice tightened. "Feelings are dangerous. They make you weak. People can use them against you."

"People can share them with you. They can share your happiness and your sadness."

"Maybe with someone. Not with me."

Chapter Forty-one

I never managed to shoot a hare or a ptarmigan, although I saw them. I did catch more foxes. After I caught the first three and made three more traps, the next day I caught five.

This time I'd done a little thinking ahead. Both Hal and Serbin had dental floss in their suitcases. I took long lengths of floss, tied them around the necks of the foxes, and dragged them back to the igloo like so many dogs on leashes. I had enough floss for four. I had to carry the fifth in my other hand. I definitely did not want to make two trips.

They weren't very fat. Jack had said if a person in the Arctic ate only lean meat, he'd starve to death, because without fat you couldn't take in enough calories to survive. I didn't tell Hal, but what we were catching was not going to keep us going very long. We needed a nice fat seal or a caribou, and we weren't going to find that. I couldn't provide enough food for us. All we were doing was slowing our rate of starvation.

I ate everything I could manage to get down, but my hunger was incessant, and my hope faded rapidly.

I thought about digging through the snow and trying to find voles, but I wasn't hungry enough yet that I thought I'd be able to put one in my mouth . . . Maybe later.

So far, the foxes had nothing much in their stomachs. Maybe that's why they came for the bait that couldn't have smelled like anything they were familiar with. I wondered what I'd do if I caught one with voles in its stomach. Would I be able to eat them?

Hal was right. I thought more and more about food. My mind seemed to fixate on baking. I found myself remembering recipes for cakes or cookies or breads. I kept envisioning opening the oven, feeling the heat, and smelling the aroma of fresh baking that emanated from the hot pan as I took it out. I started teaching Hal how to bake in an imaginary kitchen. We'd go through each recipe step-by-step and then imagine eating the results.

I tried to push negative thoughts away, but they only got stronger. I didn't tell Hal. I'm sure he was having his own struggles.

I tried not to think about Jack. That hurt too much.

The day after we'd talked about feelings, we were quiet as we played cribbage. When we finished our game, I asked, "Do you have a pen or a pencil?"

"A pen."

"Would you mind if I tore one of the blank pages out of your book?"

"No. Why?"

"I want to write a letter. I want Jack to know . . ."

"Know what?"

I held up my hand and shook my head. I couldn't talk without tears starting.

"Anne, you'll tell him when we get to Ungavaq."

"No . . . But maybe someone will find my body."

"Oh, Anne. Don't say that. Don't think that."

". . . Do you want to write a letter?"

"No. There's no one."

I tore out a blank page from the end of his book. As the daylight faded, I wrote slowly, carefully. I wanted to say the exact right thing. Jack is a strong, brave man, but he'd told me that he had been dying of loneliness before he met me. I was frightened about what would happen to him when I didn't come home. I didn't want him to die of grief. I wrote:

Dearest Jack,

I can't seem to realize that I won't see you again. As I fall asleep, I think of your face. I remember your tender caresses, the things you said to me in the night. I love you more than I could ever tell you. You're the center of my life, my heart, my soul's delight.

I grieve. I can't stand to lose you.

I know this will be a difficult time for you, but you taught me to love again. I want you to love again too. I want you to be happy. I don't want you to be lonely.

My time with you has been so wonderful. I'm sad that it was so short, but no length of time with you would ever be enough. I don't know what happens after death, but if it's possible, I'll love you for all eternity, and I know you'll love me the same way.

I wasn't injured in the crash. I'm not suffering. Hal treats me with respect. He encourages me to think we might be rescued.

You know better than I do that what's coming won't be easy, but remembering you, remembering how you made my life worthwhile will sustain me. When the time comes, I'll just go to sleep and hope my dreams will be of you.

Your loving wife,

Anne

I folded the letter in thirds and then in thirds the other direction. On the outside, I wrote "Jack O'Malley, Ungavaq, Québec, from Anne O'Malley—Private."

I handed the pen back to Hal. Then I turned my back to him and reached up under my parka and shirt to tuck the note in my bra. I could only pray that it would get to Jack.

Chapter Forty-two

The sun set on our third day in the igloo. Hal had put the cards and cribbage board away. I could tell by his breathing he wasn't asleep or even dozing, but he was silent.

It irritated me.

I'd felt low all day, and writing the letter made me even sadder. Maybe he was feeling low too. Finally, I asked, "Are you upset about something?"

"No."

I knew enough about men to know I wasn't going to get anything more than that monosyllable. Before I met Jack, I'd have tried to find out what was bothering Hal, but I'd learned a little of Inuit patience. "OK, fine. We'll be quiet if that's what you want."

We went about a half-hour more without speaking. Then he cleared his throat, and I couldn't help but feel triumphant. I'd waited him out.

"I don't want to talk about feelings," he said.

"Fine. Whatever you want."

Another long silence followed.

"Anne, aren't you going to talk to me?" he asked, a little plaintively.

"I thought you wanted quiet."

"We should talk about something."

"OK . . . What were you going to do with me in Mexico? Besides sex, I mean."

"I don't want to talk about that. It's not going to happen, is it?"

"I'll add that to the list."

"What list?"

"The things we're not going to talk about."

"Anne, don't be like that."

"Tell me what you want."

He didn't answer for a long time. Then he shifted a little on the ikliq and cleared his throat again. "I want you to care about me."

"Oh, Hal! How can you say that? You've told me over and over what you're going to take from me—my freedom, my body, my life. Now you're asking me to give to you? You don't seem to be aware of the incongruity. I'll take care of you. I can't give you more."

"I'm grateful for that. Don't think I'm not."

"We're back to feelings," I said.

"Yeah . . . What do you want to talk about?"

"Whatever you want's fine with me."

He sighed.

I waited.

"I don't want to have feelings."

"You don't want to have feelings, or you don't want to talk about feelings?"

"Both."

"Probably for the best," I said.

"Why?"

"Feelings would make it more difficult for you to kill me when the time comes."

"Anne!"

"What?"

"That's not what we're talking about."

"Oh. Excuse me. I thought it was."

I could feel his tension.

"You're not who I thought you were," he said.

"Ah, the honeymoon's over. Who did you think I was?"

"Don't be sarcastic. I thought you were sweet, but you can be really disagreeable."

"I don't understand, Hal. I've been agreeing with you."

"Other women don't behave like this."

"You pay them. You're not paying me. You get what you get, but at least it's free."

Another long silence.

"I don't want to fight with you," he said.

"No? Not yet?"

"What do you mean, not yet?"

"Later, when you don't need me, then we can fight and then you can . . . I'm not supposed to talk about it, but you know."

"Goddamn it, Anne! Stop it!"

I'd never heard him raise his voice before. I could hear him shift away from me on the ikliq. In spite of the dark and quiet, I could sense where he was and how he was. Right now, his anger vibrated in the air.

The silence stretched out again.

"I don't like yelling," he said. "I don't want to be angry with you."

Now it was my turn to be quiet.

Finally, I sighed. "I'm sorry."

He shifted back but didn't say anything.

"I am sorry." I said. "I really mean it."

"You were trying to goad me."

"No."

"Yeah."

" . . . Yes," I said softly.

"It won't work. I'm not stupid. I do need you. I'm not going to 'you know.' Why were you trying to make me angry?"

"... I want this to be over."

He sounded weary and sad when he said, "So you tried to make me fix it for you? Like I did for Serbin? You thought I'd do that? You have the pistol. You take care of it. You can shoot both of us."

"I couldn't."

"Oh, yeah," he said. "Scruples ... Anne, you frighten me."

"I frighten you?"

"Yeah."

"Because I have the pistol?"

"No." He laughed. "Because you're fierce."

"You're teasing."

"No."

"Then I don't understand."

"Because when you start, you don't quit."

"Start what?"

"You want something from me. That's what this conversation has been about all these days."

"I've never wanted anything from you. I just wanted you to leave me alone."

"But I didn't do that, and now you do want something. You want me to be different. I'd do that for you if I could. I don't know how. I don't know how to be someone you could love."

"You could start by not killing people."

"Ha! Just like a woman, changing your mind. First you want me to kill you, and then you don't want me to kill anyone."

"Well, I guess you're right. I do want you to be different."

"It's what I do, Anne ... It's who I am ... Who would I be then?"

"I don't know. But you're not a coward. Maybe you have to take a chance."

Chapter Forty-three

We were lost in our own thoughts for a long time.

Hal finally broke the silence.

"My vision and balance are getting better."

"Are they good enough that we could start walking tomorrow?"

"I think so."

We talked about the best way to carry things. We'd planned to make backpacks out of long-sleeved shirts, but then we had a better idea. I helped him over to the plane in the dark. He inspected the skis, but decided they were too damaged to be useful. Instead, he used the metal shears from Serbin's toolbox to cut a piece of curved metal off the wing that had been torn off. We made a simple sled.

I had to go into the plane again to get the rope—the one they'd planned to tie me with.

"When you're in there," he said, "look for a flare gun. I'm sure there'll be one."

I found the rope, the flare gun, and two flares. I avoided looking at Serbin.

Hal attached the rope to the metal, and we pulled the sled back to the igloo.

On the fourth morning, long before dawn, the alarms on the Rolexes woke us. We wanted to start in the dark so we could navigate by the stars.

We had finished breakfast and were packing up to go when Hal said, "You know what? I'm going to put on clean clothes before we go."

"Oh, that sounds nice," I said. "You must feel pretty grungy. I sure do." We hadn't wanted to use our precious drinking water to bathe, and I'd been so cold I couldn't face washing with snow.

"You could change. Serbin's clothes wouldn't be too big for you."

"I don't know . . ."

"Why not?"

"Maybe a shirt."

"Put on a couple of undershirts and then one of his turtlenecks. You might be warmer. You could have clean underwear too."

"I couldn't."

"I know there's an 'ick factor,' but at least think about it. We're so uncomfortable from cold and hunger. Take what comfort you can."

When I didn't say anything, he said, "Tell me what you're thinking."

"I'm afraid to get undressed with you here."

". . . I'll go outside. But Anne, the truth is, when we're lying together, it doesn't matter that I'm dizzy. It doesn't matter that it's cold. What stops me is that I promised I wouldn't hurt you. I'll change first. Then I'll go out."

"Oh . . . Don't go out. Don't get cold any sooner than you have to."

"If you need the light, I'll close my eyes."

So Hal changed, and when he was done, I used the flashlight to look through Serbin's suitcase.

I found the shirts and a pair of those knit jockey shorts with the long legs. They would fit. I changed as quickly as I could in the dark. In spite of Hal's reassurance, I was tense.

"All done," I said.

"OK. Give me the flashlight."

I did, and he rummaged through Serbin's suitcase.

"Sit on the ikliq a minute. I found Serbin's spare comb." He knelt behind me and gently combed my hair.

I hadn't combed my hair since we'd left Ungavaq. I wanted to tell him to stop. It felt good, but at the same time, it felt too intimate.

His hand stilled.

I started to thank him.

"Please, don't talk," he said softly.

He set the comb down and put his hands on my shoulders.

Even through my coat, I could feel his tension.

Without warning, he pulled me back toward him.

I was too startled to resist.

He stopped me before my body touched his.

"Oh! I want to hold you."

The whole world seemed to swell and shrink with his deep inhaling and exhaling.

My heart raced. Now I knew how the vole must feel when the wolf sniffs around its hiding place. I held very still, until his breathing slowed and his hands gradually relaxed.

"Anne, I'm so sorry."

I couldn't respond.

"We should go now."

I tried to keep my voice from shaking. "Yes."

Neither of us moved until he took his hands off my shoulders.

The silence was more than I could bear. As my heart thudded, I asked, "Do you have anything you want to take from the suitcases?"

He sighed. "The cribbage board. We had it from the first year of our friendship."

"I'm going to take the shirt I've been wearing. Jack's sister made it for me."

We didn't speak about what had just happened.

We emptied his suitcase and packed the food in it, then tied the suitcase, the tarp, and Serbin's toolbox on the sled. The toolbox was heavy, but we didn't know what kind of situations we might get in. Better safe than sorry.

We'd taken a few steps away from the igloo when Hal said, "I want to stop at the plane."

"Yes, of course."

At the plane, he stood quietly for some time, then said, "You know we have another source of food."

"Yes, I do know. But some things are worse than dying."

He nodded. "I want to say goodbye to him."

"I'll wait here." I handed him the flashlight.

He climbed in.

I could hear him talking to Serbin or maybe praying. I moved away to give him privacy.

After a while, he came out.

In the starlight, I could see tears shining on his cheeks.

"Let's go," he said.

Chapter Forty-four

We checked the traps on our way. We had two more foxes. We salvaged the bait and dismantled the rest of the traps so we wouldn't kill without reason. We secured one of the traps—the ice block, a stick, and a rock—to the sled. We didn't think we could pull more than one. We'd set a trap each night.

Hal's balance wasn't perfect. He fell many times. I suggested we wait until daylight when he could see better, but he thought we should keep going. He said the snow cushioned his falls; he wasn't hurt.

We took turns breaking trail and pulling the sled. He had longer legs than I did, and the walking was easier for him, but both chores were exhausting. Still, he didn't seem as tired as I was.

I couldn't walk as long as I wanted to. I didn't have my usual stamina, probably from lack of food, but the cold also sapped my strength. We were even colder because the north wind never let up. Some gusts were strong enough to almost stop us in our tracks. The edge of Hal's parka hood, his eyebrows, cheeks, and beard stubble were rimed with snow. I probably looked much the same.

I began to think about how this would end.

At the end of the second day of walking, I asked Hal how far he thought we'd traveled.

"We might have done as much as ten miles a day. Every hour or so, I did a calculation based on the number of steps I was doing in ten minutes. We're keeping a fairly steady pace, even though it's not as fast as we might like."

"At that rate, it might take us two weeks to get home. I didn't realize we'd be so slow. I don't know if I can do this for two weeks."

"Can you walk tomorrow?"

"I don't know. I think so."

"That's all we need to think about right now."

In the dark, it was easy to navigate by the stars. When the sun was up, I estimated the direction by where our shadows pointed. It was accurate enough, I thought. We were fortunate that the weather was good. If the sky hadn't been clear, we couldn't have walked. We wouldn't have known if we were going in the right direction. On the other hand, because it was clear, it was colder than if we'd had a blanket of clouds to trap whatever warmth the few hours of daylight gave us.

We stopped before dark each day. I said it was so we'd have light while we made an igloo, but it was really because I couldn't go farther.

Hal did more than his share of the igloo building now. I couldn't do as much. I tried not to be obvious about it though. I hung back and let him take the lead.

Life narrowed down to cold and hunger. Everything I did was harder to manage. We didn't talk or sing much in the igloo now because fatigue overwhelmed me. Mostly, I slept. I was finding it harder to wake up in the mornings too.

I tried to keep Hal from knowing, but I was scared. I knew him better now than I had before, but I didn't know what he'd do when I became a burden, as it seemed I inevitably would.

The power in our relationship had shifted over time. At first, I'd been completely under his control. I couldn't stop him from doing what he wanted with me. With his injury, he came under my rule. I controlled his survival, as he had mine. He was like a child, and I'd cared for him as I would have a child. In return, he'd treated me with courtesy and respect. Now, things were shifting again. Probably it was obvious to him I was getting weaker. At least it was obvious to me, and he was not unobservant.

At the end of the fifth day of walking, I finally had to tell him. "Hal, I'm not sure I'll be able to go with you tomorrow. I'm too tired."

After a pause, he said, "We'll wait and talk about that in the morning."

I didn't know what that meant. Maybe he needed time to decide what he was going to do. He'd never asked for the pistol. He didn't need it. He'd told me in Alaska all he had to do was put his hands around my neck, and I wouldn't be any trouble to him anymore. I knew that was true. He could still do that, whether I had the pistol or not. I didn't know that I'd even try to stop him. It might be a merciful death.

I remembered what Jack had told me about his grandmother Ivala's death. It had happened the winter before his parents adopted Quipac. She was old. One day, when they were packing the sled to move to a new location, she said to Jack's father, Piuvkaq, "My son, I am tired today. I want you to build a snow house for me."

Jack saw his father was sad, but he didn't know why.

Piuvkaq said, "Mother, we'll wait a day. You can rest. You'll feel better tomorrow."

Ivala said, "No, son. Build the igloo today."

So Piuvkaq and Maata had done so.

Ivala caressed each of her four grandchildren. Then, she took her bedding into the little igloo and laid on the ikliq.

Piuvkaq set a block of snow across the entry.

He and Maata finished packing the sled, and the family left. They didn't look back. After they'd traveled a while, Jack told his mother it was time to go back for Ivala. Maata didn't answer him. They kept going. They never went back.

Maybe I was going to be like Ivala. I was going to lie on the ikliq and go to sleep. I was tired, but not too tired to see the humor in the fact that all my life I'd worried about seat belts and vitamins and flu shots, and now maybe I was going to freeze to death in an igloo, something I could never have imagined.

I was afraid to go to sleep—I'd become afraid of Hal again. But sleep is so seductive, and I was so tired. Usually, when I'm worried in my daytime life, I have anxious dreams at night, but not now. I dreamed of Jack, of being in his arms, safe, warm. I didn't want to wake up and leave him. I knew I was dying, but I still wasn't ready to think I wouldn't see him again.

Chapter Forty-five

Hal always woke first. He didn't seem to need as much sleep as I did. When he woke me, I felt a little more rested and able. As I sat up I said, "Maybe I'll walk a little, but I'll stop early, and you can keep walking. You can go faster without me. You understand the navigating, and you know how to build an igloo. I'll tell you how to know which direction to go to find Ungavaq once you find the bay. I'll build a little igloo and stay and trap foxes. I'll use the Swiss Army knife. You can take the other knife. You can bring Jack back to me."

While I said those things, I thought about the food. I knew if he were going to kill me—or leave me with nothing, which was the same thing—he wouldn't let me eat breakfast. It would be a waste of food he could use.

It was still dark. I couldn't see how he reacted to what I said. Did he guess what I was thinking?

He was merciful. He didn't leave me wondering long.

"Anne, you didn't leave me when I couldn't travel. I'm not going to leave you alone out here."

I couldn't keep tears from starting. He'd promised if he were going to kill me, I wouldn't be afraid when it happened. And, strangely, I wasn't afraid anymore. I was sad. "We might both die."

I couldn't see him in the dark, but I knew he was reaching out to me. I didn't flinch when his fingers touched my cheek.

He could feel my tears. He moved closer on the ikliq and put his arms around me.

I leaned against him and wept.

He rocked me in his arms. "Don't cry, Anne. Don't cry. Dying with you wouldn't be so bad, you know, but we'll manage somehow. Remember, you said, 'You move forward and keep moving.' We'll try that today and see what happens. We may have to stay somewhere for a while and set traps. Then, when we have enough food, if you can't walk, I'll pull you on the sled. Dry your tears. It's time to eat so we can get going."

"I thought you'd go without me."

"No, Anne. No."

Chapter Forty-six

It was almost dawn when we finally heard what I'd prayed for—the sound of a plane approaching from behind. I turned and saw the wing lights in the distance.

I'd hoped for this. I knew it was Friday, Laura's regular day to deliver mail, but I'd been afraid we were far enough off the direct line to Ungavaq that we wouldn't see or hear her. We hadn't heard her plane the previous Friday.

Hal shot off a flare while I turned on the flashlight and waved it over my head. Then he took the flashlight from me and did an SOS.

Laura circled, waggled the wings, and continued on.

At first, I was excited, but as the lights disappeared in the distance, I was overcome with a wave of bitter disappointment. I knew she couldn't land in the dark, but still . . .

Hal must have felt the same way. We sat slumped in the snow. After a while, he asked, "Should we stay here?"

"We can't stop unless we build an igloo. We'll get too cold. If you have a light inside an igloo, it glows like a beacon. No one could miss it at night. They could easily miss a dark igloo even in the daytime. We don't know how much time is left on the batteries. I don't know if we'd hear a plane in time to get out and shoot off the other flare."

"So we keep walking."

Three hours later, in the full daylight, the plane came back. It was Laura. Again, she circled us, this time low—barely above the tundra—and slow. She dropped something out the window, waved, and turned back toward Ungavaq.

"She didn't land!" I felt like I was going to cry.

"She couldn't, Anne. Look what happened when we tried to."

The package she'd dropped was a backpack of food and a note. It read, "We're coming for you." My heart skipped a beat. It was Jack's handwriting.

The next afternoon, while it was still light, Hal said, "Look!"

I lifted my head and looked to where he pointed. There, in the blank white undulations of the tundra, I saw color and movement! I was jubilant. "That's Jack and Quipac."

"Can you recognize their faces from this far away?"

"No, but I can tell by the movement those are dog sleds, and they're probably the only ones who'd come out for us with dogs instead of snowmobiles."

Hal shook his head and sighed.

"Aren't you excited?"

"Yeah, I guess."

"You guess?"

"Whatever else, this is the end of our time together. When they get here, do you think Jack will kill me?"

He showed no more emotion than if he'd asked me what was on TV.

I couldn't answer. It hadn't occurred to me that was a possibility. Traditionally, wife stealing was one of the few things the Inuit would kill over. Strangely, this wasn't because of love or sex, although they may have been factors, but because a wife's ability to sew for her husband and children was crucial for their survival.

Often when Jack was teaching me about his people, he'd say, "That's the way we used to do things. Now things are different," but I really didn't know what he'd do.

"Jack's a peaceful man."

"We'll see."

He fired off our second flare.

"Hal, this talk of killing—are you thinking of killing them?"

"Of course. That's the kind of thing I do think about. But suppose I do. You'd rather die than show me how to drive a team. And we have no place to go except Ungavaq. I wouldn't get a very warm welcome there if we showed up without Jack and Quipac."

I turned away from him. Bitterness showed in my voice when I said, "I guess I should have realized you'd have made that calculation already. You left something out."

"What?"

"You could kill all three of us," I said, my anger rising. "There'll be enough food on the sleds for four people. You could leave the dogs and walk."

He put his hands on my shoulders and forcefully turned me so I was facing him. "Anne, let's stop this," his voice angry. "Here's the reality. I haven't had much to eat recently. I'm not as strong as I usually am. Even if I could manage to kill one of them, you know I'm not going to get both, so what's the point. And suppose I kill all of you. What'll happen when I get to Ungavaq? They'll call the authorities. I kidnapped you. Remember?" His voice back to normal, he said, "I give you my word I won't try to hurt them."

I realized I'd been holding my breath. I exhaled.

"I want to ask a favor," he said.

"Was that the truth?"

"Anne, look me in the eye."

I raised my head.

"It's the truth."

"You're not going to try to kill them?"

"Maybe this will help you believe me." He handed me the knife. I'd forgotten he had it.

". . . What favor do you want?"

"Will you keep the cribbage board for me? They won't let me take it."

"Jack and Quipac?"

"No, the police."

"Oh."

"Will you?"

"Yes," I said. "What should I do with Serbin's watch?"

"You keep it. Give it to Jack."

"I can't do that."

"It's OK. Serbin wasn't friendly, but he'd have come around. I know he would. He'd want you to have it. I want you to have it. Now, we have guests coming. We should make an igloo."

And so we began to build.

When the sun went down, we built a mound of snow, set the flashlight on it, and turned it on to guide them in.

Chapter Forty-seven

It was a long time before they arrived.

We were resting on the tarp.

Quipac pointed his rifle at Hal.

Hal sat with his hands in his lap, palms up, where Quipac could see them.

"Please. Put your rifle down," I said. "He won't do anything."

But Quipac just shook his head.

I tried to get up, but I couldn't manage on my own. Jack had to help me. He led me a few steps away, put his arm around me, pushed my hood back, and kissed me. It was like my dream, and I was floating in happiness.

He asked quietly, "My love, are you OK?"

"I am now. What are you going to do with Hal? He thinks you might kill him. I told him you're not like that."

He glanced at Hal. "Of course not. He's judging us by how he lives. We're not like him. We don't want to be like him."

"I know."

He put his cheek against mine. "I don't want to talk about him. I want to hold you and kiss you and make you warm. Your face is so cold."

"I can't get warm—even with the food Laura dropped."

He turned his head, bit the end of one of his glove fingers, and pulled his hand out of the glove, dropping it on the snow. Then he put his cheek back against mine and his warm bare hand on my other cheek.

"Tell me what happened," he said softly.

"The plane crashed. Serbin's dead."

"I was afraid they'd hurt you."

"They didn't."

"I thought maybe you weren't coming back."

"I'm here now."

"I love you," he said.

"And I love you."

He held me, and I wanted him to never let me go.

"Jack," Quipac called.

It broke us out of our reverie.

"Yes," Jack said. "We'll make tea. Maybe that'll warm you a little. Then, we'll finish your igloo and eat and rest. We pushed to get here. The dogs are tired and so are we. You must be exhausted. I don't know if you're strong enough to hold the rifle for a while."

"It's not necessary, Jack. Hal's been different since the crash. He's helped me." I turned to Hal.

"I'm too tired to do anything," he said.

"Anyway, I have his pistol and a knife." I handed them to Jack. "He gave them to me."

Jack and Quipac conferred in Inuktitut for a moment, looked at Hal slumped on the tarp, and decided I was probably right.

Quipac came to me. "Little Wife, we were very worried for your safety." To my amazement, he hugged me—astonishing behavior for one normally so undemonstrative.

He went to settle the dogs, while Jack set up our portable white-gas stove and made tea.

The tea did warm me. I felt better almost immediately, and Hal roused himself to help them finish the igloo.

I didn't have the strength to help. Jack carried me to his sled and put me in one of the sleeping bags.

I must have dozed off, because suddenly, the igloo was done, and we were on the ikliq. Quipac was fixing hot food. It should have been my job to cook, but they never even asked me if I wanted to try.

Jack sat between Hal and me. He and Quipac treated Hal with a distant courtesy I knew was a mask for their anger.

I told them some of what had happened. When I told about the foxes, Quipac laughed with delight. "I guess I'm a good teacher." He seemed really pleased.

Hal didn't try to be part of the conversation. He dozed. We had to wake him to eat, and he fell asleep again soon after. Like me, he was worn out, but I think, also, he knew sleeping was the only way to get away from Jack and Quipac.

After a while, Jack said he thought it would be good for me to sleep too.

"You seem to have faith Hal won't cause trouble," he said, "but I don't. We don't want to tie him, so Quipac and I'll take turns watching him. Quipac's going to take the first shift, and after a while, he'll wake me, and we'll trade off."

We zipped our sleeping bags together and lay down. Jack took the side nearest the cold wall. I was next to him. Quipac sat on his sleeping bag next to me. As Jack had been before, he was a barrier between Hal and me. I don't think Hal knew or cared. He was deep asleep.

Quipac turned the lamp to its lowest level.

Jack held me close and we talked quietly for a while. I could feel that he was tense.

"You knew it was me?" I asked.

"We hoped it was. When Laura reported signals, we couldn't think of anyone who might be walking toward Ungavaq, and when she returned to tell us what she'd seen, I didn't know anyone else who had a teal blue parka." He hesitated a moment. "Maybe you didn't want to talk in front of him. Maybe you didn't want to say what he did to you, but he's asleep now."

"He didn't hurt me. I was scared, but that was the worst of it. If he had . . . touched me, would it have changed everything? Would you think I was damaged or dirty?"

Jack held me tighter. "Of course not. That would never be an issue for us. Nothing will change. I love you too much." And he kissed me.

"There is something," I said.

"I'm listening." Now his voice, too, betrayed his tension.

"Hal said things to me in confidence. Will it be a problem between us that he said things I won't share with you? I ask because when we were in Alaska, you said what we said to each other was what was special and important between us. Am I being unfaithful to you if I won't share some things?" As I spoke, I could feel him relax.

"No," he said. "A wife always has a right to privacy. Now, a wife needs to stop worrying and sleep close to her husband."

After dinner, when I'd finally started feeling warm again, I'd taken off my heavy outer clothes, and in the privacy of the sleeping bag, I'd taken off the rest. As he normally was in an igloo, Jack was naked too. He kissed me, stroked my hair, and caressed my breast. Then he rolled over onto his back, and prepared to sleep.

I moved even closer to him and ran my hand gently up his thigh between his legs.

He turned toward me again and said quietly, "I think a wife doesn't know what she's doing."

"A wife is touching her husband."

"A husband has stopped thinking about sleep."

"That's what a wife hoped would happen."

"Quipac is here and he's awake."

"A wife . . . desires her husband."

"A husband desires his wife." He kissed me, and I didn't think about Quipac at all.

Chapter Forty-eight

In the morning, it felt as though the whole universe shared my joy at being with Jack again. We were under a display of the aurora—the first we'd had since the crash—that overwhelmed me with its beauty. It can be so many different colors and shapes. This morning, before sunrise, it was like enormous green and blue chiffon curtains billowing across the sky.

Hal had said, "Good morning, Anne," when Quipac woke us, but he'd kept silent after that except to thank Quipac for breakfast and to ask if he could help load the sleds.

Quipac refused his offer.

He stood out of the way now and moved from time to time so that we were never close. He'd been willing to die with me, and now we didn't speak to each other.

He even avoided eye contact. I wasn't sure who that was for. For Jack? For me? Maybe for him. Maybe it hurt too much. It had occurred to me that yesterday was the last day he'd be in charge of his own life for a long time. I felt sorry for him. Maybe that's what he didn't want to see.

Jack and Quipac thought it would be better if Hal and I rode. Hal protested a little, but they told him it would be better for us to get back to Ungavaq as soon as we could, in case the weather shifted. We could go faster if he were riding.

As Jack helped me climb onto his sled, Quipac said quietly in Inuktitut, "Of course, if Hal's on my sled, it's possible he might not be alive by the time we get to Ungavaq. There might be an accident. Who knows?"

"You're joking, aren't you?" I said.

"Yes, of course, Little Wife. I'm joking," he said, with a slight smile.

Jack was uncharacteristically quiet for the first hour or so. The only sounds were those of the sled runners cutting through the snow, his footsteps, the crack of his whip, and the dogs panting as they ran. His hood obscured his face, but his movements betrayed his tension.

Finally, he slowed the dogs a little and came to walk beside me. He broke the long silence by saying in Inuktitut, "A husband doesn't understand what happened last night. Before, a wife said, 'Never with Quipac there,' but he was there last night."

I answered in English. I wanted to be sure of what I said. "When I took an anthropology class a year ago, there was a phrase that was useful: human behavior is overdetermined."

"Yes," he said, also in English. "No human ever does something for just one reason. There are always many reasons. So you're telling me we had overdetermined sex?" He laughed.

"That does sound kind of funny, but yes, I think so."

"Tell me the first ten or so reasons."

"The first reason, of course, is that I love you. I thought about you every day I was gone. I missed you so much. But the other thing is that I wanted to be reminded of what's central for me, and that's you."

To my surprise, Jack stopped the sled. He gestured to Quipac to pass us and keep going. Then he asked, "Did you need to be reminded of me? Did you . . . maybe . . . start to have feelings for Hal?"

I shook my head, aghast. "Why would you think that?"

He spoke hesitantly—the words difficult. "Sometimes, people become dependent on their kidnappers. You seemed protective of him. I wondered . . ." He stopped.

"Wondered what?"

"It wasn't clear from your note whether they were forcing you to go."

"Oh, Jack! How could you think that?"

"I don't know. Quipac told me I was crazy. He said you'd never go voluntarily, but all those times I said hurting us was strictly a business decision for them—Hal didn't come clear to Ungavaq about business. He came for you."

"He did. But why would you think I'd want to go with him?"

"Because I can see the contrast between Ungavaq and San Diego. I can see the contrast between your life here and there. I was hunting . . . Maybe I'm not home enough . . . Maybe you were tired. Maybe you've . . . had enough of Inuit life . . . and he's not Inuit."

"You mean he's white, like me."

He couldn't look at me. "Yes."

"Have you been thinking these things while I was gone?"

"Yes." He sounded so sad.

I was sad too, that he'd been thinking those things, but I was also angry. I got off the sled and turned to face him. I said forcefully, "Jack, I understand you're not experienced in fighting, but you've said something that makes me want to yell, or swear, or throw something—I don't know what I want, but whatever it is, I know I can't do it in Inuktitut. Do you want to learn about fighting? What you're saying are words people fight about."

He shook his head. "We shouldn't fight. We should talk. I don't want you to be angry. I don't know what the right thing is to say in English or in Inuktitut. I'm confused."

"I know what to say, and I'll say it as many times as you want to hear it or need to hear it. I'll say it in Inuktitut or English or any other language you want. Listen! I love you. I am your wife. I came back to you in Alaska, and I stayed alive this time so I could come back to you again. I'll always come back to you, no matter what barriers are between us. I'm not living in Ungavaq and counting the days until I get back to Ottawa or San Diego. I'm living in Ungavaq because it's my husband's home, and it's my home. Don't confuse me with those other women you dated."

He bowed his head. He couldn't look me in the eye. "I didn't protect you as a husband should. I said you didn't have to be afraid. I said I'd take care of you. And I didn't. He took you, and I couldn't do anything but wait. I waited so many years for you. I couldn't stand the thought that you might not come back, that you might not want to come back. I couldn't think how to face the future without you."

"Jack, I was so frightened. I told him if he tried to take me away, I'd scream. He said he'd shoot one of the other women if I fought him. That's why I went. Then, at the plane, I thought it would be better to make him shoot me there than to go away from my family. But he said as long as I was alive, maybe I could get back to you, so I got in the plane."

"If I'd been home—"

I interrupted him, a terrible breach of Inuit manners. I nodded. "Oh, I see. Everything that happened—Hal and the plane crash and everything—all happened because you hunt too much."

"No, of course not."

"You won't practice fighting, so I'm practicing ridicule. Did you notice?"

Jack shook his head, looked up, and smiled. He put his arms around me. "I noticed, and we can't laugh and fight. I know that much."

"All right. No fighting, no ridicule—we'll practice some other time. For now, I'll tell you something else." I switched to Inuktitut.

"Quipac told me you love me as much as a man can love a woman, and I tell you I love you as much as a woman can love a man. If you look in your heart, you know that's true."

"Yes, I do know that." He kissed me in the long, slow way he does, and we forgot all the anger and all the sadness.

We broke apart, and he said, "So you didn't start to love him. But something happened. Things are different between the two of you. You're not angry at him anymore. And you don't seem to be afraid of him."

"Not love, nothing like that. But something just as confusing. I stopped thinking of him as a monster."

"I don't understand."

"He did all those horrible things to you and to me and to Dr. MacNeil, and to who knows how many other people, but he took care of me too. He tried to keep me warm. He tried to keep me alive. He brought me back to you when I thought I couldn't go any farther. Maybe he did that for his own needs—I don't know—but still, he was gentle and caring and honest with me.

"We talked. We shared things. That's why I asked you last night whether I'd been unfaithful to you. What Hal and I went through was . . . intimate. You, of all people, would understand that. I know now, in a way I didn't before, what you meant when you said what's most important between us is what we talk about."

"But he's still who he is."

"No, he's changed somehow . . . and I have too . . . Maybe I'm the monster now."

"No!"

And I knew I had to tell him. I'd been afraid of this, but I knew I had to do it. I took a deep breath. "We did something . . . I did something I thought was against my nature."

"Tell me."

I trembled as tears started down my cheeks. I almost couldn't say it. "I helped him . . . kill Serbin."

Jack's face went rigid with shock. His arms fell to his sides.

"I had to say it. I had to tell you."

"What happened?"

That scene was suddenly as vivid in my mind as when it happened. "The plane crashed. The lights were out. I heard a terrible noise. It was Serbin. He was screaming and moaning. His back was broken. His face was smashed.

"He pleaded with Hal to shoot him. Hal said no . . . but then he said yes. He couldn't do it alone. He was hurt. He couldn't hold his hand steady. They pleaded with me . . . so I steadied his hand. I asked you last night whether if Hal had touched me you'd think I was damaged. He didn't do anything to me, but I am damaged. I helped kill a person. I didn't ever think I could do something like that."

I spoke through my sobs.

Jack put his arms around me again. "Anne. You're not a monster. You'll never be a monster. You're you. If you were a monster, you wouldn't be upset now."

"But it was wrong. What I did was wrong."

"Sometimes you don't have any right choices."

My tears continued, unabated.

"Why do you think Hal killed him?" he asked.

"Serbin was his only friend in the world. They were like you and Quipac. He did it because Serbin was dying, and he was suffering more than I thought it was possible for a person to suffer. I never understood about that. I never saw anyone in such pain before."

Jack said, so quietly that if I hadn't been enfolded in his arms I wouldn't have heard it, "I'd do that for Quipac, and he'd do that for me."

"Is that true? You're not just saying that."

"It's true. I hope it never happens, but it's true."

"Hal said he'd never tell anyone I helped."

"What do you want to do?"

"I have to tell . . . tell the authorities."

"Why?"

"Because I did it. It would be even worse if I kept silent."

"OK." He nodded. "OK. We're going to need to radio for the police when we get to Ungavaq. We can talk to them about it. We'll do what we need to do. We'll get through this."

"What does this change for us?"

"Nothing."

"When we were in Alaska, you said you didn't want to change me from who you fell in love with, but this whole thing has changed me. I'm different, and you might not like me now."

"How are you different?"

"I don't know. I've lost my innocence—or maybe my ignorance. I didn't know there could be as much suffering and evil as I've seen since we met Hal. And still, I see him as human, not as the monster I thought he was."

"It would be easier if he were a monster," he said.

"Yes."

"Life can be cruel sometimes. You're lucky you didn't know about that until now."

"I don't know what you mean."

"I'm sure you know about Hitler and Stalin and Idi Amin and Bin Laden. You weren't really ignorant of evil, but you didn't understand what it meant—and the same thing for suffering. It's sad you found these things out, but I don't think life spares any of us. It's just that some of us come to this understanding early and some later."

"You knew about these things?"

"All humans experience evil and suffering," he said.

"Oh, I've been thoughtless. You saw people starve to death."

"Yes . . . and other things."

"Will this change us do you think?"

"Life always changes us. But I think you're asking whether this will change our love for each other, and I don't think so. We can only live a day at a time though, and I loved you yesterday, and I love you today, and I will love you tomorrow."

He pulled me close again and kissed me, and I knew whatever else happened, Jack would always be there.

"Now, there's still something I need to know," he said.

"What?"

"What was last night? Did that grow out of sadness or desperation?"

I shook my head. "Last night was whatever you want it to be. I did a lot of thinking while I was away. I wanted you to know I trust you. What's OK for you is OK for me. If you trust Quipac, I trust Quipac. As much as I now know about evil and pain, I also know you'd never do anything to hurt me, so last night was OK for me, and whatever you want in the future is OK for me. I love you more than I could ever tell you."

We kissed.

I climbed back onto the sled. The dogs had flopped down in their traces to rest while they had a chance, but they rose and were at the ready. Jack cracked the long whip over their heads, and we started to move again.

When the sun rose, the sky was bright and clear.

It took us about two hours to catch up with Quipac and Hal.

We spent the rest of that day and the next talking about my experiences again and again. I told Jack as much as I could, without breaking Hal's confidences, about what had happened after the crash.

Jack was proud of how I'd managed. He paid me the highest compliment he could. He called me a true Inuit wife. And he promised I'd never have to eat fox again.

Chapter Forty-nine

The weather held. We didn't push, but we made good time. We came into the village shortly before dinner on the second day of travel. The wind out of the north brought us the wonderful aroma of food cooking. Someone was having walrus for dinner. I laughed. I was so glad to be home.

As we approached, our dogs started yipping, and the village dogs answered.

Almost everyone came out to welcome us. Laura was there too. She'd stayed in case I needed to go to Blackwell for medical care.

I greeted everybody. While I was telling them how glad I was to be home, Jack and Quipac and some of the men started to unload our sled and carry gear into our storeroom. People started talking about a party.

Hal had been sitting on Quipac's sled. We hadn't been watching him. I guess we felt things were OK—game over or something.

But we were wrong.

"Laura!" Hal's voice cut through the rest of the conversation around me.

People quieted. Everyone looked in his direction.

Laura turned toward him.

"That's your name, isn't it? You're going to fly me out of here." He stood about ten feet away and held a pistol pointed at her.

The scene was surreal. The trouble from Hal was never going

to end. That anger I'd felt after the crash came roaring back, and something in my mind said, "Enough!" Then, strangely, the anger receded, and I felt calm. I stepped in front of Laura.

Hal said, now quietly, "Anne, get out of the way. I don't want to hurt you."

"And I don't want you to hurt Laura. Laura, step back." I didn't take my eyes off him, but I heard her move back behind me, and I could hear women moving their children away.

I stepped toward him.

"Anne, stop. Don't walk toward me. Don't make me hurt you." He no longer sounded threatening. He sounded sad.

I said softly, "Hal, do you remember what we talked about, when it was just the two of us?"

He nodded.

"It's time for you to keep your promise. I want you to know I'm not afraid, and now it's time for you to tell me whether you're going to kill me or not. These people are my family. I cannot tolerate this." I took another step forward.

No one moved.

No one spoke.

His eyes pleaded.

I stood.

I watched him move his finger to the trigger, and I knew that was the last thing I would ever see. After a moment, though, he eased his finger off the trigger, turned the pistol around, and handed it to me.

Chapter Fifty

My hands were shaking so much I almost couldn't hold it. I recognized the grip. It was Serbin's, the one I'd been unable to get out of his shoulder holster.

"It would be a good idea if you went back and sat on the sled again."

He did as I said.

Several of the men followed and surrounded him.

Jack and Quipac came over. I gave Quipac the pistol, and he engaged the safety. Suddenly I felt limp and faint. Jack put his arm around me just in time.

They were deeply angry. They didn't say or do anything, but I had begun to see these emotions even when they were hidden. Quipac once told me if I was going to be with Jack, I had to learn to read the silences. I was getting better at that.

We radioed for the police, but we didn't want to stand around in the cold for who-knew-how-many-hours waiting for them to arrive. We didn't have anything like a jail in Ungavaq. I don't even know if we had a door that locked. We couldn't foist Hal off on anyone else. I wanted to cook again in my own home. So I ended up preparing seal for my husband and my kidnapper.

There wasn't much dinner table conversation.

Sometime after we finished eating, we heard the police plane circle the village.

I went out and turned on the lights around the safe landing area. Then I showed the police officers, Sergeant Toussaint and Officer Grasse, the way to our house, where Jack and Hal waited.

Hal knew the routine. Without being asked, he rose, turned, and put his hands high on the living room wall.

Officer Grasse patted him down.

Hal put his hands behind him, but the officer said, "No, in front. You have to be able to get into the plane."

Hal turned, hands extended, and Grasse handcuffed him.

I wanted to say no, but like Hal, I knew this situation was no longer in our control.

Jack and I sat for a while with the sergeant in our kitchen so I could give my statement. I told him what Hal and I had done to Serbin.

"Madame O'Malley," he said in his French-accented English, "I have to put this in my report. We know what it's like out there. That was a terrible decision you had to make. I don't know what'll happen, but I, for one, hope you don't hear any more about it." He told me he might be contacting me for a further interview and that, of course, I'd have to testify at Hal's trial. It went unspoken that I might have a trial of my own.

I told him the approximate location of the plane, and he said he'd arrange to have Serbin's body retrieved.

We walked out to the landing strip with Hal and the officers so we could turn the lights off after they left.

There, Hal asked if he could speak to me.

Sergeant Toussaint said, "If Madame O'Malley wants to speak to you, we can give you a little time."

I wasn't sure what we had left to say to each other, but I asked Jack if he'd mind.

He was silent for what seemed like a long time. Then he said, "If you want this." He and the officers stepped back.

"This is probably the last time we'll ever speak together," Hal said. "I want to tell you the truth about something more. I know you can't love me. I understand that. But I love you. I want you to know how important you've been in my life."

"Oh, Hal."

"I never told Serbin how important he was to me. I hope he knew. I don't want to miss the chance to tell you."

"I don't know what to say."

"I wanted to say that and tell you I'm sorry for what I did to you."

I held up my hand to stop him. "I have to know. Did you go in the plane to get the pistol?"

He shook his head. "I wanted to say good-bye to him. I didn't think about the pistol until I was on my way out of the plane."

"You had it the whole time I was telling them they didn't have to worry about you, that you'd changed."

"I promised you I wouldn't try to hurt them, and I didn't."

I nodded. "Yes."

"I hope you'll let Jack know there was nothing personal in what I did to him, and I'm sorry for that too."

"You didn't tell him that while I was out turning on the lights?"

"I didn't think he'd be willing to hear that from me. That's why I'm telling you. I know that's not good enough, but I wanted to say it."

"What did the two of you talk about?"

"Nothing, really, except that he thanked me for taking care of you. I know that you told me that he sometimes expresses anger with ridicule or sarcasm, but I think he was sincere. It really surprised me."

"I will give Jack your apology. You're right. He's not ready to hear it now, but I'll tell him when the time's right . . . You know I'll have to testify against you."

"Of course. It's OK."

"It's strange. I don't want to." I had tears in my eyes.

"Are you crying for me?" he asked in surprise.

"Yes. You were willing to die with me."

"How could I have left you?"

"Oh, Hal." This time the tears spilled over in spite of my effort to contain them.

"Don't cry, Anne. It's going to be OK." He started to reach up with his handcuffed hands to touch my cheek, but he glanced at Jack and put his hands down.

When Jack saw the gesture, he stepped forward, but I shook my head. "I'm OK."

He stepped back.

Hal and I waited a moment until I was in control again.

"I told Sergeant Toussaint what we did to Serbin," I said. "I didn't want you to have to take all of that on yourself. I don't know what will happen. He said he hoped it wouldn't be an issue. We'll see."

"Thank you for caring about that."

"He said they'll retrieve Serbin's body. Will you take care of him? I thought you might want to."

"Yeah. My attorney can make the arrangements. He wanted to be buried in Mexico." He paused. "Will you remember the things we talked about?"

"I won't forget you. I want you to know I'll always keep what you told me private. I promised you I would, and I will. If they ask me anything about that kind of thing, I won't answer."

"Anne, you said you'd never be my friend, but I don't know what friends are if they aren't people who take care of each other and keep each other's confidences."

"Yes, I guess you're right."

"That's enough then. Would you shake my hand? I'd like to touch you one last time."

So I took off my glove and helped him take off his, and I held his hand for a moment. Then he turned and walked over to the officers.

I walked back to Jack.

The officers helped Hal into the plane. They attached his handcuffs to a chain anchored to the floor.

I didn't watch the takeoff—I couldn't.

Jack turned off the lights and put his arm around me. "Let's go home."

Chapter Fifty-one

Jack never asked me why I thought Hal had wanted to take me. I don't know what he figured out on his own. I thought a long time about it, and I decided not to tell him Hal had said he loved me. I didn't know if that decision was right or wrong. I know how I feel about Jack—that's one area where I'm not at all confused—and I thought if I told him, it might upset him for no reason. And the truth is I wouldn't know what to tell him, because I don't know how I feel about Hal. What had seemed so simple in the beginning wasn't simple anymore.

I also thought a long time about the letter. I finally gave it to him.

He read it, and for the first time since I've known him, tears came to his eyes. He put the letter in his pocket and kissed me with deep and quiet passion.

Over the next weeks, life returned to what we hoped was normal.

Jack and Quipac's students arrived, and the three of us conducted the survival class. I shared some of my experiences with the students. We didn't mention these experiences had happened in the context of a kidnapping. The students knew—it had been in the papers and on TV—but they didn't ask, and I didn't offer anything about that part of it. Jack told me later that he had asked them not to bring it up.

On January 2, our first anniversary, the day Jack and I told each other of our love, Quipac arranged a project for the students away from the igloo. We had nearly six hours alone together. We talked and we made love. It was wonderful.

The class was a success, and I understood why Jack looked forward to it each year. It really was a validation of his love for his culture.

We flew back to Ottawa for the winter-spring semester, and I started my new life as a faculty wife.

We hadn't been there long, when I received a letter from the chief prosecutor of the Blackwell Judicial District. No charges would be brought against either Hal or me for Serbin's death, and I wouldn't be required to testify at a trial because Hal had agreed to plead guilty to a charge of kidnapping.

"I think that plea is a gift to me from Hal."

"No," Jack said. "He was just being practical."

"Maybe."

I didn't say it, but in my heart, I knew better.

COMING SOON FROM
MADURA PRESS

Let Me Count the Ways...

by Caroline McCullagh

Prologue

I'm in the dark except for the beam of the flashlight. I hear the moans. The smell of blood is strong. Then the sound—not what I expected—and the sudden acrid smell of gunpowder. Serbin's hand loosens in mine, and his moans stop . . . forever.

Chapter One

JULY 21, 2006

Laura always circles the area before she lands in our sheltered inlet off Ungava Bay. The entire village comes alive when the sound of her floatplane breaks the quiet of Friday mornings.

That's when Jack and I usually walk to his mother's house to pick up our mail.

He goes out onto the dock to help Laura tie up and offload the cargo. I help Maata prepare tea for the visitors we know will come to hear the news Laura brings from Blackwell, our nearest city, three hours away by air.

On the way home that Friday, I leafed through the bundle of mail in my hand. "Same old stuff—ads and pleas for money." It seemed strange to live in a village as isolated as Ungavaq and still get ads for sales at computer stores and coupons for doughnut discounts. It isn't anything like the volume we get when we're at the condo in Ottawa for the spring semester, but we still get some. I'm surprised they think people living in northern Quebec might come by to shop any time soon.

My hand stopped on something different, a thick envelope. The unfamiliar return address read "Lightner, Pickerel, Robertson, and Smythe, Attorneys at Law." I guess almost anyone's heart skips a beat when they get a letter from an attorney. I'm no different.

We hung our jackets on the rack next to the door. The August sun shone through our small windows and onto the bright pink, maroon, and green floral-patterned carpet, chasing away the midsummer chill.

"Tea is pleasant when a husband and wife read the mail together," Jack said.

"It is nice."

We'd already had two cups at Maata's, but another was always welcome.

I handed him the stack of mail, the attorney's letter on top, in trade for the empty cup he'd left on the coffee table. Stepping into our kitchen, I filled the kettle and put it on the burner.

Our house is small. A smaller house is easier to heat. Barrels of heating oil, brought in by ship during the short summer, are expensive.

I put sugar in the tea. In Ottawa, we'd also use milk, but it's at a premium here—it has to come in by plane—so when we're here, we don't use it. I carried the cups into the living room.

"Thanks," he said. "There's not much of interest in the mail, except the letter from the attorney and one from Carola. I left them for you to open."

"Why would we be getting a letter from an attorney? Do you think someone's suing us?"

"It might be easier to find out if you open it."

I opened the drawer in my chairside table, found the letter opener, and slit the envelope open. It enclosed two letters, one typed, the other handwritten. I didn't recognize the handwriting, strong and plain, like printing, but I did recognize the name at the end of the second page. My heart rate shot up.

Jack looked up. "You're not saying anything."

I didn't want to answer. I took a deep breath. "I don't know where to begin."

"It's confusing then." He sounded interested.

"Two letters: one from Hal's attorney . . . and one from Hal."

"He dares to write to you!"

"It's not to me. It's to both of us."

Jack's voice had been angry. That didn't surprise me. I expected him to be upset as soon as I saw the signature. As I'd seen him do before, Jack controlled his anger. When he spoke again, the tension was gone from his voice.

"That doesn't make it much better. Read them."

I read silently for a minute. "Oh, Jack, I don't know what this means."

"Tell me."

"The attorney is someone named Alan Pickerel. The letter's dated four days ago.

> July 17, 2006
>
> Dear Dr. and Mrs. O'Malley:
>
> Enclosed find a letter to you from our client Harold Josephs. Mr. Josephs has told me you may find his letter unwelcome, but he hopes you will read it.
>
> He has authorized me to tell you he is prepared to set up a substantial trust fund to pay all expenses now and the future costs of—"

Inuit don't normally interrupt, but Jack did this time. "Let's finish that letter later. Read Hal's letter so we can have some idea of what this is about."

I set the attorney's letter down and picked up the other one. The strangeness of holding something Hal had held just four days before struck me. *Almost like touching him*, I thought. I read aloud:

> July 17, 2006
>
> Dear Anne and Jack,
>
> This greeting may seem strange and possibly even offensive to you. I know you can't be happy about hearing from me. Nine months isn't long enough for memories to fade. I wouldn't have written to you, but I don't know anyone else I would have wanted to ask this of. Please, read this letter all the way through.
>
> Anne, you once said to me that life is so strange. I knew what you meant, but I had no idea until now how strange it could be. I just found out I have a son. He's five years old. A DNA test confirms he's truly mine. He's the child of one of the women I told you about, Anne. She died four months ago, and my son is now in foster care.

I'm surprised to find that although I'm in prison I have parental rights. My father abandoned me. I know what that's like. I'd never have abandoned my son if I'd known about him, but now I'm not in a position to take care of him.

I know this will come as a shock, but I'm asking you to consider adopting him. If you'd be willing to do that, I'd give up all parental rights. You'd never have to have any contact with me, nor would he.

You know one of the reasons I'm asking you is that my circle of friends is limited. Still, I wouldn't ask this of you if I didn't believe you would be good parents.

There's a second reason. My son is of mixed heritage. His mother was Mexican.

The people in charge of his case have told me there's little chance he'll be adopted because of that fact and because of his age. He'll probably have a life in foster care until he's eighteen when he'll be pushed out into the world on his own as I was. I don't want that for him, and I don't think his heritage would be an issue for you.

Anne, I release you from your promise of confidentiality. You can tell Jack anything I said to you during the time we were together that you think would help him make a decision about this. I know it might be difficult to remember anything positive about me that would make the two of you willing to consider this adoption, but there may be something.

Jack, I know you have good reason to hate me, but my judgment is you're not the kind of man who would take anger out on a child.

Please think about this. I'd beg, but I know this isn't the kind of responsibility a person should take on because someone begs.

> I want him to have a decent home. I couldn't give that to him even if I were free.
>
> You have a large, close family—something I yearned for as a child. I know it would be good for him.
>
> I'm told he's in good health and is bright and intelligent. Anne, you said I don't think much about the results of my acts. Believe me when I tell you I have thought about this.
>
> Hal

We sat in silence, stunned.

Finally, Jack said, "I guess you'd better tell me the rest of what the attorney has to say."

"You're not saying no?"

"Hal asked us to think about it. I'll do that much. If we're going to say no, at least we should know what we're saying no to."

I scanned the rest of the attorney's letter. "It says the trust fund will cover the costs of processing the adoption and bringing the boy to Canada. It will also cover the cost associated with his acquiring Canadian citizenship after the adoption, if we decide to do that. They'd be willing to handle the associated work, or it could be turned over to an attorney of our choosing."

"I don't think 'Life is strange' begins to cover it," Jack said. "What do you think?"

"I don't know."

"Don't think then. What are you feeling?"

"Jack, I've never stopped wishing I'd had children. I got over the pain, but I never got over the regret. But this isn't just a child. This is Hal's child."

"I think you've covered it. He's Hal's child. And besides, we're both over sixty."

"I don't think that's a problem," I said. "We're in good health. We have a big family to back us up. Many grandparents are raising grandchildren these days because their children have problems with drugs or AIDS or other things. It's not unusual any more."

"It sounds as though you want this child."

I sat silent.

Jack waited. He would wait as long as necessary until I spoke or until I indicated I wouldn't answer.

I knew what I should say, but I finally decided I had to tell the truth.

"Yes, I do want this child. That's what's in my heart."

Now I waited, as I'd learned to do. I no longer need to fill every void with words.

After a time, he said, "Well. This is something to think about."

"You're still not saying no."

"I'm not."

"Why not?" I asked.

"I have lots of things going through my mind. I'll admit I'm still angry with Hal, but I don't hate him. That may seem strange. He tried to kill us and he kidnapped you. But I feel what I feel."

"You surprise me."

"Tell me some of the things he told you that might be persuasive," Jack said.

"I suppose the most important thing is that his father abandoned him. His mother died just after he graduated from high school, leaving him without anyone in the world. That's when he joined the navy, and that's when he started going bad. He may have been lying, but I don't think so."

"He mentions women."

"Call girls," I said. "He didn't date because he couldn't be honest with a woman about his life. When he wanted companionship, he'd hire a call girl. He said you could take them places, and they didn't expect any kind of commitment."

"Maybe now it's time for you to tell me why he kidnapped you."

I had a sick feeling in my stomach, but I knew I had to answer. "I thought he did it to punish you."

"But he didn't," Jack said.

"No . . . He didn't."

"What then?"

"He said he loved me."

"Well, at least that's something in his favor. He's a man of good taste."

Although we'd been married more than a year and a half, I still didn't know when Jack said something like that, whether he meant to joke or to indicate he felt irritated or angry. As educated in urban Canadian culture as he was, he still followed the Inuit way of hiding those emotions in ridicule.

"It's hard to believe," I said, "because he's so much younger, but I know it's true because of the way he treated me. When I look back, I can see he didn't really want to hurt me, but he didn't know any other way to be. Oh, Jack. I should have told you. I haven't done the right thing."

"Of course you did the right thing." He patted the space next to him on the sofa. "Come here and sit with me."

I went over, and he put his arm around me. "This is to show you things are OK between us." He kissed me. "You always have the right to privacy, and I do trust you."

"What should we do?"

He picked up his cup and took the last sip of tea as he considered. "We need to think about this, and we need to talk to the family. We couldn't do it without them. Then maybe we'll go to Blackwell to talk to the attorney. We'll need to talk to Hal too."

I listened with growing astonishment. "You're saying we're going to do this?"

"We're going to think about it. Whatever I may feel about Hal, this is about the child."

"You really mean it?"

"I've read a little about what the foster care system is like in the United States," he said, "especially for children who are not considered white. I know I'm what I am because Marcia took a chance on me when she took me to Ottawa to be educated. In a sense, you could call our relationship an adoption. And there's Quipac; he's alive because my parents adopted him. I can't imagine my life without him. I can't save all the adoptable children in Canada or the United States, but I haven't been asked to save all of them. I've only been asked about this one."

"Oh, Jack. I don't know what to say."

"Say you love me. That's enough."

"I do love you, but that's not what I meant."

"Tell me what you mean, then."

"I don't know if I'm ready to talk to the family yet," I said, "and I can't talk to Hal."

"Tell me."

"I'm afraid to tell you."

"I know," he said, "I've been waiting until you were ready. We promised we'd learn to talk to each other, to tell each other these very personal things."

"I'm afraid."

"It hurts that you're afraid of me."

I shook my head. "I'm not afraid of you. I'm afraid I'll break something I don't want to break, and I won't know how to fix it."

He took my hand in his. "Say it again."

"What?"

"Say you love me."

"I love you as I have loved you since the first time I saw you."

He hugged me and gave me a tender kiss. "All right, then. There's nothing you can break that we can't fix. Now, tell me."

I couldn't look him in the eye. My voice was so quiet, he wouldn't have heard it if he hadn't been sitting right next to me. "I don't know how I feel about Hal."

"Tell me the rest."

I'd wanted to talk to Jack about this for the longest time, but I'd lacked the courage. Now I had to do it. "When Hal came into my life . . . The intimacy of that whole time with him . . ." I shook my head. "The overwhelming feelings . . ." I shook my head again. "I'm not saying this right. I can't seem to tell you how upset I am. I wish I were at peace again the way we were before we met Hal."

"That'll come. You still need time to let everything fall into place."

"I don't know."

"Do you love him?"

I shook my head. "I don't feel about him the way I feel about you."

"Do you want to be with him?"

"No. But I still can't find peace. I thought you didn't know about any of this. Now you say you were waiting for me to be ready to talk. I didn't know. I don't know how much you're willing to put up with."

He kissed me again. "I don't think you're going to reach my limit any time soon. I love you so much and I need you so much, I'd be willing to put up with almost anything to keep you and to keep you happy. You're going through a rough patch. We'll go through it together, and it'll be fine in the end. Will you trust my judgment?"

"Yes."

"Tell me something," he said.

"What?"

"Tell me about your feelings for him."

"Too many feelings. They swirl in my brain like a merry-go-round." I shook my head. "I can never seem to deal with just one."

"Maybe now you can."

". . . I feel obligated to him. But when I try to figure out why, it doesn't make sense. It's because he didn't kill me after he said he would."

"It bothers you to be obligated to him?" he said.

"Yes . . . and also, he said he loves me. You go through life and not many people love you. It's like a gift I can't reciprocate."

"You might think about ways you could reciprocate."

"No. It flattered me that a man fifteen years younger would find me attractive, but I chose you. I love you. I'm not interested in seeing if I could love another man."

He laughed. "I don't want you to fall in love with him, but maybe loving his child would be a way to reciprocate."

"Maybe." I turned to face him. "The only thing is, if we take this child, there's no way we'll keep Hal out of our lives, even if he's in prison, and he's going to get out someday. He says he'd have no further contact with the child or with us, but if we want what's best for this child, keeping Hal away isn't it. We can't say, when the boy's eighteen or twenty, 'Oh, by the way, you do have another father. We decided not to tell you about him.'"

"I've already thought of that," Jack said. "Accepting this child means accepting Hal into our lives in some way. So what kind of relationship would Hal be willing to participate in, and what could you tolerate? Most important, would he honor an agreement he made?"

"I think Hal's life has really been all about honor, in spite of the things he's done. We talked a lot about his determination to honor his commitments, even in that perverted career he chose. I do think we could trust him."

"Well, we can't do anything about this before next Friday when Laura comes back." He gently stroked and kissed my hair. "Let's plan to have some kind of response ready by then. That gives us a week."

His lingering kiss drew my mind away from our problems.

"Meanwhile, all this heavy conversation has worn me out," he said. "Let's lie down awhile."

So we did lie down for a while, and it turned out Jack was not as worn out as he had said.

ACKNOWLEDGMENTS

Many thanks to the people who helped me so much in the preparation of this book for publication, particularly Antoinette Kuritz and Jared Kuritz of Strategies Literary Development in San Diego, who guided me through the process, and GKS Creative, who designed the covers and the interior. What a joy to see something you've written come to life.

Many thanks also to my friends and students who offered so many useful suggestions along the way.

In popular lore, writing is a solitary occupation, but that's not true at all. None of my books would have ever seen the light of day without the support and encouragement of friends, family, and professionals.

Reading Group Questions

Anne clearly loves Jack, but she also still loves Robby. What do you think it takes to balance two such loves, much less to let a second love into your life as Anne did?

Anne is a rich woman. She asks Jack if her money is going to be a problem between them. In what ways might it be? When it becomes a problem, what does that signify?

Regarding taking the job in Alaska, Jack says, "I've thought about the ethics of this. I think as long as we do what we contract to do, it's not unethical to take the oil company's money while we hope to help the people working to stop them. I know it's a convoluted argument, but that's why I'm interested." What do you think of his reasoning?

What does Jack's attitude towards the criticism he received when he read his paper to the students and professors at UCSD tell you about him? What does it tell you about science?

Clearly from different backgrounds, Anne and Jack are set to face not just curiosity but also bigotry. What do you think of Anne's response to the drunk woman's reaction to Jack? How might you have handled a similar situation?

What does it tell you about Jack that at dinner he chooses to sit next to the woman who had dismissed him as an Eskimo at the cocktail party?

Anne is unsettled from the onset of the trip. So is her dog, Kiska. Would you chalk this up to intuition or observation? Why?

What role does humor play in Jack and Anne's relationship? What role can it play in any relationship?

What do Jack's gifts tell you about his feelings for Anne? What do they tell you about him as a man?

The Inuit in Jack suppresses anger. How can doing so be healthy?

Why do you think Anne's negative response to Hal is stronger than her response to Serbin?

At the camp, Hal is functionally in a position superior to Jack. He controls everything in and out, including communication. Why does he respond as he does when Jack calls him out about disrespecting Anne?

Why is Anne so eager to embrace Jack's culture?

How would you describe Jack as a teacher? As a husband? Provide three adjectives for each.

What are some of the most pressing differences between Anne and Jack? What does how they handle their differences tell you about them?

Despite her loathing, Anne is surprised at Hal's attitude towards her. How do you think most American women would react if a younger man showed interest in them? Is Anne's reaction typical?

Jack is not jealous of René. Do you think most men might be? Why isn't Jack?

When Anne finds out Jack is missing, she flies into action. What do you think drives her response?

From where does Anne muster the strength to move forward?

Quipac says of himself and Jack, "We each see the world in two ways—the Inuit way and the white way." Discuss how living this way might affect a person.

Adoption, marriage–Quipac tells Anne that before the missionaries came, in the Inuit world these things happened because people said they did. In what ways does this differ from the world the missionaries came from? What does the difference tell you about the cultures?

What do you think about the story Quipac told Anne about what happened to the Inuit after contact?

How do you explain the confidence Quipac, Anne, and Jack have in each other? Do you have this level of trust with people in your own life? How difficult or easy is it to develop?

In what ways do Jack and Anne show their respect for each other?

What is the value of mutual respect? How does it shape a relationship?

Jack is "... one of those men who needed to be in charge and never show weakness." How would you respond to a man like that? Why?

Speaking about making love, Jack says to Anne, "I don't care what he sees. What's private for me is what we talk about, what we share that way." Discuss the pros and cons of a man who thinks like this.

Both Hal and Jack refer to Anne as brave. What is your definition of brave? And does Anne meet it?

What does it take for Anne to be fully accepted by her new community? How is this the same–and how is it different–from how American women find acceptance within a community of women?

Anne does a lot to fit in with Jack's family and friends and his culture. How would you describe the balance in their relationship?

When Serbin is injured, why is Anne able to help Hal end Serbin's misery? Why is she kind to Serbin? What would you do in the same circumstances?

When she has the opportunity, why doesn't Anne want revenge on Hal? What would you do in the same situation?

Anne says to Hal, "If you're going to change, you need to do that for yourself, not for someone else." In what ways have you changed for yourself? In what ways have you changed for someone else? Which did you find to be the more powerful and satisfying experience?

Anne and Hal share life stories. Why would people who started out as they did do so? Have you ever told someone about yourself? Were you sorry later?

Hal shares details of his life with Anne, but he has difficulty sharing feelings. Yet he can share his feelings for her. Why?

Why does Anne's fierceness bother Hal?

If not forgiveness, how would you describe Anne's attitude towards Hal once Jack and Quipac find them?

Because of the difference in their ages, Anne is thrown by Hal's attraction to her. Is it a feeling almost any woman would have? What does this say about women in general?

Anne ends up making love with Jack while Quipac is sitting next to her in the igloo. Why do you think she does this?

At the end of the book, Anne says, " . . . I don't know how I feel about Hal. What had seemed so simple in the beginning wasn't simple anymore." How would you describe the evolution of their relationship? And to what would you attribute that evolution?

The tension in this book is multi-layered. Discuss those layers and how they play into each other.

What did you think of Hal's final gift to Anne? Why do you think he did this?

Anne is a study in contrasts. She is an independent woman willing to fully share her life with someone. She is strong, proud, and capable – yet she is willing and eager to adopt Jack's way of life. What do you see as her strengths and weaknesses? Would you want to be her friend?

What do you find most compelling about Anne and Jack as a couple? Do you think their relationship has what it takes to last? Why?

Author Question and Answer

You write Anne as a woman in her 60's. Yet, she has tremendous energy and curiosity and a real zest for life. Why did you make her that age?

Two reasons: I got tired of reading about 25-year-old heroines who do foolish things because of their lack of life experience. Anne does some things that observers might see as foolish, but most of the time, she's aware of why she's made the decisions she has, and she accepts the consequences. The second reason is that in the first book of the series, *The Quest for the Ivory Caribou*, she had to be that age for the timeline of the plot to work out.

You give Anne and Jack a great sex life. What's the reason behind this?

People in their sixties can have great sex lives! Anne and Jack are emotionally passionate, deeply in love, and healthy, and they both like sex very much. Why wouldn't they?

One of the overriding questions in this book is about love. Can a woman love more than one man with her whole heart? Have you ever been in a situation where that question came up?

I look back with amazement to the time when two men asked me to marry them. I was a 39-years-old divorcée with four children. One of the men even sold his MG and bought a station wagon. Then he called the other man to try to "work things out." I guess it didn't occur to him that I might have an opinion too. I did love both of them, but I knew that the one with the station wagon would have been impossible as a husband. I had 32 great years with the other man, my late husband Bill.

You have lived and breathed Anne through two books now. How would you describe her?

With each book I write, I learn more about Anne. Writing her is like making a friend. Bit by bit, over time, she reveals herself to me. I think the best thing about her is that she is honorable. That honor forces her to be courageous. Being courageous doesn't come naturally to her, and she pays a price for it. Also, she's passionate. She's able to feel deeply and commit deeply. She's far from perfect though. As you get to know her, she'll reveal that part of herself to you too.

Anne is remarkably willing to compromise with Jack about a number of things. Do you see him as compromising also? In what ways?

Jack has done most of his compromising long before he met Anne. He learned how to live in the "white world," but as their friend Marcia points out, "His heart is Inuit and will always be." Anne's emotionality is difficult for him to deal with, and she knows it. The only time he's comfortable with it is when they're in bed. When that little voice says to Anne, "Be more Inuit," that's her voice, not Jack's, chiding her. She recognizes how much he compromises for her.

Is Jack a figment of your imagination or a conglomeration of men you know? When writing him, how conscious were you of the qualities with which you wanted to imbue him, and which of those qualities do you find most attractive?
I haven't met a man like Jack yet, but I live in hope! I didn't consciously choose to imbue him with qualities. He revealed himself to me as I wrote. Sometimes I would write a section or even a chapter, and when I was finished, Jack would say to me, "No! I would never do that. I would never say that," and out it went. I had to throw out the entire first chapter of the third book, *Let Me Count the Ways...*, because of that. It's a strange process. I don't understand it, but all the characters live in my head and sort of tell me what I should write.

What I most admire is his courage and his passion for Anne, for his family, for his teaching, for science. Jack has lived close to nature most of his life. He understands about the realities of life and death. He focuses on the important things.

You create a situation where a younger man is obsessed with an older woman. What drew you to this dynamic? In reality, what are the obstacles to such a relationship? When might it work?
In truth, these kinds of relationships exist, and like any relationships, some work and some don't. Social and cultural pressures are intense on anyone who lives outside the norm. People who want to do that must have strong self-confidence.

You seem to deal with several themes in this book. In order of importance, can you enumerate them as you see them?
All five (so far) books about Anne and Jack are about the nature of love and the possibility of forgiveness. Those are the most important themes. And when I say "love," I don't mean just sexual

love. I also mean the kind of love Anne has for Carola and Ernesto, the feelings she has for René and Marcia, the yearning she has for family.

I think a second theme has to do with the innate dignity of the Inuit. They were not "lesser people" waiting for us to come along and bring them into the modern world. They had a rich society and culture and still do, but they've been through some hard times in order to maintain that. The same is true of many other cultures.

A third theme is the importance of the balance of nature. Jack speaks for me when he talks about what will happen if drilling is allowed on the North Slope. There are some things in life that just cost too much, and you and I will pay for them—probably sooner than later.

What attributes would you ascribe to Anne's character? Which do you consider most important?

Perseverance, curiosity, loyalty, optimism, and honor are all characteristics I would ascribe to Anne. Additionally, Anne finds much joy in life. She's willing to try new things. She's a real fish-out-of-water in both Canada and Alaska, but most importantly, she believes in putting one foot in front of the other and keeping going.

When did you first get the idea for this series of books, and how long did it take you to write the first one?

I started reading about the Inuit and the Eskimos when I was a teenager. I've always been interested in transition characters—people like Jack who have to learn to live in two worlds. I thought these books were going to be about him, but—surprise!—I had no idea what the inner life of an Inuit man was like. I know a lot about older women, however.

I started the actual writing about twelve years ago. The first book took about two years, but you're never really done with a book until someone takes it out of your hands.

How much research do you put into your books? And do you do it yourself, or do you have a research assistant?
I don't have an assistant. I do and enjoy research. My husband and I used to go to second-hand stores to buy old *National Geographic*s that had stories about the north. I have a huge scrapbook that I made from those. I also have a number of books on the Inuit. And I've put in many hours on the internet looking for technical details such as how long a sled is, how the Inuit carried water when they traveled, and the significance of the various tattoo designs. I really enjoy that kind of thing, so I can get lost for hours researching.

Tell us a bit about your writing schedule and process.
I'm just a tiny bit compulsive about writing and editing. Some might say I'm addicted. Usually the first thing I do in the morning is work for a couple of hours before I get dressed and eat breakfast. The amount of writing I do the rest of the day is dictated by what other responsibilities I have. And I don't just work on the Anne and Jack books. Right now, I'm also working on my memoir, editing and fact checking a book for a friend, and working on the monthly book review column I write for a national magazine, the *Mensa Bulletin*. I also teach creative writing at a senior center and trade editing chores with a friend. We meet once a week to go over what we've been writing. Unfortunately, this doesn't leave much time for housework and such like.

How much easier–or more difficult–was this book to write than the first in the series?

This one was easier because I've learned more of the craft of writing (I'm still learning) and I've gained self-confidence. I'd learned that I can write. And I knew my characters better than when I started the first book. The third book in the series (*Let Me Count the Ways...*) was a little more difficult. I knew the beginning and the end, but I had to fill in the middle writing about some things I didn't know much about, so lots of research involved.

What's next for Anne and Jack?

Many of my beta readers thought Hal should have died at the end of the book, but real life isn't like that. Bad people don't usually conveniently die to make a tidy package of an ending. Life goes on. Anyway, Hal was too good a character to abandon, so he comes back in book three. He writes to Anne and Jack from prison and asks them to adopt his five-year-old son, Victor, whose mother has been murdered. They agree, and they live happily ever after—until they find out who Victor's maternal grandfather is. Cue the scary music!

ABOUT CAROLINE MCCULLAGH

Caroline McCullagh, writing teacher and award-winning author, earned a master's degree in anthropology at UC San Diego. Besides *Quest for the Ivory Caribou*, her published books include *American Trivia* and *American Trivia Quiz Book*, both with Richard Lederer, and *Sing for Your Supper: Opera Memories & Recipes*. She has extensively published in newspapers and magazines. When not writing, she spends time with her daughter and granddaughters, playing with her dogs, gardening, and listening to classical music.

Visit CarolineMccCullaghAuthor.com

Made in the USA
Las Vegas, NV
16 March 2024

87320603R00204